FOUR FIANCES & I

D. E. BARTLEY

By D.E. Bartley

O'Reilly Fight Club

Four Stepbrothers & I

Four Daddies & I

Faking it with the SEALs

Three Stepbrothers Save Christmas

Four Fiancés & I

To every single person who has read and loved these books, thank you from the bottom of my heart.
Now, be a good girl and turn the page.
The O'Reillys are waiting for you.

Vinci Books

vinci-books.com

Published by Vinci Books Ltd in 2025

1

A CIP catalogue record for this book is available from the British Library.
Paperback ISBN: 9781036709693

Trigger Warnings

During this story, we learn a lot about the characters' childhoods, some of which are very dark and sensitive subjects are discussed that may trigger some readers. I hope I have done justice to Jasmine and the guys' stories and have handled everything appropriately.

Please ensure you check the trigger warnings before continuing.

Your mental health matters, and so do you.

Chapter One

JASMINE

"Please tell me this is the last one," Layton whines beside me as we make our way down the busy high street. "Why couldn't you have brought your fiancé, who loves to shop? That would have made more sense than making me deal with all these people. I hate people."

Count to ten, Jaz. Daddy and Terry will not be happy if you stab your security.

"Because I'm shopping *for* Jason, so he couldn't come," I point out, rolling my eyes. "And yes, this is the last one, so stop sulking. Otherwise, I will tell Daddy you threatened to shoot me." I warn, but looking at Layton, I know he's not threatened.

"He would ask what you did to annoy me," he points out. "They are all surprised I haven't done it yet."

I open my mouth to argue with him, but as I turn to do so, I see the way his eyebrows have disappeared under his hairline, daring me to try and prove him wrong.

"Yeah, fine. I'll give you that one," I sigh, shaking my

head. "Why don't you put the bags in the car, and I'll meet you there. I will only be in here for ten minutes."

"Yeah, like that's going to happen," he laughs, shaking his head.

"I won't tell anyone you left me. It will be our secret."

"Please, you can't hold your own piss when it comes to the O'Reilly's. Do you really believe you won't let it slip that I left you unsupervised?"

"I'm not that bad!" I argue, turning back towards the jewellers I have an appointment with. I notice the security signs and smile. "See, you can watch me go in and leave. I will be perfectly safe." I turn back to Layton and can tell he's assessing the situation.

Honestly, he's not the only one fed up, but I have to get the last Christmas gifts today, or I risk not having anything for the guys. Performances only finished yesterday, and with everything that's been happening with Verity, who is still hiding with her men, I am stupidly behind. It doesn't help that the constant worry of them being found has left me exhausted, thanks to being unable to sleep properly. I'm terrified she will be forced to marry the prick like her arsehole of a father has arranged behind her back. Thinking about it makes me so angry that I force myself to concentrate on everything around me.

Turning to Layton, I see him eyeing the multi-storey car park before us. The car is on the third level, and would only take a few minutes to get to it. If it weren't for the fact that I still need to find Christian a Christmas present, I would be demanding Layton take me home.

"Come on," he sighs, reluctantly walking to the door of the jewellers. He knocks on the door, and a gentleman in a suit appears.

"Do you have an appointment?"

"Yes, under the name O'Reilly," Layton explains. The gentleman's eyes widen when he recognises, and his whole persona changes.

"Of course, Mr O'Reilly, please do come in."

"I'm their security team, she…" Layton nods at me, "Is their fiancée. You are to treat her with the same respect as you would them. Is that understood?"

"Yes, of course, sorry." The gentleman smiles nervously as I watch him tremble slightly before turning his attention to me. "Congratulations on your engagement, Miss …"

"Connors. Thank you for seeing me at such short notice, Mr …"

"Cooper, but please call me Trent."

"Mr Cooper is fine," Layton warns. He can sometimes be a little overprotective, even more so when he is tense, tired, hungry, or all of the above.

"Layton," I say through gritted teeth whilst trying to force a smile. "Why don't you sit outside while I get what I need from here? You will be able to see the door and will be only a call away should I need you."

Layton stares at me momentarily before looking down at the bags, which I know must be hurting his hands. I offered to carry them myself, but he went all macho man on me and told me I was being ridiculous.

"Fine," he sighs, walking towards the door. Mr Cooper quickly steps around and opens it for him. "I'm going to drop these bags off at the car and come straight back. Do not leave this shop until you see I'm out there," Layton snaps at me before rushing towards the car park.

"Feel free to grab me a coffee on the way back," I call out while giving him a little wave. I can see him muttering under his breath, no doubt calling me every name under the sun. I smile, stepping back as Mr Cooper closes the door behind him and turns to me nervously.

"Let's try this again without the hangry guard," I say with a relaxed smile. "Hello, Mr Cooper, I'm Jasmine Connors, but please call me Jasmine." Holding out my hand. His body visibly relaxes before he reaches out and shakes my hand.

"It's lovely to meet you, Jasmine. Please, call me Trent."

"Thank you, Trent," I reply happily before turning my attention to the display cabinets around me. "The O'Reillys all speak very highly of you and the quality of your products." I spot Trent's chest expanding at the praise. "I know you know their style, so I need to find something special to gift Christian for Christmas. I also need something for each of the brothers as wedding gifts. The wedding is in just over a month, so I want to order them now. Do you have anything unique that can be personalised?"

His face lights up as he almost skips around the counter, holding up a finger.

"How about I show you a few options, and you can decide if any would match what you are looking for," he declares, walking over to a cabinet.

"That sounds like a great idea," I reply, hoping he will have something to fit the bill and show my men just how important they are.

Fifteen minutes later, all wedding gifts are picked and ordered, and Christian's Christmas gift is hidden safely in my bag. I look out the door to see if Layton is back, but he's nowhere to be seen. But I spot two people I haven't seen in a very long time, and my heart jumps into my throat. My old best friends Sophia and Amber sit on a bench giggling together. I have conflicting feelings seeing them. Part of me wants to hide away, remembering the last time we saw each other, but another is desperate to make peace whilst we can. I don't know if it's because I'm missing Verity so much or if it's because I still think of the girls regularly, when I decide to speak to them and put the past behind us.

"I'm going to wait for Layton outside," I declare as I walk to the door. Trent quickly rushes out from behind the counter and places a hand on the handle as if to stop me.

"I think you should wait here until your security comes back," he says nervously, looking around.

"I promise I will be fine. Layton is probably just waiting in the queue at the coffee shop and will be here any minute," I reassure him. Sometimes the whole 'save the little lady' attitude pisses me off.

"Then please let me stay with you until he returns." He doesn't realise that I am better equipped to defend myself out of the two of us. Sean has trained me every other day since I was recused.

I open my mouth to point this out but am interrupted by someone calling my name. I turn to see Amber and Sophia walking towards me, both smiling. I wave and turn back to Trent.

"My friends are here and will wait with me. But thank you for everything, and I look forward to coming to collect the other gifts when they're delivered." Before he can reply, I step away from the shop and hug my old friend.

"Where the hell have you been? We haven't seen you in months!" Sophia yells as she hugs me tight.

"Here and there, you know how life is," I answer with a smile. I know I should be pissed with them; they abandoned me when I needed them the most. But I've changed, and I'm sure they have, too.

"Did you just come out of that jewellers? Do they sell anything in there for less than a grand?" Amber asks.

"Yeah, it's not cheap. I think I just spent a huge chunk of my savings," I start but stop myself from saying any more. I don't know how much of my life I want them to know right now. I also don't miss the way they smile at each other. "What are you two doing with yourselves?" I ask, hoping to change the topic of money.

"Nothing much; going out, enjoying life, same old," Amber smiles before looking me up and down and then at the shop I had just walked out of. She has noticed that my outfit is designer, as Jason only buys what he classifies as 'the best' for me.

"We should go out and catch up. You can tell us all about what you've been up to."

"Definitely, it's been so long since we had a night out like we used to," Sophia chimes in. "We were just saying the other day how much we missed you and how much fun we used to have on weekends together."

I'm nodding in agreement when I hear someone shouting.

"Jasmine! What the hell did I tell you!"

I spin around and see Layton storming towards me, holding a take-out cup of coffee. He doesn't pay any attention to the girls, but I notice the girls are paying plenty of attention to him.

"I told you to stay inside the shop until I got back!" he snaps, stopping in front of me and thrusting the coffee cup into my hands.

"I'm fine. Don't get your panties in a twist," I sigh, rolling my eyes.

"Is this your boyfriend?" Amber asks, checking Layton out.

"What? Hell no!" Layton and I respond in unison. If it wasn't Layton, I would probably take the look of disgust personally. But with him, the feeling is mutual.

"Good to know," Amber grins with that look in her eye, which she gets when she sees something or someone she likes. "Hi, I'm Amber. Single and always up for a bit of fun," she declares, holding her hand out for him to shake.

Layton looks at her for a moment and obviously thinks better of commenting as he rolls his eyes and turns back to me. Sucking my lips between my teeth, I attempt to ignore the look of disappointment on her face.

"Maximus just called to see if you had finished. He said he would meet us here."

"What? Already?" He's meant to check out a new property for a potential club. He had asked me to go with him, but Christian gave him a list of things to do first. I was expecting it to take him the majority of the day.

"Your stepbrother?" Sophia asks excitedly. I'd forgotten how obsessed she was with Maximus. She was determined to have at least one night with him and would throw herself in his direction whenever she had the chance. I hated it then, but now it leaves me feeling protective as well as jealous. Layton looks from me to her and back again.

"Who are these girls?" he asks, nodding towards them. This is what I love about Layton, he never pretends to like someone. He shows it if he doesn't deem you important or worthy of his time.

"They used to be my best friends; I've known them most of my life," I answer, sipping my coffee. Layton's eyebrows disappear under his hair before looking back at them.

"The ones who left you the night Maximus offered me the job?"

I nod, knowing what night he's referring to.

Layton got his job as my bodyguard after Maximus saw how well he looked after me one night. I was so drunk I couldn't stand and was throwing up everywhere. He had been a bouncer at the club, and the girls had left me to chase after some guys, leaving me with the moron I was dating at the time.

"Who is this if not your boyfriend?" Sophia asks, watching Layton and me.

"I'm her bodyguard," he answers, standing tall beside me. Amber and Sophia look at each other and burst out laughing.

"What the fuck do you need a bodyguard for?" Amber laughs. "Thinking very highly of yourself, Jaz."

"It's to keep her safe from lowlifes like you."

My heart skips a beat as Maximus steps into view in his jeans and black shirt, looking like a god.

"Max!" Sophia screams and goes to launch herself at him. He growls as he stops her before she can touch him.

"For the last time, it's Maximus," he growls.

"But Max will be so much easier when I moan it," she smirks, causing me to choke on the coffee I was sipping.

"Oh shit!" Layton gasps as he looks at me. I'm staring at the girl who has the audacity even to suggest my man would touch her.

"Shorty never has any issues moaning my name," he replies, wrapping an arm around my waist and tugging me close to him before kissing me so hard that it takes my breath away.

"You're sleeping with your stepbrother!" Amber yells before laughing again. I smile at Sophia as I lean against my man, leaving my hand resting on his chest. I can tell she's put out that I have what she has always wanted.

"Oh, this could be interesting," Layton mutters under his breath, unable to hide the massive smirk on his face, as Maximus chuckles in my hair. The girls seem oblivious to the fact, and the guys are trying, but failing, to hold it together.

"I always thought she would end up with that stuck-up fucker Christian," Sophia adds.

And just like that, all the humour from the situation has gone.

"What did you call him?" I demand, stepping out of Maximus's arms.

"Oh, come on, he was always telling you what to do and that you should stay at home and be a good little girl," she answers, rolling her eyes.

"Maybe he was looking out for me as he could see I was on a slippery slope and was going to end up throwing everything away," I point out, annoyed.

"You wouldn't have thrown everything away; you were just trying to have fun. He was a killjoy, and you know it."

I step forward and close the distance between us a little. I hear Layton asking Maximus if he should intervene, but he knows, as well as anyone else, that this is overdue.

"At least he helped me when I hit rock bottom. He didn't force me out onto the streets with nowhere to go or money to eat."

"We didn't force you out; we gave you a couch to live on. You're the one who disappeared in the middle of the night without so much as a word!" Amber snaps, taking a step forward.

"Because I couldn't afford to stay! You wanted two

hundred pounds a week from me!" I yell, throwing my empty hand up in the air.

"It was to go towards the rent and bills," she screeches back.

"Yeah, the whole amount! What were you going to pay towards?" I ask. "I heard everything you two said that last night when you thought I was still at rehearsal—laughing about how you were going to get me to pay for everything so you guys could enjoy the free ride and have more money to spend at the weekends. You figured you would get more money out of me that way, not like you ever paid for the nights out anyway; it was always me. You even said it was the only reason you kept my sorry ass around." I had been so hurt hearing how my best friends didn't really care about me, and it was always my generosity they loved.

I leave out how I heard they would try to get money from the O'Reillys for putting me up. I can already sense Maximus's anger radiating behind me. I don't need to add fuel to that fire. Feeling him there reminds me that I don't need them anymore. I have more than they ever will.

"Let's face it, you were always well off and could afford it! You would have asked your stepbrothers for help eventually." Amber shakes her head and looks at the guys over my shoulder. "You did fine anyway. You bagged a millionaire, and I'm sure stick-up-his-arse Christian still has his say over what you can and can't do."

I jump forward, all anger taking over. I feel an arm slide around my waist, holding me back as someone takes the coffee from my hand. Maybe lashing out wouldn't be the best thing to do right now, but I will not let anyone talk shit about my man.

"Say one more thing about my fiancé, I dare you," I

snarl, desperate to teach her a fucking lesson once and for all.

"Fiancé? I thought you were with him," she frowns, nodding to Maximus behind me.

"Oh, I am," I reply, grinning. I stand tall and look her dead in the eye. "I haven't just got one fiancé; I have four, and in less than two months' time, I will be Jasmine O'Reilly."

A grin spreads against Amber's lips as she shakes her head.

"Who would have thought the fridged bitch would become a slut."

"Watch your fucking mouth," Maximus growls behind me, but I place a hand over his, which rests on my stomach. I sense Layton standing closer to me and know he will be just as furious as Maximus right now. Layton and I call each other every name under the sun, but if anyone else does it in front of him, he reminds me why he's my security.

But I realise I'm not angry; I know these girls, and I expected nothing less than them becoming nasty bitches when they found out about me and the guys. So, instead of getting irate, I lean back against Maximus smugly.

"It's okay, let her say what she wants. She's just jealous. I have four men who love me, whereas she's always struggled to keep a man longer than a few months."

"I never thought you would turn out like her, but here we are. Both of you are unable to keep your legs closed and happy to take whatever dick is offered as long as you get something out of it. Like mother like daughter." The smug look on her face tells me all I need to know. She wants to hurt me, and in many ways, she has. The one person I never want to turn out like is my mother, but with the guys' help, I have realised I never will. So, I smile instead of letting her think she's getting one over on me.

"If you had said that a few months ago, it would have destroyed me to be compared to her," I start, taking a step forward to close the distance between us as I stare my childhood friend in the eye, refusing to let her get to me. "But now I know I will never be that bitch. I will never abuse my children, and I certainly won't ever let someone touch them or try to sell them. You can say what you like about me, but I can hold my head high, knowing that I have not one but four men who love me more than anything in this world, and there is nothing they wouldn't do for me, as I would do anything for them. I have the love and stability you could only dream of." Taking a step back, I lean into Maximus's arms.

"You know, I've actually missed you. Even after everything I heard, I've been thinking about reaching out. But you just reminded me why I'm better off without you and my bitch of a mother. I'm stronger, wiser and loved in a way you will never understand. You once told me you felt sorry for me, but how the tables have turned." I resist the urge to punch her, and instead, I take my coffee back from Layton and sip it as I watch the two of them.

Sophia looks like she's trying hard not to cry, and Amber looks furious. I can feel the two guys tensed and ready to intervene if they have to. But they won't without my say-so.

"You can sugarcoat it as much as you like, but it won't work. You still think you're better than everyone else, but you're not. Let's face it, no one wanted you, so you had to settle for your stepbrothers like the desperate whore you are," she snarls whilst staring at me.

"That's enough!" Maximus shouts as he steps around me and gets into Amber's face. "You need to watch your fucking mouth because I will not stand by and watch you trying to upset my fiancée when you have no idea what she has been through. And you," he turns his attention to Sophia. "When will you get the picture that I'm not interested? It's pathetic how you throw yourself at me every chance you get. Why would I pick someone like you compared to the woman behind me."

"Fuck you, both of you," Sophia yells before grabbing Amber's arm and dragging her away.

"Nice seeing you both; we will have to catch up again," I call cheerfully as they flip me off.

"Well, that was unexpected," Layton sighs beside me. I turn to face him with a smile on my face.

"You are so fucking hot when you stand up for yourself," Maximus growls before pulling me against him and kissing me hard.

"I'm ready to go home," I point out, smiling as the two girls hurry away. "Are you finished with whatever you were doing?" I ask, hoping to go back with him and show him how much I love him.

"I've got her from here," he tells Layton, not looking away from my eyes once. My whole body has come alive with need. I want this man inside me now.

"But Christian wants-" Layton starts, but Maximus stares in his direction, daring him to keep arguing.

"I will deal with my brother if he gives you any hassle. Now go." Layton doesn't say another word. I catch him nodding once and walking away. Maximus looks back at me and grins.

"Daddy needs some alone time with his Shorty. You

fancy a short weekend break?" he whispers in my ear as I nod, grinning from ear to ear. "Good." He kisses me once on the lips, takes my hand and marches towards the car park as I giggle, trying to keep up.

Chapter Two

JASMINE

Maximus starts tapping away on his phone as soon as we're in the car. Pulling my coat off and throwing it in the back, I ask what he's doing, but he flashes me his devious grin and tells me to wait and see. I playfully try to look over his shoulder to peek at his phone, but he just looks at me with one sexy arched brow.

"Brat, don't think I won't pull you over my knee and spank you in this car in front of everyone," he warns. My thighs clamp together as my sex throbs. Is it wrong I want that?

Maximus looks down at my lap, slowly letting his eyes roam up my body. He stares deep into my eyes as I chew on my bottom lip. "Behave." The deepness of his voice makes me want to do anything but behave. He reaches over and takes my chin between his thumb and forefinger.

"Put your seatbelt on and do as you are told for a little while. I promise it will be worth it." The way his eyes burn into mine, I know he's about to blow my mind. "Are you going to be a good girl?" I nod slowly, unable to look anywhere but at him. "That's what I thought," he winks before kissing my lips and returning to his phone.

We sit silently for a moment as he grins at whatever he's organising. As soon as he's finished, he connects the phone to the car and pulls up the number for the house phone. It starts to ring as he pulls out of the parking space and heads for the exit.

"O'Reilly." Jason's voice calls out through the speakers.

"Hey, it's just me," Maximus starts. "Just giving you all a heads up that Shorty's with me. We won't be home until tomorrow evening," he explains whilst swiping his card at the barrier, allowing us to leave.

"Where's Layton?" he asks.

"I sent him back. We don't need him; I've got her."

"No worries, I will give him the day off if he can't get hold of Terry to see if he needs him for anything."

"Are Terry and Daddy still away?" I ask. Christian was only meant to be gone for a few hours the other day, and it's now been three days. I've hardly heard from him, which is very unusual as he always makes a point of calling me at least three times a day when he's forced to be away. But I've had nothing this time besides three very short text messages.

"Yes, Jazzy. Don't worry, though. I spoke to Terry less than twenty minutes ago, and everything is fine. He reckons they will be home tomorrow evening, so don't worry about them. Concentrate on having a good time with just the two of you. I will see you when you get back. Love you."

"Love you too," I answer with a smile as Maximus reaches over and places a hand on my thigh.

"Have fun, you two, and try to stay out of trouble," Jason laughs.

"Where's the fun in that?" Maximus laughs, his hand sliding further up my leg. I can't help grinning as I slide my butt closer to the edge of the seat, giving him better access to the part that's throbbing for his touch. Knowing what I'm after, he grins but removes his hand and winks, leaving me aching for his touch.

"You okay after seeing the two bitches?" Maximus asks as we head out of town.

"Yeah, I am," I answer with a smile. "It sucks to know that our friendship meant so little to them, but I'm happier than I've ever been, and I don't need them in my life." Maximus lifts my hand to his lips and kisses my knuckles.

"You have come a long way, Shorty, and I know I speak for all of us when I say we couldn't be prouder of you." Leaning my head against his shoulder, I close my eyes and smile.

"Thank you, Daddy."

Maximus kisses my head before I sit up, letting him concentrate on driving.

"You're welcome, Shorty. Now, why don't you sort some music out? We have a thirty-minute drive ahead of us."

I don't need telling twice, especially as I know Maximus will have my favourite band ready for us to listen to. As much as he sighs, just as he is now, I know he would never stop me from listening to them.

Nickelback starts playing from the stereo, and I place my hand on his thigh as he drives and tells me about the building he visited this morning and his plans for it.

Thirty minutes later, Maximus pulls off the road and heads down a smaller one. I look ahead, hoping to get some idea of where we are heading; it's then that a huge hotel comes into view.

"Where are we?" I ask excitedly.

"Somewhere I've wanted to bring you for years," Maximus grins as he stops outside the main entrance. A guy around the same age as me jogs down the steps to the car and stops beside my door.

"Open that door, and I will break your legs," Maximus warns as he climbs from behind the wheel. The guy instantly jumps back and looks like he is going to soil himself, stumbling over an apology. Maximus storms to my door and opens it as the guy jumps back further, wanting to put as much distance between them as possible. The door opens, and he holds out his hand to help me out of the car.

"Was that really necessary?" I ask under my breath. He places a hand on the base of my back and leads us up the steps, chucking his car keys to the trembling valet.

"For the first time in weeks, I don't have to share you with anyone. So yes, it was necessary. No one will touch you except me for the next thirty hours." It takes everything in me not to stumble as my heart rate skyrockets and my body shakes with need.

Until I moved in with the guys, I had no idea they could be so ruthless or that I would like it as much as I do. At some point, every single one of them has shown me just how dangerous they can be and why everyone who knows the name O'Reilly understands what will happen to them if they get on the wrong side of the brothers. Well, everyone but me. I know that the guys would never hurt me in any way. Nothing will ever come between us again; people have tried and failed. Our parents included.

Maximus leads me through a beautiful entrance hall to a reception desk where a woman is smiling. I don't miss how she looks at him, and only him. I can see the lust in her eyes, and I don't like it. Maximus may be drop-dead gorgeous, but he's also mine.

As we come to a stop at the desk, I lean into his side and place my left hand with my large engagement ring on his chest to ensure she knows he is taken. I feel, rather than hear, Maximus chuckle under his breath as he kisses the top of my head affectionately. The woman does a double take at the ring and then quickly looks at me as she introduces herself and welcomes us to the hotel and spa.

"Mr and Mrs O'Reilly, I booked online half an hour ago," Maximus announces. I smile as warmth rushes through my body. I love it when they guys already refer to mc as their wife. I'm rarely introduced as their fiancée, and I will never get bored hearing it.

"Of course, I have already made sure everything is ready for you in the suite," the receptionist smiles as she types something on her keyboard before lifting a key card and placing it on the desk on top of some papers already there.

"Here is your key and all the information about the facilities available. Do you require someone to take your bags?"

It suddenly dawns on me I have nothing with me, not even a hairbrush or change of underwear. But as I'm about to point this out, Maximus's hand slides around to my hip and gives a quick squeeze.

"They aren't here yet; my brother will drop one off in about an hour. His name is Sean O'Reilly. Give him a key card, and he will drop them off in the room before returning the key. No one else is to enter unless we say so."

"Of course, Mr O'Reilly. Is there anything else you need? Would you like to book a table for dinner?" she asks, but Maximus shakes his head.

"No, we will eat in our suite."

"That's absolutely fine," she smiles and notes something on the system. "Do you have any questions?" Maximus shakes his head and picks up the paperwork and key card.

"Okay, if you go to the end of the hall, you will find an elevator. The suite you booked is on the third floor. The elevator opens, facing the door to the suite." The two of us thank her before Maximus takes my hand and leads me in the direction, she pointed us towards.

We stop in front of the elevator, and Maximus presses the button. He looks at me with a devious smile on his face. Leaning in, his lips stop just before they touch mine.

"I've wanted to bring you here for so long," he whispers as his lips brush against mine.

"Why haven't you?" I ask, leaning forward to close the distance between us, but he moves back, grinning further.

"Things get in the way, like you not knowing how I felt, brothers, arsehole parents and work." The door opens in front of us, and we step inside. The second, the doors are closed, and Maximus presses the button for the third door; he walks me backwards until my back is pressed against the mirrored wall.

"Give me your phone, Shorty," he demands, his hand held before him. Retrieving it from my handbag, he takes it from me and unlocks it before turning it off.

"As I said outside, I'm not sharing you for the next thirty hours. You will not be contacting any of your daddies until I say so. Is that understood?" When I nod, he arches one brow in warning.

"Yes, Daddy," I answer quickly. It's usually only Christian who demands I always use my words. But when the others are feeling particularly spicy, they demand the same thing. It's their way of reminding me to use my safe words if things become too intense.

Maximus leans closer so his whole body is pressed against mine, sandwiching me between him and the mirror behind us.

"I can't wait to spend this time just you and me. No interruptions or having to share you." He grinds up against me, rubbing me in just the right spot through my jeans.

"Daddy?" I gasp, my eyes rolling back as he rubs against me again.

"Yes, Shorty?" Maximus whispers against my neck.

"I need you."

Maximus lifts his head and grins, a look I've come to associate with him being ready to blow me wide open.

"Where do you need me?"

"Everywhere!"

I barely get the word out as my whole body tightens with desperation. His hands leave the wall behind me as the door pings to signal we have reached our floor.

Chapter Three

JASMINE

Grabbing my ass, he lifts me so I can wrap my arms and legs around him as he carries me out of the elevator, coming to a stop in front of the door and pulling the key card from his back pocket.

In seconds, we are inside the room, and doors closed behind us. I know I should be paying attention to where we are and where Maximus is taking me, but I can't tear my eyes from him.

Maximus carries me into the bedroom and kicks the door closed before placing me on my feet. The second I'm out of his arms, I want to jump back into them, wrapping myself around his body so I never feel empty again.

"When you look at me with those fuck me eyes, I swear everything else stops existing." Maximus slowly steps back into my space and places a finger under my chin, forcing me to look up at him.

"Tell me what you're thinking," he whispers, releasing my chin and running a knuckle gently down my cheek. His other hand slowly slides from my hip to my lower back.

"That I love you," I whisper, tears burning my eyes. "That I don't think I have ever loved you more than I do at this moment," I add, placing a hand on his chest whilst leaning into him. "That I want and need you, now."

Maximus's eyes darken whilst he stares deep into mine. For a moment, time stills as we absorb each other, unable to look away or move. It's him who breaks the spell by leaning forward and kissing me as his fingers thread into my hair. He kisses me like he's been starved of me but is holding back.

Maximus is a dominating lover, but now and again, he will make love to me and shower me with nothing but affection, and it is just as mind-blowing as when he fucks me into next week.

"I love you, Shorty," he whispers against my lips. "I have since the moment I saw you, and I will continue to love you until my last breath." He kisses down my neck. His lips only leave my skin when he takes hold of the bottom of my jumper and pulls it over my head, leaving me in a lace bra.

Maximus looks into my eyes as he unfastens my jeans. I undo each button on his shirt, revealing his broad, muscular shoulders and eight-pack. Leaning forward, I place kisses along his chest as I slide his shirt from his back, desperate to get my lips on every part of him. But he pulls away with a smile as his fingers hook into the waistband of my jeans. Maintaining eye contact, he lowers himself so he is kneeling in front of me whilst pulling down my jeans and helping me out of them completely, leaving only my lace thong in place.

Sitting back on his heels, his eyes slowly make their way up my body, leaving a burning sensation in their wake. I try to control my breathing but fail when his eyes finally find mine.

"You are so perfect," he whispers, reaching out to take

hold of my hips. He stands from the floor, lifting me with ease. Placing my hands on his shoulders, we continue to look into each other's eyes as he walks forward and lays me on the soft bed so he is lying over me. One hand remains on my hip, the other cupping my head as he lies between my legs.

I don't know how long we lie there, my hands on his shoulders, his hands on my hip and head, but neither of us makes a move. We just look into each other's eyes and take this moment just to be us.

"I am so proud of you." The words are barely a whisper from his lips.

"Why?" I laugh nervously.

"Because you have come so far and are no longer the pushover you let your friends mould you into." His fingers brush some hair from my forehead lovingly, and my eyes start burning again.

"I have hated how those girls have treated you from the moment I met them. We could all see that they were not the right friends for you, but every time we mentioned it, you would pull away; we were forced to stop and wait for you to realise on your own." His hand that rests on my hip lifts as he trails his fingers from my hip up my side and across the breast he leans away from. His eyes follow the trail of his fingers as he moves my bra to one side, and he cups my breast, causing a gasp to leave my lips as I watch his eyes, watching my body.

Maximus takes my nipple between his thumb and forefinger and pinches slightly.

"Today, you stood up to them," he whispers, finally looking back into my eyes. "And I'm going to show you how proud I am of you." I cease to breathe as he takes my nipple between his teeth. Pleasure blooms in my chest as he flicks the nipple with his tongue whilst massaging the breast with his hand—my back arches off the bed when he bites down on it slightly.

Slowly, he moves his lips from one breast to the other, peppering the skin with soft kisses and nips of his teeth before giving the other nipple the same amount of attention. As my back arches from the bed again, he reaches around and unfastens the bra with one hand before sitting up a little to remove it completely.

Leaning back down, he lets his hand slide up between my breasts, only stopping once he has hold of my throat. He doesn't tighten his hold as his mouth moves to mine.

"You held your head high today, Shorty. You stood up for yourself, our relationship, and your other daddies." Maximus kisses me on the lips as his hand tightens ever so slightly around my throat. "I fucking love the way you stood tall and took no shit." His lips leave mine and move down the side of my throat, peppering the skin with soft kisses again.

"I saw the way your eyes changed when that little bitch tried to throw herself at me." His lips move from one breast to the other, as the anger I had felt at that moment threatens to take hold of me.

"I always hated the way she wanted you," I gasp as he starts kissing down my stomach, his hand still around my throat but not tightening.

"I know." His lips reach my stomach as his hand leaves my throat and starts massaging my breast. "I used to see how you glared at her when she would call me Max or flutter her eyelashes at me." Lifting his head, he looks into my eyes with a devious smile. "It would make me rock hard, knowing you were jealous." A memory flashes before me and nearly takes me under, but the feel of Maximus kissing the thin material that sits at the apex of my thighs pushes all coherent thoughts from my mind.

"Fuck, I love the way you smell," Maximus growls as he buries his face between my legs, smelling me through the material I know is soaking wet.

"Daddy," I gasp as he pulls away from me.

"What do you need? Tell me what you want."

"Lick me," I beg, feeling so close to finding my first release before he's even touched me down there.

"Like this?" I look down to see him looking up at me as he slowly licks the material of my thong, applying just enough pressure to tease me but not enough to make me come.

"No," I groan as his finger starts toying with the edges of the material.

"How about this?" his tongue sweeps up the inside of my thigh, and I groan with frustration.

"No," I cry out, getting desperate for his touch. I hear Maximus chuckle before the sound of fabric ripping. Before I can ask why he did that, I feel his tongue lick me from entrance to clit. I cry out as the sensation consumes me.

"Yes," I gasp as he does it again.

"Like this, Shorty?" I feel his tongue flick the sensitive tip of my clit as he pushes a finger inside of me.

"Yes! Don't stop!" I cry out as he devours me, pushing me closer and closer to the release I'm so desperate for. I feel rather than hear him chuckle as he continues to feast on me. I can't stop myself from grinding against his face, desperate to come. I cry out with frustration as he pulls away from me and quickly lies on the bed beside me.

"Come here." I move to lie on top of him, but he shakes his head. "Sit on my face." I don't need telling twice. I need his head back between my legs now.

"That's it, Shorty," he whispers as I straddle his head. I feel his tongue brush against me as he begins licking me again. "Use Daddy's face to make yourself come."

I start rocking my hips and grinding against his face as he uses my movement to give me as much pleasure as possible. I reach up and thread my fingers through my hair as I grind my pussy across the light stubble on his face. With his hands on my hips, I lose myself in his touch and his tongue.

"Daddy." The word barely a gasp as every muscle in my body coils tighter, and I know I'm so close. Maximus doesn't say anything; he continues his assault on my pussy. I feel the tip of a finger slip inside my back entrance, and I cry out as I fall apart and explode with pleasure. Maximus continues to lick and fuck me with his tongue, dragging out my orgasm until I'm completely overstimulated. I slide down his body, desperate to feel him inside of me.

"Daddy."

"I've got you, Shorty," he moans as he takes my hips and helps me slide down so I'm in just the right spot. With one hard thrust, he enters my already contracting pussy, filling me to the point it almost hurts.

"That's it," Maximus growls as he thrusts into me again. "You were made for me," he growls through gritted teeth, encouraging me to sit back up.

"Fuck yourself with my cock, Shorty." With his help, I start bouncing on his dick as his hands stay gripping my hips to the point I know they are going to leave bruises, which turns me wild.

"Fuck you are so perfect."

I can't open my eyes; I'm so close. I love how these guys can make me come, only to do it again seconds later. Running my fingers through my long hair again, I continue to fuck myself with his dick. Maximus's grip on my hips tightens each time he moans or calls my name, which pushes me closer to the edge.

"Fuck," Maximus roars as his fingers dig deeper into my hip, and I know he is getting close. "Rub your clit, show it to me."

Sliding my hand across my stomach, I use one finger to rub my clit, just how I like it. I look down and watch Maximus watching me. The look on his face is enough to push me over the top, and I orgasm, covering his cock with my release.

"Shorty," Maximus roars as he slams me down onto this pulsating cock, once, twice, three times before I feel him filling me. I stay sitting until my body slumps forward, well and truly spent. Maximus wraps his arms around me and holds me close as we both gasp for breath.

"I love you." The three words whisper across my shoulder before Maximus's lips gently follow. "I love you so fucking much it hurts." I feel tears fill my eyes again as I close my eyes and enjoy the way his soft touch feels.

"I know," I whisper before lifting my head to look into his rich chocolate eyes. "I love you just as much, Daddy."

"I know," Maximus whispers with a smile. I lean in and kiss his lips before placing my head back on his chest and looking at the bed for the first time.

"I didn't realise the bedding was white," I say with a smile as Maximus roars, laughing.

"How haven't you realised?"

I shrug whilst sitting up so I'm straddling his lap with my hands on his chest.

"I was a little preoccupied," I wink as he smiles at me, putting his hands back on my hips.

"You are so beautiful," he whispers, reaching up with one hand and tucking some hair behind my ear. "Even more so when you are riding my face," he winks back at me.

"How would you know? I could have been pulling weird faces the whole time, and you would have had no idea," I laugh. A big grin spreads across Maximus's face as he bursts out laughing.

"You really haven't been paying attention to the room, have you." He looks up at the ceiling, and I follow his line of sight.

"There's a mirror on the ceiling!" I exclaim, shocked. "Why is there a mirror on the freaking ceiling?"

"I think the bigger question is, how didn't you notice when you were lying under it for a good five minutes." He sits up and wraps an arm around my waist while the other stays behind him, propping us up. "Was I so good that you completely ignored our surroundings?"

I lean in and kiss his lips while wrapping an arm around his neck.

"Daddy, you are so good; I don't know what anything other than the elevator looks like, and even that's a blur."

His lips crash into mine as he stands, lifting me with him. I wrap my legs around his waist as I start laughing.

"Where are you taking me?"

"To give you the guided tour of the suite," he announces, walking back through the bedroom door and into a sitting area. He carries me over to the table and picks up two champagne flutes. "Hold these, please." I take them quickly before placing my arms back around his neck.

"This is the sitting area; you won't be seeing much of this," he winks before turning to a curtain on the right. "That's the door to the balcony, where I may let you sit out later. I need to see how private it is first." He looks down between our naked bodies and smiles. "I haven't decided if

I will let you get dressed yet." Our eyes lock for a moment, and I smile.

"I'm not sure I will let you get dressed either." A devious grin appears on his face, and I can't help but laugh. Maximus marches us to the coffee table, picking up an ice bucket with a bottle of champagne before returning to the bedroom. I wait to be thrown on the bed, but he walks past it and to another door.

"This is one of the main reasons I wanted to bring you here."

I look around and realise we are in a massive bathroom with a huge tub, which is floor-level. It's filled with water and lots of bubbles; the air smells amazing.

"I want to go in there!" I cry excitedly. Maximus laughs and walks us over to the tub.

"I had them fill it ready for us, and it's temperature controlled so it won't be cold." He walks us into the water and sits with me still on his lap. The water is warm, and I instantly melt into my amazing man.

"This is perfect," I sigh as he kisses the top of my head.

"No, Shorty, you are perfect, and I can't wait to spend this time just you and me." I lift my head and look into his eyes as a smile spreads across my face.

"Neither can I."

Chapter Four

JASMINE

"Thank you," I whisper, taking another glass of champagne from Maximus.

We are sitting in the huge tub together. I'm between his legs, leaning back against his chest, feeling more relaxed than I have in ages.

This is what I needed, what *we* needed. I try not to spend more time with one of the guys than the others, and I don't have favourites. I love each of them in their own way. But sometimes, I just want to hide away with one of them and not get interrupted or even see the others. It always feels like I have to keep everyone happy, which can be exhausting sometimes.

"Do you ever regret it?" The question slips from my lips before I'm even sure I want to ask it.

"Regret what?" Maximus asks, wrapping his arms around me.

"Agreeing to share what we have with the others," I ask nervously.

"No, Shorty, I don't regret it," he replies, kissing my

cheek. "Do I wish we could get more time alone like this? Sure, we all do. But I would never make you choose between me and my brothers. I wouldn't do that to you or them."

I nod while trying to push all the worries to the back of my mind, but I'm struggling for some reason.

"Do *you* regret it?" he asks, turning slightly so he is looking at me.

"No." I'm unable to hide the sadness in my voice.

"You don't sound so sure. What's the matter?"

"I'm scared," I admit out loud for the first time in a while.

"Of what? Us?"

"No. Well, yes, but not in the way I think you are thinking," I'm rambling, I know it. Taking a deep breath, I try to pick out the right words. "I'm scared one or more of you will regret it and leave. I'm worried that me marrying Christian legally is going to make the rest of you feel like I have a different relationship with him than the rest of you."

"But you do have a different relationship with him," Maximus answers, taking me by surprise. I turn my head to look at him, expecting to see him angry or upset, but he's smiling. "You have a different relationship with each of us, and we all know that. We know you don't love one of us more than the others, but we also know that you need us for different things, and we are all okay with that." Maximus takes my drink off me and turns me around so I'm straddling his lap, facing him.

"You don't need to be the one to worry that we will leave you, Shorty. We are the ones that have to worry about *you* leaving *us*," he says softly, running his knuckles down my cheek. I open my mouth to argue, but he shakes his head, stopping me. "Let me finish." He watches me momentarily as if waiting for me to continue arguing before continuing.

"I know you have no plans to leave, that you love us all in various different ways. But there is more chance of you choosing one of us over the others. We all had to discuss that before we agreed to share you, which we did at length. I don't think there is a scenario we haven't made a plan for, and one thing we all agreed on is that your happiness will always be our priority. If this relationship became too much for you, we would let you make your own choices, even if it meant that three of us had to let you go."

"I don't want to lose any of you. Not now, not ever," I whisper as my eyes fill. "I could never love one of you over the others. Since the day we all met, I knew you were all equally important to me, and I was terrified of the day you would leave me." A single tear slips down my cheek as the truth consumes me. Maximus smiles at me softly, brushing it away with his thumb, and cups my cheek.

"We quickly realised that you wouldn't want to choose and were scared we would run. Why do you think we waited so long to tell you how we felt?"

"I thought you were waiting for me to be twenty-one?" I ask, frowning. That's what they all told me.

"That was part of it," Maximus starts. "We figured our arsehole parents wouldn't be able to come between us if you were classed as a full adult. But that's not the main reason. We wanted to show you that we weren't going anywhere." He wipes away another tear whilst keeping eye contact.

"We knew very early on you believed we would only be in the picture whenever our parents demanded it, and that wasn't what we wanted. We wanted the type of relationship where we would be there for every event in your life, even if you didn't know at the time. We wanted you to know how much we cared about you and how important you were to us. Most importantly, we wanted you to know that we loved you and you were stuck with us, whether you liked it or not. Even if it meant letting you make bad choices and being there to help pick up the pieces afterwards, it was all part of the plan of making you feel loved."

I lean forward and hold my man whilst resting my cheek on his broad chest.

"I didn't make that many bad choices," I sigh, smirking. Maximus starts laughing as he wraps his arms around me.

"Shorty, you made some of the worst choices in the three years we watched over you. Your friends being a big one. Don't think we didn't know about the boyfriends because we did, and they were all terrible, to and for you."

"Is that why you kept an eye when I was out? Why you would show up, even though Sophia would throw herself at you?" I ask, sitting up a little before looking down at the water. The bubbles have long gone, but the water is still warm, thanks to the jets that turn it into a hot tub.

"We were there whenever we could be. If we weren't, then a member of our security team would be. Why do you think we suggested the various clubs for you to try? Because we controlled them and had someone watching your back the whole time." I remember all the times I was helped by bouncers and people behind the bars. They called me a taxi or just ensured I had some water. Everyone always joked about how I was pampered; I guess I was, I just didn't realise it. But as those memories arise, so does another.

"I thought you were going to give in one night." The words are out of my mouth before I can stop them. Maximus is looking at me, but the memory is at the forefront of my mind. One that I pushed back earlier when he was between my thighs, but now there is no distraction and the pain I felt that night hits me in the chest.

"To what?" When I don't answer or look at him, he places his finger under my chin and lifts my head, not allowing me to blink back the burning tears. "What did you think I was going to give in to? You?"

I shake my head and try to look away, but Maximus turns my head to the side, so I'm looking at him again.

"To Sophia," I whisper, remembering the pain I felt that night.

"Never-" he starts, but I shake my head.

"You saw us out one night; you were with friends and sat with us. Even though you sat next to me, you kept laughing with her and putting your arm around the back of the booth where she was sitting." Maximus thinks for a moment before the realisation appears in his eyes.

"To make you jealous," he admits; with a sigh, he lets go of my chin and runs his fingers through his hair before looking deep into my eyes. "I was tired of hiding how I felt. I wanted you to know but knew I couldn't tell you. That night when we saw you, I was being nice to your friends, hoping for a reason to spend the night out with you. She was all over me, and I could tell you were jealous. I wanted you to finally admit to me and yourself that you wanted me as much as I wanted you. So, I flirted with her, but my eye was always on you." He lifts my arms, places them over his shoulders, and rests his hands on my hips, tugging me tighter against him.

"I'm sorry; I only did that because I'd had quite a bit to drink and was determined to make you so jealous you caved into me."

"I nearly did," I sigh, tightening my arms around his neck to lean against his chest. "I was so hurt and angry. But

I thought if I did anything, you would reject me, so instead, I told you I was going to the toilet and went outside for some fresh air before heading home."

Maximus's arms tighten around me, and for a moment, I think he's going to say something, but instead, he takes a deep breath and kisses the top of my head.

"All of us wasted so much time trying to do the right thing and even doing the wrong thing completely," Maximus sighs. "But I'm sorry for what I did that night. I shouldn't have tried to make you jealous; it wasn't fair to mess with your feelings like that. I saw the pain in your eyes, and that's why I stopped as soon as you went to the toilet. When we all heard you had gone home, I was furious with myself. I … I sat in my car outside your house all night and most of the following day, wanting to see that you were okay and to let you know nothing had happened." Maximus buries his face into my hair and sighs. "I'm sorry, Shorty. I never wanted to hurt you."

"You haven't. I mean, you did at the time, but I get it now."

"You are too good for me." Lifting my head, I frown at him. "Yes, you are. I have done things I'm not proud of, like that night hurt you. I'm sorry, and I promise that I will spend the rest of my life making it up to you and showing you how much I love you."

I look deep into his eyes with a genuine smile.

"You have already made everything up to me and more. I love you, and I know you love me too. Nothing will ever change that." Leaning forward, I kiss his lips at the same moment as I feel him hardening underneath me, and I know just how to show him how much I love him. Lifting, I lower myself, impaling myself on his cock. We both moan together as our hold on each other tightens, and we show each other just how perfect we are for each other.

Chapter Five

MAXIMUS

The sound of someone banging on a door wakes me with a jump.

"Was that our door?" Jasmine asks as she lifts her head from my chest where she had been peacefully sleeping in my arms. I tighten my arm around her and lie back on the pillow.

"I don't care if it was. I'm not leaving this room until I have to." I kiss the top of her head and pull her on top of me to kiss her.

"I can get behind that," she giggles as her smooth skin sends shockwaves through mine. Her pussy rubs against my hard cock, which is desperate to enter her again.

The banging sounds out again, and I realise it *is* coming from the door of the suite.

"What the fuck?" I curse as it happens again.

"What if something's wrong?" Jasmine states next to me as whoever it is bangs again.

"Maximus! Jaz! I know you can hear me!"

What the actual fuck?

"You have got to be kidding me," I growl, climbing from the bed, grabbing my discarded boxers and pulling them on. "Stay there, Shorty," I order, walking out of the room and into the sitting area as he bangs again.

"Alright!" I yell, reaching for the door and throwing it open. Grabbing his collar, I pull him into the room and slam the door behind us.

"Am I not allowed two fucking days where I can keep my fiancée for myself?" I roar, slamming Layton into the wall next to the door.

"Don't shoot the messenger. I'm only here because I was ordered to find you when no one could get hold of you," he answers, holding up his hands defensively.

"That's because we wanted to be left alone, so we turned our phones off!" I snap, slamming him into the wall one last time before walking away from him. "Just one night! That's all I wanted!"

"Daddy." I turn to her soft voice to find her standing with a hotel robe around her. "Layton would have just been following orders." Her voice is calm and collected. I know she's right, but I'm still pissed off. Holding out one arm, Jasmine walks to me, and I hold her tight as I smell her hair, using the scent of her shampoo to centre myself.

"What's so important you needed to find us?" Jasmine asks, looking at Layton.

"There's been a development at the safe house."

Jasmine stiffens in my arms as she gasps, and I suddenly hate myself for throwing a tantrum. Of course, they would have tried to contact us. No matter what's happening with us, Jasmine's best friend is her priority.

"What's happened?" I ask, leading her to the sofa and

pulling her onto my lap. Holding her close, I ensure she is covered whilst signalling for Layton to sit on the other seat and explain.

"We had word this morning from Logan that Travis has left the safe house. They think he has gone to Nicholson to get this all over and done with."

"Why would he choose now to go?" Jasmine asks in my arms.

"Travis loves Verity, Shorty. He would not willingly leave her unless he thought it could save her." I kiss the top of her head whilst running a hand up and down her back.

"What's going to happen now?" Jasmine asks. Layton shrugs and gives her a sad smile.

"We don't know. Travis left notes and told them to run if he's not back in three days, and he will find them. Ryan is worried as it's just the two of them keeping an eye on things at the moment, and Calvin can't lend us any more guys as they are needed elsewhere. He's got more starting in the new year, but that's no good for him now."

Jasmine looks up at me with tears in her eyes as I see her bottom lip tremble.

"Why is her dad doing this? I hate him for ruining everything for her," she sobs before burying her head into my chest and bursting into tears. I tighten my arms around her and hold her as she cries. I can see from Layton's face his heart is breaking for her. He might be her security guard, but he is also a great friend to Jasmine and Verity. Let's face it: you can't have one without the other.

"Do we not have anyone to send?" I ask. But Layton shakes his head.

"Terry is still with Christian, and others are on holiday for Christmas, so we are stretched as it is."

"What's Christian said?" I ask, running a hand up and down Jasmine's back as she cries.

"I don't even know if he knows. No one can get hold of him, and Terry didn't respond to my message before coming here."

I can see from the look on his face that there is more to it, but when he glances at Jasmine, I know he won't say anything in front of her. Something is going on with Christian; we all know it, but we have no idea what. He only communicates via text messages, and that alone is unlike him. It usually means he is worried he is being followed, so we haven't pushed anything yet.

"Why can't anyone get in touch with him?" Jasmine asks in my arms, and for a moment, I have no idea what to say. Luckily, Layton comes to the rescue.

"When Terry called yesterday, he said Christian was having issues with the screen and speakers on his phone because he accidentally knocked it into the sink. He is going to buy a new one today."

I call bullshit, but I won't say anything in front of Jasmine.

"Why can't everyone just be home and safe?" Jasmine sniffs into my chest. Listening to her worry like this is breaking my heart in two. I wish there was something I could do to help put her mind at ease.

"Take it you have your car?" I ask Layton, who nods. "Then you take her home, and I'll go and help keep watch at the safehouse with the Donavons until we have a better understanding of what's happening."

"What?" Jasmine exclaims, looking up at me, panicked. I place a hooked finger under her chin and tilt her head back so I can look her in the eye.

"I'm going to the safe house and will help the others

keep an eye on Verity until we know if Travis is safe or if they have to run." Leaning in, I press a kiss on her lips. "I will make sure your best friend is safe, Shorty."

"But will that put you in danger?" Jasmine asks, her eyes wide. "I don't want you to go missing as well." I smile and shake my head.

"I dare anyone to try and stop me from returning to you." I press another kiss on her lips and smile down at her. "Go get showered and dressed. I'll just let Jason know what's happening." Jasmine climbs to her feet and kisses me on the cheek before rushing towards the bathroom. I hold my hand out for Layton's phone, knowing mine will take too long to load up.

"It's me," I answer as soon as the phone stops ringing.

"I'm sorry. I know you wanted this time alone, but the shit has hit the fan-"

"It's fine," I answer, standing up and listening into the bathroom, where I can hear the water splashing as Jasmine showers. "I don't have long, so tell me what's happening with Christian."

"Nothing that we are aware of, but it's not like him to only communicate via Terry."

"Do we think he's been compromised?" There is always the possibility that someone has Terry's phone and is trying to lead us off track.

"If I hadn't spoken to Terry myself, I would say yes. But he ensures that Christian is safe and well and hasn't used a single safe word or trigger. All we can do is sit back and wait to see what happens." I know he's right, but my gut is telling me something is going on.

"Layton is bringing Shorty home. I'm going to lend a hand with the Donavons. They will need another set of eyes on the place."

"Calvin has found someone who will be there in forty-eight hours. So stay until they arrive, then get out."

"I will," I sigh, pinching the bridge of my nose. I now have a roaring headache and feel completely deflated.

"How is Jazzy?" Jason asks. I hear the shower turning off and know I have to be quick.

"Devastated and worried. It's why I'm going. I'm hoping it will give her some peace of mind."

"You're probably right. I'm staying at the house in case anything else comes to light with Christian, so send her home, and I will keep an eye on her. Sean is on his way back after staying with a mate last night. He should be home by the time Jazzy arrives."

I hear Jasmine leaving the bathroom and want to get off the phone before she hears something she shouldn't.

"I'll let you know when she is on her way. Speak soon." I don't wait for my brother to answer before hanging up and tossing the phone back to Layton. Jasmine is my priority until she is safely away with Layton.

"We will be ready to go in ten minutes," I tell him before walking into the bedroom and closing the door behind me. I turn to find Jasmine pulling on her underwear. I can see she's been crying again, and I hate how much her mood has changed from last night when she fell asleep in my arms, happy and relaxed.

"Sorry this break hasn't ended as you would have liked, Shorty," I sigh, grabbing my jeans and pulling them on.

"Me too, Daddy. We will have to try again when everything has calmed down." She walks over to me in her bra and tight jeans with a sad smile. "Thank you for a lovely time. I really did love that it was just the two of us for a bit."

"Me too, Shorty. We will do it again soon." Leaning down, I thread my fingers into her wet hair and tug until her head tilts back. "I promise I will always make time for us, no matter what."

"I know you will. You always have," she replies before I kiss her once more and release her so we can get dressed and out of here as quickly as possible, even though it's the last thing I want to do.

Chapter Six

CHRISTIAN

It's been four long days, and I have never been more relieved to finally be home.

"You ready to face the music?"

I turn to look at Terry as I take a deep breath.

"No time like the present," I answer, grabbing a bag from the back seat. It's a good job I'm rich as a few hours away turned into four days, and I had to keep sending Terry out to buy me new stuff, including a new phone.

"Remember to keep your mouth shut," I warn as Terry shakes his head.

"The truth will come out eventually, Christian. You need to be honest with them now."

"I don't remember paying you for your advice," I snap through gritted teeth and instantly regret it.

"No, you pay me to protect you, and sometimes that includes from yourself!" he snaps in retaliation. "Just remember I've had your back since we were kids, and I always will, even if you do pay my wages. But I'm not saying this as your employee; I'm saying this as the closest thing you have to a best friend. Don't push them away when you need them the most." He grabs his things from the back of the car and slams the boot shut.

"I will keep your secrets. I always have and always will. But don't expect me to put your pride over the safety of others. I wouldn't be doing my job as your head of security or your friend if I did."

I watch as he storms off towards the back of the building where the security hub is—no doubt to get all the details from our time away and then head home.

Letting out a deep sigh, knowing I need to face the music and walk through to the kitchen from the garage, where I'm surprised to find Mrs Brown making herself a hot drink.

"Look what the cat finally dragged in," she snaps, standing with her hand on her hips. "Do you have any idea how worried everyone has been?"

"Something came up…" I start, but Mrs Brown stops me by throwing her cloth onto the side and standing in front of me.

"It's not me you have to explain to; it's that poor girl upstairs. She is beside herself with worry about her best friend, and then her fiancé goes missing and doesn't even bother to pick up the phone to reassure her that he is okay."

"My phone was broken. They know-"

"Whatever your reasoning, you need to stop and think," she snaps, cutting me off. I turn around to drop my bag by the utility room as she continues to berate me. "Your brothers are used to you going off and doing your own thing, but young Jasmine isn't. She needs you right now, and you have only bothered to message a handful of times. And now, with everything going on, she is heartbroken and scared and needs her Daddy."

I spin around on the spot to look at her, it's then I realise how worried she looks.

"What's going on? Is Jasmine okay?" I demand, looking around.

"No. There seems to be some trouble with poor Miss Stevenson and the Donavons. Maximus left to help out. Poor Jasmine is worried sick."

"Where is she?" I demand, dropping my new overnight bag on the floor.

"Upstairs."

I don't waste any more time as I turn on my heels and rush out of the kitchen, heading straight for the stairs. Taking them three at a time, I charge towards her room to find it empty.

"She's in with Jason."

I turn at Sean's voice to find him walking towards me from his room.

"What the fuck's happened?" I demand, charging into Jason's room to find Jasmine curled up on his lap, her eyes red from crying.

I don't have to say a word; she leaps from him and straight into my waiting arms.

"You're finally home," she gasps as she hangs on to me tight, and her whole body starts to shake as she cries.

"I'm here, Sweetheart. I'm so sorry." Guilt like never before engulfs me as I hold her, running a hand over her head as she cries. I hear Sean moving something and turn in time to see him nod to the chair he has placed behind me.

I sit, pulling Jasmine onto my lap as she curls up small.

"What's happened?" I ask again, looking at my two brothers.

"We should be asking you the same question," Jason

replies. He doesn't snap or yell, but I know we will be having some strong words about my silence later.

"You know I was dealing with some shit. Now, fill me in on what's been going on here." Jason continues to stare at me for a moment, and the tension in the room builds. Just when I think I will have to demand someone answer me, Jason sighs while shaking his head.

"We got a call this morning that Travis had left the safe house. He has gone to find Nicholson to confront him about everything."

That stupid prick. He has always been reckless and leads with his heart. I've been waiting for him to do something stupid this whole time.

"What's Maximus got to do with it all? Mrs Brown said he wasn't here, but his car is in the garage."

"He went to help keep an eye out for trouble. He saw how worried Jazzy was and wanted to do something to help." Jason climbs off his bed and stretches. I know he would have been curled up on there with Jasmine for as long as she needed him, ignoring his own discomfort.

"That sounds about right. How is Verity doing with Travis leaving?" I ask, knowing she won't be taking it well.

"We don't know. She's run off."

"What?" That was the last thing I expected. Verity has never come across as the act first, think later type of girl.

"Yep, that's why Maximus's car is here. Layton met with Calvin to pass over Maximus's spare car key. Turns out she stole his before running, so they couldn't chase after her," Sean explains, shaking his head. "Maximus is driving Logan's car as he got to the safe house first."

"I'm going to kill her if Nicholson doesn't," Jasmine whispers against my chest.

"Nicholson won't hurt her," I whisper into her hair. But

I know I could be giving her false hope. I don't have any dealing with the man for a reason. He is known for hurting anyone who gets in his way, regardless of their sex and age. His son, who Verity has been promised to, is no better.

"When was the last time you heard from anyone?" I ask absentmindedly, running a hand over Jasmine's head.

"Two hours ago. Last I heard, Maximus was driving the remaining Donavons to Nicholson's place to see if they were both there."

"He better not get involved; he will bring a ton of shit to our door if he does," I warn. It's the last thing I need on top of everything else.

"But what about Verity?" Jasmine asks, leaning away from me.

"Sweetheart, we will do what we can, but we cannot be seen helping them," I explain, but I see the disappointment in her eyes. She is still so new to this world she doesn't understand how people like Nicholson work.

"Jazzy, Christian's right. Like I tried to explain, making enemies with someone like Nicholson is bad news for everyone involved." Jason sighs, sitting on the edge of his bed; he reaches over and takes her hand. "If we could storm in and take her, we would, but it's not that simple. Nicholson would ensure there were repercussions for our actions, and we will not put you in harm's way like that."

"But she's like a sister to me," Jasmine sobs as she looks at us all. "I can't sit here doing nothing when she's in danger." She looks to Sean as if hoping he will back her up, but he shakes his head.

"We won't do nothing, but the others are right; we can't be seen intervening."

My brothers and I share a look as Jasmine bursts into tears and leans back against me. We know that if anything happens to Verity and we don't prevent it, she will never forgive us. We have discussed it at length since the whole situation Verity's father has gotten her into came to light. We have considered paying off his debts to Nicholson, but again, that puts us in the middle of it all, and we need to deal with it without our identities being known.

I wish we could do more, but I will not risk my brothers' or Jasmine's lives for the sake of one another. She may hate me for it, but there is nothing I'm not willing to do to protect our family.

We all turn to Sean as his phone rings, and he pulls it from his pocket.

"It's Maximus," he declares before answering. "Hey, you're on speaker, what's going on?"

"I've left the Donavons at Nicholson's. Travis and Verity are there; they are okay and in no danger. I don't know the ins and outs, but the marriage is off, and Verity is free. Travis has to stay there for a few days, so the other two will take Verity home. But it's over from what I can gather."

We all let out a sigh of relief as Jasmine visibly relaxes into me. I tighten my arms around her and kiss the top of her head.

"Were you seen?" I ask Maximus.

"Oh, you're back, are you?" he snaps. "Of course, I wasn't seen. I'm not completely stupid."

I try to ignore the way he speaks at me, he has probably had a shitty day, but I need to know so I can do damage control.

"Shorty, if you even think about doing something as reckless as your friend just did, I will tan your ass so hard, you will never sit down again. Is that understood?"

"Yes, Daddy." She curls up smaller on my lap, and I

have to stop myself from laughing as she tries to use me as a shield against Maximus. "Are you heading home?" she asks.

"Yeah. Is there any chance there is some food left over? I'm starving," Maximus answers. Glancing at my watch, I see that it's already coming up to midnight, and he will be out for at least another two hours.

"Mrs Brown was going to plate up your food and leave it in the microwave for you. I will check that she has," Sean says as he hands his phone to Jasmine. "Jaz has my phone, as I'm sure she wants to talk to you before she heads to bed," he adds before walking out of the room.

"I'm going to wait for you to get back," she says into the phone.

"No, you're not. Go to bed, Shorty. I will see you in the morning."

Jasmine turns the loudspeaker off and stands from my lap before walking away as she talks to Maximus quietly.

"Everything sorted in Bristol?" I hear Jason ask as I watch our girl.

"Yeah, the building's been destroyed on the inside. Police think it's squatters or a bunch of ASBO kids. There have been a few similar cases recently."

One of the premises we have been converting into a new fitness centre was broken into, and a fire started a few days ago. Luckily, we were far from ready to open, and none of the equipment was inside. But they have destroyed the walls and some of the flooring. They had taken advantage of the windows still being boarded up so no one could see inside.

"Is this a one-off, then? Or will there be more?" Jason asks, standing from the bed.

"I don't know. Hopefully, it'll be a one-off," I reply, thinking about the damage I saw this afternoon.

"Do we need to talk when she isn't around?" he asks. I shake my head quickly, looking back to Jasmine, who walks over to us, no longer on the phone.

"I've sorted it," I answer quietly, hoping Jasmine won't hear. I know he's not going to drop it, but I'm too tired to deal with his nagging right.

"You okay, Jazzy?" Jason asks, placing an arm around her shoulder. She nods as she leans into him.

"Can I sleep in with you tonight?" she asks, looking at me. I stand with a smile and run a hand over her head.

"You know you don't need to ask," I reply, pressing a kiss to her head. "Why don't you go and say night to Sean and get ready for bed? I'll be right in."

Jasmine turns in Jason's arms and hugs him as she lifts onto her tiptoes to kiss his lips.

"Thank you for sitting with me all day," she whispers. Jason cups her cheek with his hand before kissing her gently.

"You know you don't have to thank any of us for looking after you, Jazzy. You are always our main priority."

"Doesn't mean I can't show how grateful I am for you all, though," she smiles before kissing his cheek and stepping back to face me. "I'll see you in a minute." She flashes a seductive grin, and I reach out, pulling her into my arms.

"You going to be in bed ready for me, Baby girl? So I can show you just how much I've missed you." She nods eagerly, so I press my lips to hers hard, claiming her, leaving her with no doubt that I'll be making her scream tonight.

I pull away, leaving her gasping for breath.

"Go and say goodnight to Sean, Baby. I'll be right there."

She rushes from the room eagerly, with a small giggle, as she goes to find Sean.

"She's been worried sick about you," Jason says beside me as we watch our girl rushing out of sight.

"I tried to get the phone sorted sooner, but the insurance guy and police were difficult from morning until night. I've hardly eaten or slept. All I've had time to do is pass messages through Terry." Running my fingers through my hair, I know I need to give him more information, even if it's the last thing I want to do.

"Going back to your question, I don't know what to think. My gut's telling me we need to be on the lookout for trouble, but I could be wrong."

"Or you are worried that something is going to go wrong with the wedding, and you are projecting those worries onto everything else." Jason cocks that one eyebrow at me, daring me to say he's wrong when I know he might not be.

"Maybe," I admit. "No harm in keeping an eye on things through."

"Well, just remember that it isn't just us you need to keep in contact with; it's her too. You dropped a ball this week, and it hurt her, even if she would never admit that to you."

"I know. I will speak to her. I really didn't mean to worry her or you," I answer before leaving his room. "I'll speak to you in the morning," I call, heading into my room to wait for my beautiful girl.

Chapter Seven

JASMINE

"How you feeling now, Princess?" Sean asks as he places an arm around my shoulder, keeping me close as we walk up the stairs.

"Better. I don't think I will completely relax until everyone is safely away from that house, though." My heart's been racing since Layton told Maximus and me what had happened. I just knew Verity would do something reckless, and hearing she had gone missing herself was terrifying. I am going to kick her ass when I get ahold of her after I've hugged her to death first.

"Maximus won't be too long, and I know Christian will be waiting for you in his room." He kisses me as we reach the landing where all five of our rooms are situated. "I know he upset you by not keeping in contact, but I'm sure there was a good reason. Don't go too hard on him," he smiles. "Good night, Princess."

"Good night, Daddy." I kiss him again before turning around and heading straight to Christian's room.

I enter, expecting to find him already in bed. But

instead, he's sitting on it with his back to me, holding his phone to his ear.

"Don't give me that bullshit! You need to remember who you work for," I hear him snap as I head straight for the en-suite, closing the door behind me, not wanting to disturb him whilst he's working.

I head to the sink and start my nightly routine of removing my makeup and cleansing my skin. I have toiletries in all four of the guys' bathrooms as well as my own. That way, I always have everything I need at hand, no matter what room I'm sleeping in. If I'm honest, I've hardly slept in my room in the eight months the guys and I have been together. If I do sleep in there, it's usually with all four guys, as my bed is the biggest. Even on rare occasions, all four of them are away simultaneously. I usually sleep in one of their rooms as I feel closer to them.

After I wash my face, I realise I can hear Christian's raised voice from the bedroom, not enough to hear what he's saying, but whoever is on the other end of the call is getting a telling off. I'm just glad it's not me.

I brush my teeth and apply my face cream to give Christian as much time as he needs to finish his phone call.

I look down at my hands and rub the last of the cream into them. I notice my engagement ring and remember the night the guys proposed.

We had all sat on our beach at the villa in Majorca, the same way as the first time we met, watching the sun go down. I had already told the guys I was ready to make our relationship legal, and I wanted us to get married so I could officially be the O'Reilly everyone keeps telling me I've become.

The four men surrounded me that night, and each declared their love to me. Maximus said he would never want another brat or for me to change. Sean promised to treat me like the princess he's called me since day one. Jason vowed to guide me and shower me with all the love he had to give and more, and Christian swore to protect me from whatever life would throw at us. Christian pulled out a jewellery box that contained five rings and placed one on my finger, asking me to marry him legally. A blessing of our polygamous relationship will follow straight after.

The wedding is a little over a month away, and I couldn't be more excited and happy. Looking down at my engagement ring, I know nothing will stop me from marrying my four guys. They are my whole world, and that will never change.

"Look, I have dealt with your crap for the last four days!" Christian growls as he opens the ensuite door and walks over to me, his phone still in his hand. "All I care about right now is making it up to my fiancée that I had to leave her for that time to sort shit out. Now fuck off, and don't get in touch until you have some good fucking news for me!" He ends the call and slams his phone onto the counter beside me.

"You got it fixed then?"

Christian looks at the phone and sighs, rubbing his face.

"It's a new one I picked up on the way home. I've just turned it on, and all your messages and some work came through."

I lean back and look up at my man, worried he is lying to me, but all I see is how tired he looks.

"I'm sorry, Sweetheart. I should have made more of an effort to contact you." He runs his knuckles down my cheek lovingly as I lean into his touch.

"It's okay; I know you have a lot going on," I reply, reaching forward to rest my hands on his chest.

"That's not the point. I was worried you would hear how stressed I was or I would snap at you by mistake, so I thought communicating through Terry was the best option. But I was wrong, and I'm sorry. I hate how much work is dragging me away from you at the moment," he sighs, leaning forward to kiss me.

What I thought was going to be a gentle kiss is anything but. It's strong, which he deepens by threading his fingers into my hair and wrapping an arm around my waist, keeping me held tightly against him.

I can feel his hard length, constricted by his suit trousers, and I can't help grinding up against him. A deep moan leaves Christian as I reach down and unfasten his belt before working on his trousers. Grabbing hold of his hips, I turn us so he is now leaning back against the counter as I break the kiss.

"Let me help you unwind, Daddy," I whisper against his lips before dropping to my knees, pulling his trousers and boxers down at the same time.

"Baby girl, you do that just by being here," he replies, running a hand over my head, his fingers tightening in my hair as I take his rock-hard cock in my hand. I look up at him through my lashes and can't miss how he hardens further.

"This may help a little more," I whisper with a grin before licking up his full length. Christian's eyes close as his head falls back. A deep growl-like noise sounds in his throat as I take him in my mouth, letting my tongue lick the tip before sucking him deeper.

I watch his whole body tense as I take him deeper. Watching the guys when I suck their dicks is as much a turn-on for me as it is for them. There is something about bringing these powerful men to putty in my hand that makes me almost orgasm from the sight of them alone.

"Fuck, Baby," he gasps out as I take him deeper again and nearly bottom out as his cock slides down my throat. I hum around him as his moans heighten my arousal.

Christian continues to hold his head back to the point I can't see if his eyes are open. The brat in me comes out before I can stop it.

"Eyes on me, Daddy."

Christian's head snaps down as he stares at me, my mouth once again filled with his cock as I smile around it.

"Oh, Baby girl." There is a warning in his tone, even though he has a big smile. He wraps my long ponytail around his fist before pulling my head back, so I have no choice but to let his cock fall from my mouth.

"What have I told you about topping from the bottom?" he asks, looking down at me as his grip on my hair tightens. "On your feet."

I stand whilst keeping eye contact. Christian grips my chin and tugs my hair, forcing me to look up at him.

"Do I need to remind you why I'm your daddy?" he asks with a playful grin, his dominating tone causing my sex to clinch.

"Maybe?" I tease, smiling as sweetly as possible, and I give him my best puppy dog eyes.

Christian doesn't give me a chance to argue or brat any further as he spins me around and pushes me forward so I'm bent over the counter—his hand slides across my throat before tightening slightly.

"Look at me in the mirror," he demands. When I look at our reflection, I see my strong, sexy man standing behind me, his hand around my throat as he dominates me just the way I like it.

"I'm going to fuck that cute little pussy of yours. The whole time, I want your eyes on me in our reflection. Every time you look away, I will spank you, reminding you who's the top in this relationship. Do you understand, Baby girl?"

"Yes, Daddy," I reply as my sex clinches and his hold on my throat tightens slightly.

I love being choked; it's a serious kink of mine. But then I was kidnapped and strangled in a way that nearly killed me. It took a long time to recover and to trust the guys, but slowly, they reminded me that just because one arsehole treated me that way, my four men never would. They were always patient and reminded me how much I could trust them until I could enjoy it again.

Christian grabs my underwear and leggings, pulling them down roughly. I know I won't be able to spread my legs far with them only around my knees, but that just adds to the thrill as I know when he impales me, I will feel it more.

Christian places his hand between my legs and spreads my sex open, running one finger through my lips, feeling how wet I am.

"I think you've been enjoying yourself. Does it make you wet sucking on Daddy's cock?" He leans in further, so his lips press against my neck as I gasp before moving to my ear. "Use your words, Baby girl," he warns, causing my stomach to tighten.

"Yes, Daddy. I love the feel of your cock in my mouth, but I prefer it somewhere else."

Christian grins at me in our reflection as his fingers slowly push into me, making my knees shake as the pleasure builds from that one simple touch.

"Good, because I have no desire to come down that sweet throat of yours. There's somewhere else I would much rather finish." Not giving me any warning, Christian removes his fingers and thrusts up into me, filling me with one move, causing me to cry out as my body is pushed against the counter. It's not pain that makes me gasp for breath is the utter overwhelming pleasure that overcomes my whole body every time one of my guys enters me.

"Eyes up, Baby," Christian chastises before spanking me. Each of the guys knows every one of my limits, and even though I have safe words with them all, I nearly never have to use them. I know Christian demanding 'eyes up' is his way of watching for any show of discomfort or displeasure.

"You are so beautiful," he moans as he starts working his cock in and out of me. "I love the way your eyes come alive as I fuck you, giving you everything I have," he growls as his grip on my throat tightens again as he forces my head a little higher, controlling everything from the pace he fucks me to the direction I'm looking. His spare hand flattens against my lower stomach before sliding down so he can start rubbing my clit as he picks up speed. His grip on my throat loosens a little, just enough for me to catch my breath. The flood of oxygen pushes me closer to the point I'm about to orgasm.

"Daddy!" I cry out as he lets go of my throat altogether and wraps my ponytail around his hand again. This time instead of pulling my head back, he leans me further over the counter and starts pounding into my pussy, as if to destroy it and me, for all other men, bar his brothers.

"Daddy's got you, Baby girl," he growls through gritted teeth as his assault on my clit intensifies, and I scream through an orgasm which destroys me on the inside and out.

"Fuck!" he curses as I know I must be clamped around

his cock, which is now pulsing inside of me. Christian roars out as he climaxes, filling me with his seed.

"Your greedy little pussy is milking me of every last drop," he moans as he leans his head into my shoulder. "I think it wants you pregnant as much as I do," he adds, kissing my shoulder and letting me up from the counter where I've been gasping for breath, trying to recover.

"Not yet," I smile over my shoulder. "You promised."

"I know; it doesn't stop me from wanting it more than anything in this world, though," he answers, stepping back and pulling his trousers back over his hips. I turn so I'm leaning back against the counter.

"There was me thinking you wanted to marry me more than anything in this world."

Christian closes the distance between us and places his hands on either side of me, caging me in so I can't do anything but look into his eyes.

"Nothing in this world will stop me from marrying you. Being your husband will be my greatest honour." Wrapping an arm around my waist, he pulls me against his as he cups my cheek. "Being a father to your children will just be the icing on our perfect little family," he adds, kissing me gently. "But I promised not to rush you, and I will always keep my promises to you."

"I know," I smile, looking deep into his eyes. "It's one of the reasons I love you as much as I do," I add.

Christian grabs my hips and lifts me so I am sitting on the edge of the counter. He removes my leggings and underwear and throws them into the washing basket.

"Let's get cleaned up and into bed. I've missed having you in my arms the last three nights."

Christian makes short work of cleaning me and

spending a few minutes helping me get into some sleepwear and under the covers.

Promising to return quickly, he gets himself washed and stripped down to his boxers before climbing into bed beside me.

"Come here, Sweetheart." Curling up on my side, I rest my head on his firm, tattooed chest as he wraps an arm around my shoulders.

"Will you be working away again soon?" I ask as I start tracing his tattoos with my fingertips whilst he plays with my hair, which I have released from the ponytail.

"I don't know, Sweetheart. There is so much going on at the moment."

I lean up so I can look into his tired eyes.

"Anything I can help with?" I would do anything to take some pressure off him if it meant he would be home more. Christian reaches up and tucks some hair behind my ear whilst I see the slightest smile on his face in the dark.

"No, Sweetheart, and I don't want you worrying about anything. Everything is fine; it's just a busy period. Things will settle down soon," he whispers before encouraging me to lie back down. "Get some sleep; you've had a long day."

Lying back down, I close my eyes as sleep takes me.

"Just remember you aren't alone; I can and want to help you in any way I can, Daddy," I whisper as he kisses the top of my head.

"You already do in so many ways. I really can't wait to make you my wife."

"I'm already your wife. We don't need a piece of paper to show we belong together," I whisper, smiling as I drift off to sleep, confident that my big, strong man knows how much he means to me and that I would do anything to help him.

Chapter Eight

CHRISTIAN

It's been two days since I got home, and I don't feel like we have stopped.

It's seven Christmas morning, and we have all been busy trying to ensure this will be the best Christmas our girl has ever had.

"I can't believe she's still asleep."

I turn to see Jason walking from his room. I smile, looking through Jasmine's open door, where she is asleep in bed.

"I was sure she would sneak into someone's room during the night," I chuckle. We are waiting for Maximus and Sean to join us as planned before waking her up. This will be our first Christmas all together in one house.

Before she moved in, we only spent Boxing Day with Jasmine and always at her place. The four of us went around for breakfast with presents for our girl, spoiling her as much as we could get away with. It wasn't easy as she didn't like us spending a lot of money on her, but she has slowly come around and accepted we want to spend money on her; it makes us happy to give her anything she may need or want. We tried every year to get her to come to ours for Christmas, but she always had an excuse not to.

Jasmine finally admitted a few months ago that she hasn't celebrated Christmas since her dad left. Even when our father was still married to her mother, Jasmine would say she was spending Christmas with them or with friends, and we failed to pick up on the lies; like so many she told us, to hide how alone she really was. So this year, we are making it up to her and giving her the Christmas she deserves, including making her sleep alone in her own room. We wanted to ensure we could get everything ready without her seeing anything.

"Do you think we will need to wake the twins up?" Jason asks, smirking.

"No, we've been up for a while," Sean announces as he appears, walking up the stairs behind us.

"Where have you been?" Jason asks. The twins hate getting up early; even when they know it's essential, they will still drag their feet and try to stay in bed as long as possible. It's always been the same. Usually, we don't see them before midday at Christmas.

"You know I said it felt like something was missing last night when putting the gifts under the tree?" Sean asks as we both nod. "Turns out all of Jasmine's were there, but I forgot my gifts to you three. I spent the last hour wrapping them and putting them with the others," he grins as Jason and I try not to laugh out loud.

"So, where's Maximus?" I ask, looking around. "Did he forget to put something out as well?"

Sean shrugs as he looks around.

"I saw him grabbing a coffee about six, mumbling

something about retrieving his present for Jasmine, and heading out the door."

Jason and I frown at each other before looking back to Sean.

"Did he say how long he would be? I'm not waiting around for him all morning," I argue as we hear footsteps on the stairs behind us.

"I'm here. Keep your hair on, old man." Maximus walks into view with a bundle in his arms.

"You have got to be kidding me," Sean groans as Maximus grins at us.

"What the fuck have you done?" Jason growls through gritted teeth.

"Did you not think you should have spoken to us about this?" I ask, trying to keep my cool. Maximus looks at me with a deep frown on his face.

"I don't need your permission to buy my fiancée a gift, Christian. If I want to get Shorty a puppy, I fucking will." We glare at each other for a moment, but before I can respond, Jason steps between us.

"Look, we can discuss this later," he states, looking between us. "We did all say we may get a dog in the future, as Jazzy wants one," he adds. Maximus and I continue to stare at each other before I let out a deep breath and rub my face.

"You're right. Let's concentrate on the main thing: giving our girl the Christmas she deserves." We all share a nod in silent agreement. But I don't miss how Maximus looks at me, and I know there will be words between us at some point. We've been butting heads a bit more recently, and I worry that it's something that's only going to get worse. Someday soon, we need to have it out, and I need to find out what the hell has gotten into him and why he is fighting me so much. But like Jason said, now is not the time, and we need to focus on Jasmine.

The four of us all head to her room and quietly walk in. Maximus, leads the way, we all stand at the bottom of the bed and watch our girl sleeping for a moment.

"Should we let her sleep longer?" Sean whispers.

"Nah, she would never forgive us," Jason grins.

"I know how to wake her," Maximus declares, putting the puppy on the bed. It looks at us all for a moment before Jasmine groans in her sleep. It quickly turns and rushes to her before pawing at her hand, nestling up to it.

Jasmine groans as she starts to wake up. But as soon as one eye opens, she jumps into the sitting position and stares at the puppy, who looks up at her with its tongue hanging out.

"Oh my god! Where did you come from?" she squeals, picking up the puppy and hugging it.

"Merry Christmas, Shorty!"

Jasmine looks up at us as we all call Merry Christmas as well.

"You gave me a puppy?" she asks, tears in her eyes.

"That was all Maximus," I smile as it licks her face.

"Oh my god! Thank you, Daddy Max," she cries, jumping from the bed, nearly tripping over her blankets in her haste before throwing an arm around Maximus, hugging him and the puppy.

I hate to admit it, but she looks so happy. The puppy does, too, as it looks up at her with the biggest eyes, desperate for her attention.

"You're very welcome, Shorty. Merry Christmas." When he looks into her eyes, I can see how much he loves her and wants to make her happy, just like the rest of us.

"Merry Christmas, Daddy," she whispers before looking

at the rest of us. Stepping away from Maximus, she walks to Sean and gives him a one-arm hug and kiss, wishing him a Merry Christmas before moving to Jason and eventually me.

"Happy Christmas, Sweetheart," I whisper in her ear before kissing her.

"Merry Christmas, Daddy." Stepping back from me with a smile, she looks around at us all before bouncing on the balls of her feet. "Can we go downstairs?"

"Sure thing, Jazzy," Jason laughs as she squeals and rushes for the door, still holding the puppy in her arms.

The four of us laugh as we follow her. Sean quickly catches up so we can all enter the large lounge, which we have decorated with a tree and various decorations.

"You okay?"

I turn to Jason, who gives me the look he gets when he knows I'm stewing on the inside.

"Why wouldn't I be?" I ask, frowning.

"The whole dog thing. Is it going to be an issue later down the line?"

We look down the stairs together, where Jasmine is excitedly playing with the dog as she shows him to Mrs Brown, who has joined them. It sounds like Maximus has asked her to take the puppy while Jasmine opens her presents.

"I would have preferred for him to have checked with us, but it's done now. She is happy, and that's all that matters."

I can feel Jason watching me as I start to descend the stairs. I didn't lie; all that matters to me is her happiness, and I know there will be times when my brothers make her happier than me. It's something we have all had to come to terms with quickly. Otherwise, this relationship would never work.

"Come on, you two! Hurry up already!" Jasmine exclaims happily, which only lightens my mood further. This is a side of her I love to watch. I don't think she has ever had the chance to enjoy being her true self before. She is so full of energy and enthusiasm she's unable to stand still, so she bounces from one foot to the other with a massive smile and her eyes sparkling with excitement.

As we head to the room and watch her bouncing around excitedly, waiting to go inside, I wonder what age her Christmases stopped being about the excitement and magic and just became about surviving her abusive drug addict of a mother.

"You ready, Princess?" Sean asks with his hand on the door handle, looking at us all to check we are ready to enter.

"YES! Hurry up already!" she laughs.

"Okay. Three. Two. One," Sean throws open the door, and Jasmine freezes.

Inside is the biggest tree we could find, and it's all lit up, with lights and ornaments she hand-picked or made with Mrs Brown. A big pile of presents is underneath the tree, much bigger than we usually have under there, not that we bother with a tree when it was just the four of us.

"Shorty? Are you okay?" Maximus asks as we all notice how silent and still Jasmine has become. He reaches and places a hand on her shoulder.

"Sweetheart, if it's too much, just say," I whisper as she continues to stare at the room.

"I …" Jasmine's voice breaks a little as a tear escapes and slides down her cheek. Looking at my brothers, I find them all looking exactly how I feel—terrified that we have overwhelmed her. That this is all still too much after everything she has been through.

"Jazzy? We can come back or do things differently,"

Jason starts, but Jasmine finally seems to snap out of it when she turns around and throws herself at him.

"It's perfect," she sobs as she takes a step back before throwing herself at me as she starts to cry.

"Sweetheart?" I hold her as she sobs into my chest.

"I'm sorry," she whispers before stepping out of my arms and turning to Sean to hug him before finally holding Maximus.

"What are you apologising for?" he asks, running a hand over her head, looking around at us all worried.

"For being an emotional mess," she giggles, stepping back and wiping her face. A big smile reappears as she looks at all four of us. "Did you do all of this for me?"

"Of course we did, Princess. We told you we wanted to give you the Christmas you deserved," Sean answers, putting an arm around her shoulder.

"Thank you, all of you." Jasmine makes a point of looking at each of us individually, showing us how much we mean to her.

"You're more than welcome, Angel. Now come on, let's see what Santa has brought you," Jason announces as Jasmine squeals excitedly, grabs his hand and pulls him into the room.

Walking in behind the twins, who are laughing happily, I take a moment to watch them all as they shower each other in love and know that no matter what, I will always strive to give them everything they need and want because nothing else matters more than our family.

No matter what comes our way, I will always protect them to the best of my ability, even with my life, if that's what it takes.

Chapter Nine

JASMINE

I look around the dining room table and smile as I watch my guys and our friends laughing and joking together. The table that usually sits twelve has been compacted so eight of us can sit together comfortably.

The guys, of course, pulled out all the stops today. They have spoilt me and spent far too much money as usual. But it's something I'm starting to come to terms with.

The O'Reillys have a lot of money and want to spend it on me as it brings them joy, so I let them. Do I wish they would tone it down a little? Of course, but whenever I bring it up, they just shrug and say they work hard for what they have and want to spend it on me.

"Okay, here's mine," Terry laughs as he lifts the joke from the cracker he pulled with Maximus. "What is Santa's favourite pizza?"

"I know this one!" Layton calls out excitedly.

"No, you don't!" I tease. He looks at me from across the table, grinning smugly.

"Yes, I do, it's meat feast!"

"Nope!" Terry laughs as the rest of the table laughs along.

"Why would it be a meat feast?" Sean laughs next to me.

"As in mincemeat, you get in mince pies," Layton explains, frowning.

"Do you know it, Jaz?" Terry asks, shaking his head at Layton's horrendous answer.

"Of course, it's one that's deep-pan, crisp and even." Everyone groans as Layton frowns at me.

"How does that even make sense?" he asks. The table goes quiet, and the two of us stare at each other.

"Do I really need to explain it to you?" I ask, arching one brow. When Layton just continues to stare at me, I shake my head and repeat the words in the tune of Good King Wenceslas.

"Ahh shit, she's right."

The table erupts with laughter as Layton sinks into his chair with embarrassment.

"No more drink for the rookie!" Terry laughs as he tosses the screwed-up joke across the table, aiming for Layton. "It's okay, bud. I will find you an easier one."

Layton reaches across so his hand shields Mrs Brown's eyes before flipping Terry off.

"Christian, have you seen the abuse your staff give me?" Terry laughs.

"I've seen the train regiment you put them through; I think you deserve it now and again," he smirks while reaching over and taking my hand, which rests on the table.

As always, Christian is sitting at the head of the table with me on his left and Jason on his right. Maximus is beside Jason and Sean next to me, with Mrs Brown at the other head of the table, Terry and Layton on either side of her.

As soon as I heard that Terry wouldn't see his daughter until Boxing Day and had planned on spending Christmas with Layton in the security room, I asked Christian if they could join us. I, of course, had to include Mrs Brown as she has become like a mother to me, especially after the whole kidnapping drama. I don't know what I would have done without her.

I turn to look at Christian and notice he's looking at the silver bracelet I had engraved for his Christmas present. It reads, *"To my amazing Daddy, love your Baby girl xxx."* Luckily, Trent hadn't asked too many questions when I had told him what to engrave. Although I'm sure he will never look at me in the same way again.

"Does it fit okay?" I ask, turning in my seat so I can give him my full attention. Christian lifts my hand and presses a kiss to my knuckles.

"It's perfect, Sweetheart. Just like you."

Even after all this time, the way he speaks to me makes butterflies erupt in my stomach and I have to stop myself from jumping on him.

"Everything I am, is thanks to you four," I whisper before turning my attention to the other three, who I find are all watching us, smiling softly.

I'm not exaggerating when I say I'm the person I am thanks to them. If it hadn't been for the O'Reilly brothers coming into my life four years ago, I wouldn't be a professional ballerina, living my dream life whilst studying in the best dance school in the UK. They did so much for me behind the scenes, and now they may not need to hide it, but simply by encouraging me and helping me learn and grow, they have shaped me into the person I always wanted to be.

"And everything we do is for you, Jazzy," Jason winks before turning his attention back to our guests.

Content just to relax and enjoy the day together, we invited the others to join the five of us for the whole day. We are currently sharing a few drinks and nibbles in the sitting room and haven't stopped laughing and joking all day; everything has been magical. But my mind has constantly wandered to my best friend, and I can't help worrying that she isn't having the day she deserves. Verity will do anything for anyone, and I just hope her three men are all back with her and showing her the love she deserves.

"Princess, your phone's vibrating." I turn to look at Sean, who is standing on the other side of the room, chatting with Layton and Maximus. I quickly place the puppy on the floor and rush to where my phone is charging.

"Hey! I was just thinking about you!" I answer, looking around the room to find the puppy trying to get Christian's attention as Verity laughs down the line.

"I wanted to call quickly and wish you a Merry Christmas."

"Merry Christmas, Ver. Have you managed to enjoy your day at all?" I ask, walking back over to the sofa where I'd been sitting with Jason. I curl back up beside him as he places an arm around my shoulder and hands me my half-filled glass of wine.

"Believe it or not, it's been amazing! I woke up to find Travis had been to the other house and picked up the tree and decorations. He decorated the whole downstairs as I slept. Jasmine, after everything that's been going on, it was perfect just because all three guys were here with me."

I know there is a lot we need to talk about, and we will, very soon, but not today.

"I'm glad your daddy got home in time for Christmas. You deserve to be spoilt." Jason kisses the top of my head as his arms tighten slightly.

"So do you, Jaz. I bet you've been spoilt rotten today by your daddies." Before I get a chance to answer, the puppy starts barking at Christian, still desperately trying to get his attention. "Did I just hear a dog?" Verity asks as I hear the shock in her voice.

"Yep. Daddy Max got him for me. He's trying to get Daddy's attention and doesn't like that he's not picking him up," I giggle. Christian looks at me with that Daddy look he gives when I'm pushing my luck. But I don't miss the way he's trying desperately not to smile.

"Aww, send me pics! I obviously have my phone again. I need to see him! Has he got a name?"

"No," I admit. "I need to think of one, but nothing suits him.

"Send me pics, and we will work one out together."

The puppy starts yapping again whilst trying to jump up Christian's legs. I can't help smiling when Christian sighs, picks him up and places him beside him. The puppy ignores him, curls up on his lap, and settles as Christian glares down at him. When Christian's eyes meet mine, I don't miss the warning in them. I smirk and lean further into Jason, who's chuckling at his brother.

"I need to go. Ethan's cracked open another bottle of champagne and demanded that I help him drink it," Verity laughs as I hear a couple of other voices on her end of the call.

"Okay, I'll send the pictures over now, and we can call and talk more tomorrow or something."

We end the call, and I place my now empty glass on the coffee table before smiling at Christian.

"Are you going to take the mutt back now?" he asks with an arched brow. I grin, shaking my head and snap a quick picture of them on my phone.

"He looks happy now he's having cuddles with Daddy."

The whole room looks at Christian and starts laughing, which wakes the puppy, who cuddles closer to Christian, looking for protection. Instead of letting him rest, Christian sighs and stands whilst holding the puppy, only to drop him onto my lap.

"I think he needs letting out," he mutters, heading to the bar.

"Come on, Shorty, we can take him for a walk around the garden," Maximus says as he moves over with the lead. The puppy instantly jumps down and runs around his feet, almost tripping Maximus up in his excitement.

"Remember the rule!" Christian calls as Maximus and I head out of the sitting room.

"He poops, I scoop," I call back. "Don't worry, I won't forget!" If Christian replies, we are too far away to hear it. Maximus laughs beside me as he passes me the lead and takes my hand in his.

We head straight to the kitchen and out of the back door, where we start to walk the puppy around the dark garden.

"Have you had a good day, Shorty?"

I smile, nodding and giving his hand a quick squeeze.

"It's been perfect, thank you."

He pulls me to a stop and wraps an arm around my waist, holding me tightly against him before kissing me.

"I'm glad to hear it. You deserve so much happiness after everything you have been through."

I smile back before kissing him again.

"I am the happiest girl alive and will be even happier in a few short weeks when I will be married to all four of you."

"It couldn't come soon enough, Shorty. I can't wait until you are finally my wife." He kisses me, but this time, it starts to deepen quickly. But before it can go any further, the puppy pulls against the lead and whines. We both look down at him and laugh.

"Come on, let's see if we can think of a name as we walk." Maximus holds out his hand, and I happily take it, so we walk around hand in hand, laughing at all the ridiculous names we can think of, ending the day happier than I have ever been at Christmas.

Chapter Ten

JASMINE

As much as I love my men and our lives together, sometimes I like nothing more than to lock myself away to enjoy a book in peace. So that's what I'm doing. I'm curled up on my bed with Embry, the puppy. Of course, I had to pick a name from *Twilight* as I read a new book on my Kindle underneath a new blanket Jason gave me at Christmas.

I'm absentmindedly scratching Embry's head when there's a knock at my bedroom door. Embry instantly starts barking and jumps from the bed, or more like flops off it, and rushes for the door.

"It's open!" I call, turning to face the door as Sean walks in and grabs the puppy before he can run out. "Why do you all knock before entering?" I ask as I move to sit up a little more and rest my back against the headboard.

"Because we promised you this would be your safe space, somewhere you can go when you need some time to yourself," Sean answers as he steps around the puppy whilst trying to get to the bed.

"But you all tell me off if I knock before entering your rooms. What if you guys want some time to yourself?"

Sean sits on the side of the bed as he reaches over and tucks a piece of hair behind my ear.

"Your time is divided between the four of us; why would we not jump at any time we get with you alone?" Leaning in, he kisses my lips while smiling. "I, for one, never want you to feel like you need to knock before entering. If you want or need me, you come and find me. I don't care what I'm doing or how tired I am. It's not my room; it's our room, and I will never stop you from being in it."

Tucking my legs underneath me, I lean forward to wrap my arms around Sean's neck.

"You always know the right thing to say," I point out with a smile before brushing my lips against his. "I think I might marry you before someone else snatches you up."

With a primal growl, Sean pounces, startling a scream from me as he pushes me onto the bed and leaps over me, so I'm pinned between the covers and his hard, muscular body.

"No one would ever be able to snatch me away from you, Princess, and you know it." lifting my hips, I rub against his growing bulge, milking another growl from his throat.

"Is that so, Daddy?" I tease whilst grinding up against him again. He closes his eyes briefly before burying his head against my shoulder.

"This is the hardest thing I've ever had to do." The way he groans against my neck causes my body to freeze and my smile to vanish.

Sean lifts his head and looks down at me as I frown at him.

"What is?" I ask, all my old securities rushing to the

surface. Sean must realise where my mind has gone as he cups my face and presses a soft kiss to my lips.

"Not fucking you until we break this bed," he sighs against my lips before standing up, leaving me lying on the bed and feeling a little rejected. "But Christian is waiting for us."

I know better than to make him wait; it always puts him in a bad mood, especially when he has places to be and people to shout at.

"Fine," I sigh dramatically as Sean reaches down and pulls me to my feet. Wrapping his arm around my waist, holding me against him, he thrusts his fingers into the hair at the back of my head and tightens his hold so I can feel him everywhere.

"Spend tonight with me, and I promise I will make it up to you, Princess." Looking deep into his eyes, I can't find my words, so I nod with the biggest smile. His lips capture mine, and for a moment, he takes my breath away. How is a girl meant to say no when his kisses alone have my thighs tightening and my sex clenching?

Too soon, he pulls away, grinning, knowing exactly what he does to me. Removing his arm from around my waist, he takes my hand and pulls me towards the door.

"Come on, pup," he calls, opening the door, and Embry follows us onto the landing.

The three of us make our way downstairs, and Sean guides us towards Christian's office.

"What does he want to see me about?" I ask, quickly running through the last twenty-four hours in my head, wondering if I've done something I shouldn't.

"You'll see," Sean answers, smiling as he opens the door.

Embry rushes past us, heading straight for Christian and yapping happily. Christian is in front of his desk with his phone in his hand. He looks so freaking sexy standing there with his free hand in his black trouser pocket, his dark grey shirt sleeves rolled up to his elbow. Instead of wearing a tie today, his top two buttons are undone, adding to the hot factor. Whenever I see him looking like the hard-ass businessman he is, I have to remind myself that he's mine and no one will ever take him from me.

"Sweetheart." Christian's eyes go from mine to Embry, who is still trying to get his attention, signalling me to deal with him.

"I'll let him out."

We all turn to see Mrs Brown walking into the office behind me and scooping up the puppy, giving me a wink before leaving the room. She loves that pup and has set aside time in her busy schedule to ensure he is always let out and given lots of attention when I'm not here.

I turn my attention back to Christian and catch the end of the conversation he is having on the phone.

"No worries, I will fill them in on the way to yours … not a problem, see you in twenty minutes." He hangs up as I reach his side. Lifting onto my tiptoes, I kiss his lips quickly.

"Where are you going?" I ask as he leans back against his desk, crossing his arms over his chest. His shirt tightens around his biceps and broad chest, making me swoon just a little.

"Sean will explain. It's his big news," Christian answers, smiling at his brother. I turn to see Sean sitting casually on the sofa with one arm over the back, his left ankle resting on his right knee.

"What's going on?" I ask, giving him my full attention.

"As you know, I've been toying with the idea of branching out into managing fighters rather than just being one," he starts. I nod as we had a long conversation about it a month or two ago. "Well, we are heading out to sign my first fighter."

I scream excitedly before launching myself across the room at him. Throwing my arms around his neck as I straddle his lap, I squeeze him tight as I burst with pride and admiration for this amazing man. Sean's arms wrap around my waist as he laughs.

"I am so proud of you!" I declare, meaning every word as I sit back so I can kiss him. "Why didn't you tell me you were speaking to someone?" I demand, slapping his chest.

"Ouch! Because I didn't think he would agree," he laughs, rubbing where I hit him.

"Who is it?"

"Ryan Donavon," Sean answers with a wide smile. I knew the twins had been training with him before they all went into hiding, but I had no idea it was anything serious. "He messaged me last night and told me he wanted to sign."

I turn to Christian as I climb off Sean's lap and sit beside him.

"Is that who you are going to see?" I ask, hoping they will let me go with them so I can check in on Verity. We have only shared the odd message since she returned, and I want to check on her properly.

"It is-" Christian starts and holds up a finger to stop me when I open my mouth to speak. "Yes, you can come with us."

Again, I squeal excitedly, launching myself at Sean and then Christian.

"Sweetheart, calm down. There are a few things you need to know before we get there," Christian adds, taking hold of my shoulders to keep me still.

"What's happened?" My excitement plummets as I worry for my friend.

"I will explain everything in the car. But Verity is safe. A few things came to light over the last few days, which Travis thinks you should be aware of before getting there so that you don't say anything that may trigger her." I nod as I blink back the burning in my eyes.

"Okay, Daddy," I remember seeing the girls for the first time after being kidnapped. Christian had pre-warned them what had happened to me during that time to ensure they didn't cause me any upset. I remember thinking one word about the sexual assault, and I would break all over again. The last thing I would want is to cause Verity more pain than she must be going through.

"Good girl. Go and get your coat and shoes on, and we will head straight out," Christian kisses the top of my head as I turn towards the door.

"I'll walk with you, Princess. I want to change my shirt," Sean says, stepping beside me. I turn my head and nod, worried that if I open my mouth, I might be sick.

"She really is okay, I promise," Sean takes my hand and squeezes it.

"Do you know what it is Daddy wants to tell me?"

Sean shakes his head but gives me a small smile. I know he's trying to reassure me, but it's not working right now.

"No, but I have spoken to Ryan and know that she was dealt a few very difficult blows, which have caused her a lot of upset. But physically, she is completely unharmed." Sean lifts my hand and kisses my knuckles as we climb up the stairs. "She has missed you and has been wanting to see you for a couple of days now, but things have been complicated, and decisions had to be made before her daddies were happy for her to see people from outside the family." He lets go of my hand and places an arm around her shoulder. "They weren't trying to keep you away, but they needed to protect Verity, not from you but everything."

I remember the way the guys protected me when I got home. No one but the doctor and anyone assisting with my care was allowed to see me. That only consisted of Mrs Brown, Terry and Layton once he was healed from his injury after being shot.

Sean and I reach the top of the stairs and part ways. I quickly change out of my yoga pants and put on some jeans and a warmer jumper. Grabbing some fur-lined boots, I pull them on before putting a jacket over my arm and rushing back down the stairs to where Christian is waiting for me.

"Ready, Sweetheart?"

"Yes, Daddy." I know I won't stop worrying until we are in the car, and he tells me everything he knows. He must realise how anxious I am as he puts an arm around my shoulder and pulls me tightly against him. He doesn't say anything, but he knows how important Verity is to me and how worried I have been about her the last few weeks.

"Ready?" Christian asks over my head. I look at the stairs where Sean is walking down, looking sexy. He's changed from his jeans and polo shirt and is now wearing black trousers and the light blue shirt I got him for Christmas. It fits him perfectly around his chest and shoulders but isn't too tight to restrict him. He sees me watching him as he rolls up his shirt sleeves and gives me a cheeky wink. He knows exactly what it does to me when I watch them rolling up shirt sleeves. Oh, that's right, he does, because I always tell him.

"Shirt looks good on you; someone has great taste," I tease as I try to ignore the worry for my friend.

"They really do," he whispers before kissing me. The

scent of his aftershave almost makes me weak at the knees. This man is getting *so* lucky tonight. I already planned on putting on some sexy underwear before bed, but now he's getting the full works, whilst he wears that shirt and nothing else.

"Come on, we are going to be late," Christian announces as he takes my hand but drops it when he sees Sean stepping beside me and taking my other hand. I give him a quick smile, knowing it's his way of letting Sean take the lead today.

"Terry is in the car. Do you want Michaela with us?" Christian asks. Sean shakes his head.

"Nah, she is off today anyway." Michaela is Sean's bodyguard. She doesn't usually have to go with him as much as Terry does with Christian or Layton with me. I used to get jealous of Sean having a female guard, but then I got to know her and realised I had nothing to worry about. I might not have known about all of their guards in the past four years, but all their guards have known about me, how important I am to the guys, and what would happen if they upset me.

We make our way through the house and into the garage, where Terry is waiting in the car. We all say hi as Christian climbs into the back passenger seat. Sean sits in front of him, and I sit behind Terry.

"Never thought I would be driving you to see a Donavon, Christian," Terry teases as he pulls out of the garage.

"Me neither," Christian sighs, shaking his head.

I want to bombard him with questions and learn about Verity, but I know he will be on edge.

Christian and Travis Donavon have spent the last ten years at each other's throats. Christian was with their father when he was killed in a car accident and fled the scene, leaving Mr Donavon to die alone, surrounded by drugs. Travis blamed Christian for the accident for a long time, but earlier this month, the Donavons realised Verity was in trouble and asked the O'Reillys for help. Knowing how much Verity means to me, Christian put his dislike for Travis on the back burner and helped keep her safe. I will be forever grateful to him for that.

"You okay, Sweetheart?"

I lift my head from where I had been watching, my hands on my lap and nod.

"Is Verity okay?" I ask.

Christian lets out a big sigh and nods as he reaches over and takes my hand.

"Let me tell you what I know before we get there. Hopefully, it will put you at ease a little." I nod in agreement and listen as Christian tells me everything, making me want to get to my best friend even faster, knowing how much she will need a hug.

Chapter Eleven

JASMINE

As we stop outside Verity's home, I wipe away the tears which have fallen whilst listening to all she's endured. I've hated Henry for a long time; he was never there for her when she needed him. After we discovered he tried to force her to marry someone she didn't want, I hated him even more. But even then, I thought there must be a small part of him who loved her; I mean, what's not to love about that girl?

But hearing how he treated her and stole from her not only money but her auntie and her actual father. The man was sick, and I'm glad he's dead.

Christian gives my hand a small squeeze before climbing out of the car as I check my makeup in the camera function on my phone. Luckily, I'm not wearing much, so the damage is an easy fix. The last thing I want is to let Verity see how much I've been crying.

"Ready, Sweetheart?"

I look to my right at the open passenger door as Christian's hand appears. Taking a deep breath and swallowing my anxiety, I take his hand and let him help me from the car. He leans in and kisses my temple as his arm settles around my waist.

"I know this will be hard, but Verity needs her friend."

Tilting my head up so I can look at him and offer a small smile.

"I know, she was amazing after I was kidnapped. There's no way I could ever let her down."

Christian kisses my lips this time and smiles at me sweetly.

"I know you couldn't."

Walking around the car, we come to a stop next to Sean. I squeeze his hand before lifting onto my toes and kissing his cheek.

"You ready to sign your first fighter?" I ask, smiling excitedly at him. My heart is full of pride. This man is taking the next step to fulfilling his dreams, and I'm honoured to stand beside him as he achieves them.

"I think so." He looks over my head to his older brother before pushing back his shoulders.

"You've got this. But if you need any advice, remember, I've got your back. I will help you every step of the way until you are ready to stand on your own two feet." Christian has always been a fantastic brother to his younger siblings. He wants them all to succeed and will do anything to help them. Even if they don't notice how much he does, I do.

"Thank you, Christian," Sean whispers before looking towards the front of the house and taking a deep breath to settle his nerves.

I look around us and see two skips filled with stuff and a large van next to three cars.

"Looks like they are getting rid of anything that wasn't Verity's," I point out as we walk towards the doors.

"Wouldn't blame them. It must be tough having the constant reminder of the arsehole who ruined your life everywhere you look." Looking at Sean, I wonder if that's how he felt after everything Tommy put them through. I know they stayed in their childhood home for a while after Christian threw Tommy out because an argument between Tommy and Maximus became physical. They were always a nightmare when living together. This one was particularly nasty and the first in many things that made the guys realise they no longer needed Tommy as much as he needed them. They have been living in the house we call home for nearly three years, and I now know they bought it so we could all be together.

"Here goes nothing." Sean's voice brings me back to the present as he knocks on the front door. It opens almost instantly, and a smiling Ryan greets us.

"Hey! Come on in, but watch your step; it's a building site here," he laughs as he steps out of the way. As soon as we walk through the door, I see Verity standing with Travis. She looks so much thinner than the last time I saw her, and she looks scared. Travis has his arm around her shoulder, protecting her as she clings to a ballerina doll.

I don't stop to think; I rush out from between Christian and Sean, wanting to hold her. Before I reach her, she throws herself at me, and we meet in the middle in a fierce embrace. The two of us instantly start sobbing into each other's shoulders as we cling to each other.

Eventually, we let go, and I place my hands on the tops of her arms keeping her in front of me to ensure she's paying attention.

"From now on you don't go anywhere without me. You

were only gone for three weeks and look at all the trouble you created. I'm meant to be the bad influence, not you," I laugh through my tears as a short hard burst of laughter escapes Verity before she wipes her face.

"Okay," she smiles. I let go of her and wipe my eyes.

"Why don't you two go and have a chat in the kitchen whilst we all talk in the lounge," Travis says, stepping forward and offering us a small smile.

"I want to watch Bear sign the contract," Verity answers, looking at Ryan as he steps up next to Travis.

"We will call you before he signs. I need to go over a few things with him first, which will take a little while," Sean says as he steps beside me. Verity looks at me and grins before taking my hand and pulling me towards the kitchen.

"Come on, I just got a new coffee machine!" she grins.

"Now you are talking my kind of language!" I wink, not bothering to look over my shoulder as we hear the guys laughing behind us.

"Come back if you need us," Travis calls. We both hold up a thumb in acknowledgement, making the guys laugh again.

I've only been to Verity's house a handful of times, she didn't like having people around when her dad, I mean Henry, was away. A couple of times we came to pick something up before a show, but never for longer than an hour. One room I know is the kitchen; it couldn't be more different than the last time I was here.

One thing you expected when visiting Verity's place was that it was spotless, with no sign of anyone living in it. There had been a breakfast bar in the middle of the room and a table and chairs. Both are now missing. The flooring has been ripped up, the cabinets destroyed, and the walls are being stripped of tiles. There is a much smaller version of the old table and chairs in place of the previous ones.

"Like what you've done with the place," I tease as Verity points for me to sit in one of the four chairs.

"The whole house looks the same. We are stripping it right back to the foundations and doing what we want with the place," she says putting her doll down on the one sideboard that's left, next to a fancy-looking coffee machine.

"Good, if you need any help just shout."

Verity turns to look at me with an arched brow.

"Aren't you scared you will break a nail?" she teases.

"I never said I would help; I'll send the guys round. We can drink coffee and watch the men get all hot and sweaty," I wink as she giggles. For a moment, she looks like the Verity who doesn't have a care in the world.

"Now that's something I could get behind, she replies.

I sit and watch as she loses herself in making the coffee. Now and again, she seems to zone out and stare into space. I want to pull her back but know to wait until we can talk properly. Sometimes, the moments we spend staring into space are the moments we need to come to terms with something that pains us.

A few minutes later, she walks over with our coffees and sits beside me. I don't miss how she looks longingly at the doll she left on the side, chewing on her bottom lip, showing how much she wants it. I think about telling her to get it, but I stand and retrieve it for her instead. She looks up at me with tears in her eyes as she holds it to her chest.

"Thank you," she whispers. "I was worried you would think I was being pathetic."

I sit back in my chair and lift the mug to my lips to take a sip.

"I have a light brown bear, which I hug when I'm feeling down or overwhelmed. Jason picked it up for me one day when we were in Majorca after the whole kidnapping drama. I don't think he realised how much I would come to depend on that small bear. But sometimes it's the only thing that helps." I offer her what I hope is a reassuring smile. "So I understand why you would want to keep it close at the moment."

Verity buries her face into the top of the doll for a moment with her eyes closed. I know she is trying to hold it together, and I don't want her to think she has to do that with me.

"Do you want to talk about it?" I ask not wanting to push her too quickly. Christian told me what he knows but we both think there will be a lot we don't know.

Verity looks up from the doll, towards the entrance of the kitchen.

"Let's talk outside," she says quietly before standing with her cup in hand. she nods towards a door at the back of the kitchen, and I quickly follow her out through a laundry room and into the large spacious garden I have never seen before. I turn to close the door behind us but see Verity shake her head out of the corner of my eye.

"Leave it open. That way, the guys will know where we are."

I nod and follow her further into the garden. A little part of me worries that Christian will wonder where we've gotten to, but it's not like we are going far.

Walking around the side of the house, we come to a stop at a two-seater love chair that hangs overlooking a large field where horses are grazing, wrapped tight in their winter coats.

Verity sits in the chair, and I sit beside her. We sit in

silence for a moment, watching the horses and drinking our coffees.

"This was my mum's favourite spot. This swing is the only thing of hers left." I turn my head and see her staring ahead. "How much did Travis tell Christian?"

"That Henry isn't your father, and how he had been stealing your money for years." Verity nods in confirmation, not looking away from the horses. "He also told me about your auntie and how Henry had her sectioned or something."

"We delivered the paperwork for her real diagnosis yesterday. We are expecting a call later today to tell us what the next steps will be to get her out."

"Can't you just walk out with her?"

Verity shakes her head and lets out a deep sigh as her arm around her doll tightens.

"She has been on medication for years; they are worried that stopping it too quickly will cause real issues for her. Plus, she has nowhere to go, he sold everything of hers." She finishes her drink before placing it on a table beside her. "I hate him. There are moments when the hatred I feel towards that man is so overpowering that I throw up. It takes over my whole body, and all I can do is scream and cry." Her jaw clenches as she starts blinking faster. "But then there are moments I would give anything to see him again and for him to say that he loved me really and I was still his pumpkin." Verity finally looks at me and my heart breaks as her lip trembles and tears roll down her face. "How can I love him and hate him at the same time? Why can't I just hate him and lose this pain that's tearing me apart? I want to heal, to move on, but …" A sob bursts from her chest and that little control she's been holding on to breaks.

I pull her into my arms and hold my best friend as she

falls apart in my arms. I close my eyes and listen to her pain and wish I could take it away from her. I would give anything for her not to hurt like this. If anyone understands the pain she's feeling, it's me.

"I know it hurts," I whisper into her hair as I run a hand over it. "I know that whenever you feel like you are taking a step in the right direction, you are pulled ten steps back. But I promise one day, it will start to feel a little better, and it won't be the first thing you feel when you wake up or when you are alone. Slowly, you will realise you are able to think of him without the confusion and pain. He will be a memory that haunts you now and again, but he no longer has the power over you he once did."

"I hope so," Verity sniffs in my arms. I hold her for a while until, eventually, her tears dry up, and she pulls away from me, wiping at her face.

"I'm sorry."

"Don't apologise to me for crying. You have held me enough times over the last six months." I take her hand, which isn't holding her doll. "I am always here for you, you know that, right? I know I've been preoccupied with the wedding and the guys. But that will never mean you can't come to me, about anything."

"I know. You will always be the most important person to me, Jaz."

"So I should be," I tease with a playful smile. Verity smiles at me for a moment before looking back at the horses that seem to have come closer. I can just imagine them sensing her pain and wanting to check on her. Verity has always seemed the type to attract forest animals and have them help her with the chores.

"Did Travis tell Christian much about my mum?"

I turn my attention back to my friend and am surprised when she smiles at me.

"Only that she was super rich, and you had no idea." A grin spreads across my face as I nudge her playfully with my elbow. "Don't start thinking you are above us now you're, what? A millionaire?"

"Multi-millionaire, to be precise."

I whistle, impressed.

"Bet that feels weird to say?"

"It really does. A few weeks ago, I was worried about whether I could afford to find a place after graduating. Now I own this huge house and have a bottomless bank account; it's crazy!"

"Yeah, I was like that when I first moved in with the guys. I remember Danielle making fun of me because my shoes were dead and crying all the way home. When Sean took me out and bought me six pairs, I felt like a charity case. But slowly, I've learnt that they mean it when they say what is theirs is mine. Plus, my bank account is looking better than ever as my performance pay doesn't get touched."

"I don't want people to know I'm rich," Verity sighs, looking back to the horses. "I don't want to be treated any differently than I was before."

"Then don't tell anyone. No one needs to know what goes on outside of the school unless you want them to."

Verity nods in agreement, and we are quiet for a moment before she speaks again.

"So Travis never told Christian about who my real father may be?" I shake my head and am surprised when a smile appears on her face.

"Do you know who it is?" I ask, shocked. Verity giggles and shakes her head.

"Not exactly; we know it's one of two guys." Watching the way her smile widens; I feel my jaw drop.

"No?"

"Yep, my mum lived in this house with two guys. They were in all in a relationship with each other."

"Your mum was like us?" I ask, sitting forward suddenly, making the seat underneath us rock, causing us both to start laughing as we panic; we are about to fall off.

"Yeah," Verity answers, still giggling. "My auntie has been telling me more about them. We've actually met one of them. He's the one Mum and Auntie always believed was my father."

"Who, damn it!" I demand, desperate to know.

"Remember the guy Dave who comes to a few shows a year and has even talked to us a few times."

"Of course, he is a sweetheart, always talking about how much his wife loved to dance."

"Well, it looks like he was talking about my mum."

"So you think he knows?" I demand. Verity shrugs and looks back towards the horses.

"Auntie Trish thinks that he suspects, which is why he watches a couple of shows whenever he is in the country." Verity looks down at her doll and starts playing with its hair. "She says that he never got over losing my mum. That he fought for her, but my… Henry was a bastard and made sure my mum had no idea he was still around."

"Christian said something about Henry stalking her."

Verity nods.

"Yeah, he scared the other two guys off. One of the guys has married and has kids but knows there is a chance I'm his and would be happy to find out if I choose to. Then there's Dave, who has always checked in on me, even from afar, and apparently, I look a little like him."

"Do you want to find out which one it is?" I ask carefully. Verity nods her head but lets out a deep sigh.

"I do, but not yet. Travis thinks I need to come to terms with a few things before I learn more life-changing information. I agree with him and am scheduled to start therapy on the fourth. I want to ensure I'm in the right frame of mind before coming face to face with the father that was kept from me."

"What if he hears about Henry and comes looking for you?" I ask, worried the decision may be taken away from her. But Verity shakes her head.

"He won't. We aren't going to tell anyone Henry's dead. We will act like he has returned to the States and slowly stop mentioning him. If people ask, we will just say there was a family falling out, so Linda and him are no longer talking to any of us. I will admit he's not my real father and leave it at that." A sad smile appears on her lips. "Let's face it, no one will question it as he was never here anyway."

"And what's happening with Linda?" I ask. "Have the guys heard from her?"

"Not since Boxing Day. She turned up at Travis's and called me every name under the sun, blaming me for everything that had happened. We didn't know Henry was dead at that point, so as far as we are aware, she still thinks he's alive. Hopefully, she will go back to the States and live off all the money they have over there. Travis left a message telling her we don't want anything and she can keep it all. But if she ever contacts any of us again, we will take it all back, leaving her with absolutely nothing."

"Go Daddy Travis!" I laugh as Verity smiles, nodding.

"He is rather epic. They have all been amazing, and I know I wouldn't be here without them."

"Don't say that; you are one of the strongest women I know; you would have survived, even without them."

Verity chews on her lip for a second before whispering.

"Jaz, I haven't been strong. I've caved to pressure so many times over the years I … I ended up doing things I'm not proud of."

I want to ask her to explain, but the second she looks up at me with her eyes once again filled with tears, I know she has done enough talking for one day.

"Whatever you have done, I know you would have thought you had no other option. You don't need to tell me. I can see in your eyes that you are worried about me knowing. So tell me when or if you are ever ready. I am always here for you. Bratties before Daddies," I grin proudly.

"That's not a saying," she giggles. It's good to see her smiling, showing that the old Verity is still in there. She just needs a little help right now.

"Since when have we stuck to the rules?" I laugh. "That's the fun of being a brat; rules don't apply to us unless we want them to."

"I've missed you," she giggles, pulling me in for a hug.

"I've missed you more," I tease back.

"I'm wondering how you have missed that it's freezing out here, and neither of you have a coat on?"

We both slowly look to where Travis and Christian are standing together, staring at us. Christian's arms are folded over his chest, and Travis has his in the pockets of his jeans.

"It's not that cold," I point out, earning me an arched brow from Christian.

"Plus, we were drinking coffee, so we didn't notice," Verity adds beside me.

"Get in the house, both of you, before you catch a cold," Travis demands, pointing back towards the house.

Verity and I stand up and slowly walk over to them with our heads down, knowing better than to ignore them. But as we pass, Verity looks at me and whispers.

"I think I preferred it when our daddies didn't get along."

"Right! They would have spent more time shouting at each other than us," I point out.

"Sweetheart, we can hear you."

I look to Verity and smirk.

"Was that my daddy or yours?" We both look over our shoulders as we hold hands while walking toward the house. The guys are behind us, watching every move we make.

"I don't know. Them both calling us sweetheart is a little confusing," she points out.

"I would suggest I start calling you brat, but I think you would both answer to that as well," I hear Travis announce behind us. Verity and I share a look before bursting out laughing as two deep growls sound behind us, making us squeal, running the rest of the way to the house and rushing for the lounge into the safety of our other men's arms.

I look over at Verity as she laughs in Ethan's arms. She whispers in his ear, and he laughs as Travis and Christian walk into the room.

"Causing trouble, Princess?" Sean laughs into my hair.

"I never cause trouble! It was Verity's fault! She dragged me out in the cold!" I protest.

"Hey! It's not like you argued. What happened to 'Bratties before Daddies'?" Verity argues.

"Shush!" I snap with my eyes wide as I stare at her. "Are you trying to get us a spanking?"

"No! But I'm not getting one because you can't stop being a brat!"

"Takes one to know one, sister!" I stick my tongue out at her, and she does it back in return.

"Girls! Have you quite finished, or do we need to separate you?"

We both look to Ryan, who is looking between us.

"You can't do that!" Verity demands stepping away from Ethan. I step next to her and link my arm through hers.

"Yeah! We can't be separated; she's my sister from another mister!"

"Do we really know that though? I mean, we don't know who my father actually is."

The room falls deadly silent; you can hear a pin drop as we all stare at Verity open-mouthed. She looks deadly serious for a second before a smile appears on her face, and she winks at me. I burst out laughing, pulling her into my arms.

"That's my girl! Welcome to the toxic parent group; we are all brats here!" I cheer as I hold my best friend at arm's length and let her see how fucking proud I am of her.

Things become serious after that, and we watch together as Ryan signs the contract and becomes Sean's first fighter as a manager. Verity and I stand proudly, watching our guys as they both shake and start new chapters in their lives.

After a short while, Christian, Sean, and I are ready to leave, and we say goodbye to everyone, promising to help as they redesign the house. As Sean chats with Verity and Ryan, Travis pulls me to one side and engulfs me in a huge hug.

"Thank you," he whispers in my ear.

"What for?" I frown up at him.

"For being the best friend my girl could ask for. I don't

know what you talked about out there, but you made her laugh and smile, and that's all I want for her right now."

"You don't need to thank me for that. She is my best friend, and there is nothing I wouldn't do for her. Including murder," I add a little warning in with the last word. "I will kill you if you break her heart. Don't think I won't because I have four daddies to help me hide your body, ensuring you will never be found."

Travis stares momentarily before looking over me to where I know Christian is standing.

"She's perfect for you guys. She may even be scarier than you, O'Reilly."

Christian stands behind me so I can lean against him as he wraps his arms around my waist, holding me close.

"She sure is, and we couldn't be prouder." He leans to the side to kiss my cheek. "Come on, Baby girl, let's get home where Maximus and Jason are waiting for us."

I step out of his arms and head straight for Verity. Holding her tight, I whisper.

"Remember, you can message or call at any time. I'm always here for you."

"Bratties before Daddies?" she smirks, holding up her little finger.

"Bratties before Daddies," I smile back, wrapping my pinky around hers, knowing that it's a pinky promise I never plan on breaking.

Chapter Twelve

JASMINE

Curling up under my blanket, I rest my head on Sean's lap while my feet are on Christian's.

It's New Year's Eve, and when asked what I wanted to do, there was only one answer: I wanted to spend it with my four men, watching movies and seeing the new year in with a bang, and I'm not talking the fireworks kind either.

I think it's safe to say this year has been the worst and best year of my life. I started it alone, feeling like no one would ever love me for me, and ended it by being loved by the four men I had pined for for years.

When I think of all we have been through: the Hudson drama, which left Jason scarred on the inside as well as physically, me being kidnapped, and all of us losing a parent in that house, it's no wonder we are all happy to see the end of this year. I had started it on the road of self-destruction, but as much as I tried to hide it from the guys, they saw. They rushed in when I needed them the most, picked up all of my broken pieces, and placed them back together.

Whenever I've started to crumble again, or someone else tried to destroy me, they've held me together and cared for me in a way only they could.

"You okay, Princess?" Sean's hand tightens around my shoulder as he tucks the blanket around me. Lifting my head, I smile, nodding, and blink back tears. He notices and gives me a look, telling me to be honest.

"I was just thinking that I will feel better once we can put this year behind us," I smile, letting him see that I am, truthfully, okay. Christan's hand, which rests on my ankle, squeezes slightly.

"I will second that." Glancing up, I find him watching me as his thumb strokes against my skin.

"It's been a roller coaster, that's for sure," Sean chuckles as his hand runs over my head.

"Everything happens for a reason, and as much as it hurts at the time, it has led us to where we are now, Sweetheart." Christian has said this to me a few times over the last six months, and he couldn't be more right.

"Next year will be everything you want it to be and more," Sean says as he continues to play with my hair. "Starting with making you our wife and hopefully ending with you pregnant with our first baby." I can hear the smile in his voice, and I can't help but look at Christian, who is grinning at the two of us.

"You promised no pressure," I remind him. But a devious element appears as he grins at Sean over my head. "Daddy! You promised," I warn.

"I know I did. I promised I would wait until the next show was cast before I threw out your pills. I will never go back on my promise to you, Baby girl; you know that." Christian continues to smirk while looking back at Sean. "I never promised to stop your other daddies if they decided to do it instead."

My jaw drops as Christian pulls away my blanket before removing my feet, making it easier to pull me away from Sean and onto his lap so my back is pressed against his front.

"I also never promised to stop your other husbands from impregnating you by holding you down so they can do what they want to you." His deep, sexy, husky voice whispers into my ear as he takes my wrists and holds them against my chest. My heart starts to race as I realise that my legs are on either side of his at the same time as he does. He spreads his legs, forcing mine to open further as Sean stands and looks down at me. Pinned by Christian, who is opening me up and leaving me at their mercy.

Adrenaline curses through me as I realise the guys may plan on doing as they wish to me tonight. There have been nights we have played with them taking *complete* control, using my body in any way they want. I may put up a fight and even try to escape, but I know if I use my safe word, they will stop instantly.

Christian takes both wrists in one large hand and holds them tight against my chest as his other hand slides down my stomach until he has my aching pussy in his hand. His grip tightens as Sean watches with a smirk, his eyes boring into mine.

"This is ours, Baby girl. It belongs to all four of your daddies, fiancés, and soon-to-be husbands. If we decide to fill it until our child is growing inside of you, we will." His grip tightens until it's more than a little uncomfortable, causing me to hiss from the pressure. Christian's stubble rubs against my cheek as his grip tightens again.

"Shall we show you how it could go if we really wanted to take it in turns to fill you?"

Fuck I want that.

"You promised," I gasp as he tightens his hold on my wrist as I try to move, testing how he will react.

"You're right, I did." Christian's teeth skate over the skin on my shoulder before he bites down, not hard enough to break the skin, but enough to shock a cry out of me. "But like I pointed out, I never promised not to be the one to restrain you so my brothers can do it for me." He lifts his head and looks at Sean as I try to get out of his hold. "You got your knife?"

"Always," Sean grins as he pulls his flip knife from his pocket. Christian chuckles as he removes his hand from between my legs.

"Cut them off."

"What?" I explain as Sean looks at the knife in his hand and then grins at me.

"You heard me. Time for you to be naked."

"Don't cut them off!" I protest. "I'll do whatever you ask."

I can tell from Sean's face that he's unsure if he believes me. But he looks at Christian and nods once.

"If she runs, I'll get her."

I freeze, waiting to see if Christian is going to loosen his hold on me, and for a moment, I don't think he is until the iron grip he has on my wrists loosens slightly.

"Fine, but you know the rules, Sweetheart. You run, and we catch you, you are ours to do with as we please."

"And if I do get away?" I ask as my heart starts to race, remembering the times I've gotten away and the guys have been my slaves for the day. But all hope is dashed when Christian's teeth graze my earlobe before he whispers.

"You won't."

I swallow deeply as he chuckles into my ear. I love it when he relaxes enough to play like this. It's been a while since he has relaxed in any sense of the word. I want to keep him this way for as long as possible.

"Okay, Daddy. I'll behave." I look at Sean and can see how hard he is. His noticeable bulge showing from inside his sweats. He gives me a look I have named his *"I want to see you on your knees choking on my cock,"* look.

Christian's grip on my wrists loosens further until I'm able to move my arms away from my chest and twist them to try and get some of the blood flow back. Sean holds out his hand for mine and helps me to my feet.

"What's going on?" Jason asks as he walks into the room.

"Jasmine is about to learn a vital lesson," Sean answers as I turn to Jason.

"Daddy is going back on his promise about not forcing me to have a baby as soon as we're married," I pout, pointing at Christian.

"No, we've been over this. My promise doesn't cover your other men."

"Well, in that case, I'll just withhold sex. If you throw out my pills, I won't let any of you sleep with me until I'm ready." Crossing my arms over my chest, I act braver than I feel.

Excitement builds inside me as I think of all the ways the guys could take what they want. Christian and Jason share a look, and a smirk appears on Jason's face.

"Yeah, that's not going to work, Jazzy," he says, stalking towards me. I go to take a step back, but Sean blocks me. Jason stops at my front and reaches up to wrap my hair around his hand. Tugging it hard, he forces me to look at him as he grins. "We all know you couldn't go more than a few days without begging for one of us to fuck you."

"I'm sure I could find a way," I reply, refusing to back down. "I managed just fine before I moved in here." I cross my arms over my chest, desperate to appear bolder than I am. Jason looks me up and down whilst grinning.

"You did." He takes a step forward, so I'm almost completely boxed in by Sean and him. I look to the side where Christian grins, watching the scene unfold. "But that's because you had no idea how good we could make you feel." His hand cups my aching pussy, and I know from the way he smiles that he can feel how hot and wet I am. "Now, you can't even manage a few days without begging for our attention." He takes hold of the strap of my top between his fingers and slowly lowers it, letting his knuckles gently rub along my skin, leaving a trail of goosebumps in their wake. "Even when you deny it, we can tell what you need," he whispers against my neck. "We can read your body like a book."

"You really think so?" I try to sound confident, but my head instantly leans to the side to give him better access to my neck, showing him how badly I need him.

"Oh, I know so," he chuckles as his fingers lightly graze against my side, causing my breath to catch. "Do you want to play, Angel?"

"Maybe," I tease, taking a step closer so there is almost no space between us. "Maybe I want to do things my way." Before he blinks, I jump from between him and Sean and rush towards the door.

"Oh, it's on!" I hear Jason shout as I manage to dodge Christian, who has jumped over the back of the sofa. I know the three of them are going to be held up as they all try to get through the door at the same time. I'm laughing out loud as I run around the corner and hit a solid wall. A scream escapes as I almost hit the floor, only to be caught by Maximus.

"What the fuck?"

I try to run past him, but he holds on to me tight as Sean flies around the corner, quickly followed by the others.

"Is it playtime, Shorty?" Maximus asks, grinning down at me.

"No, let me go!" I yell, trying to escape him, but I have no chance.

"Not happening; you know the rules," he smirks.

"You weren't playing, it doesn't count!" I scream as he knocks my legs from underneath me, dropping us both to the floor before straddling my waist.

"Oh, it counts," Christian grins down as Maximus pins my arms above my head. Christian drops down and takes control of my hands. "Do you want to do the honours of getting her out of these clothes?"

Maximus grins down at me as he pulls his knife from his pocket.

"Do you all just walk around with knives in your pockets?"

"Yep," all four answers together as Maximus flips the knife in his hand and brings it down to my top.

"You never know when it will come in handy," Maximus grins, lifting the neckline of my vest top and cutting it before ripping the top in half. "Like now."

"You gave me this set for Christmas!" I had hoped he would at least seem a little disheartened, but he winks at me instead.

"I know, and it will look so much better shredded on the floor instead of hiding your body from us all."

Well, damn, there goes that argument. I wait for him to

lift the knife away from the skin and start trying to wiggle my way out from under him and Christian.

"Stay still, Jazzy, otherwise, he may cut you."

I freeze as my eyes find a grinning Jason standing over me.

"Anyone want to fill me in on what I missed?" Maximus asks as he moves so he's sitting on my legs and starts shredding my shorts.

"Somebody tried to argue with their daddy about what he did and didn't promise when it came to us getting her pregnant," Sean answers as I glare at him.

"Please tell me her pills have been thrown out. I am so ready to impregnate her!" Maximus asks. I don't miss how his eyes light up with the idea; he's as bad as Christian.

"No! I'm not getting pregnant yet!"

If I'm being completely honest, every month, I'm a little disappointed when my period arrives. If I said the word, the guys would be more than happy for us to start trying, but I also want to wait. I want to be married when we try and not worrying if I'm pregnant whilst on our honeymoon. I won't tell them I'm ready yet; this is more fun.

"I simply pointed out that although I promised I wouldn't throw out her pills, it doesn't mean I can stop you guys from doing it."

"You said you would hold me down whilst they tried to get me pregnant!" I yell, trying desperately not to laugh.

"Yes, I did, and look where we are," Christian grins, tightening his grip on my wrists as Maximus laughs. I shouldn't find this as arousing as I do, but the thought of these four getting rough with me and taking what they want causes my pussy to flood.

"Shorty, you're so wet, your panties are soaked," Maximus grins, cutting through the last of the material of my underwear and shorts so I am left completely naked for them all. I try to clamp my legs closed, but he gets his hand between them and runs a finger through my lips. It takes everything in me not to moan, but he already knows how excited I am.

"Let her up," Christian orders as he lets go of my wrists. Maximus grins while standing and helping me to my feet. The four of them surround me as I stand naked and aroused.

"Here's what will happen: you get four chances to run. Each time we catch you, one of us is going to fill that pussy, showing you how quickly we could get you pregnant if we wanted to," Jason says.

"Four against one isn't very fair," I point out, putting my hands on my hips. I used to worry about being naked in the house with all the security cameras, but I know now that when everyone is home, and it's only Terry on duty, they are all off, which means no one can see what we get up to, which is usually a lot.

"Angel, it's always going to be four against one, so get used to it," he smirks as the others laugh. Well, when he puts it like that, it is what I signed up for by being with them all.

"Then there should be rules," I argue.

"What rules would you like?" Christian asks. His eyes are sparkling, and his mischievous grin always makes him seem younger and happier.

"Uhhh …" I try to think of something, but my mind comes up empty.

"Face it, Shorty, there are no rules. Now you have to the count of four to put some distance between us and you." Maximus grins at his brothers, who all start counting together.

"One."

I scream and spin on my toes, squeezing between Sean and Maximus.

"Two."

Finally getting past them, I run towards Jason's office, hoping to close the door behind me.

"Three." I know they are all watching me. I can feel their eyes roaming up my body as I run naked through the house.

Grabbing the handle, I throw open the door as I hear them shout, "Four!" I scream as I jump into the room and lock the door, laughing as the handle rattles.

"You never learn!" I don't get to gloat for long, though, as the door flies open and Sean rushes into the room before his brothers.

"How?" I don't get to finish, as he takes advantage of my shock and tackles me to the floor.

"We learnt, Princess, and now we know how to unlock all doors from the outside." Before I can argue, his mouth is on mine, and all coherent thoughts are lost for a moment.

Remembering I'm meant to be fighting this, I start to struggle underneath him, but Christian grabs my arms again.

"Do you really think you could stop me from putting a baby in you if I wanted to?" Sean chuckles as his hand goes between my legs. "You are so fucking wet and ready; you love to play, don't you, Princess."

"No," I argue, but the moan that leaves me as he slides a finger on me gives it all away.

"No? So you don't want me to do this?" he presses a second finger into me before rubbing my clit with his thumb. I open my mouth to argue, but a long moan escapes instead, making him grin down at me.

"Your body gives you away every single time," he smiles as he removes his hand and releases his cock from his sweatpants. "So you don't want this?" rubbing his head up and down between my clit and entrance, I shake my head, not trusting what noises will come out of my mouth if I open it.

"Remember, Princess. Say the word, and it all stops." He's giving me the chance to use my safe word, but I won't. Instead, I shake my head as he grins. "That's what I thought."

With one thrust of his hips, Sean fills me as I cry out.

"That's right, you can deny it all you want, but I can feel how wet and close you already are to coming on my cock." He starts to grind into me as Christian finally lets go of my arms. "Are you going to be a good girl, Princess, and come for all your daddies tonight?"

"No!" I cry out, making Sean laugh.

"From the way your pussy is squeezing me, I think you're lying to not only your daddies but yourself as well."

The noise that leaves me as he continues to rub his cock against every single button inside of me tells them all they need to know. I am fucking loving my life right now. Sean, like the others, knows what drives me wild and can have my orgasm in no time at all.

"Fuck, you are so close I can feel your walls vibrating," Sean curses, reaching down and rubbing my clit as he starts going harder.

"How does she feel, Sean?" Maximus asks as I look up to find him grinning down at me.

"Like fucking heaven," Sean answers as he gets harder and faster.

"Oh my god!" I cry out, gripping his body with my nails, knowing they are going to leave a mark.

"Fuck, you're crushing me," Sean moans as he starts

picking up speed. It doesn't take long until all I can hear is the sound of our bodies slapping together as we both cry out through our orgasms. Not giving me a chance to catch my breath, Sean's mouth is on mine as he kisses me to the point I think I'm going to pass out.

When he finally pulls away, he grins down at me whilst pulling away.

"This time, you have until the count of three." The others roar, laughing as I struggle to understand what he means.

"What?"

"One."

Oh shit. I try to jump to my feet, but my body is too relaxed after the mind-blowing orgasm.

"Two." Maximus is the closest, grinning at me as I finally reach my feet.

"Wait, that's not-"

"Three."

I scream as I turn to get away from him, but my legs aren't quite working, and he catches me with ease.

"That was just too easy," Maximus grins before his lips crash into mine. I know I'm meant to be fighting him, but fuck I want him so bad right now. Putting my arms around his neck, he lifts me so I can wrap my legs around his waist.

"Maybe I wanted you to catch me," I tease as he carries me over to the wall.

"Oh, I know you did. You want me to fuck you until you think you can't take anymore, only to get fucked by my brothers." My back slams against the wall, knocking the air out of my lungs.

Leaning against my body so I can't go anywhere, Maximus frees his dick and thrusts me onto it.

"Daddy!" I cry out as he fills me to the point it almost hurts.

"I'm going to fuck you hard and fast because I don't think I can cope with how tightly you are squeezing my cock."

Not holding back, Maximus keeps to his word and starts pounding into me; all I can do is hold on as I cry out through the pleasure.

"Fuck, Shorty." His lips press against mine as I hold on for dear life. Maximus has been wild in bed recently, and he's not holding back this time, either. I hear a bang in the room, followed by Christian cursing and the others laughing. Opening my eyes, I see them all sitting on the sofa with a drink, watching us as Christian moves a picture frame while keeping his eyes on me. Fuck I love it when they watch. Jason's eyes collide with mine, and I know from the way they darken that he will be next.

"Daddy, don't stop," I cry out as the pleasure becomes overwhelming, and I can't keep my eyes open anymore. Throwing my head back, I cry out as he grips my ass so tight I feel his nails cutting into the skin. My nails dig into his shoulders as I get closer and closer to my orgasm.

"Fuck, Shorty, come on my cock and take it all," Maximus cries out as he finds his release at the same time as I fall apart around him.

"Daddy," I gasp as I try to breathe, but there isn't a part of me that isn't overstimulated. I can feel him everywhere. Where he ends, the wall begins, and I know my back is going to be scratched up, and I don't care.

"I fucking love you, Shorty." Lifting my head from his shoulder, I look into Maximus's eyes and smile. "You are perfect." He kisses me slowly, this time as he lowers my feet to the floor and holds me close. "But I hope you can run because you have until the count of two."

"What?" I snap, looking behind him, and Christian and Jason smirk at me.

"One."

I don't know why I even bother trying; there is nowhere to go. But I attempt to move to the left as Jason rushes forward.

"Two."

I scream as Jason grabs me next to the desk, pinning me between him and the wood.

"Was it worth trying to run?" he whispers in my ear while taking the lobe between his teeth. "Did you like looking at me as your other Daddy fucked you?" he continues as his hand cups my pussy which is still contracting after my last orgasm. One sweep of his finger over my clit, and I cry out from the pleasure. "I'll take that as a yes."

Jason steps back a little, giving me a bit more space. I use it to try and run but quickly realise that's what he was hoping for. Grabbing my hand, he pulls me back to him and turns me so I'm facing the desk.

"Bend over, Angel." I don't have much choice as he places a hand in the middle of my shoulder blades and pushes. Leaning over me, he whispers in my ear again.

"Colour?"

"Green," I whisper back. Jason presses a kiss to my cheek as his hands grip my hips and knock my legs apart to make room for him between them.

"That's what I thought." I barely get a second warning before he thrusts forward and impales me on his rock-hard cock. I cry out as my extremely sensitive body makes room for him.

"Look at me." I lift my head the best I can as Christian stands in front of the desk while Jason fucks me from behind. "Do you see how easy it would be for us to get you pregnant if we wanted to? How we can take control and fill you with our sperm until your belly swells with our child."

I can't answer with more than a nod as Jason picks up the pace, and I cry out from the pleasure. I always become more sensitive after one or more of my men fuck me. Especially on nights like this when they aren't being gentle.

"Fuck, you look so hot right now," Christian curses as he rubs his bulge while watching Jason pound into me.

"She's even fucking hotter from this side," Jason growls through gritted teeth. The sting of his hand on my ass has me crying out.

"Do it again," Christian orders. Jason slaps the other side, and both men moan as I cry out and come hard.

"Fuck, that sound," Christian gasps as Jason slaps me a third time.

"Daddy!" I cry out as his hand lands for the fourth time, sending shockwaves to my core as a powerful orgasm rocks me.

"Fuck!" Jason roars behind me as he thrusts into me three times before emptying his release.

I can't move; I'm spent. Leaning against the desk as I gasp for breath. My whole body is over-stimulated, so every touch, whether with an object or just the air, has me recoiling.

"Red," I sigh across the wood.

Two strong arms wrap around me and pull me from the desk until I'm being held against a muscular chest. I see the rune tattoo and know it's Christian. He carries me over to the sofa and sits with me on his lap. My eyes close as my body becomes exhausted.

"Have you had enough, Sweetheart?"

"For now," I nod into his chest. "Let me rest, and I will do anything you want," I add, smiling at him.

"Anything?" he asks as someone drapes a blanket over my sticky, sweaty body. I realise I'm shivering, but I don't think it's from the cold but from the overwhelming senses. I nod whilst pulling the blanket up to my neck as Christian tucks it around me.

"So if I told you to crawl and beg me to take you?"

"Give me five minutes, and I will happily beg for your cock."

Christian shakes his head and uses my chin to ensure I am looking at him.

"You crawl for no one, not even us. You are our equal, the queen of our empire and nothing less would be acceptable." The way he looks at me makes all feelings of exhaustion disappear. When he looks at me like I could rule the world after he hands it to me on a silver platter, I go weak at the knees, and my already soaking wet pussy, gets wetter.

Pushing off the blanket, I straddle his lap, thread my fingers into his hair and kiss him hard. His hands land on my hips as he pulls away, grinning.

"I thought you needed a break?"

"I need Daddy's cock in me, showing me how amazing he can make me feel."

Christian lifts his hips and frees himself from his jeans.

"Then take what you need." He breathes in through his teeth as I slowly lower myself down onto him, feeling the tip going deeper and deeper into my pussy. I start bouncing slowly on his cock, loving how he struggles not to throw me onto the sofa and take over.

Christian lets me take control, and it doesn't take long until his head is leaning on the back of the sofa, his eyes closed, and I know he's trying everything to stop himself from reaching his climax until I do. He loves to watch, so he will be close by the time I am all his.

"Daddy," I cry out as the pressure builds inside me. I'm so close, but I'm struggling on top.

"I've got you, Baby." Christian tightens his grip on my hips and thrusts up into me. He takes control but keeps me on top. We stay together, both rushing to our own release, before finding it and crying out together, my whole body becoming rigid, before slumping onto him, resting my head against his chest as we both try to catch our breath.

"Three months."

Christian's eyes open, and he looks down at me.

"Until what?"

Sitting up, I look around at the others, each now dressed with a drink.

"Until the next production is cast. If I don't get a lead, I will throw away my pills."

"You going to let us put a baby in you, Jazzy?" Jason asks, walking towards me, picking up the blanket and placing it back over me. Christian helps me sit across his lap.

"In three months, IF I don't get a lead in the next production. Then, I want to start trying."

"I think that's fair enough, Shorty," Maximus grins as he leans in to kiss me.

"Me too," Sean smiles. "We all know how hard you've been working, and we may joke about throwing your pills out, but I can promise you we wouldn't do that." He looks around at his brothers with raised brows. "Would we?"

Everyone shrugs before laughing as I roll my eyes and lean back into Christian, closing my eyes as he holds me and the blanket against him.

"It's a good job. I know the truth," I whisper as my eyes get heavy.

"And what's that, Sweetheart?" Christian whispers into my hair.

"That as much as you all try and pretend you control me, I'm the one with the final say." Grinning to myself, I listen to them all trying to protest, but I can hear the truth in their playful tones. They will never make me do anything I don't want to.

Chapter Thirteen

JASON

"Have you heard from Terry or Layton?" I ask Gordon as I climb into the car. The two of us have just been to check on the latest shipment of equipment delivered for Calvin and his team. When I heard how they use their knowledge and training to dig out criminals and sexual predators the police can't find, I knew we had to do all we could to help them. With the contacts we have with weapon production as well as other items of detection and destruction, it was easy to come to a deal with them to ensure they always have the best equipment to hand. At the end of the day, that's why we took over these contracts. To make sure the equipment didn't end up in the wrong hands.

"Nothing, but neither would contact us unless something were wrong," he answers as we pull away from the warehouse.

Glancing at my watch, I see it's ten past five, which means Jasmine should be out of therapy by now. I hate that none of us are there if she's had a painful session. The twins have both been to a meeting with a new chain of gyms to encourage them to buy our gym equipment, which Sean has designed and pushed since leaving university. It's his side business, and it's blooming. He organised this meeting weeks ago, so he had to be there. I tried to reschedule the handover, which Gordon and I just left, at the last minute, but it was today or never, so I had no choice. As for Christian, I have no idea where he is. We woke up to find him gone this morning, and no one can get a response from him. Even when Jaz messaged to see if he was still taking her to therapy, he didn't reply, which upset her, even if she was unwilling to admit it.

We drive silently as I watch my phone, waiting to hear from my girl. She always sends a message in our family chat to let us know she is out of therapy and how she's doing. I don't know what it is, but something's telling me I should be with her, that something's happened, or she is upset after whatever they discussed. It's not the first time I haven't been able to be there, but we've always ensured that one of us is.

I quickly check the trackers and see that Layton's car is approaching the house. The new security system sends me a notification showing them pulling up at the back door. Jasmine jumps out of the car and heads straight for the house, not looking up at the camera and giving it a wave like usual, knowing one of us will see it.

"Head home. I want to check on Jaz before we head to the bar." Gordon takes the turn without question.

I repeatedly try to tell myself everything is okay, but my gut tells me to get to the house as quickly as possible. I message the twins to see if they have heard from her, but Maximus immediately says they haven't, and they are heading back to the house as well. I'm about to message him back when Layton's name flashes up on my phone, and I answer it in less than a second.

"Hey, is she okay?"

"No," Layton sighs before I hear *Nickleback* blaring in the background. "I tried to call Christian, as I know you are busy, but he's still not answering, and neither is Terry. She needs one of you here. Who's the closest?"

"Probably me. We will be there in five minutes. Have you spoken to the twins?"

"No, you were my first call when I couldn't get Christian. I'm checking the tracker now, and I think Sean may be closer than you, but I can't see where Maximus is."

"He's in Sean's car. Tell them I'm on my way, and we will deal with whatever's upset her together." I hear Layton agree as the call ends. I don't have to tell Gordon to speed up as he already has. I might miss Calvin having my back, but Gordon is proving just as good at reading the room and knowing what I need without saying it.

"Of all the days for therapy not to go well," I sigh, rubbing my face as the guilt settles in my gut.

"You can't all be there every time. The four of you run several very successful and stressful businesses. Jaz knows that and understands why she had to go alone today," Gordon points out.

"We have a schedule and are meant to keep to it, but Christian disappeared when he was meant to be with her." I don't know what has gotten into my brother recently, but I never thought he would put anything before Jasmine. He could have asked me or the twins to deal with whatever cropped up, but once again, he is keeping us out of the loop, and it's getting old fast, especially now Jasmine is suffering because of it. He can think again if he thinks I will keep my mouth shut this time.

We pull up outside the back of the house, and I tell Gordon to wait for my call before jumping out and heading through the back door. As soon as I leave the kitchen, I hear Jasmine's music and know it's not a good sign. Taking two stairs at a time, I reach the landing and find Maximus and Sean standing outside her bedroom. The music is deafening, even though her door is closed.

"Have either of you been in?" They turn to look at me and shake their heads.

"We spoke to Layton downstairs, and he's worried. Apparently, she ran out of her therapist's office and was beside the car quicker than he could unlock it."

"Fuck," I groan, rubbing my face.

"Where the fuck is Christian? He was meant to be with her!" Maximus hisses through gritted teeth, his eyes ablaze with anger.

"I don't know, something important must have come up, especially for him not to be here for her therapy," I know I need to keep the peace; if Christian is up to something dodgy, I want to keep the twins out of it as well as Jasmine. But with me, he doesn't have a choice. I need to know what the fuck is going on.

"Stop making excuses for him. He's dropped the ball and hurt her in the process; he needs to sort his shit out!" Maximus snaps, getting angrier.

"I know, and he will be told, but getting angry right now isn't helping Jaz. She needs you to be calm, so if you need to take a minute to sort your head out, go and do it. Do not let her see you like this."

Maximus glares at me for a moment before his face softens. He nods slightly before taking a deep breath and forcing himself to calm down.

"We were saying before you arrived that we think you should go in and see what's going on," Sean explains.

"If we all go in together, it might be too much for her,"

Maximus finishes. I nod in agreement as we've all noticed that one of us is sometimes better than all.

"Wish me luck," I sigh as I knock on her door. I wait a few seconds and listen for her, but I can't hear anything over the music. I look at the twins and sigh before knocking again as I open the door.

"Jazzy?" I stop as I look at the bed, expecting her to be on it, but all I can see is her bag. "Jazzy?" I call again, heading to the bathroom to check if she's there, but I find it empty. "Jazzy, where are you?" I shout, rushing over to her stereo to shut off the music.

"Where is she?"

I turn to see the twins entering the room. Sean heads straight for the walk-in wardrobe but curses when he doesn't find her there.

"Check the other rooms," I order, rushing out of Jasmine's and heading to Christian's. I call out to her and check everywhere, but it's empty. As I leave his room, planning to head to mine, I see Sean rushing out of it.

"She's not in yours. Maximus is checking mine."

"She's not in either of ours," Maximus adds as he joins us at the top of the stairs. "She must be downstairs," Maximus declares as he turns and storms down the stairs. We all rush, taking them as quickly as possible.

"You two search here; I'll check the studio and gym." The twins nod once before rushing off in different directions before I head for the underground gym and studio.

I can hear more music as soon as I enter, but not the type she usually dances to. I'm about to check her studio when I hear something coming from the sparring room where we keep the punching bags and boxing ring.

Hearing the sound again, there is no mistaking what I hear. I slowly open the door.

Inside, I find Jasmine in a pair of shorts and a sports bra, wearing boxing gloves and hitting a punching bag. From how she is breathing and going for it, I think it's safe to say something has really upset her today.

"Jazzy?" I call softly as I walk into the room. The way her shoulders jump for a second tells me she heard, but she doesn't stop her assault on the bag. I approach and stand slightly behind it so she can see me, but she doesn't have to stop what she's doing if she doesn't want to.

"Hey, what's happened?"

Jasmine's eyes lock with mine briefly before she hits the bag twice. It starts to swing, making it a little more difficult for her to hit, so I hold it in place for her. She freezes for a second when she sees me holding it, but I nod at the bag in my arms.

"Keep going." She says nothing but starts punching again, each time getting harder and faster. I watch as the tears slowly slide down her cheek, and it takes everything in me to keep holding the bag and not pulling her into my arms.

"I hate her." The three words spill from her mouth with such venom that it takes me a second to realise it was Jasmine speaking and not a voice from the sound system.

"Who?" I ask, even though I can guess the answer.

"My fucking. Bitch. Of. A. Mother." She punches the bag with each word. The tears are flowing freely now, and I can see she's starting to break.

"I hate her," she hisses through gritted teeth. "I'm glad she's dead." She's never voiced much about Carol's death. We always assumed it was because she killed her to save Christian. But I'm starting to think it may be more than that.

"Say it again," I demand as I watch how her body responds to the mini outburst.

"I hate her." This time, I notice a wobble in her voice, and I know she will break soon, which is what she needs.

"Again."

This time, it's not a word that comes out of Jasmine's mouth but a small scream of frustration.

"Again," I order as she punches the bag, but there's not as much power in it; she's losing focus.

"Again," I say as she hits the bag one last time with such force I struggle to stay on my feet. The exact second she punches it, a scream erupts from within her, and her whole body becomes ridged.

I let go of the bag and only just catch her as she falls and continues to scream. She's expelling so much pain and anguish it's hard to watch. Now she's started, she can't hold it in as she continues to scream and cry in my arms as I hold her on the padded floor.

It feels like she screams for minutes; by the time the last scream ends, her voice is almost non-existent. She sobs and shakes in my arms, and I don't know what to do. What the hell happened for her to have this much of a reaction to her therapy session?

Jasmine shivers in my arms, and I know she will feel the air conditioning down here. It's enough to make me think and act.

"Put your arms around my neck, Angel," I whisper as I lift her from the floor and head towards the exit, planning on carrying her to her room. I notice the twins for the first time and can see the pain in their eyes. I know they will want to do something to help her, but I am unsure how.

"Can you grab her a bottle of water and one of those protein bars she likes? We'll be in her room."

Sean nods before rushing off to get what I requested.

"Her favourite blanket is in the sitting room; I'll go get it," Maximus says as he walks out of the gym, holding doors open for me as we go. I thank him as I head towards the stairs and continue to carry her in my arms, unsure if I can put her down.

As I enter her room, I know the best thing for her will be to rest, but I also know she hates getting into bed before showering after a workout. So, instead of placing her on the bed, I walk into her bathroom and squat down next to the bath, keeping her on my lap as I turn the taps on.

"Let's get you bathed and into bed, Angel," I whisper as I hold her close and wait for the bath to fill. I hope I'm doing the right thing and won't make matters worse.

Twenty minutes later, Jasmine lies in the bath as I sit on a stall beside the tub. I've washed her hair and hopefully helped her to feel a little better. She hasn't said a word, only responding with nods and shakes of her head when asked a question. The twins are giving us a little space and waiting for us in the bedroom. Neither of them wants to be too far away.

"Are you ready to come out, Angel?" I watch her nod; her usual bright eyes have lost all sparkle, and her face lacks emotion. For someone who usually always wears a smile, it breaks my heart to see her like this.

Not caring about my shirt getting wet, I lift her from the bath and place her on my knee, where I have a towel ready for her. Wrapping her in two towels plus one for her hair, I carry her into the bedroom. Maximus and Sean both jump to their feet as we enter, but I shake my head, signalling for them to stay back until I have her settled.

Sitting her on the edge of the bed, I dry her off and help her put on a pair of pyjamas she loves. I brush her hair and towel it dry before twisting it into a plait and tying it off at the end with a hair elastic. Helping her to stand, I pull back the covers and watch as she climbs in, picking up her teddy from where it sits and holding it close to her chest.

"Do you need anything, Angel?" I ask, sitting on the edge of her bed as I run a hand over her still-damp hair. She shakes her head, so I reach over to kiss it before standing, but she grabs my hand.

"Stay." That one word is barely a whisper, but the pleading in her eyes speaks volumes.

"Of course, I'm not leaving you. Move over." Jasmine slides across to give me some room, and I lie on the bed beside her before pulling her into my arms. She looks at the other two, and they slowly slide onto the bed, so they are close too.

"What do you need, Shorty?" Maximus whispers as he holds her from behind.

"Time," she croaks, her voice raw from screaming as she did.

"You can have all the time in the world, Princess. You don't have to tell us anything until you are ready." Sean whispers as he sits at the bottom of the bed, running his hand up and down her leg. She nods once and closes her eyes, no doubt exhausted after everything that she's been through. I look at my brothers over our sleeping girl, and they share the look of disbelief and pure heartache for the woman we love and all she is going through.

Chapter Fourteen

JASON

The three of us stay by Jasmine's side as she sleeps. We don't say a word at first because we fear waking her. But also, because there are no words for what we witnessed in the sparring room.

Jasmine has always been so unbelievably strong; we have seen breakdowns and what the effect of nightmares have done to her, but not once have I witnessed what we did today. That was a new level of pain, breaking us all to watch.

"You okay?"

I lift my head from where it's been buried in her hair and look at Sean to find both of them watching me.

"Better than she is," I answer, forcing myself not to kiss her head in case I wake her.

"What happened?" Maximus asks.

"How much did you see?"

"We heard her yelling 'I hate her, ' and then the screaming started."

I fill them in on what they missed, and we sit in silence again.

What I wouldn't give to kill Carol for the abuse she caused our girl. Jasmine is an absolute sweetheart who wouldn't say boo to a goose unless provoked. But Carol has caused all kinds of fucked up issues, and it's going to take years for the therapist to unravel it all.

"Have either of you contacted Christian?" I ask quietly, a while later. Both of them shake their head, but I don't miss the way Maximus's jaw clenches.

"If he wants to know what's going on, he should be here, not swanning off doing whatever he feels is more important than her," Maximus mutters through gritted teeth.

"He has a right to know," Sean starts but stops when Maximus glares at him.

"What right does he have? He should have been here or at least told us what was so important that he couldn't be."

"I know, and I will deal with him when he gets back."

"Will you, though?" Maximus snaps.

"Of course I will."

"You said that last time, but here we are, with Shorty suffering and him being AWOL again!" I know he's right, but if I don't stay in control of this, Maximus will deal with him, and that will be all kinds of fucked up, which is the last thing Jasmine needs, us all to be falling out. It's the last thing any of us need.

"Look, I know things are crazy at the moment, and I'm not making excuses for him," I glare at Maximus to stop him from arguing with me. "But something is going on, and he is hiding it from us, me included. He's only ever done that a handful of times, and each has been because he needs to keep us safe."

"That's no excuse anymore; we are old enough to deal with shit," Sean sighs, but I shake my head whilst turning my attention to him.

"Do you really think age matters to Christian? He took on the father role at fifteen, when Mum first started getting ill, for fuck's sake. He has spent his whole life protecting us, if not from Tommy, then from the shit he had gotten us into. Now that Jaz is involved, he will take even more on to keep her protected, even if it means staying away and dealing with shit on his own." I look to Maximus and know he will want to have his say, but I'm not finished. "I know our brother, and I know he is dealing with something that he wants to keep us safe from; all of us," I nod down to the sleeping Jasmine to show it includes her.

"I will not attack him about today, but I will make it clear how fucked up it is that he doesn't trust us to help or to know what's going on. He needs to stop trying to protect us all and include us so we can take some of the pressure off him." Letting out a deep breath, I briefly close my eyes and try calming myself a little.

Looking down at Jasmine asleep against my side, holding her bear, I worry again about what Christian has gotten himself into. It's got to be something terrible for him to let her down like he has. I'm just about to climb out of bed and call him when I feel Jasmine tighten her grip on me. Looking back at her, I can see she is starting to wake up. I'm surprised she has slept as much as she has. It just shows how draining her breakdown was.

As her eyes flutter, I run a hand over her head, letting her know she isn't alone. Her bloodshot eyes open and look up at me.

"Hey, Angel. You okay?" I ask softly. Maximus leans in and kisses the top of her head as she nods slowly.

"Do you need anything, Shorty?" he asks softly. She opens her mouth to speak but has to clear her throat, which is no doubt sore from screaming earlier.

"Water," she croaks. Sean leans towards the floor and grabs a bottle he placed there earlier.

"Here you go, Princess." He hands it to Maximus, who helps Jaz to sit up. I don't miss how she keeps her bear tightly in her arm. It's a sign that she's hurting and feeling vulnerable. I've not seen her with it for a while and knew it was a good sign. But now, she's back to clinging to it again, and it's hard to watch her take these steps backwards.

Sitting up myself, I lean back against the cushioned headboard and hold out an arm so she can lean against me whilst sipping the water. Once she's finished, I take it and place it on the cabinet beside me. I want to ask her what happened that caused her so much pain and if there's something I can do to help her heal, but I don't know how to ask without upsetting her. As usual, Maximus doesn't think about such things.

"What happened, Shorty?" He takes her hand to kiss her knuckles.

"Maximus, give her time," Sean sighs. Jasmine looks at him before looking to Maximus, then me.

"I need time to work through it all," she whispers as she plays with the bear's ear, not looking up at us. "I asked Dr Gold not to send his usual report to Daddy." When Jasmine looks up, she seems like a small, vulnerable child. Her eyes fill with tears, and she looks scared. "I know he's going to be cross, but I need to understand this myself before explaining it to the rest of you." I offer what I hope is a reassuring smile before running a hand over her head.

"He won't be cross; he will understand. Therapy is about you and not any of us. You do what you must to heal from whatever has come up." Jasmine tries to look away, but I place a hooked finger under her chin and gently encourage her to look at me. "The only thing I want you to promise me is that you will always come to us if things become too much. If something ever makes you feel like you need extra support, or if you feel like you can't cope, please know we will help you. Don't ever do anything reckless because we love you more than life itself, and we would never cope without you." Looking deep into her eyes, I know she is reading between the lines as she nods slowly.

"I promise." I release her chin, and she leans into me. "Thank you, Daddy."

Kissing the top of her head, I look to see my brothers looking at me, both looking devastated and as unsure of what to do, as I feel.

Sean's phone vibrates on the bed at the same time as Maximus's and mine. I know it will be the security system letting us know someone has arrived.

"It's him." Maximus's jaw clenches as he starts to fight the urge to go to Christian and have it out with him. I know I need to intervene quickly and ensure there's no fighting while Jasmine is this vulnerable.

"I'll go and speak to him and let him know you are okay and what you have asked," I say softly into her hair. I hear the slightest thank you from her before I kiss the top of her head and nod at Sean for him to take my place. He nods and moves once I am out of his way.

"I'll be back in a bit," I smile at Jasmine, leaning against Sean now as Maximus holds her hand and plays with her hair. I glance at the other two and nod, hoping they will understand that I heard them, and I will not be going easy on Christian.

Walking from the room, I close the door to ensure they

won't be able to hear anything and head for the stairs. As I reach the top, I find Christian standing at the bottom of them, looking frantic.

"Where is she?" he demands as he moves up a few steps.

"Resting. We need to talk," I reply coldly. Seeing him there looking worried gets my back up. It's been a couple of hours since her session finished, and as far as I'm concerned, he hasn't contacted any of us.

"We can talk when I've seen her for myself," he starts, but I place a hand on his chest as I reach him.

"No. You will listen to what I have to say first." I add firmly. Christian looks at me for a moment, and I can see he knows I'm pissed, but when he opens his mouth to argue with me, I shake my head. "Don't. You are not getting near her until I have said what is needed, and I will not do this where she may hear us." I stare at my brother, showing him I will not change my mind. I will not back down and mean what I said. He will not get near her until I have spoken to him.

He looks like he will argue for a moment, but when he sees I'm not backing down, he turns around and heads back down the stairs. I follow a few steps behind as he storms through the house and heads for his office. I know it's his way of trying to keep some power right now, but I don't care. He may be my older brother, and he may have saved my life a number of times, but I have saved him as well, and he needs to remember he is my brother, not my boss.

As we enter his office, he walks over to the desk, pulling off his suit jacket and placing it on the back of the chair. He looks up at me, and my control snaps a little.

"Are you having an affair?"

Christian's eyes bulge as he stares at me from his seat.

"What the fuck did you just ask me?"

"I asked if you are having an affair because it's the only reasonable explanation as to why you are still being so secretive!"

"Of course, I'm not having a fucking affair! Are you insane?"

"Then where the fuck have you been?" I demand, marching over to his desk.

"Out." That's all he's got to say whilst sitting back in his chair.

"Where?" I ask again.

"It doesn't matter where I've been." The proud, stubborn bastard is actually going to continue hiding shit from me.

"It matters when you ignore your responsibilities to your fiancée," I point out. "Did you forget it was your turn to be here for her today?" The look on his face tells me he didn't.

"Something came up, and I had to take care of it," he answers.

"And you couldn't pick up your phone to give us a heads up so we could move things around? Or is your phone broken again?" I point to the door as my anger starts getting the better of me. "She tried to call you herself, and as much as she tried to hide it, she was gutted when you didn't answer!" I stand tall whilst crossing my arms over my chest.

"I didn't have time to call and left my phone in the car. Things progressed quicker than I thought they would, and time got away from me."

"Are you going to tell me where you were? Or what you were doing?"

"There's no need, it's sorted." It's like talking to a goddamn robot. He is giving nothing away, which is starting to get on my last nerve, and I have no doubt he knows it, too.

"How long are you going to keep doing this?" I ask, shaking my head in disappointment.

"I wasn't aware I was doing anything." There he goes again with that stubborn streak of his.

"You are well aware of what you are doing, and it needs to stop. Whatever is going on, you need to tell me. How can we help you when you shut us all out?"

"I don't need your help."

"Yes, you fucking do!" I snap, slamming both hands on his desk, and I lean against it, staring at my brother. "I know about the other buildings, Christian. I know that it hasn't just been one vandalised but eight! I also know that something has got you so worked up you are letting Jaz down!"

"I am not letting her down!" he yells, jumping to his feet as he, too, slaps his hands on his desk and glares at me. "Everything I do is for her!"

"Except being here when she needs you the most!"

"I'm here now!" he states, standing tall and waving his hand towards the door. "I would be with her finding out what's been going on if you hadn't stopped me!" He shakes his head and starts marching towards the door.

"She doesn't want you to know!" The second the words are out there, he stops in his tracks and frowns as if he had misheard.

"What?"

"She asked me to tell you that she doesn't want to discuss what happened today. She doesn't want to talk about the session or what caused her to have a breakdown."

"What breakdown?" he asks as his eyes widen. Shit. I forgot he doesn't know everything. He probably only knows that she was upset.

"Layton called after he brought her home to let me know she was really upset. He tried to call you, but you weren't answering. I rushed back, and at first, we couldn't find her, but then I found her in the sparring area. She was beating the shit out of a punchbag. She started shouting that she hated that bitch Carol before she broke down and screamed until her voice was gone. She then shut down completely."

I watch as he pulls his phone out of his pocket and starts tapping it, looking for an email from her therapist.

"There isn't a report to read," I say, stepping forward.

"I've told him I want a report after each session!" he snaps and lifts his phone to his ear.

"She told him not to send one." Christian stares at me before lowering the phone and ending the call. "She knows you get sent them as she has to agree to it; otherwise, it goes against client-therapist confidentiality." I point out, taking another step towards him. "But today, she didn't consent. She begged him not to send one, so he can't."

"Why would she do that?" I can see the pain on his face. "How can I help her if I don't know what's happening?"

"You help by letting her accept whatever she's dealing with. All she's asking is that we give her time, and we have to respect that." Running my fingers through my hair, I let out a deep sigh and wish I could just go back upstairs and take all her pain and suffering away.

"Jazzy never asks us for anything. But she has asked us for this, and we have to give it to her, even if it's the last thing we want to do. We have to give her the time she has asked for."

Christian walks over to the sofa against the far wall and leans against it whilst rubbing his face. As he lowers his arm, I realise there are marks on his shirt.

"Is that your blood or someone else's?" I ask, nodding towards his arm. He looks at it and curses.

"Someone else's," he answers, unfastening the shirt and pulling it off. "It's why I left. I was given a tip-off about who was behind the destruction. It all progressed quickly, and I ended up taking out the threat," he explains, obviously realising he has no other choice but to tell me now.

"So it's over? Whatever you have been dealing with on your own has finished?" He nods once before screwing the shirt into a ball. "Why didn't you tell me?"

I look at my brother properly for the first time since he returned and see how tired he looks. Not just because he left early this morning, but like he hasn't slept in weeks. His skin looks pale, and he has lost a little weight. All signs that he has been pushing himself too hard and dealing with more shit than he should have handled on his own.

"Because I was furious and wanted to deal with it myself. I wanted to ensure no one got near you guys or Jasmine. They made this personal, and I had to ensure I ended it."

"I would have helped," I point out, and a small smile appears on Christian's face.

"I know. But this was something I needed to do."

"Okay," I answer, knowing there is no point fighting over it. "If you are sure it's over, then nothing else needs to be said on the matter." I walk over to my brother and cup the back of his head whilst leaning my forehead against his. "But stop thinking you are the only one who can take people on. If they threaten one of us, they threaten all of us, and we deal with them as a family. It's the one thing that we all stand by. What have you always told us?"

"You hurt one O'Reilly, you hurt us all," he replies as his eyes close.

"So take your own advice and let us help you."

He nods in agreement, but I can't help thinking he's

only saying it because he's been caught. But there's nothing more I can do. The ball is in his court now, and I can only wait to see if he will start including us or keep playing on his own.

"Come on. Let's get you a clean shirt, then you can see Jazzy. She will be glad you are home," I tell him, hoping it will put him in a slightly better mood.

As I follow him out, I can't help but wonder if things are as over as he says they are or if I should be worried. One thing I do know for sure is that no one will stand a chance against us. Now I know I need to be on the lookout for trouble; I will be, and God help anyone who attacks my family because it will be the last thing they ever do.

Chapter Fifteen

JASON

Walking down the stairs, I try to push down the constant worry that's been consuming me the last five days since Jasmine's breakdown. The first twenty-four hours were rough to witness.

As soon as Christian walked into her room, she started crying again until she fell asleep in his arms. I have never seen him look as grief-stricken with guilt; if he needed any confirmation of how much he fucked up, that did it.

Jasmine's therapy was Monday evening, and none of us left her side until she was ready to leave the room Wednesday morning. She hardly spoke and cried silently into her teddy or in the arms of whoever was holding her at the time. When she slept, it wasn't peaceful; the nightmares she had woke us all as she thrashed and screamed in her sleep until she woke herself up. Even though we managed to get her to drink plenty of fluids, she couldn't stomach food, so Mrs Brown made her all her favourite snacks and meals in small portions. The four of us cancelled all meetings and training to give her our undivided attention.

We all woke up on Wednesday morning and found Jasmine writing in a journal on her vanity table. She told us she was okay and wanted to carry on as best she could, and she has. If you were to see her now, you wouldn't think anything was wrong. She's smiling, laughing, and acting like everything is fine. But now and again, she starts staring into space, lost in her thoughts. Her nightmares have increased, and she's back to having them nightly. As much as we all want to ask her what's happening, we are giving her the time and space she requested. I'm surprised by Christian as he hasn't tried to get out of her what's going on. But I think he knows better than to push any of our buttons right now.

Something tells me that Jasmine is not telling us anything because she worries about Christian and how stressed he has been. I believe her when she says she needs time to work everything out before telling us, but I also think she's protecting him. She is sleeping in my room more than anyone else's. Christian has also noticed and seems to be taking it a little personally, but what does he expect? He wasn't here when she needed him the most; I was. He has stayed close since the whole ordeal, which could mean everything is taken care of, as he said.

On Thursday afternoon, when Mrs Brown and Jasmine took the puppy out for a walk, Maximus charged into Christian's office and had it out with him. It wasn't pretty, and for a moment, Sean and I were worried it would come to blows, but they managed to clear the air a little, at least. When Jasmine is around, you would not know they had fallen out. Over the last day or two, they have been civil and hopefully, tonight, they will be able to put their differences behind them.

Tonight is our stag party. We wanted to cancel it and spend the time with Jasmine, but she insisted we carry on as usual. Apparently, she and the girls will use the time to organise a few more things for the wedding and her hen party. It feels wrong to go out when she has been so troubled, but if it's what she wants, then that's what will happen.

I walk into the sitting room, tugging at my shirt cuff and checking that the cufflink is positioned correctly. I'm not surprised the twins are already in here with a drink in their hands and dressed in trousers and shirts as they laugh together.

"Here you go, Jason," Sean grins, holding a glass for me.

"Thanks," I say, taking it. "You ready for this?" I ask, smiling at them.

"Hell yeah, going to be a great night," Maximus laughs, knocking me with his shoulder. "It's not every day you get to share your stag do with your brothers."

He's not wrong. Before Jasmine, I figured if I ever got married, I would have the three of them there as support, not as fellow grooms.

When I think about how I thought my life would go before our amazing, beautiful fiancée danced her way into our hearts, I can say getting married was the furthest thing on my mind. I was content to follow my brother's orders and help him build and protect the empire we have developed through a lot of blood, sweat and tears, and those haven't always been our own. Sure, I loved to fight and had fun when I did, but I realised the business side of things was a better fit for me and started to concentrate on that.

But now, things are different; our lives have changed and will continue to do so as our family grows. It's made me wonder if all the stress is still worth it. What if we took what we built, kept the legal stuff and stepped away from the weapons and illegal shit. Would it make Jasmine and our future children safer than they would be if things continue as they are? I can't decide, so I haven't said anything to Christian about my thought process yet. I need to work out an easy, safe route out of this life, if there is one.

"Everything organised at the club for tonight?" Sean asks, bringing me back from my busy thoughts.

"Yeah, security has been given a list of people invited. Calvin and the guys are guests, but they have loaned us a few of their people to help out our security. Personally, I think our lot will be enough, but Christian was adamant we needed more."

He's still on edge, even though he says everything is fine. I know him as well as I know myself, and I can tell when he hasn't slept well or is overthinking everything. It's embedded in him to analyse everything and to prepare for the worst. But sometimes, I wish he would just stop and enjoy the moment. But I don't think it will be possible until he knows what to do to help Jasmine. It's hitting him hard being unable to fix this for her.

"Yeah, well, you know what he's like. He needs to relax now and again," Sean sighs.

"Well, hopefully, he can relax a bit tonight and enjoy himself," I smile as I hear giggling from the corridor outside the room.

Jasmine rushes in, looking happy in her leggings and one of Sean's old hoodies. Verity, Danielle King and Abigail Young walk in behind her, smiling.

"Why are you all still here? I thought you were leaving at eight?"

"Eight-thirty, Jazzy. We will be gone as soon as Christian graces us with his presence," I wink as she leans against Sean's side. He wraps an arm around her waist before leaning in and kissing her cheek.

"Are you eager to get rid of us, Shorty?" Maximus asks, taking my glass to top up.

"Yes, we have things to organise which the grooms can't know about!" Danielle answers from the sofa, where she and the other girls sit.

"Are you all staying tonight?" Sean asks, looking over the top of Jasmine's head to her friends.

We have three guest rooms on the floor above ours, which Jasmine's friends have stayed in a few times. Each has their own room and stays to keep Jasmine company when we are working away or if they are doing something together.

"And be here when the four of you come home drunk and want a loud orgy? No, thank you," Abbi replies as Verity giggles behind her hand.

"Don't be so vulgar, Abigail," Christian declares as he walks into the room whilst shoving his phone in his pocket. "Are we all ready to get this over with?" he asks, looking around at us all.

"You could pretend you are looking forward to it," Sean sighs, rolling his eyes as he takes a glass and hands it to our older brother. "Even if just for the three of us," he adds. Christian's shoulders visibly slump a little as he realises tonight isn't just about him.

"You're right, I'm sorry. I'm sure I will relax once I have a drink or two." He knocks back the bourbon in his glass and holds it out for a top-up, a playful smirk appearing as he winks at Jasmine.

"That's more like it!" Maximus laughs as he downs his own, picks up shot glasses from the small bar that are already filled, and hands them out. I sniff the liquor and realise it's the expensive tequila we keep for nights like tonight. He holds his glass out in front of him with a big grin. "Here's to us showing others that no one throws a stag do like the O'Reillys." My brothers and I tap our glasses against his before all knocking back our shots and laughing. I smile at Christian, who puts his empty glass on the table.

"Right, come on. There is a bottle in the limo with our name on it and a whole load of arseholes waiting to get us drunk."

"Will there be strippers there tonight?" Verity asks from the sofa.

"There better not be since I wasn't allowed to book any for Jaz's hen party," Danielle adds, giving us a look. If it weren't for knowing she is all bark and no bite, I would sometimes feel slightly intimidated by that woman.

"Usually, that's down to the best man, and since we are all each other's best men, I can guarantee there will not be one," Sean answers, looking at each of us as if daring us to say he's wrong. We all smirk whilst shrugging, knowing how much it will irritate Jasmine.

"There better not be any strippers, or I will not be held responsible-" I cut her off by taking her hand and pulling her from Sean so I can wrap an arm around her waist whilst threading my fingers into her hair before kissing her until she is left gasping for breath.

"Why would we have a stripper when we are coming home to you?" I ask, looking into her eyes. "Which room will you be in later, Angel?" Even after only a few drinks, I'm ready to lose myself in this woman.

"My room," she answers, smiling. "Do you think you will be joining me? Or will you be too drunk?" I let her go as Maximus steps forward and pulls her into his arms to kiss her with as much passion as I did.

"I don't think I could ever get drunk enough to stop myself from fucking you into next week," he growls as

Jasmine melts in his arms. He grins before turning her around so she faces Sean and Christian, who both look ready to skip tonight and spend it buried deep in our woman.

"Will you be our stripper, Princess? Can we get a lap dance when we get back?"

Jasmine grips the front of Sean's shirt and pulls him close to her.

"If you behave tonight, I will give you more than a lap dance," she whispers just before his lips slam into hers.

"How is a guy meant to refuse an offer like that?" he teases, then kisses her lightly. "I will be on my very best behaviour," he adds with a wink before letting Christian finally get to our girl.

"Will you be behaving, Daddy?" she asks, fluttering her lashes and looking as sweet as honey.

"No one on this Earth could take my attention from you, Sweetheart. Each and every one of us is a one-woman man." Christian lets his lips brush against hers as he grins. "And we all plan on getting back and fucking you to the point you won't even be able to walk tomorrow." Not giving her a chance to reply, he briefly kisses her hard before smirking and walking towards the door. We all follow suit, knowing it will be killing her to watch us leave, knowing we won't be back for many hours and by that point, she will be ready for everything we throw at her and more.

"Don't forget the no-touching rule, Shorty. We will know if you do," Maximus warns before closing the door and shutting the four women in the sitting room.

"Well, that was fucking hot!" we hear Danielle exclaim as we walk away smiling.

The four of us make our way through the house,

heading to the front door where Terry and a couple of guards are waiting for us.

"Do you think she'll be okay?" Sean asks quietly.

"She has promised to call if she's not," Christian answers.

"We all know she won't though, she would be worried about ruining our night," Maximus points out.

"Which is why security will contact me if they see her upset or struggling," Christian adds, coming to a stop beside Terry. "I thought I told you not to work tonight," he points out, arching a brow at his friend, who is smiling at him.

"I'm not. You didn't think I would be working on your stag do, did you? After all these years, you should know I will be partying with the rest of you. Let's face it, we never thought you would find someone to put up with your shit, let alone all your brothers too," he winks as Christian calls him an arsehole. Terry turns his attention back to the guards. "You know what to do here. Verity, Abbi and Danielle are all being collected just before midnight by Travis Donavon, Miss King's driver, Frank Laws and Mr Young Junior. Walk them to the car and check everyone is safe before leaving. If there are any issues, contact Layton, as he is the one with the phone tonight. If anything happens with Jasmine, you call Christian."

Both guys nod and hold the door open as the five of us head out and climb into the limo. Terry and Sean start pouring each of us drinks as we sit back and take a deep breath.

"You all ready for this?" Terry asks, looking at us all.

"As ready as we will ever be," Maximus replies, grinning from ear to ear. I think out of all of us, he is the one looking forward the most to this evening. He has always been the one to enjoy partying, and the rest of us are happy to drink a few bourbons and head home at a reasonable hour.

"Well then, all that's left to say is happy stag do, you four!" Terry declares, holding up his glass. We all smile with a chorus of cheers and sip our drinks. All sharing a look that tells me we are all shocked that we are here, celebrating our future marriage to the woman of our dreams. It still amazes us every day, and we can't wait to get to the wedding in two weeks and marry the love of our lives once we have made it through tonight.

Chapter Sixteen

CHRISTIAN

"How many people have told you not to do it and run?"

I smirk sipping my drink as I watch everyone talking and enjoying themselves.

"Everyone has said it at least once," I reply, turning to Logan. "How many people have asked you if you actually like sharing your woman with other men?"

He rolls his eyes, places his empty glass on the bar, and tells the server what he wants.

"Everyone has asked at least once, nosey fuckers."

"Every man wants relationships with multiple women, but it takes a real, confident man to share one woman with multiple men." I have had every man and his dog ask me if I'm sure I want to share my woman with my brothers. When I tell them I have no doubts, they joke about none of us being able to satisfy Jasmine on our own. The first couple of times, I defended our family with violence and threats, but as Jason pointed out one night. No one will ever understand it until they have experienced it themselves.

"I'm going to have that printed on a T-shirt," Logan says, causing me to laugh into my drink.

"I'll take four." I look around again to see all three of my brothers laughing with friends in different areas of the club. They look so at ease, and not just because they are half-cut. They have always been great at things like this, being around people for reasons other than business. But it's a privilege I didn't have growing up. From age fifteen, every time I was out of the ring or not being forced through rigorous training, thanks to Tommy, I was in business meetings or learning about the workings of the underworld. I was never allowed to just go out and interact with people on a social basis. Besides the occasional drinking session with Travis or Terry, usually, while our fathers talked business or were out somewhere, I never got the whole social life experience. But I made sure my brothers did; I pushed them to experience as much of life as possible. I didn't want them to turn out like me.

"How's Chelsea and Luna doing? Is everything going okay with the pregnancy?" I don't miss the sheer pride on Logan's face as he thinks of his new partner and the little girl he has adopted as his own.

"They are both doing great. Luna is really looking forward to the wedding. She has been practising walking down the aisle nonstop. It was sweet of Jaz to ask her to be the flower girl."

"Jasmine has a soft spot for that little girl. I think she enjoys spending time with her more than anyone else." A few times, Jasmine has watched Luna for her parents. Luna wants to attend Jasmine's dance school, so they've been having little lessons together. It's adorable to watch the way they interact with each other. Luna has become a family member and refers to Jason as Uncle Jason.

"Someone doesn't look happy," Logan declares, nodding towards the other side of the room. I turn to look when I see Sean arguing with someone and Maximus charging in to stand with his brother.

"What the fuck?" I curse, jumping to my feet and heading over to where the argument is breaking out. I spot Terry, who frowns when he sees me. I nod towards Sean and see the realisation on his face.

"We have a breech," I point out as he joins me. We are only a handful of metres from the twins when the guy Sean is arguing with throws a punch. Sean blocks it and quickly restrains him, pulling a gun from the back of his trousers.

As Sean took that guy down, two try to jump Maximus.

"Fuck," Terry and I curse together as we throw ourselves into the fight.

Suddenly, all hell breaks loose, and about twenty people pile into the area, all gunning for a fight. At first, I assume they are defending us, but when I see who they are, I realise not a single one of them was on the invite list.

"Layton, there's been a breech!" Terry shouts as his second grabs a guy and throws him to another security team member to remove.

"You don't fucking say!" Layton shouts back as he rugby tackles someone heading towards Sean, who has his back turned.

"Get the O'Reillys out of here!" Layton shouts before being punched hard in the face.

"Christian!"

Instinct has me ducking whilst spinning on my heels to find a guy standing behind me with a knife in his hand. Grabbing his wrist as I come up, I use to momentum to twist his arm, causing the knife to drop from his hand. Before it hits the floor, I grab it and thrust it into his gut.

The blood sprays across my hand and wrist as I pull the knife from the wound, wanting to cause him as much pain as possible.

"Christian!" I look up as Jason punches a guy and takes out his legs by kicking him behind the knee.

"I want every fucker cuffed and in the arena!" I shout over the ruckus. Then I realise our security and friends have surrounded us and are doing all they can to protect us.

"Get in the office now!" Terry shouts as someone kicks him in the ribs. I can tell from the sheer pain on his face that at least one of them is broken.

"What the fuck is going on?" Jason shouts as a member of the security forces him and me into a corner and stands in front of us. I see two other security members ushering the twins towards us. Both look furious and ready to kill someone.

"Get in the office and stay there!" Terry snaps, pointing to the door.

"I'm not hiding!" Jason shouts as Terry turns to stare at him.

"No, you are making sure you don't look like shit when you see Jaz!" I'll give it to him. He knows that the only way to get my brothers or me to do anything we don't want to is by pointing out that Jasmine would disapprove.

"I want them all in the arena!" I shout, knowing he wouldn't have heard me before.

"Already on it!" he yells back before grabbing someone off one of our guests and throwing him towards Layton, who has just finished knocking someone else out.

There must be at least twenty security members here, each one fighting someone. I see Logan disarming someone and holding a gun to their head before passing them over to a member of security.

"Fuck this."

I push past the security trying to block me in, jump on a table and fire my gun three times into the air before holding it in front of me, ready to take out any fucker who tries anything. I don't have to look to see my brothers standing with me. All four of us, back-to-back like it's always been.

"The next fucker to move is getting a bullet to the head!" I yell as the sound dies down around us. Someone lifts their gun and aims it at me, but I take them out without a second thought. "Anyone else want to fucking try it?" Everyone freezes, and I take in the scene before me.

There are people lying on the floor; at first glance, most look alive, bar a few. Alasdair McIntire is on the other side of the floor, and I can see he has at least four security guards around him. This wasn't his fight; he could have left, and I wouldn't have blamed him. Instead, he stayed, and I can see he's been involved.

"Fucking arsehole!"

I spin just in time to see Calvin tackling someone to the ground, a gun skidding towards Drew, who kicks it out of everyone's way whilst pointing his own one at the guy Calvin has just tackled.

"You need to fucking pay O'Reilly!" the guy yells. He lifts his head and looks straight at me. "You really thought you could kill Taylor, Flint and Hudson and get away with it!" he looks to Jason, then the twins, whose backs are to him as they watch those behind me. "You all need taking down. You need to realise you're not fucking invincible, you piece of-" he gets cut off as Calvin hits him hard with his gun, knocking him out. Other people start shouting and trying to fight back again, but they've lost and know it. Some people managed to escape before they could be restrained, leaving about fifteen being held by security and friends as someone rushes around handing out zip-ties to use for cuffs.

Logan and Drew start dragging off the unconscious ones as Layton shouts for everyone to get the rest to the arena. My eyes fall on Terry, leaning against a wall, his hand on his side, looking like he's just gone twelve rounds in the ring and lost every one.

"Get in the office," I order, walking to the door and unlocking it with the code.

"I'm fine," he argues, but I just give him a look. I see Layton talking to two guests a few feet away.

"Layton!" He turns to my voice and rushes towards me. "I'm taking Terry to the office to get him cleaned up. I want everyone down in the arena—invited and uninvited guests. I want a count of injured, names and who stuck up for us. I will message you when we are leaving the office. Make sure no one comes in unless cleared with me first."

As I've come to expect from Terry's second, he nods once with a firm, "Yes, sir." Before turning to Terry. "Get your ass cleaned and checked out, old man, I have everything under control."

"Fucking arsehole, forgets he's the rookie," Terry mutters under his breath before following me and my brothers into the staff area. I can see Jason looking around before following and know he will be looking for Calvin. Once again, it seems his old guard has saved his life.

"We will find him before heading to the ring," Sean says as he stands waiting for his brother. Jason nods before following and letting the door close behind him. As I turn from watching him, I see Terry struggling to walk. Stepping beside him, I place my arm around his waist and let him lean on me a little. At first, he tries to resist, but I shake my head.

"No one can see. Just accept help for once in your life, you stubborn arsehole." Terry stares at me angrily for a moment before his head drops slightly, and I feel him relaxing into me the best he can.

The five of us walk in silence until we get to our office. Maximus unlocks the door, and we all enter. I lead Terry to the desk and get him to sit in the chair, as it's higher than the sofa. Once I can see he's settled, I turn and look around the room, needing to check each of my brothers is okay.

Maximus heads straight for the bar and pours five drinks. Whilst he's busy, I walk over to where Jason's with Sean, who is holding a napkin to his eyebrow.

"Let me see." Sean looks at me for a second before lowering the cloth. He has a split eyebrow, but nothing worse than he's had in the ring. "Jason, can you grab a first-aid box? We may need a second just for Terry."

"Yeah, I'll sort it," he replies. Before he can walk away, I grab his arm and force him to look at me.

"Are you okay?" I ask, giving him a warning with my eyes about lying. Jason nods before looking me in the eye.

"You?"

"Nothing a strong drink won't fix," I reply, forcing a smile. Jason watches me momentarily before nodding again and walking over to the cabinet where we always keep a fully loaded first-aid kit.

I turn back to Sean and signal for him to sit on the sofa. Maximus heads over and places three glasses on the coffee table beside the seat before helping Sean out of his shirt. I hadn't realised it was ripped until Maximus held it up.

"Were you stabbed?" I ask as Maximus lifts Sean's arm and checks out a wound.

"It's only a scratch; you got lucky," Maximus says, lowering his arm back down.

"I was lucky Mykela was there to knock the guy over before he could do some real damage," Sean sighs. It seems there's another personal guard who I need to thank. I work in silence as I go through the box Jason brings over and set up everything I need to clean the wound.

"Want to tell me what happened?" I ask, wetting some gauze. Sean sighs as he takes a sip of the drink Maximus hands over.

"I have no idea. One minute, I'm laughing with a few friends; the next, Flint's son is standing in front of me, shouting that I killed his dad. I haven't seen him in years it took me a second to realise who he was." Sean hisses as I dab the wound. I apologise under my breath but don't stop, knowing it will only make the pain worse.

"I want to know how he got in," Jason asks behind me.

"I will find out," Terry answers from the desk. Looking over at my oldest friend, I can see how much he is struggling.

"If Sean needs stitches, I want you to do them," I whisper to Jason, nodding to Terry. He looks at the guy and nods, knowing I want to take care of him myself.

"So there was no warning; he just jumped you?" Jason asks Sean, who nods.

"Logan noticed before I did. We were at the bar. I was already heading to Sean when I saw the first punch being thrown," I explain. "All hell broke out from there."

"Do we even know how many there were?" Maximus asks. "As well as why they chose tonight? How did they even know about it? We have kept it quiet for a reason."

I shrug, not knowing how to answer. We have hundreds if not thousands of contacts in both lines of work, but we agreed to keep anything wedding-related under lock and key. The only people invited to anything, such as the wedding or parties, are people we have known for years and trust to keep their mouths shut if they see anything they shouldn't. That doesn't mean I won't have to put a warning out tonight. That's why I have asked everyone to be put in the arena; I have no intention of repeating myself.

"I will get to the bottom of it. As for how they got in, I have no idea. They must have had inside help because security was tight, and I trust our guys as well as Calvin's," Jason says behind me, sighing. I nod in agreement.

"Did everyone put all the names of those invited on the list?" I ask, sitting back on my heels and checking Sean's wound. Thankfully, it doesn't need stitches; butterfly strips should do. I hear all my brothers confirm before getting up from the floor.

"Strips are all he will need. Can you sort that?" I ask Jason, who nods and takes my place. I mutter a thanks before grabbing the kit and heading over to Terry.

I look at him, almost asleep in my chair, and for a moment, I consider calling an ambulance.

"I swear to God, O'Reilly, if you make a fuss, I will kick your ass." He doesn't even bother to open his eyes as he scolds me.

"Please, you struggle to take me on a good day. You have no fucking chance right now," I smirk. "Let's get you out of that jacket." From the effort it takes, I know there is no denying Terry needs X-rays. He has at least fractured his collarbone and ribs. I don't think there is a part of him that isn't injured.

"I thought you were meant to be good at your job?" I mock, trying to keep the atmosphere light.

"I'm fucking brilliant at my job. You're not injured or dead, are you? I'm meant to protect you, not myself."

"Good point," I laugh as Terry smiles, and the split on

his lip bleeds again. "You know you will need to go in, though, don't you." Terry rolls his eyes and instantly flinches. I don't think there is an area of his face that isn't bruised.

"I'm fine; it's all superficial," he tries to argue, but I know one way to ensure he stops.

"Do I need to call Jasmine?" Terry freezes and stares at me for a second before looking defeated. "I thought as much," I laugh. I love how threatening him with Jasmine makes him listen each time.

"You know the staff are more scared of her than you, right?" he chuckles before regretting it. I laugh out loud, nodding.

"Don't tell her, but so am I. That woman is a force to be reckoned with, and I couldn't be prouder."

"I will second that," Maximus calls.

"Third," Sean adds.

"Fourth!" Jason laughs as he continues to tidy up Sean's wound.

"She is going to be so mad when she sees the state of us all," Maximus points out. I shake my head and point to the wardrobe. We keep one in every location we own to ensure we can change if we need to. Each contains at least one suit for each of us.

"She won't know. We can shower and get changed before heading home." I look at Sean and nod at his face. "We will say a small fight broke out, but that's expected at these kinds of events." The others look at each other before Jason answers.

"Don't you think we should tell her something more than that? She deserves to know the truth."

"No," I interrupt. "That's all she needs to know. I don't want her worrying that this was more than it was. We will deal with those who were here tonight and make sure the world is reminded why they shouldn't fuck with us." I turn my attention back to cleaning Terry.

"Christian, I know you mean well, and fuck, I want to keep her as much in the dark as possible too, but she is about to become our wife and deserves to know everything about us. The good, the bad and the downright ugly," Sean points out. I turn and look at my brothers, who are all watching me.

"And she will, just not yet. She is dealing with so much already. It's only been five days since she had a full breakdown after therapy, and the last thing she needs is us bringing this shit home. Let's get through the wedding and ensure she is stronger. I don't want shit like this taking away what a magical time this should be for her." I look at each of them and see deep down that they know I'm right. "She has never had what we are trying to give her with this wedding. I want it to be perfect for her, and I will do whatever it takes for that to happen." I watch them momentarily, waiting for them to continue questioning me, but they don't. "Thank you."

Turning my attention back to the job at hand, I clean Terry up whilst making a plan with the others on how we are going to deal with people waiting for us in the arena.

Chapter Seventeen

JASON

I walk down to the arena with my brothers. All of us are in clean suits and looking as deadly as ever. Each furious that someone decided to attack us at our own stag party. I can guarantee more than one of those fuckers downstairs will leave in a bag tonight.

Layton is standing outside the staff entrance door as we exit. Now all the lights are up in the bar, we can see the extent of the destruction left from the fight. There are broken chairs, tables, pools of blood and broken glass. On the bar is a collection of weapons ranging from handguns to various knives and even a couple of bats. These guys came with the intention of causing as much damage as possible and nearly succeeded.

"How many were injured?" Christian asks Layton as he falls into step beside us.

"Twelve guests injured, eighteen of the intruders as well as two dead. I think the most serious injured on our side was Terry." Layton glances behind us, looking for his mentor.

"I want someone to take him to the hospital. He needs

X-rays. Our doctor has already been informed and will meet him there," Christian says, placing a hand on Layton's shoulder. "That means you are in charge until he can return to work."

Layton nods, and I can see the cogs already turning in his head as he tries to implement a plan.

"Okay, I will send Mykela up now to go with him. As for everyone else, they are downstairs. No one has managed to leave, and those who tried got an earful from McIntire, who is furious on your behalf."

"That still doesn't sit well with me," Maximus mutters behind us.

"Alisdair and I have an agreement. We do not get involved in each other's business and focus on the things that are important, like the Youngs and keeping the peace," Christian answers, not looking at our brother. It's an argument they have had several times, and I understand both sides, so don't get involved.

"I take it the uninvited guests are in the ring?" I ask, trying to prevent any further discussion on the subject.

"Yes, ten out of eighteen. The other eight will not be talking any time soon. Some have broken jaws; others are still unconscious or in too much pain to do anything other than whine."

I know I should be sorry, but I'm not. Don't come into my place of business and attack my family.

"Any issues at the house?" Sean asks. We'd asked Layton to check on things there and let us know if there were any problems.

"Nothing at all. Calvin sent two extra bodies over to help keep watch from outside for any intruders. So far, there's been nothing, and the girls are none the wiser." He pulls his phone from his pocket and watches the screen for a moment. "Danielle and Abbi have just left. Verity left a few hours ago, so she was already home before everything kicked off."

Even though we knew he would never prioritise anyone's safety over Jasmine's, including ours, we were still on edge about what could be happening at home.

"Seems I owe Calvin thanks for something else tonight," I point out as Sean smirks at me.

"Too right you do. I thought I was done saving your ass!"

I turn to see my old security walk into view with Logan beside him. Smirking, I approach him and pull him into a hug.

"But you do it so well," I laugh, stepping back. "But seriously, thanks, brother."

"I didn't do it for you," he smirks back. "I was too scared to face Jaz if anything happened to you."

"Is everyone really that scared of our fiancée?" Christian asks, smiling.

"Hell yeah! She scares the hell out of everyone who works for you!" Calvin laughs, winking at me.

"That's my Shorty," Maximus says proudly before glancing at the door to the entrance of the arena as we approach it. "You guys ready for this?" he asks, looking at the three of us. We all share a look and nod, taking our positions outside of the double doors. Christian and I are at the front, with the twins behind us. The way it's always been. Christian and I share a look and nod at each other once, signalling we are ready. In unison, we face the doors again and throw them open before storming into the arena, the four of us as a team.

The whole arena descends into silence. Other than the

sound of our shoes clicking as we walk over the hard-tiled floor, you could hear a pin drop.

None of us say anything or look anywhere other than the ring. In the centre, there are ten people, as Layton said. Their hands are still tied behind their backs, kneeling on the hard, cold ring floor. Five armed guards stand behind them, as well as one in each corner of the ring. No one had a chance of escaping.

We approach the ring, and I hold the ropes open for Christian to enter, followed by the twins. As soon as we are in position, Christian looks at each of the arseholes in front of us before facing the crowd outside of the ring.

"We wish to apologise for how the evening turned out. As you can imagine, it was not how we planned tonight ending." He turns his attention to the guys in front of us. "We will be dealing with each of you in a moment," Christian warns before returning to our friends.

"You will, or your pal McIntire?"

I turn to see a blonde guy who must be in his forties looking at Christian with a smirk on his face.

"I don't need anyone to fight my battles, I assure you." He turns back to the crowd around us. "I want to reassure everyone that there are not going to be any repercussions for those who are victims of tonight's attack. I would appreciate any information you may have, whether you recognise any of the people up here or heard anything during the attack. If you could inform a member of our security on the way out, I would appreciate it." Christian continues to stand tall, and you can see the power radiating from him. This is the man Tommy moulded him into—a force to be reckoned with and one who will kill in a heartbeat.

"As I'm sure I don't need to remind you all, but I will, to ensure there are no mishaps, please do not repeat anything that happened here tonight. I'm sure you all respect the level of discretion needed after such an incident." Christian turns to face the security when the bastard who mouthed off a second ago laughs.

"Something funny, arsewipe?" Maximus demands, stepping forward.

"Yeah, your joke of a family. So much for the big scary O'Reillys; you are nothing but wannabes like your father was. I bet he's real proud."

Before I have the chance to grab him, Maximus punches the bastard so hard that he falls to the side, knocking into the guy beside him. Sean and I both grab Maximus to stop him from beating a tied-up man.

As we pull him away from the arsehole, Christian approaches.

"Untie him," Christian demands in a calm voice that causes every warning bell in my head to ring.

"Keep it together. Can you do that?" I warn Maximus before letting him go. He looks to the guy now standing smugly before Christian whilst rubbing his wrists, red from the cable ties. Christian is staring at him; every single muscle in his face and body is primed and ready.

"Who are you?" Christian asks.

"The guy who's going to knock you off the pedestal, your daddy dearest, put you on." The guy looks Christian up and down, still grinning. "You might have had it a few years back, but let's face it. If you can't even pleasure that pretty little thing on your own and need your brothers' help, you are probably as washed up as you look these days."

I feel Maximus and Sean both react to the guy mentioning Jasmine behind me but put out both arms to stop them from charging forward. From the look on Christian's face, I can see that he plans to make an example of this guy.

"How does it feel, knowing that your girl has to go from you to your brothers just to get off?"

Christian smirks.

"I remember you. Your ex-wife is Maya Robinson. Why don't you ask her if I need any help in the bedroom department? She covered my sheets in blood when I took her virginity ten years ago and loved it so much she kept coming back for more. The last time, she begged me to remind her how a real man fucks, saying she was finally leaving you. When was that five years ago?"

"She left me four years ago," he growls back. Christian looks shocked.

"Well, it looks like one of us has their dates wrong because I've been loyal to my fiancée for four years, and I met her a year after I spent a full weekend in Maya's bed, making her scream over and over again. Oh wait, she said you were in Spain on a stag do?"

The guy roars as he launches himself at Christian, but he is prepared for it. In the blink of an eye, the guy is pinned to the ropes, Christian holding him in a sleeper hold.

"If I was my father's puppet, it was because I'm fucking good at what I do. I can make you wish you had never been born. Or I can make sure your body is never found." He releases the prick, who turns to face Christian with a look of murder.

"You better kill me because otherwise, I'm going to enjoy knocking all four of you out, tying you up, then fucking your little slut in every hole whilst all you can do is watch helplessly as she screams." He leans in closer as he grins. "You might have made my whore of an ex-wife bleed, but I bet it was nothing like the way your slut bled on Hudson's hand. I was there that night, and her screams of pain as he taught her a lesson was so sweet. I've always loved the way she cries out with pain. I still think about it when I jack off at night."

This time, there is no holding back the twins. They roar as they charge towards Christian and the guy, but by the time they get there, Christian has released his inner beast, and the arsehole doesn't stand a chance. I watch as he swings punch after punch. Nothing is holding him back as he destroys the prick. For all the talk of what he wanted to do to us, he's not getting a chance to fight back.

With every punch Christian lands, the sound of bone and cartilage being destroyed fills the air around us. The blood is spraying everywhere and covering the other attackers and even some of the guests. He won't know that because when Christian finally stops and steps back from the body lying in a growing pool of blood, I look at his face, and it's hard to believe he was once a man. He is unrecognisable. I can hear the guy choking on his own blood and know he will be dead in moments.

"See this!" Christian roars. "This is what will happen to anyone who thinks they can try and attack any member of our family. O'Reillys are not weak! We have not forgotten who we are! And we will kill to protect our future wife and each other!" He looks at the guys still tied up before returning to our guests. "Remember that before you leave here today! Tommy O'Reilly may have hidden behind us, but we hide behind no one! No O'Reilly will ever back down to idol threats, and we do not let those who attack our family live!"

Chapter Eighteen

MAXIMUS

The car journey home is much more sombre than the one to the club. Each of us has had to do shit we don't like tonight after we were left with no choice.

After Christian killed that prick, we had the rest of the arseholes to deal with. Thankfully, after they saw what Christian did to their little friend, most played ball, but that doesn't mean we weren't forced to play the arseholes and beat the shit out of them. Two tried to fight back, and Jason took one out whilst I was forced to break the neck of the other. I hate killing, especially when it's hands-on. When you pull a trigger, you can switch it off to a point. But breaking someone's neck is personal, and you feel the moment you send them to hell.

I look at Sean sitting with his eyes closed and his head resting on the back of the seat. Tonight, when I saw that arsehole pull a knife on my twin, I lost it. I would have killed him for having the nerve even to consider hurting him. I love my brothers, each of them, but they aren't wrong when they say twins are closer because we are. We know each other inside and out. He knows if I'm hurting or need him, no matter where I am. It's the same with me; I can tell when he is in trouble without having to be there. It comes in handy at times, for example, tonight. I was on the other side of the room to Sean, but I just felt that I had to find him and managed to do it before he found himself in real danger.

"So what's the plan now?" His voice drags me out of the dark place.

"Well, now we know that I haven't been paranoid and our enemies are trying to rise above us; we need to devise a game plan," Christian answers as he rubs his knuckles absent-mindedly. It's not surprising they hurt, given the mess he left of that guy's face or what was left of it. He deserved everything he got and should have suffered more. Hearing that he was there when Jasmine was assaulted and how she screamed in pain made the red mist descend. If Christian hadn't killed him, I would have.

"We can deal with all of that later," Jason declares, sipping from his glass. "All I want to do right now is collapse into bed and pretend for a few hours that tonight never happened." He finishes his drink before pouring another big one. Jason has his demons, which he fights with daily, and I can see he's fighting them now.

Christian looks at Jason, and for a moment, Christian looks furious. He looks like there is more he wants to say, but instead, he shakes his head, downs his drink and pours another one.

We continue to travel in silence for the rest of the journey. The tension surrounding us doesn't improve; if anything, it's worsening. I don't miss how Christian's jaw clenches whenever he glances at Jason. I try to think what could have happened to make Christian pissed at him. It must have been one of the times the rest of us were removing the bodies or cleaning up the mess. Usually, we leave that to Terry's team, but with them being a few guys down, Christian demanded we all stay and help. It was the last thing any of us wanted to do, but it needed to be done properly.

The car stops, and I realise we are finally home. Climbing out one by one, we make our way to the back door, where a member of security is waiting for us.

"Any issues?" Christian asks.

"No, sir. Whatever happened there wasn't planned for here as well. But it helped to have the two extra staff members to watch the perimeter," the security guy says. Christian nods and tells them to stay on duty until their relief comes in the morning.

"Hopefully, we dealt with everything, but I want everyone to be on alert for a few days to be sure. I will be holding a staff meeting at midday. I will send a message out now, letting everyone know. I don't expect you three to be there, but I will ensure you are informed of what's said."

The security guard nods before stepping back and out of Christian's way.

"We will be there, sir."

Christian nods, and the four of us head out of the kitchen and straight for the stairs.

As we walk into the hallway, I spot the clock and realise it's three AM. I was convinced it would be later. I haven't checked my phone in hours as I didn't want to see any messages from Shorty, as it would make the guilt I feel from what I have done tonight worse.

"Everyone, head to bed. I want to meet in the office at ten to discuss what we learned tonight," Christian declares.

We all agree through various types of grunts. I'm too tired to speak.

"I'm going to sleep in with Shorty," I mumble as I head to her room. I'm stopped by someone grabbing my arm. I look up to see it's Christian stopping me.

"No, you're not, let her sleep. Go to your room."

"Excuse me?" I snap, pulling my arm from his grip as my eyebrows disappear into my hair. "Since when do you tell me what I can and cannot do with my own fiancée?" I demand, turning to look at him.

"When it's for her own good. She will know something's wrong when she wakes up and sees you with a bruised cheek," he answers.

"She will know when she wakes up alone," Jason points out. "At least if Maximus is in there, he can distract her enough for everyone to get their story straight since you won't let us tell her the truth about what happened tonight."

Christian turns his attention to Jason, and I see the rage he was trying to hide when in the car.

"I told you why I want to do that," he snaps.

"Fine, you know best as always. But that still doesn't give you a right to dictate what we do when it comes to Jazzy. If Maximus wants to sleep in with his fiancée and isn't interrupting any of our alone time with her, then he can."

"And you think you should have any right to make decisions when it comes to Jasmine?" Christian asks through gritted teeth. Jason looks at him, shocked for a second, before frowning.

"What's that supposed to mean?"

"It means you, of all people, have no right deciding what is right for her when she was sexually assaulted because of you!"

"You think I don't know that?" Jason shouts. "You think

I haven't relived what that arsehole said about what happened to her? I wanted to throw up hearing how she screamed, how Hudson made her bleed."

"None of that would have happened if you had just fucking killed him when you had the chance the first time!" Christian shouts back.

"Guys, you're going to wake her," Sean warns, trying to get between them.

"Fuck you, Christian! You, of all people, know how tough this life is."

"Yeah, I do, especially with you hiding behind me and expecting me to fix your mistakes all the fucking time." Christian takes another step towards Jason, who doesn't back down. "How long until another one of your fuck ups puts her in danger again?"

"Fuck you," Jason snaps. Before any of us see it coming, Christian punches Jason in the face. Sean and I stand shocked as Jason stares at Christian as he wipes blood from the corner of his mouth.

"Feel better now?"

"No," Christian answers as he swings to punch him again, but this time, Jason is expecting it and lets out a roar before rugby-tackling Christian. The two of them go down hard. Jason manages to straddle him and get in a hard punch before Christian rolls them and starts punching back.

"You fucking piece of shit!" Jason yells as I see blood on the side of his face.

"Guys, pack it the fuck in!" I yell, trying to pull Jason off Christian, who quickly rolls them out of my reach and manages to get a few punches in.

"Christian, stop!" Sean yells as we both manage to grab him and pull him off Jason, who jumps to his feet and charges towards us.

"Let him go!" Jason shouts, grabbing Christian's shirt and pulling him to his feet. Christian grabs Jason's shirt in return and, after a few turns, manages to pin Jason to the wall.

"Daddy!"

We all turn to find Jasmine standing at her door, staring at us wide-eyed.

"Get in your room, Jasmine," Christian snaps before slamming Jason into the wall. "Now!"

"Don't fucking speak to her like that!" Jason yells, pushing Christian away from him. "It's not her fault you are an arsehole!" Jason shouts. He goes to turn towards Jasmine, but Christian grabs him and throws him in the opposite direction. Jason falls and slides across the wooden floor, before coming to a stop closer to his room.

"You don't go near her!" Christian warns, stepping between Jason and Jasmine.

"What the hell is wrong with you?" Jasmine yells, going to rush towards Jason, but Christian grabs her arm to stop her.

"Get in your room, now."

"No!" Jasmine snaps, staring at him straight in the eye. She has balls I'll give her that.

"Jasmine Rose, do as you are fucking told for once in your life!" Christian yells as he turns to drag her back to her room. Jason, Sean and I all charge towards them as we hear her cry out.

"You're hurting me."

Christian stops in his tracks, looks down at his hand and lets her go immediately. I grab her and place her behind me as Sean stands beside us, keeping Christian away from our girl.

"Sweetheart, I'm. I-" I watch as the realisation hits, and

he stares at Jasmine while she stays behind me. He takes a step forward, but Sean gets in the way.

"Go to bed and sleep it off," Sean warns, holding a hand up. "You've had too much to drink and a lot of shit to deal with. Sleep it off, and we will all talk tomorrow."

Christian goes to speak to her again, but I've had enough.

"Don't even look at her! If you try to go near her again tonight, you will have me to deal with."

Christian looks from Sean to me and then finally to Jason. Now that they have stopped fighting, I can see how beat up they are. Neither of them held back.

"I'm so sorry, Sweetheart," Christian whispers as he tries to look at Jasmine again. I reach round to move her further behind me, only to find she has moved away from him, herself.

"I know," she whispers before leaning into my back. I want to punch him for scaring her like this, but one look at him and I can see how much he hates himself for what he just did. He doesn't say anything or look at us before turning on his heels and storming into his room, slamming the door behind him.

"Are you okay, Princess?" Sean asks, turning to look at Jasmine. I continue to watch the door for a moment, checking that he isn't coming back out.

"No," Jasmine gasps as I hear her voice wobble. "What the hell happened?" she asks, sobbing. The three of us share a look, all wanting to tell her the truth but not knowing how badly Christian will react if we do.

"Nothing for you to worry about, Jazzy. It was just a stressful night, and we had to deal with some shit. I pushed his buttons when we got back, and he lashed out." Jason rubs his face and hisses when he catches a gash on his cheek.

Jasmine steps forward and reaches out to touch him, but he stops her hand before she can touch his face.

"I'm okay, Jazzy. Nothing a shower, some painkillers and a good sleep won't cure." Kissing her palm, he closes his eyes briefly, savouring what little touch he will allow himself. "Stay with Maximus or both of them tonight. I will come and see you in the morning." He lowers her hand and gives her a small smile before turning around and heading to his room, closing the door behind him.

When Jasmine turns to face me, I can see the tears streaming down her face.

"Come here, Shorty," I whisper, pulling her into my arms and leading her towards our room. I look at Sean and nod to the door. Silently asking if he will be joining us.

"I'll be a moment. Let me just get changed," he whispers, kissing her cheek before heading to his room next door.

Leading her into our room, I encourage her to sit on our bed. Reaching for the bedside cabinet, I grab a box of tissues and hold them out for her. Jasmine takes one and starts to dry her face, but the tears really begin then, and she breaks down.

Sitting beside her, I pull her onto my lap and hold her as she cries into my chest. I start shushing her gently whilst running a hand up and down her back.

"You're okay, Shorty. I've got you," I whisper into her hair, pressing kisses to it every few moments in the hope of calming her. She's still crying when Sean walks in a few minutes later and sees how upset she is.

"Oh, Princess," he sighs, sitting beside me so he can hold her hand.

"What happened?" she asks between sobs. She looks up at Sean and sees his taped cut. "Did he do that to you?" she demands. He shakes his head before looking at me.

"No, Princess. Someone who wasn't meant to be there tonight turned up and caused an issue. But everything is okay now. Christian's just struggling with some things someone taunted us with." Sean cups Jasmine's cheek lovingly, ensuring she is looking at him. "But he would never purposely hurt you. He loves you so much that hearing what he heard tonight pushed him over the edge."

"What did he hear?" she asks, holding his hand. I can see Sean isn't sure about telling her or just doesn't want to say the words, so I take over.

"Apparently, the guy was in the house Taylor kept you in. He told us he was in the room when Hudson hurt you. He went into detail to rile Christian up, and it worked." I feel my poor woman's body tense as she realises what I'm referring to.

"Did he have blonde hair and tattoos on his neck?" she asks.

"Yes, Princess," Sean answers. "Was he in the room?"

Jasmine nods, leaning into me as I tighten my hold on her. My brother and I share a look, and I know he wishes he could kill the bastard himself.

"Why were they fighting just then?"

I look down so I can see a little of Jasmine's face.

"Christian and Jason?" She nods into my chest, and I let out a sigh. "It's hard to explain, Shorty. It doesn't happen often, and they will have forgiven each other by the morning. That was just the two of them carrying their demons a little too close to the surface after tonight."

Jasmine sits up from my lap and looks from Sean to me.

"He still blames Daddy Jason, doesn't he."

I nod, knowing there is no way we can hide that from her. There has been tension between Jason and Christian a few times since we rescued her. If Jasmine has a bad therapy session or a nightmare about everything that happened in that house, Christian will try to keep his distance from Jason. Jasmine rolls her eyes and looks to the door.

"Will they be okay?"

"They'll both be fine, Shorty. Just give them some space."

She nods and climbs off my lap.

"I'm tired." She doesn't say anything else, just climbs into the bed on her usual side. I look to Sean, who appears as tired and defeated as I feel.

"I'm going to bed. Shout if you need me."

I nod and stand as my brother walks over to where Jasmine is lying on her side, looking to the other side of the bed.

"Good night, Princess. If you need me, come to my room okay." Jasmine nods but doesn't turn to face him. he leans over and kisses her head, whispering a quiet "I love you" before standing and looking at me. He runs one finger down his cheek, signalling that she's crying. Closing my eyes momentarily, I try to let out a deep breath quietly before nodding.

For a moment, when I open my eyes, my twin and I stare at each other before Sean steps forward and hugs me.

"You did what you had to tonight." He leans his forehead against mine as we hold the back of each other's heads. "We will go for a run tomorrow and talk. But tonight, I think you need her as much as she needs you." I nod in agreement and step back from my brother, my best friend.

"Night."

"Night, Maximus."

He walks out of the room, and I quickly strip and wash my body and face over the sink before brushing my teeth.

When I return to the room, Jasmine is sitting in bed, with her legs up against her chest, resting her chin on her knees.

"Why are you still up, Shorty?" I ask, climbing into bed next to her. She instantly leans into my side, allowing me to wrap an arm around her.

"He hurt me." Those three words cause my jaw to clench. I know he was angry and caught up in the fight with Jason, but to treat her the way he did is unacceptable. I have given him the benefit of the doubt tonight, emotions were running high, and we all drank a lot on the way home, but if I ever catch him treating her like he did tonight again, I will beat the shit out of him. I will always defend my Shorty before any of my brothers.

"I know, Shorty." For a moment, I want to tell her he is an arsehole and doesn't deserve her, but that's the anger talking, and I know he will hate himself for what he did tonight. "Please don't be scared of him. He loves you more than anything in this world and will do anything to protect you. Tonight, things just became a lot; there were too many factors he couldn't control, and it became too much." Part of me doesn't want to defend him, but he's my brother, and I know he loves her. He killed a man with his fists tonight for threatening to break her. He will hate himself for grabbing her like that.

"I know." The pain and confusion are evident in her voice.

"Come on, let's try and get some sleep. Hopefully, everyone will be calmer in the morning, and we can all sit down and talk about what happened."

The two of us slide down the bed, and I hold my girl as she rests her head on my bare chest. This isn't how I planned on ending tonight. I thought the four of us would be rocking our girl's world, but then what part of tonight went to plan?

"I'm sorry tonight wasn't as great as it should have been. You all deserved a good stag do."

Looking down, I press a kiss to her head.

"It's just one night, Shorty. We are getting a lifetime with you, which is more than we deserve." I can feel her moving to say more, but I don't want to hear her telling me I deserve more than I think I do, not after some of the things I did tonight. I don't deserve this woman in my arms, and I'm terrified she will realise that and leave one day. I lift a hand and place it on her cheek. "Go to sleep, Shorty."

I kiss her head one last time before closing my eyes and lying back on the pillow.

"Good night, Daddy."

Chapter Nineteen

JASMINE

I can't sleep. I've tried everything to stop thinking about what I saw on the landing tonight, but I can't.

I never thought I would see the day Christian and Jason came to blows. They rarely have a cross word, let alone raise their voices to each other.

I've known for a while that Christian has held some level of blame on Jason for what happened to me, but I honestly thought he would get over it with time. Now Christian and Maximus, yes, that's a fight I think we are all waiting for. They seem to be butting heads more and more recently, something they haven't been able to hide from us. But Jason and Christian aren't only brothers, they are best friends and more alike than the twins at times.

There is also the fact that tonight, Christian did something he has never done before: he laid his hands on me. When he grabbed my arm and dragged me towards my room, I was terrified. No one has manhandled me like that since I was rescued from Taylor and my mother. The irony is that I think Christian killed someone tonight for being in that house and being present when I was assaulted. Then he came home and treated me like that.

Maximus rolls away from me in his sleep, and I use it as an opportunity to get up and check on the puppy. Maybe some cuddles from Embry will make me feel a little better. Slowly, I climb out of bed, not wanting to wake Maximus and tiptoe out of the room. Closing the door quietly behind me, I head towards the stairs, planning on heading to the conservatory where the puppy sleeps because he still has the odd accident at night, and Christian doesn't want him peeing everywhere.

As I walk quietly past Jason's room, I notice a light coming from under his door. I stand outside it for a moment and remember the way he looked at me after Christian had gone to his room. He didn't want me to touch him, and he looked like he was guilty of so much more than he is. I can't let him blame himself for what happened to me anymore.

Not stopping to knock, I walk straight into the room and look at the bed where I expect Jason to be. When I don't see him there, I look to his bathroom and see another light on. I walk quietly to the door and push it open, finding Jason standing in nothing but a towel wrapped around his waist as he checks out his injured face in the mirror. There are tissues covered in blood in his sink, as well as a few other first-aid bits.

As I open the door further to enter, Jason turns around and stares at me for a moment.

"Jazzy, are you okay? What's happened?" I notice that he doesn't come closer. I refuse to let him hold himself back, so I walk up and wrap my arms around his waist.

For a moment, he freezes before letting out a deep breath and holding me back whilst burying his face in my hair.

We stand there like that for a few moments. Neither of us saying anything, just taking a moment to be in each other's arms.

"It wasn't your fault." I lean back a little to look him in the eye while staying in the safety of his arms.

"Jazzy, you weren't here. You don't know-"

"And you weren't *there*. Nothing you did, even letting Hudson live, caused what happened to me. If it hadn't been him, it would have been someone else. Every man that I saw in there had the face of someone who no doubt thrived off causing pain. I was always going to end up there; my mother would have made sure of it." I reach up and cup his face, and I look deeper into his eyes, which look like they are filling with tears. "It was not your fault, Daddy. I need you to realise that and stop beating yourself up. I hate watching you blaming yourself. It needs to stop; *you* need to stop."

For a moment, Jason looks like he's struggling. But slowly, he nods and closes his eyes while leaning into my hand.

"I will never understand what I did to deserve your love," he whispers before opening his eyes. "You are far too pure for our world, and I hate that we are dragging you into it."

"You aren't dragging me into anything; I'm choosing to be part of it. I'm choosing you four, and I always will, no matter what." Lifting up, I kiss his lips before smiling.

"I'm going to check on the pup before going back to bed." Stepping back, putting some distance between us, I smile, hoping to slightly lift his mood. "Go to bed and rest. I will see you in the morning."

Jason wraps an arm around my waist and pulls me to him, pressing his lips hard to mine.

"Good night, Angel. I love you."

I can't help but feel lighter after seeing a genuine smile on his face.

"I love you, too," I whisper before kissing him again and leaving the room.

Standing on the large landing, I feel a little better knowing that he at least knows that I don't blame him for what happened. Looking towards Christian's room, I realise I'm not ready to see him yet. I'm scared of what will happen if I go in there now and he's awake. Am I afraid of him? No. Even after he grabbed and shouted at me like that, I know he would have never done anything worse than that. He would never, ever hit me. Sure, he spanks me and disciplines me, but that is different, one word, and he would stop. Tonight was different, but I'm still not scared of him. I'm scared of what I will do. Being handled like that brought back some memories I have been trying my hardest to forget. The last thing we all need is me having another breakdown, adding more fuel to the fire. Knowing I'm doing the right thing by leaving him to it, I rush down the stairs and head to check on the pup.

Approaching the conservatory, I feel a slight draft coming from under the door and quickly start to panic. Throwing it open, my worst fear is confirmed. The back door leading into the garden is open, and the pup is nowhere to be seen.

"No. No. No." I rush out of the door, not stopping to put anything on my feet. Desperate to check where my puppy is.

"Embry, where are you, baby?" I whisper, not wanting to scare him away. I walk a little away from the conservatory and listen out for the sound of my pup. I listen for a moment while taking a few more steps, my heart dropping when I hear the tiniest bark. I rush around to part of the garden, where I thought I had heard him. I move around a large bush and whisper yell his name when I see him playing around someone's feet. Not just anyone, Christian.

I watch silently as he picks up a ball by his feet and throws it for Embry before taking a sip out of a large bottle. Even in the dark, I can see he's struggling as his head and shoulders are sagging. He rubs at his face, and I hear him letting out a deep sigh as he watches Embry running back with his ball. But on his way back to Christian, he spots me and lets out a yelp before running over. Christian spins around and sees me for the first time.

For a moment, we stare at each other. For the first time ever, I don't want to rush to him. I don't feel that excitement I get from the mere sight of him, and that hurts.

I'm thankful when Embry jumps at my legs, begging for my attention. Squatting down, I pick him up and make a fuss of him. As I pay attention to my pup, I notice Christian taking a deep drink from his bottle.

"Where are your shoes?"

My head snaps up to stare at him.

That's how he's going to start this conversation. By going into Daddy mode? No. The fact he tries to chastise me after everything that happened upstairs seems to flick the switch in my brain from sad and hurt to damn angry.

"Inside, as I had no idea where my baby was! I thought he had gotten out by himself!" I snap, shocking myself at the level of anger in my voice. I stand with the puppy in my arms, staring at the man I am marrying in a couple of weeks.

"Watch your tone-"

"No!"

Christian stares at me for a moment, but I'm not done. "I will not watch my fucking tone!"

Christian opens his mouth to say something but seems to think better of it as I storm forward, closing the distance between us until I'm directly in front of him.

"You and I are going to have a conversation. For the duration of it, you are not Daddy, you are Christian, and I am Jasmine, your fiancée, do you understand? You will not discipline me or tell me to watch my language; you will listen to what I have to fucking say for once. Is that understood?"

Christian stares down at me for a moment, and I think he's going to argue. But instead, his face softens, and he nods before lifting the bottle to his lips. I snatch it from his hand and pour it onto the ground beside me.

"What the fuck?" he snaps as he goes to snatch the bottle from me, but I continue to pour it onto the grass. "Do you have any fucking idea how expensive that bottle is?" he demands. The fact he is swearing and sounding like a teenager watching their mother pour away their hidden vodka tells me that he is in a worse state than I initially thought.

"What's the difference between pouring it down your throat and onto the ground?" I ask, and he shuts up showing he has no answer. "Are you going to tell me what the hell that was about upstairs?" I demand. Christian looks at me again, and the pain is back there in his eyes.

"I am so sorry, Sweetheart. I don't know what came over me, but I would never hurt you-"

"I'm not talking about that yet. I want to know why you felt the need to try and kill your brother?"

Christian's shoulders tighten as he stands taller, obviously still angry about everything, but as he does, he sways slightly. Any other time, it would worry me that he had drank so much it was having an effect on him. I don't think

I have ever seen Christian get to the point of being tipsy, let alone drunk.

"Get in the house right now!" I snap, pointing to the building angrily. "We will finish this conversation when you are sat down and not in danger of falling over!"

Christian stares at me for a moment, but the higher my eyebrows get, the more he seems to realise I am not playing. Christian turns and starts walking towards the house when he stumbles a little. I sigh and grab his arm to keep him stable.

"I'm fine."

"You are far from fine in every sense of the word. This is why we are going to sit down, and you will listen to me for once."

"I do listen to you," he argues as we reach the conservatory, where one of his security guards, Justin, stands waiting for us.

"Is everything okay, Miss Jasmine?"

"Why did you let her outside?" Christian snaps at him.

"Because I thought she was heading to see you, sir. I stayed close until I knew she was safely by your side." Well, that goes to show how preoccupied I was, as I never even noticed him there.

"Thank you, Justin, I've got it from here." But he looks between Christian and me as if he isn't sure if he should leave or not.

"Leave," Christian snaps. I roll my eyes and offer Justin a small smile.

"Yes, sir," he stutters before heading to the security office.

Once inside the conservatory, I close the door, and he falls onto the sofa. Embry instantly jumps down from my arms and heads straight to Christian, who picks him up and places him on his lap.

"For someone who said they didn't want anything to do with the dog, you seem very fond of him now."

Christian doesn't say anything immediately; he just looks down and strokes his head.

"I think he's the only one in this house that doesn't hate me at the moment."

His words shock me as they are the last thing I expected him to say.

"No one hates you," I sigh, wanting to feel more sympathy for him than I do. He deserves some of this pain, especially after everything he has done to the rest of us. But I also know he carries more pain than he lets on. "Want to tell me what that was about on the landing?" I ask.

"Not really."

"Fine, if you won't talk, then you will listen," I snap, my anger rising again. "You want to know what I think. I think tonight, the four of you had a good night turn into a shit one. I know that the blonde guy from *that place* told you a few things, and things escalated to the point Sean was injured, and you all had some sort of fight."

"What did they tell you?" Christian snaps, causing me to push away from the wall I've been leaning against.

"Oh no, I gave you the chance to speak, but you turned it down. So now, you can shut up and listen to me." I don't give him a chance to interrupt again and carry on talking. "As usual, they won't tell me anything, and I know that's because of you. I know you think you are protecting me, but you aren't, Christian. You are pushing me away." I want to tell him how much it hurts and how much of a divide it's putting between us and our whole family. They all think I don't notice the way they whisper together or change the topic when I walk into a room, but I do. But once again, I don't get to voice my concerns as Christian shakes his head and stands from the sofa, placing the dog down before heading for the door.

"Where are you going?" I demand, following him, being sure to close the door behind us so Embry is safe.

"I need a drink."

"No, you don't," I snap, storming after him. We are in the main hallway when I realise he is heading to the sitting room. "Christian, stop!" I shout as he turns down the corridor towards the room, where I know there are plenty of bottles for him to choose from. I rush towards him and stand in front to try and stop him from going further.

"Stop!" I warn firmly as I place a hand on his chest. "Drinking isn't going to help this. All I want is an adult conversation, and you are shutting me out again!" my voice is getting louder, but my anger and hurt are getting the better of me.

"I love you, Jasmine, but you need to get out of my way." His voice is firm, and I know he is getting angry, too.

"No!" I shout, surprised by my own tone. "I'm not getting out of your way. You are going to talk to me. You are going to listen-"

"Listen to what? How precious Jason isn't to blame for you being assaulted more than once? How he did nothing wrong by letting that fucking arsehole live? How I'm meant to just forget that you were not only assaulted with a knife but sexually assaulted by the same arsehole? How everything you have been going through this past week is all because of what happened to you? Yet here's the kicker: you still go to him for comfort, not me! No, I won't listen; I know what I know, and it's all his fault!"

Christian spins on his heels and heads away from me,

and for a moment, I panic he's heading to the stairs to attack Jason again.

"Christian, stop!" I shout trying to get in front of him. But he doesn't stop at the stairs; he heads straight to the kitchen. "Stop!" I shout again, terrified, as a load of different scenarios rush through my head of what he's going to do. Sure, he's going for a knife or something. I grab his arm and try to pull him to a stop. Christian grabs my wrist to pull me from him.

"Get off her!"

I look up in time to see Jason jumping down at least ten stairs and landing beside me. He grabs my hand and pulls me behind his back, pushing Christian away and getting between us.

"What the fuck is going on?" Maximus demands, appearing beside Jason, Sean on the other side. All of them blocking my view of Christian.

"Get out of my way!" I yell, trying to push between them so I can see Christian and talk to him, but Maximus tightens the gap between him and Jason. I hear footsteps behind me and turn to see Justin and another security woman beside him. I hold up my hand to stop them. "Stay back," I order.

"Oh, here we go! Once again, I'm the bad guy when precious Jason is the knight in shining armour," I hear Christian laugh, all of them oblivious to the fact we have company.

"Are you drunk?" Jason asks, the surprise evident in his voice. Maximus and Sean both curse under their breath.

"What did you do to her?" Maximus demands.

"Nothing, you idiot, we were arguing," I yell, trying to get around them again but failing. "For fuck's sake, fucking MOVE!" I scream as loud as I can, causing all three to spin around and look at me surprised. I use their shock to my advantage, push past them, and stand between them and Christian, keeping my back to him so I can look the others in the eye. Sean reaches out to grab me, but I move out of his way.

"I'm not in any danger," I sigh, staring at them all. "He won't hurt me again," I add quickly.

"That's not how it sounded," Maximus answers, staring at his brother.

"What did you do to her?" Jason demands again.

"Nothing, it was me stopping him from doing something like going to the kitchen to get a knife to kill you!" I yell, throwing my arms up in the air dramatically.

"I wasn't going to kill him; I was going for a drive," Christian sighs behind me. I spin around and stare at him.

"Yeah, that's so much better, considering you couldn't stand without swaying five minutes ago!" I snap, shaking my head at him. "Moron" I mutter under my breath as I turn to face the others again.

"Jazzy, come here. Let him do what he needs to get this out of the system, and we can talk to him tomorrow," Jason says softly whilst giving his older brother a death stare.

"Yes, don't want to upset prince Jason," Christian scoffs. I spin around and stare at him, furious.

"I swear to God, Christian, if you don't shut up with the name-calling, I will lose my shit!" I snap, glaring at him. "I have never had a favourite, and you fucking know it. If the tables were turned, I would fight as hard for him to hear me out. I don't know how many times I have tried to tell you, but Jason was not to blame for what happened."

"He let that bastard live when he should have killed him years ago. It was his fault."

"It wasn't his fault; when are you going to stop blaming the wrong person," I yell, throwing my hands up in the air.

"The only other people to blame are dead, Sweetheart if you haven't already noticed."

"Oh, I noticed! Especially as I killed one of them to fucking save you, arsehole!" I yell. I step closer to him, but someone grabs my arm, stopping me.

"For fuck's sake, can I not even argue with my fiancé without someone trying to save me?" I yell, throwing my hands up in the air before turning and staring at Christian. "The only reason you are going so hard on Jason is because you can't go any harder on yourself without causing physical harm to yourself." I step closer and see that I'm right. The guilt is there all over his face.

"You want to blame Jason for not killing Hudson in the first place. You blame Layton and Terry for the fact I was taken. You blame Maximus because he hired the guy who helped kidnap me, but most of all, you blame yourself because you let me go out and went against your better judgment. You blame yourself for not killing Hudson when you wanted to, but none of that would have stopped what would have happened. Either way, I had a target on my back, and someone was going to cash in on it."

"You had that target because of us, so it's our fault!" Christian snaps, tears in his eyes, the only indication that I've hit the nail on the head.

"No, Christian, none of it was your fault. None of you played a role in what happened to me. That target has been there longer than I have known any of you," I say softer. "My mother was never going to stop. She was never going to stop using me to get what she wanted. Either it was money for her addictions or something else. She has been willing for me to be a form of payment for my whole life." I reach up and cup his cheek. "Nothing that happened to me was due to any of you. Do you really think I would have never been assaulted if Jason had killed Hudson? She was sending men into my room when I was still a young child. That is what caused my pain the last few days, not what happened in that house, but what happened long before I even met you.

"She tried to sell my virginity more than that one time Christian. I slept at Amber's house more than once because I had run from what should have been my safe place. I often woke up to find her letting men into my room." I want to close my eyes and hide from the images that flood my mind, but I don't. I do what I've always done and look for sanctuary in his. "Hudson was not the first to assault me, and if you four hadn't saved me, he wouldn't have been the last. Nothing he did to me hadn't been done before." I reach out with the hand that's not on his cheek and take his before squeezing it.

"That woman is to blame for everything that ever went wrong in my life. She forced me out of the first place I ever thought of as a home. She tried to take my dancing from me and stole my innocence. She killed my grandparents and tried to kill me. She abused me physically and mentally, and worse of all, she took everyone who cared away from me. But do you know the one thing I can never forgive her for?" I ask, ensuring he looks as deeply into my eyes as I am his.

"I cannot forgive her for what you were forced to do when you were just fifteen years old," I whisper as he looks at me with wide eyes. "My father's death is completely in her hands, and so is the fact his blood has been on your hands all this time. She let a fifteen-year-old boy spend a lifetime beating himself up for being forced to kill someone who was just trying to give that woman what she wanted. I hate her for every second you have blamed yourself for a death that wasn't your fault. You may have pulled the trigger, but you did not kill him; his blood was on her hands, and she didn't give a shit!"

Letting my hand slide from his cheek, I keep it pressed against his chest above his heart, which I feel beat strong and fast under my palm.

"You, Christian O'Reilly, are the strongest man I know. Each of your brothers behind me will agree. You take on so much and do so much to protect us that you forget we are here to protect you, too.

"Stop trying to do everything yourself. Stop blaming your brothers and yourself for what you had no control over. You were as much of a victim as I was during all of that. Taylor and our parents played us all, wanting to get as much out of us as possible, but they didn't count on one thing: our love for one another would conquer everything they threw at us. Nothing they did was ever going to stop us all fighting until the end to get back to each other." Closing the gap between us completely, I grip his shirt and hold it tight, forcing him to look at me.

"You always say I belong to you, well guess what, Christian O'Reilly, you belong to me too, and there is nothing I am not willing to do for you. I just need you to stop blaming yourself and your brothers for what was out of your control. I need you to let us help you and for you to realise we will protect you just as viciously as you will protect us. Understand?"

For a moment, Christian looks at me as a single tear rolls down his cheek. I reach up and wipe it away before laying my hand back on his cheek as I look deep into his tear-filled eyes.

"Use your words, Daddy," I tease with a small smile. It

has the effect I hoped for as a short burst of laughter escapes him as his eyes close and arms tighten around me as he buries his face in my hair.

"Yes, Sweetheart," he mumbles against my head. We stay in each other's arms for a moment as he breathes deeply. Eventually he pulls away enough to look deep into my eyes again.

"I am so sorry, Baby," he whispers, cupping my cheek. "I could never hurt you, I don't know what happened, I just-"

"Stop," I whisper, shaking my head softly. "It was a shock, but I was never scared. No matter what, you would never hurt me, not really."

For a moment, he rests his forehead on mine and breathes deeply.

"If I had hurt you, I would have-"

"Enough!" I snap this time. "You wouldn't have; no matter how mad you get; you would never physically hurt me. I could feel you holding back." I glance over my shoulder and spot Jason with even more swelling and bruising evident on his face.

"Shit, Jas. Did I do all that?" Christian asks. I turn so I'm beside him and able to see everyone.

The other three O'Reillys are still standing together, facing their eldest brother. I hadn't noticed how close they were. They must have moved to ensure they could get to me if needed.

"Yeah, but I'm not sure if you've seen your face," he shrugs, forcing a smile.

"No, I haven't," Christian smiles before approaching his brother. "I'm so sorry; all I could see was Hudson hurting her and nothing else. My anger blinded me, and I should have spoken to you about my feelings regarding it long before now."

"Until tonight, I would have agreed with everything you said. That's why I didn't hit you back straight away; I deserved at least one decent punch."

"Do I need to repeat myself?" I sigh dramatically, hoping to break up the tension in the air.

"No, Jazzy, you don't," Jason smiles, rolling his eyes. When they find me again, I watch his face become more serious. "But we will discuss a few things you just told us. I have questions, like why didn't you tell us before?"

I look down at my feet, knowing I'm not ready to answer questions about everything.

"Not tonight. I think it's safe to say we have all been through enough," Sean says, stepping forward. The brothers all look at each other and nod.

"I know you will be having talks about whatever happened tonight, and I want to be there. I'm sick and tired of being kept out of the loop," I snap, looking at Christian. "Hiding things isn't protecting me; it's making me feel like you think I'm too weak to deal with anything, and I'm not." I step back, and all four look at me as I stand alone. "I want to prove to you that I am worthy of your love and the O'Reilly name."

"You showed us that long before you realised it, Angel," Jason says, stepping forward to take my hand and pulling me into his arms. "I don't think you realise how strong we know you are. But yes, you deserve to know more." I don't miss the way he looks at Christian. "She's right. It's not protecting her."

Christian looks at me in his brother's arms and nods.

"I know that now. You've shown me once again how strong you are."

"She must be strong to have the courage to stack up the number of punishments she earned tonight," Sean laughs. I look to Christian with an arched brow, who is smiling whilst shaking his head.

"She told me under no uncertain terms that there would be no punishments issued for anything said or done. Tonight, we were just two people arguing, like any other couple." A smirk appears as he stares at me. "Although Maximus, you might disagree when you hear she poured over half a bottle of your favourite bourbon on the grass."

I stare at him, shocked, before looking at Maximus.

"I didn't know it was yours! I was trying to stop him from drinking himself into a coma!" I protest as Maximus takes a step forward.

"Do you have any idea how expensive that bourbon is?" he demands.

"Well, he was drinking it straight out of the bottle, so you wouldn't have wanted to drink any more of it anyway."

His head snaps up as he goes from staring at me to Christian.

"You owe me a bottle, arsehole," he declares before rubbing his face. "I'm going to bed. Are you coming, Shorty? Or are you staying with one of the others?"

"I'm going to my room. I need some time to think," I admit. Maximus nods before kissing my lips and wishing me a good night. Sean is behind him and kisses me quickly before the two of them head to bed, leaving Jason, Christian, and I standing in the hallway. I glance to where the security had been, but they have also gone, probably realising it was a family matter and no one was in any further danger.

I look between the two brothers and realise they need a little time to talk.

"Did I get through to the two of you?" I ask. "Do you finally accept that neither of you is to blame, and this arguing needs to stop." I check I have both men's attention. "I will never choose one of you over the other, but I cannot handle the two of you arguing and fighting. You are more than just brothers; you are best friends and have been through too much to act like a couple of spoilt rich kids." I look between the two of them, hoping it's sinking in. "I hate violence, but I accept that it's a part of being with you and have come to terms with that. But I will not accept it in our home, especially with each other." I turn to Christian with raised brows.

"Now, you two obviously need to have a long chat, and it's up to you when that is. But I suggest it is soon because otherwise, I will be forced to activate nagging wife mode before we are even married."

"Yes, Sweetheart," he smiles before looking at Jason. "I *am* sorry."

"I know, me too. I think talking sometime soon would be a good idea. We've gotten so good at reading each other that we are also good at hiding shit too."

Christian nods before looking to the stairs.

"But not now; I need to pass out and sleep off some of this alcohol before dealing with anything else." He rubs his face as I smile at him.

"Yes, you do, as well as shower. You smell like a brewery." I rush towards the stairs as Christian goes to grab me.

"Your time of being just Jasmine is coming to an end, Sweetheart. I will start punishing you again," he warns with a smile. I stand on the bottom step and look at the two of them.

"On that note, I'm going to bed before I start being

bratty then," I smile before turning around and skipping up the stairs.

"Sweetheart?" I turn to Christian's voice to find him standing at the bottom of the stairs, looking up at me seriously. "Thank you. I think you were the only one who could have gotten through to me tonight, and you did it without a moment's hesitation. I don't know what I did to deserve you, but whatever it was, I'm grateful for it. I'm forever grateful for you."

I stand on the step for a moment, looking at this man. When I saw him in the garden, I hadn't gotten that loving feeling I always get when I look at him. But now, all I can feel is my love for him. I nearly trip as I rush down the stairs and throw myself into his arms. He catches me with ease and holds me close as I wrap my arms around his neck and bury my face into his shoulder.

"I've always got your back, even when you think you don't deserve it," I whisper before lifting my head and looking at him. "I love you, Daddy."

"I love you too, Sweetheart, more than you will ever know." I kiss him once on the cheek before he lowers me back onto the step. I smile one more time before heading back up the stairs.

"Oh, one more thing," he calls. I turn around, rolling my eyes.

"Daddy, I'm tired," I groan dramatically, hoping to keep the smile on his face, and it works. Christian grins before nodding up the stairs.

"I was an arsehole tonight and stopped Maximus from coming in to see you when we got home. He wanted to be with you tonight, and I think it may be what he needed."

I look up the stairs and think about how tightly he held

me when we got into bed. I smile at Christian and nod before rushing up the stairs.

I don't stop until I get to Maximus's room, where the door's open a little. I walk in to find him sitting up in bed. His head snaps to the door, and he looks confused.

"Shorty? I thought you wanted some space tonight?"

I climb into bed and snuggle up to him. He's warm, and I realise how cold I had become since slipping out of bed earlier.

"I decided I would rather be back in here with you," I whisper, smiling into his chest as he settles us back into bed. "As long as you don't mind," I add, already knowing the answer.

"I would spend every night cuddled up to you if I could. You know that."

"I do," I whisper as Maximus tightens his hold on me for a moment and kisses the top of my head.

"Get some sleep, Shorty."

"Night, Daddy," I whisper as I find sleep a lot easier this time while safe in Maximus's arms.

Chapter Twenty

CHRISTIAN

Leaning back on the sofa in the sitting room, I sip coffee and pray for some relief from the constant headache. I remember now why I don't let myself get drunk; I always suffer from the worst hangovers.

I glance up at the clock and see it's five to nine in the morning. I only managed to get about three hours of sleep this morning. I don't think I could ever admit to my brothers how hard I crumbled when I got to my room last night. I locked the bedroom door, needing some time to myself, and broke down in the shower. I haven't cried like that in years. Probably because I don't think I have let myself feel what I did last night in years.

All I could see was the way I yelled and fought with my brothers and the way Jason had looked at me when we were fighting. But the most painful of it all was the look in Jasmine's eyes when I grabbed her.

"You're hurting me."

Those three words were like a knife straight into my heart. I always swore I would never hurt her, but last night, I not only hurt her physically, but I was hurting her emotionally as well. That's something I don't think I will ever forgive myself for.

Looking down at the bracelet on my wrist, which my girl gave me for Christmas, makes my heart ache. She called me her amazing Daddy, but I've been anything but. It just took me nearly throwing everything away for me to realise.

What the fuck happened to me last night? I lost control in a way I haven't for a very long time. Even when Jasmine was taken, I didn't lose it to the extent I did last night. I'm so ashamed of how I handled it all. It's like as soon as I got home, everything just collapsed in on me. All the pressure I've been trying to hide from my brothers came to the forefront and boiled over drastically. I have a lot of apologising to do, as well as being honest with my family about how bad things have really gotten.

After Jasmine went to bed, leaving Jason and me, we agreed to leave it for the night and meet here at nine, knowing the others won't be up until at least ten. That gives us an hour to get a few things off our chests and for me to catch him up on a few things.

"Hey."

I look up to find Jason walking in and heading straight to the coffee machine.

"Morning," I mumble, closing my eyes as I keep my head on the back of the sofa.

"Hungover?" Jason asks as he approaches. I hear him sit on the sofa opposite mine.

"Yep." I slowly lift my head and look at him, the hate I feel for myself increasing when I see the patchwork of bruising and cuts on his face.

"Fuck, Jas." I sit up, place the mug on the coffee table

and force myself to look at my brother. "Is your nose broken?"

"Yeah, reset it last night. It's fine; nothing I haven't had to do in the past," he shrugs.

"That's not the fucking point! I broke your nose! Shit!" Jumping to my feet, I start pacing with my head in my hands. All the guilt I was trying to push down rushing back to the forefront.

"Hey, it's okay. Looks like I got you good, too." I know he's trying to calm me down, but it isn't going to happen. I can't believe I attacked him like that; I wasn't even that drunk by that point. I just lost control.

"Hey, stop." I hadn't heard him move as I paced around the sitting room. I lift my head to find him standing in front of me. He places his hands on my shoulders and forces me to look at him. "Speak to me. You've never had a problem before, so what's making it start now?"

He's right; it's always been me and him against the world. I love the twins just as much as I love Jason, but they were young when Mum got ill and then died. I took on the parent role with them more than with Jason.

He had been forced into this world the same night as me when he knelt there with a gun to his head as I was being forced to kill Jasmine's father, Connor Grant. Every time I think of him now, I want to be sick. His death has always consumed me, but now, knowing how much she missed him and knowing what taking him from her meant, and how she suffered without him there to protect her from her abusive mother. The guilt I've felt my whole life has become even more unbearable.

"Hey, where have you gone?"

Jason's voice brings me back to the sitting room and out

of the warehouse, where everything started all those years ago.

"I'm sorry." It's all I can seem to say when I look at my brother's battered face. He's right; I don't look much better, but that's what I deserve.

"I know you are, Christian. I have been waiting for you to lose it for a while now; I just never expected it to be to that extent." He looks towards the open door. "Hang on," he sighs before heading over to close it, checking outside for anyone else before turning around to face me.

"Last night, I agreed with you; I believed I was to blame for everything that had happened with Jazzy. I wasn't arguing that part. It was the fact you tried to stop Maximus from going to see his fiancée when you knew he wouldn't want to be alone after everything that had happened in that arena. You thought you could control everything, including our relationships with Jaz. It was you who drilled into us how important it was to never do that; then you did it to the point I thought Maximus was going to punch you," Jason sighs as he rubs his own face, hissing as he catches his nose.

"Look, Jasmine is right; we have all been blaming ourselves for everything that happened with Taylor and our parents, so we all missed the bigger picture. Us turning against each other was exactly what the arseholes would have wanted. They wanted to destroy us and are succeeding from the grave." He stops in front of me again, places a hand on my shoulder, and starts leading me to the sofas.

"Let's sit down like we said we would, and you are going to start from the beginning and tell me what's been going through that head of yours. Then we are going to decide on the next step in how to deal with all the shit we learnt last night before filling Jazzy in on everything."

It's five to ten when I stand to get another cup of coffee. We haven't managed to get through much, thanks to my mini freak-out, which took up a lot of our time. We were then interrupted by Mrs Brown, who came in and left a hot tray of breakfast bits for us all, guessing we would be hungover. She was furious when she saw our faces. She even hit us with her tea towel, scolding us for fighting. We didn't dare point out it was with each other. Whenever Mrs Brown acts just like a mother to us, which in all fairness is most days, it makes me miss our mother even more.

"Our lives would be so different if Mum were still alive," I say out loud without thinking. Jason looks at me and smiles a little.

"Mrs Brown got you thinking about her?"

I nod, sipping my drink, not focusing on anything other than trying to remember how she looked or sounded.

"I don't remember her voice," I admit. "I will never forget the way she smiled, but I can't remember how she sounded."

"I do," Jason says, looking into the corner of the wall where a picture of her is next to one of the four of us with Jasmine. "Do you remember that song she used to always sing?" I shake my head, but I do remember; it's one thing I will never forget. "I do," he continues, turning his attention to the picture of Jasmine and Verity dancing. "I had forgotten too until I heard Jazzy humming it to herself the other day. It was like it opened a floodgate, and all the memories of Mum came back to me. Her baking in the kitchen, planting in the garden, and cleaning around the house with Mrs Brown. She used to sing it everywhere, especially when he wasn't home."

I shake my head, looking into my mug.

"I don't remember." I do; I just don't want to. It's always been something I refuse to reflect on. It's too painful to think about, so I pretend it never existed.

"You will, maybe, when you are in a better place." He looks back over to the photo of our mum and smiles. "I can imagine the fun she would have had with Jazzy. They would have been like two peas in a pod and up to all kinds of mischief, especially once grandkids started arriving."

"They won't have any grandparents," I point out, realising it for the first time.

"No, they won't. But there again, the ones that could have been alive would never have been allowed access to them anyway." I can hear the venom in his voice and know he's right. There was no way I would have allowed Tommy or Carol within ten miles of our kids.

"But they will have four fathers who love them more than anything else in this world." Without meaning to, this has brought us around to another conversation I wanted to have with him.

"Do you think Jasmine still needs us to be her daddies?"

Jason's eyes widen for a second before a small smile appears.

"Did she scare you that bad last night?"

"You didn't see the worst of it. She ripped me a new one, stitched me up, then ripped me open all over again!"

Jason laughs, trying to hide the smug look on his face.

"Yeah, she was brutal from what I saw." He finishes his coffee and places the mug in front of him before putting an arm over the back of the sofa he's sitting on. "Do you want to still be her daddy?"

"Of course I do! But she has grown so much in the last

nine months; I don't know if she needs us like she did." I lean back into my own sofa and try to relax.

"When we decided to take on that role, she was lost, and we knew she needed guidance, even if it was much more than we originally realised." Jason nods but doesn't say anything signally for me to continue. "But now she's thriving. She is smashing every goal she makes, whether it's with her personal growth, dancing or the fact that she will stand up for what she wants now. As Terry said, everyone knows she's becoming just as scary as we are."

"If not more," Jason laughs. I can't help laughing in agreement.

"She's amazing, and I worry that she thinks we want to control her, or we are holding her back."

"She doesn't, and I don't think she would let us hold her back."

"I know that deep down, and you know that, but it doesn't stop me from worrying." I rub my face and regret it as I hit a bruise. "Last night, when she told me to shut up and that for the duration of the night, I wasn't her daddy, I was just Christian, and she was Jasmine, it hit me hard how much she might not be Jasmine the rest of the time. She might be the woman we think she should be, the one we moulded her into."

"Then ask her, Christian. I know I will love her the same as if I'm her daddy or just her husband. The twins will love her the same as well, will you?"

"Of course I will. Whether I'm her daddy or not, she's my whole world!"

"Then we will discuss it with her today. We will tell her that it's now up to her whether we are her daddies or just Christian and Jason, her husbands."

I nod, knowing he's right; it's time to approach the topic.

Her laugh fills the air before someone knocks on the door.

"Is it safe to come in?" Sean asks as Maximus and Jasmine laugh together. Jason looks at me and winks.

"No, we have the stripper from last night in here."

My eyes widen simultaneously as the door flies open with such force that I worry it will come off the hinges.

"You better be kidding me!" Jasmine yells, storming into the room and standing before the two of us with her hands on her hips.

"Oh, someone's feeling brave!" Maximus whistles as he walks into the room.

"Braver than me," Sean adds, smirking. Jasmine holds up one finger, silencing them both. She turns her attention to me.

"Sweetheart, can you see a stripper hiding anywhere?" I ask, waving my arms around.

"I know you wouldn't dare have one here; that's not the problem!"

"Then what's the issue, Angel?" Jason asks, sitting forward and smirking at her.

"That you even had one when I can't!"

"We didn't have a stripper," I sigh before looking around at my brothers. "Did we?"

"No!" the others laugh.

I'm surprised when Jasmine walks over and slumps onto the sofa next to me, instantly leaning into my side. For a moment, I freeze before lowering my arm and wrapping it around her shoulder.

"You okay, Sweetheart?" I ask into her hair. She looks up at me and nods.

"Just tired." She reaches up and runs a finger lightly over a bruise on my face.

"Did I hurt you?" I ask, looking down at her arm. She shakes her head and shows me both arms, knowing I need confirmation.

"I'm fine."

Needing to calm myself before we go any further, I bury my nose in her hair and close my eyes, reminding myself that she is still here, and I didn't fuck everything up royally.

"You both look like shit," Maximus says, handing Jasmine a cup of coffee.

"Trust me; I feel like it in more ways than one," I admit into Jasmine's hair before looking up to see Maximus looking at me. "I'm sorry to you all, but I'm especially sorry I tried to get between you and Jasmine last night. It won't happen again."

"Yeah, it better not because I will take a lot from you, Christian; you are my brother, and I love you. But if you ever try to stop me from going to Shorty again for no other reason than you say so, I will go full Jason on your ass." Jason and Sean both laugh as Maximus smirks at me. I know he's trying to keep the mood light, but his eyes tell me he means every word, and I don't blame him.

"Tell you what, if I ever do it again, I will let you go one better."

"Oh yeah, and what's that?" Maximus asks, frowning.

"I will let you set Jasmine on me." My brothers burst out laughing as Jasmine protests in my arms, which I tighten around her to ensure she can't hit me. My body went through enough last night, and I'm aching.

"Damn, I wasn't going to go that far!" Maximus laughs, winking at Jasmine before sitting down next to her.

"I don't know how to take that?" she admits, sitting back with her arms over her chest, sulking.

"Take it as it's meant, a huge compliment," I say, kissing her head again.

"If you say so," she sighs before sitting up and looking around. "Is there food?"

"Over there, let's grab some and then we can all have a long chat," I smile at her.

"Sounds good to me; I'm starving," Sean announces.

Jasmine stands and looks down at me in my seat.

"I'm glad you are okay, Daddy."

"I will be Baby girl, and it's all thanks to you."

She leans down and kisses me. "I'm here to remind you that you are not alone whenever you need me to."

"Thank you, Baby," I smile as I kiss her again and stand up.

I watch as Jasmine and the twins head to the bar where Mrs Brown has laid out the breakfast bits.

"It will be okay; we can come up with a plan together. Just remember you are not alone anymore."

I nod once and squeeze his shoulder.

"Thank you."

"Stop thanking me. We have always had each other's backs. That will never change. Now come on, I want to grab some food before they eat it all."

I laugh as the two of us go to grab some food, which the twins are already squabbling over. I look around at my family and realise Jason's right. I've never truly been alone. I just didn't realise that until I nearly pushed them all too far.

Chapter Twenty-One

JASMINE

Usually, when the five of us sit together for a meal and catch up, the air is alive with chatter and laughter, but not today. There is still a lot of tension between the brothers, and I don't miss how they are all watching me, as if they are waiting for me to fall apart or explode angrily. I'm too tired, physically and emotionally, to do either.

When I woke up this morning, I asked Sean and Maximus not to give Christian a hard time, and they agreed that enough had been said and done last night. They promised that no matter what Christian decided today, they would insist on me being present and knowing everything. I knew Christian had been hiding stuff from us all. They think I don't realise everyone is on edge, but I do. I know my men as well as they know me, and I know Jason and the twins have been worried about their brother.

Seeing Christian sitting in his grey sweatpants and loose t-shirt, I realise how much he needs a break. I can't wait for the next couple of weeks to get here so we can all get married and disappear for a short while. I think it's something every one of us needs for one reason or another. I know I'm ready to hide away from the world with my men. I sometimes wish it could be longer and that we would never have to deal with all this crap again.

Since coming downstairs, I haven't wanted to leave Christian's side. I've sat beside him or curled up against him and listened, as now and again, his heart rate picks up as he stares off into space. Every time I've placed my hand over his heart or taken his hand in mine, just to remind him through contact that he's not as alone as he seems to think.

I look up and watch him for a moment. He's leaning his head against his right fist, staring at nothing whilst running his left hand up and down my arm. The other three are all talking among themselves, occasionally including Christian or me, but they know he needs space and are giving it to him.

"Daddy?" I whisper, looking up at him, realising he hasn't looked away from the one spot on the wall. I startle him as he looks down at me as if he'd forgotten I was there.

"Sorry, Sweetheart. I'm useless when I'm hungover," he sighs, kissing my head. He sighs and looks at his brothers, who have stopped talking and are now watching us.

"Why don't we get this over with, and then we can all crash for a bit if we need to?" Jason suggests, turning his attention to me and giving me a small smile. "I think you could do with a nap," he points out with a raised eyebrow. I nod while leaning further into Christian, liking the idea of curling up with him and going to sleep. But as much as I want to curl up and close my eyes, I know I can't. Christian needs me right now, and I want to be here for him like he has always been for me.

Forcing myself to sit up from his side, I reach for my

bottle of water on the coffee table and look around at my four men, who are all looking right back at me.

"I think you will need to start from the beginning. I'm guessing we don't know everything, and Jasmine will know even less," Sean starts looking to Christian, who nods before placing a hand on my leg.

"I know you are all going to have questions and will be angry at me for hiding stuff, but I swear I did it out of love and wanting to protect you." Christian lets out a sigh before running his hand over his head. "That goes for all of you," he adds, looking at his brothers. "All I've ever wanted is for you all to be safe, and Jasmine loved in the way she should have been her whole life. I didn't want you worrying about the shit that I've been dealing with or worrying about me when I'm not here." Christian looks down at me as he runs his bruised knuckles over my cheek. "I wanted you to be able to focus on your dancing, and for you to do that, I have hidden stuff from not only you but my brothers, too."

I hear the others curse under their breath and know that things must be worse than I ever dreamt.

"How much stuff?" Jason asks from his seat.

"Enough."

I glance at the others and see them all giving their undying attention to their eldest brother, who runs his hand over his head again before taking my left hand and playing with my engagement ring.

Watching Christian, I don't miss how vulnerable he looks. He's not making eye contact with anyone and has lost the dominance he holds when in any room.

"The reason I've been away so much is that we have had a large number of properties burnt down or vandalised. There's been sixteen in total." All three of the guys curse under their breath. "Most of them were ones we took over from Taylor. People haven't been happy and made sure they would be useless to us."

I frown, wondering what he means.

"When we killed Taylor, we took procession of his businesses. The majority of them had been started with money we had given him, or Tommy had, so in theory, they were ours," Christian explains.

"Over the last few months, more and more of our properties have been torched or vandalised. At first, it was the odd one, which you can expect now and again, especially as they were empty and ideal places for kids to hang out and cause trouble. Squatters took over one, and instead of kicking them out, I had it made it into a shelter for them. But over time, more and more things happened to the properties. Before Young's death, there had been one, maybe two properties affected a month, which could all be put down to them being empty. I sold a few more off, and things seemed to calm down."

"I take it things are getting worse," I ask. Christian nods and closes his eyes for a moment.

"There has been something every other day: a break-in, broken windows, fires started, equipment damaged, the list goes on. It's been exhausting, to put it mildly. It's why I have been away so much. I've been dealing with everything that gets thrown at us."

"Is that why you said I couldn't go with you on the occasions I asked?"

Christian nods as he looks at me.

"Where were you when you said your phone was broken?" Jason asks, leaning forward and looking at his brother.

"I'd been arrested."

"What?" all four of us cry out together. I look around and realise that I wasn't the only one who had no idea.

"On what grounds?" Jason asks.

"Someone called and told them that I was lighting a fire in my own building to claim on the insurance, knowing that I was heading there after a tip-off about some squatters."

"Let me guess, when you got there, the place had already been set alight?" Jason sighs as Christian nods.

"The police turned up as I was on the phone to the fire brigade. They arrested me and kept me as long as they could get away with. They tried to pin all kinds on me, and I had to prove to them I wasn't involved in each property that had been damaged. It took the solicitor hours to get all my known whereabouts together for the previous few weeks."

"Have they dropped all charges?" Sean asks. Christian nods, and I let out a sigh of relief.

"They had nothing to go on, but they are keeping an eye on me, which is why I've been away more than usual."

"So, in other words, people aren't happy about you taking Taylor's buildings and are what? Claiming them back?" I ask, trying to get my head around it all.

"More like trying to get rid of him full stop," Maximus adds, standing and walking away from the sofas. I look to Christian, who is back, staring at my hand and avoiding all eye contact.

"What aren't you telling us?" Jason asks from across the room. Christian continues to look anywhere but at any of us. I look between the two of them, then the twins. No one is saying anything, just staring at Christian, who won't look up. It's Jason who breaks the silence.

"No!"

"I've had the details confirmed," he starts before looking

at Jason, who stares for a moment before jumping to his feet angrily.

"If you are saying what I think you are, I'm going to kick your fucking ass again." Christian and Jason stare at each other before Jason snaps. "You fucking stupid, stubborn, proud bastard!" he starts pacing around, and I can see the twins don't know what he's on about.

"What?" Maximus asks as he stares at his brother. But Christian looks at me, and I know he doesn't want to say it in front of me, which means it must be bad.

"Tell me." The words barely a whisper, but I see the fear in Christian's eyes. "Whatever it is, we can deal with it together." I'd hoped to reassure him, but from how he turns away and refuses to look at me, I know I failed.

"Tell her!" Jason snaps, standing in front of his brother. "Fucking tell the woman you claim to love what you have been hiding from all of us," he shouts, pointing at me.

"I don't *claim* to love her. I *do* fucking love her! Which is why I've been protecting her!" Christian shouts, jumping to his feet. "Everything I have been doing is to protect the four of you, especially her!"

The rest of us are on our feet now. All waiting for Jason and Christian to start fighting again.

"Protecting her? You've been putting her in even more danger, you fucking stupid moron!" Jason yells.

"Why do you think I've been away so much? Why do you think I never take her out anywhere anymore? The only time I spend with any of you is in this house where we are safe!" Christian shouts.

"Have you got a fucking price on your head?" Maximus's loud voice brings the world to an abrupt standstill. Everyone turns to look at him in unison, but the only person he has his sight on is Christian. Slowly, I force myself to look at Christian, staring at the floor.

"Daddy?" I'm not even sure the word made it past the lump in my throat. Everything around me fades into black when Christian turns his attention to me, and I see Maximus is right.

The lump in my throat thickens as my chest starts to burn with a lack of air. I instinctively try to breathe in, but I can't.

"Shit," someone curses as I hear the others move around me as if in another room. My heart's pounding so hard that I can hear it. I know I should be doing something, anything to get air into my lungs, but all I can see is Christian and that someone wants to take him from me.

"Baby, breathe." He's so close now, and I know he has his hands on the top of my arms. He is all I can see as my vision becomes even more blurred.

"Jazzy, look at me." Jason is beside him, but I'm too focused to see him; all I can see is Christan. With my eyes and chest burning, I subconsciously realise I'm having a panic attack. I know I'm gasping for breath, but nothing is happening; I'm locked in my own body, which is starting to give up.

"Baby, I'm here," Christian whispers, touching my cheek. "I'm right here, Sweetheart, and I'm not going anywhere."

Tears are streaming down my face as I continue to try and get some air into my lungs. My panic taking hold. All I can think about is that someone wants to take my daddy from me. Someone wants to take another person from me.

No.

That one word sounds louder in my head than anything else.

No.

It's there again, and this time, I throw all my panic into the small hole my strength has created. Sounds start coming back to me, and I realise I can hear people arguing and talking over each other.

"Baby, you need to breathe."

"Shorty needs you to fuck off, this is your fault!"

"Shouting at each other isn't going to help!" Jason growls through his teeth before looking back at me.

I try to slow my breathing a little, trying to calm my racing heart. My chest is on fire as I struggle to see anything through the darkness. I try again to slow my breath, and again, I can take in a little more each time.

"Get back all of you," Sean snaps as he pushes Christian out of my narrow tunnel of vision. His face appears in front of me, even disfigured through the fog I would know him anywhere. "Get over there and stay there until I tell you!" He doesn't wait for a reply before cupping my face between his hands and looking deep into my eyes.

"I know you are scared and want answers, which you will get, but we need to calm you down first, Princess." His voice is soft and soothing, which I need right now.

Again, I try to slow my breathing, and Sean gives me a reassuring smile.

"You're attempting to take control, aren't you? I can see you fighting. Do you want me to help?" I nod, and Sean smiles again. "Okay, close your eyes, Princess." I do as he asks without question. He keeps holding my face with one hand and lifts my hand with his other. Once he has hold of my wrist, he lets go of my face, ensuring that he always touching me so I know he's there even when I can't see him.

"Good girl, Princess, keep trying to breathe." He repositions my hand so it's up as if to high-five someone, and I spread my fingers out. "Do you remember what to do?" he asks gently as I feel him running his finger up and down mine. He used this technique one night when I woke from a nightmare after they rescued me. "Breathe in as my finger goes up and out when it travels down." Starting on my wrist, he traces the outline of my thumb as I try to breathe. Once at the top of my thumb, his finger slides down to the skin between my fingers, and I attempt to breathe out. He repeats this until he gets to my wrist on the other side and then starts making his way back to my thumb, going up and down my fingers. Slowly, I begin to control my breathing a little better and soon, I'm almost breathing normally.

"That's it, Princess, you've got it," Sean encourages. He continues running his finger up and down mine until I ball my hand into a fist, signalling that I'm okay. Taking one more deep breath, I let it out slowly before finally opening my eyes.

I blink until my eyes adjust to the light in the room, and I can see better; I lift my head and look at Sean, who is kneeling on the floor before me. I have no idea when I went from standing to sitting. Sean holds my water out, and I take a small sip.

"That's it, Princess, take another sip for me." I do as I'm told as Sean runs a hand over my head. I want to thank him for helping me through the panic attack. I want to tell him I love him and am so grateful for him knowing exactly what I need when I need it. But I can't. There's only one thing I want to say right now. Only one word matters.

With unsteady legs, I climb to my feet. Sean tries to help me, but I shake my head at him before standing tall. Looking to the other end of the room, I see the other three watching us, all looking terrified and at a loss for what to do.

Right now, I don't care how they feel; for once, what I think is the priority, and I will make myself heard.

I walk to Christian standing behind his brothers, for once not leading them like he always has. Jason and Maximus both part as I reach them, giving me access to Christian. I stop in front of him and can see the shame and loss of pride on his face. I'm furious.

The sound of flesh hitting flesh sounds out in the silence of the room, shocking me when I feel the pain in my palm. Christian stands with his hand over his cheek, his eyes wide with shock. I step forward to close the distance between us as Jason and Maximus step closer.

"No." I shake my head as I glare at him.

"I'm sorry," Christian whispers but stops when I shake my head.

"I don't want to hear it," I say louder than I expected. "I don't want to hear you've been protecting us, how you don't want us worrying. Because I, for one, am sick of it." The venom in my voice spills from my mouth like acid, words burning their way out of me. "Did you really think we would let anything happen to you? Do you believe that you are on your own in this world? Because you're not." I step back and try to ignore how my head is pounding in time to my heart.

"You are part of the glue that holds this family together, but you are not all of it. We all work together to keep this family what it is, and the rest of us deserve to know when one of us is in danger. How can we protect you when you don't tell us you need protecting?"

"I don't need protecting I have-"

"The only thing you have is a stubborn streak that's going to kill you, literally," Jason yells beside me before storming away.

"Who took out the hit?" Sean asks, placing a hand on the bottom of my back. I hadn't realised how much I needed that slight touch until that moment. He always knows what I need and never fails to provide it.

"I don't know for sure, but I know it's for me alone. No one else's name is on it nor is there another." Christian looks down at the floor and sighs. "They want me and only me."

"Well, they can't fucking have you," I snap, crossing my arms over my chest. "If they think they can take you from me, they can think again." Taking a step forward, I look up to Christian and he has no choice but to tip his head to look down at me. "You promised me a lifetime. How can you fulfil that promise if you are not here?" Christian's eyes stay on mine, even though he has no idea what to say.

"Does Terry know?" Jason asks behind me. Christian nods but doesn't take his eyes off me when I step back.

"The whole security team does, it's why Layton's been so on edge recently," I point out, shaking my head, wondering why I didn't think of this sooner. It was bound to happen one day; someone would put a price on one of my men's heads. But they can take it off because my man is going nowhere.

Jason and Christian stare at each other. For a moment, I can't work out whether Jason wants to deck him or hug him. I know exactly how he feels.

"How long have you known?" Maximus asks.

"Four weeks. Someone tried to set a booby trap in a property I was going to see. Terry realised before we set it off." My chest threatens to tighten again as I realise we have already come close to losing him. "He did some digging and found the contract. He wanted to tell you all, but I told him no. I don't want you guys trying to get involved." Christian looks to each of us before continuing. "I won't risk your names being added to the contract." Maximus and Sean walk away, their heads in their hands, as Jason stares at his brother. "When I left the other day before Jasmine's therapy session, I had word that someone knew who had taken out the hit, and I went to confront them. I ended the threat. Or I thought I had."

"Last night?" Jason asks as I frown.

"Could have been arranged as a way to take me out. I don't know. But from all we learnt from what the arseholes who stormed the place said, I have a better idea of who set it up."

"Who?" I ask, keeping my arms crossed over my chest, and I tighten my hold, keeping my anxiety from taking over again.

"Mitchell," Sean says behind me as Christian nods.

"What the fuck did you do to piss him off?" Jason asks.

"I killed Flint, remember? They were lovers; it all came out after Flint was dead."

"How did they find out you killed him?" I ask. "Surely no one goes around boasting about who they killed," I remember how lost and broken he had looked after that. I had washed him in the shower and held him as he recovered. People may think he is a heartless bastard; it's a reputation he has worked hard to achieve. But so much of it is a show that sometimes I think even he forgets where Christian, the loving, protective man finishes, and the highly feared man, starts.

"They don't," Jason sighs. "But there will always be speculation. There will be someone somewhere that knows Flint was pissed with Christian and planned on having it out with him." The room falls into silence as we all try to take in the fact that there is a hit contract for one of us.

"So, what do we do?" I ask, chewing on my nail. I feel all four men look at me.

"*We?* Shorty, you're not getting involved. I'm shipping your ass off to a safe house or at least your little friend's where the Donavons can keep you safe," Maximus declares next to me. My head whips to the side so fast I'm surprised I don't end up with whiplash.

"I would like to see you try!" I snap back.

"Watch me," he growls, stepping closer so I have no choice but to look up at him. I know he means to intimidate me, but I stand firm.

"I'm not hiding when one of my men is in danger."

"If one of us is in danger, we all are," Sean says behind me. "We stay together; we are stronger that way."

"Sean's right," Jason adds from where he is standing. "If we send Jazzy away, we will be so busy worrying about her that we could miss a real threat."

"I'll go."

We all turn to see Christian rubbing the back of his head.

"The hell you will," I snap. Christian frowns at me momentarily, but I close the distance between us again. "You are not leaving, not happening. You can forget it." He looks down at me, and I see the pleading in his eyes. "Are you sure it's this Mitchell who took out the hit?" I ask, looking at Christian.

"About eighty percent. One of the guys who crashed last night mentioned him and the hit. But then he realised what he had done and did everything he could to get out of saying more."

"Where is he now?"

Christian looks at me and shakes his head.

"Dead, so there is no way to know for sure. He was

killed before I could find him again and question him." I don't miss the way Christian glances at Maximus quickly. Neither does Maximus.

"The guy who I -?" He doesn't need to finish the sentence; I can see what he did written on his face. "Shit!"

"So, what happens if you take this Mitchell out? Will the hit be cancelled?" All four heads snap in my direction. "What? I'm new to this; I don't know how they work," I point out, shrugging.

"I don't know how I feel about your talking about taking someone out," Jason sighs.

"I do, it's fucking hot," Maximus grins at me before winking. I roll my eyes at him before looking back to Christian.

"Well?" I ask, waiting for someone to answer.

"We would have to be sure it really was him who took it out," Christian sighs before walking away from the wall he's been standing in front of since I came out of my panic attack.

"How could we do that?" I ask, following him as he walks to the sofa and sits down before placing his head in his hands. I sit on the coffee table in front of him and wait for him to answer.

"We could kidnap him?" I suggest when he doesn't answer.

"Jazzy," Jason sighs, walking up to stand next to me.

"What? Why couldn't we?" I ask. "People have no issues kidnapping me!" It's meant as a joke, but with one look at the guys, I can see it hasn't been taken as one. "Fine," I huff, crossing my arms over my chest. "If you guys have a better idea of keeping my future husband alive, I would greatly appreciate it if you could speak up."

"You know, it's not the worst idea." We all turn to Sean,

who shrugs. "It wouldn't be the first time we've kidnapped someone to get answers from them. Even if he didn't take out the hit, he may know who did."

I look around and can see each of the others thinking about it.

"The problem with that is that he may have heard about last night and run or hired extra security," Christian points out.

"You know you still haven't told me about last night," I point out.

"Basically, we were having a great time; all hell broke loose when a bunch of twats we didn't invite turned it into one giant brawl. People were hurt, mainly on their side. We killed a few and beat the rest, making an example of them and what happens if they turn against us or mention you," Maximus shrugs. I look at him wide-eyed before looking at the others, who just shrug in confirmation.

"And you say I cause all the trouble," I sigh, shaking my head.

"We just know how to end parties with a bang," Maximus smirks.

"Yeah, the wrong kind," I add, rolling my eyes. "I never did get my promised hot night of sex."

"We will make it up to you," he replies.

"Can we get back to trying to save Daddy first, please," I sigh. "Then we can have hot sex to celebrate," I add in the hope of getting at least a smile out of two of them, but instead, all four have a smirk on their face. I'm taking that as a win.

"Fuck it, I think she's right, and not just about the sex," Christian says, sitting back on the sofa. I climb onto his knee needing to remind myself he is still here, and I will make sure he stays here.

"You want to kidnap him?" Sean asks. Christian looks at Jason and shrugs as he wraps his arms around me.

"What do you think?" he asks. Jason seems to think about it for a moment before nodding.

"I think it's the best option, but we will have to move quickly before he can run," Jason confirms. The guys all nod and start to move towards the door. Christian taps my hip, encouraging me to move so he can stand up.

"So, when do we leave?" I ask, trying to keep up with them. All four turn around and stare at me with wide eyes and open mouths. I only manage to keep a straight face for about five seconds before I wink at them all, and they visibly relax.

"This is all down to you four; I'm just the brains in this family," I tease, walking past them, grinning.

"Is it just me, or is she getting scarier by the day?" I hear Jason ask as I walk away. Maximus chuckles, and I listen to his response.

"She is, and it's sexy as fuck."

Chapter Twenty-Two

CHRISTIAN

"How long does it take to see what's going on?" Maximus asks behind me as we hide in the car down the road from Mitchell's place, waiting for Sean to return from looking around.

"As long as it takes to get all the information we need," I sigh, looking at the house across the street. Placing my elbow on the car door, I lean against it, glad the headache is slowly easing. I'm going to be feeling like shit for days, though. I swear, the older I get, the longer the hangovers last.

We've been in this car for three hours waiting to see if Mitchell was coming home. He finally arrived fifteen minutes ago with another male I don't recognise. The two of them entered the house and have been there since. I sent Sean to look around as he is the best man for the job. He can hear through any wall or window and has a much better memory for layouts than Maximus. Jason and I are too beat up to be sneaking around, plus neither of us wants to be seen looking like this.

When we were talking this morning before the others joined us for breakfast, we decided to keep a low profile for a few days until some of the bruising goes away. Or until it fades enough for us to cover it with some sort of makeup. It's not ideal, but people know we weren't badly hurt after last night's brawl. They will all start talking if they see the two of us now. The last thing we need is for people to realise there's tension between us. They will try to divide us further. Not that they can do as much damage as it seems I have done all on my own.

"Here he is," Jason mutters.

Sitting up, I see Sean walking towards us out of the windscreen. His hands are shoved in his jeans pocket, his head down as he hides his face under his baseball cap.

"He looks like a fucking drug dealer," Maximus teases as Sean opens the back door and slides in. He removes his hat and runs his fingers through his hair.

"What did you see?" I ask, looking at Sean through the rearview mirror.

"The other guy is one of Mitchell's dealers. He's come to pick up some stash. I heard them arguing about missing stock, and then Mitchell forced the guy to give him head. The guy got onto his knees, and I think you can guess where it went from there."

"Fucking joy," Jason sighs, rolling his eyes. "I've heard a few times that Mitchell is known for using the guys who deal for him."

"Well, when you look like Kermit the Frog on crack, you ain't going to get people lining up to suck your little cock are you," Maximus groans, turning up one side of his lips. I burst out laughing, no longer able to see the bastard Mitchell as anything other than Kermit the fucking Frog. "So, what's the plan?" Maximus asks.

I look out the window into the darkening sky and check my watch.

"We wait for the guy to leave, give it fifteen minutes, then go in," I answer, looking at Jason, who nods in agreement.

"Sounds like the best plan."

"Can someone check on Jasmine? She was putting on a front earlier after her panic attack. This has upset her more than she would admit in front of me." I can't get the sight of her gasping for breath out of my head. I've seen her struggle before or have a panic attack, but I have never caused it, and that made this one a lot harder to deal with. I always swore I would never hurt that girl; she is everything to me, and I honestly thought I was dealing with all this shit on my own was best for her. I was wrong.

"I've just checked the cameras; she's in your bed," Jason replies. "I'd leave off messaging in case we wake her."

"How did she sleep?" I ask Maximus, who shrugs.

"She tossed and turned all night. I'm not sure how much rest she got."

I close my eyes and take a deep breath to try and calm myself.

"I fucked up." I don't know if I mean to say the words out loud, but getting them out of my head into the open doesn't help the guilt as I had wished it would.

"No shit."

"Maximus," Sean warns. As always, he's the peacekeeper between the two of us.

"What? He did, in more ways than one! I'm not going to pussy foot around that!" The tone in Maximus's voice confirms how pissed off he is. When I look at him in the rearview mirror, the anger is there at the forefront. But there is also pain, and I know I put that there, too.

"What did you think was going to happen? Did you really think none of us would find out what was going on?" Jason asks next to me.

"Well, you hadn't yet, so I thought I might have a bit longer," I shrug, knowing how blasé that sounds. But it's true. I've been waiting for one of them to hear about the hit, but there's been nothing. I'm surprised by how long it's taken one of them to find out.

"I knew something was going on, especially when you started finding reasons to deal with everything alone, but I would have never guessed this," Sean sighs. "There again, I never thought you would be as careless as you have been with Jasmine's safety."

"I was protecting Jasmine," I snap.

"No, Christian, you weren't," Sean answers firmly. "If you had been, you would have made sure we were all aware of what was happening. You have put her in danger every time you have been in the same building as her."

"Terry has been aware of it all from the start and put extra security in place. No one would have gotten near the house or her without someone knowing."

"But we wouldn't have known." Jason looks at me, and I see the hurt in his eyes. "We wouldn't have known to be weary and what we were looking out for. What if they tried to get to you through us and Jaz? We haven't been on guard like we should have been."

I rub my face, knowing that he's right.

"I know, okay. I know I fucked up, and I'm sorry." I turn in my seat so that I can see my three brothers. "All I have tried to do is keep you as safe as possible. Let's face it Tommy didn't give a shit; if he had, he wouldn't have dragged us into this mess. Without Mum to protect us from his crap, I had no choice but to step up."

"We know that, and we are grateful for all you have done for us," Sean starts, but I shake my head.

"I don't want you to be grateful; I want you all to be safe!" I'm feeling overwhelmed with it all again, and it shows as my voice gets louder. I take a deep breath in an attempt to calm myself. I look at Jason, who has been by my side for as long as I can remember. "Which means, at times, I have hidden things from you, keeping you out of the loop and protecting you in any way I can.

"Do you really think this is the first time someone has put a price on my head? After all the shit I've pulled over the years, do you believe that I haven't pissed off the wrong person a few times? Because I have, and I have kept you out of it so that you are safe."

"For fuck's sake, Christian. How many times have I told you over the years not to hide shit from us!" Jason curses, looking away in anger. "You aren't the only one Tommy threw to the wolves. I know you were the first to kill, but it was me who had the gun held to his head that night. You think I wasn't with you every step of the way? Because I was! You aren't the only person who Jaz's dad's death has haunted. He died, so I didn't; you don't think I feel guilty about that because I fucking do. Even more so now we know who he was to Jaz and how it affected her." He takes a deep breath and runs his hand over his face.

"This shit needs to stop, Christian. You need to stop trying to protect us and let us work with you. We only discussed it this morning."

"You are asking me to go against every instinct I have. You are telling me to ignore my gut, the one thing that has kept us alive for this long. I know it needs to change, but it's hard."

"What about when we have kids? Will you continue to

pull this shit?" I turn to look at Maximus, who is red in the face. "You keep going on about wanting Shorty pregnant as soon as possible. You know we all want that, but how can we bring a child into this mess? How can we trust you to be the father we know you can be if you don't keep us in the fucking loop!" He slumps back into his seat and closes his eyes. "I want nothing more than to get married and live our lives with our girl and any children that come along. But right now, I worry that we are putting her in danger just by living with her." When he opens his eyes, he looks deep into mine; for a moment, I think I see tears.

"I love you, Christian. You have been the only father figure I needed. But-" Maximus takes a deep breath, obviously to calm himself before he continues. "But, if I have to choose between you or Shorty, she will win every time. I will protect her over you, even if that means taking her as far away from you as possible. I will not let her get hurt again, not because of who we are. I will not lose her."

"I think it's safe to say we all feel like that," Jason sighs as I look at him. "We are a team, the four of us. We always have been, but if I had a choice, I would walk away from our lives and never look back. I want nothing more than to pack Jazzy up and take her as far away from this mess as possible. Because losing her isn't an option, not anymore."

"I would never ask you to choose me over her," I point out, looking at each of them. "She is my world and protecting her is my priority. If it ever becomes a choice of saving her or me, then I want you to grab her and run as far away from me as possible. I want you to give her the life she deserves."

"Yeah, well, hopefully, it will never come to that because, like I said, we are a team, and Jazzy losing a husband isn't something she will survive." Jason sits back in his seat and looks out of the window. "There's movement."

We all turn our attention to the house across the road and see the guy walking out of the house, Mitchell, standing at the door in a dressing gown.

"Take it he had more than a blow job," Maximus mutters under his breath. I hate people who use their authority over others to get sexual favours out of them. It's just another form of rape in my eyes.

"Fuck waiting fifteen minutes; I say storm the place now," Maximus announces behind me. Anxious to get in there and end this shit as much as I am.

"Then let's get this shit done and go home," I answer, looking to Jason, who nods in confirmation.

We all get out of the car and give each other a quick nod for encouragement before heading off to our chosen places. Maximus and I head for the front door, Jason and Sean at the back. We have checked everywhere, and there are no other exits other than the windows.

I wait momentarily, giving the others a chance to get into position, as I pull on my leather gloves before knocking on the door.

"I never get why you attempt to be civil. Why don't you just kick the door down?" Maximus whispers beside me.

"Because this way doesn't cause anyone to be suspicious of us hanging around." I look around to check to see if there is anyone walking a dog or driving past, but luckily, the streets are quiet.

I knock again, this time a little louder, to ensure that he will hear me. Checking the windows at the front of the house, I try to work out which room he might be in and if he has seen us. My curiosity is answered when I hear the door being opened.

Mitchell is standing at the door, flicking through some money in his hand, not looking up at us.

"I hope you have change 'cause I don't," he mutters, moving some notes into one hand and holding it out in front of him. He finally lifts his head and sees me looking down at him.

"Afternoon, Mitchell."

"Fuck!" he tries to slam the door in my face as he turns on the spot and attempts to run. But fails and trips over his own feet, causing him to face-plant on the hard-tiled floor in his hallway.

I don't say anything as I sigh whilst stepping into the house. Maximus closes the door behind us and drags Mitchell to his feet as he tries to escape.

"Whatever you think I have, I don't!"

"I think you know exactly why I'm here." I nod towards the door I know is Mitchell's office, and Maximus drags him in there. I walk to the back door and open it for Jason and Sean. We walk into the office together to find Mitchell sitting in a chair in the middle of the room with Maximus standing over him.

"I hear you don't like me very much," I say, pulling up a chair and sitting with my eyes firmly on the piece of shit in front of me.

"I never hid that fact," Mitchell answers, trying to look in control. "In fact, I think I've told you exactly how I feel about you to your face on more than one occasion."

"You have, and I've always admired your balls for doing so," I nod in agreement. "However," I continue. "I don't admire the hit you took out on me. I'll admit I was surprised. I figured you weren't much of a coward, but I have been known to be wrong occasionally."

I don't know how I'm keeping my cool right now. My

brothers are right. Whoever has taken a hit out on me is at the same time putting our girl at risk. That is something I will never let stand.

"Prove it."

Well, he's not denying it straight out. Turning my attention to Sean, I nod to Mitchell's desk. He takes the hint and moves to the computer to start going through it for any proof he might be able to find.

"I have plenty of reasons to believe it was you. The biggest was only last night; I beat someone who confirmed that my suspicions were correct, that you have put a fairly pricey sum on my head."

"Who the fuck talked? … I mean, they're lying."

A typical dealer who uses his own stuff can't keep the truth from falling from his vile mouth.

"I think you've just given me all the confirmation I needed, don't you?"

Mitchell snarls at me before noticing the sounds coming from his desk.

"Get the fuck away from my laptop O'Reilly, that's fucking personal!" he goes to jump to his feet, but Maximus is there, placing a hand on his shoulder and shoving him back down. Mitchell looks at him and snarls. "Don't you ever get sick of being his lackey?"

"Do you ever get sick of being a fucking piece of shit?" Maximus retaliates.

"I'm not!"

"And I'm not his lackey; I just enjoy causing others pain." Mitchell looks Maximus up and down, and I don't miss the way he swallows deeply. Maximus smirks as he sees it, too. "Don't worry, Christian has put me under strict orders not to hurt you too badly … yet." he grabs Mitchell's arm with no warning and pulls it until it pops from its socket. The scream that leaves Mitchell hurts my ears, but I force myself to keep a straight face.

"Found something."

We all turn to see Sean looking at Mitchell's computer screen. Jason looks at me, and I nod, telling him to check it out.

"You've found fuck all; there's no way you could hack into my protected space that quickly," Mitchell moans through the pain from his shoulder.

"It's easy, considering your password is written on a piece of paper pinned to the board beside it," Sean answers, shaking his head. He moves out of the way and starts pointing things out to Jason.

"It's all here, not only the contract but a list of properties we own and what's happened to them, as well as plans for others."

I look at the piece of shit with a raised brow, but he just stares at me.

"There's also a schedule for each of us; someone's been following us and …" I don't miss the way his voice trails off. When I look back, I can see the rage taking over. "You need to see this."

Knowing it takes a lot to rattle Jason's cage, I get to my feet and stand beside my brother, who is pointing to the screen.

Everything is there. Where we go, eat, sleep, what will get us to change our plans and what we will never change them for. But when I look to where Jason is pointing, my blood starts to boil. Jasmine's name and a list of nicknames we call her.

Clicking on a link, I realise it brings up her class schedule and her appointments for the wedding, therapy sessions and who will take her; my heart drops when I see the following list: the times she's home alone.

Pulling my phone out of my trousers, I dial his number on instinct.

"Yeah?" Terry's voice comes through thick and heavy.

"I know you are meant to be resting, but the cat's out of the bag. Everyone knows, and I have who took out the contract. I want someone with Jasmine, now. Find out if she is still in my room and place someone outside. Whatever room she is in, someone stands guard outside, and I want people on foot checking all entrance points. But I don't want *anyone* to know why."

"Where are you?" Terry asks as I hear him moving around, no doubt to give the orders to others.

"We will be home in an hour. I have something to take care of first." I don't wait for him to answer before ending the call. I trust him to do as he's been ordered and know he will ask questions when I get home.

"I want that contract down and bring his laptop and any other devices you can find in the house."

"There's information here he shouldn't have been able to get hold of," Jason whispers as we both turn to see Mitchell sweating in his chair.

"I know, and it only means one thing," I answer, looking at the screen as Sean does his thing. "We have a mole in our team."

Chapter Twenty-Three

SEAN

I'm hiding in my room, needing five minutes to clear my head before I face everyone else again.

How the fuck did we get here?

Mitchell is currently in one of the makeshift cells we have at a hidden location. Christian and Jason have already managed to get a lot of information from him, and I know they plan on returning to get the rest. Once they are satisfied they know everything, they will end him. I used to hate the idea of killing; I still do in many ways. I remember begging my brother to find another way of dealing with people, and I never truly understood why he said that sometimes there isn't one; until today.

When I sat there looking through Mitchell's files and saw just how much he has on not only us but Jasmine, too, I wanted to be the one to kill him. I wanted to end his life for trespassing on hers.

We have no idea how he knows some of the things he does, and so far, he hasn't given us any solid evidence of who is telling him everything, so now everyone is under suspicion.

Everyone we hire and trust, even those we classify as friends, is now a suspect. It's going to be hard to ever trust anyone again after this and our girl's protection being jeopardised.

If you had asked me this time yesterday if we would be dealing with possibly the biggest threat we have ever faced as a family, I would have laughed in your face. I knew things were bad; I'm not as blind as my brothers like to think I am. I've noticed the tension in the house; it's impossible not to. I knew Christian was hiding stuff from us with how much he's been away. But never did it even cross my mind that someone would have put a price on my brother's head. We might have pissed some people off over the years, but the thought that someone wants to take Christian out terrifies me.

My brothers and I have never had it easy. It may look like it to outsiders, but our family has been through hell and back. From our selfish prick of a father to the world he dragged us into, nothing has ever been handed to us on a silver platter. But for once, I thought we had a chance of knowing what happiness and contentment were now that we have Jasmine, but I guess that was too much to hope for.

Taking a deep breath, I lean forward in my chair and place my head in my hands. I can't lose it now. I need to stay strong for my brothers and our girl, who I know will be beside herself and terrified she is about to lose one of her men.

When we got home, we found her pacing around the sitting room. She had woken up just after Christian had called Terry, who had taken it upon himself to watch over her so that the rest of the team wouldn't know there was a problem; how that man is functioning at all, I don't know. He's meant to still be in hospital but refused. He instructed our doctor to give him some pain meds and a follow-up appointment. When we are threatened, he takes it personally, and we should have known better than to expect him to rest.

Luckily, a team meeting was scheduled for this afternoon, which we moved back a few hours. The team are none the wiser, which is what we want. We need to see their initial reactions when we tell them about the mole. Hopefully, it will help us work out who it is quickly.

"Jazzy?"

I lift my head from my hands and look at my closed bedroom door as I hear Jason outside.

"What are you doing?" he asks, his voice getting louder as he gets closer. I hear Jasmine let out a deep sigh and I climb to my feet.

"I wanted to see if my blue hoodie was in Daddy Sean's room, but I don't want to bother him; he looked stressed."

I freeze with my hand on the door handle, shocked that she thought I would ever want time away from her. I don't get enough of it as it is. That's the downside to sharing her with my brothers. I will take any second I can get just the two of us; no matter what's going on, she is always my priority.

"He would never turn you away, Angel. You know that," Jason says from outside my door.

"I know; I just don't know what to do for the best right now," Jasmine sighs, and I can't take hearing how her voice wobbles as she tries to stop herself from crying. I step out to find Jason holding her. She turns at the sound of the door opening and looks at me with tear-filled eyes.

"Come here, Princess," I smile as she steps out of

Jason's arms and straight into mine. "What have I told you? I don't care what's going on; this is our room; you never need to worry about entering," I say into her hair before looking up at my brother, who winks at me before heading towards the stairs.

"I know, but everyone is so wound up and on edge; I don't want to make things worse," she admits, which breaks my heart.

"Nothing you could possibly do would make things worse; you are the one thing that makes everything better," I tell her, looking down into her eyes. "Now, how about you come in and get your hoodie? It's hanging up in the wardrobe."

Jasmine nods, smiling. I just wish it reached her eyes. Keeping an arm around her shoulders, I guide her into the room, and we quickly find her hoodie. Once she has it on and is comfortable, we leave our quiet space and head to the sitting room, where I know Christian and the others are waiting for us.

"Who's going to be in this meeting?" Jasmine asks as I lead her down the stairs.

"The five of us, Terry and Calvin," I answer; Jasmine looks at me and frowns.

"Why's Calvin coming? He doesn't work for you anymore."

I open my mouth to answer but spot Jason and Calvin walking towards us from the kitchen.

"Because Jason can't survive without me, apparently," Calvin winks at her as Jason rolls his eyes. "Did he tell you about how I saved his life *again* last night?"

"What? No!" Jasmine stops and stares at Jason, who rubs the back of his neck.

"When I said she knows everything, I didn't mean the finer details," he scolds Calvin, who holds his hands up.

"How was I meant to know that?"

"Who else was nearly killed last night?" she demands with her hands on her hips.

"Well, I guess you could say all of us, as we were the targets," Jason shrugs. I can tell he's trying to keep everything as calm as possible for Jasmine, but I don't know how long that will work.

I reach out and take her hand before pulling her back towards me.

"Come on, Princess. Christian and the others will be waiting for us." Jasmine looks towards the sitting room and nods before turning to walk beside me.

"Don't think this conversation is over, though. Later, you are going to tell me the *finer details*, understood?" She looks over her shoulder at Jason, who nods, looking slightly less confident than he had been a moment before.

"Yes, Angel."

Calvin and I make eye contact for a second, fighting to keep a straight face. We all know Jasmine is quickly becoming the boss of us all, whether we like it or not, which, of course, we secretly do.

All joking ends when we enter the sitting room and find Terry, Christian, and Maximus already there.

Christian is standing behind his desk, reading through some papers. Maximus and Terry sit on one of the sofas with a cup of coffee. Letting go of her hand, I tell her to go and sit down before heading to the coffee pot and pouring us each a cup. Holding up a mug towards Jason and Calvin, both nod, letting me know they want one too.

"So, other than you both looking far worse than you did

when I left you last night. What's going on?" Calvin asks as he makes himself comfortable on one of the sofas. I glance at Christian before handing out the coffees I've just made.

"We found out we have a mole in the team," Terry answers, looking at his previous second-in-command. "That's how they knew where to attack last night and organised a few other incidents the last month or two."

"Shit," Calvin curses as he sits forward, rubbing his face. I place a hand on Jasmine's back, letting her know I'm here if she needs me. "So why am I here?" he asks, looking at Jason, who is now standing beside Christian.

"Because we need your opinion on who we can trust and who could be the mole," Jason answers.

"Jason trusts your opinion more than anyone else's. Plus, you know the team better than anyone," Christian adds. I can see Calvin looks uncertain, and I'm unsure if it's because he doubts himself or if he's questioning whether it's the real reason we want his opinion.

"I've been out of the team for a while now; people could have changed since then," he points out. Christian nods and looks to Terry.

"But we would still appreciate your opinion, as well as you being present when we hold a team meeting in half an hour to see if anyone is looking suspicious."

Calvin nods and takes a deep drink of his coffee before sitting back in his seat again.

"Okay, I'll help in any way I can."

Christian and Jason share a look, and I notice how they both glance at Jasmine simultaneously. I can already guess who they want to talk to first, and I don't think Jasmine will be too happy about it.

"What do you know about Layton and his loyalties?"

Before Christian's even finished the sentence, Jasmine bolts upright and stares at him.

"Layton isn't the mole. There is no way he would betray any of us," she argues. Running my hand up and down her back, I try to calm her.

"Princess, we need to confirm that, as he's the one who will have the most inside knowledge when it comes to you and your whereabouts." I hoped to put her at ease, but from the look on her face, I know I've failed.

"He would never put me in danger like that. He wouldn't turn his back on any of us."

"I agree with Jaz." I turn my attention to Calvin, who is looking at her with a small smile, before turning to Christian. "That man is as loyal as they come. I do not doubt that he would protect Jaz or any of you with his life. He takes his job seriously and has the utmost respect for you all."

"I agree," Terry adds, nodding. "That kid would put himself between you and a bullet without a second's thought. He's still beating himself up over the time Jaz was attacked when at school. He would never willingly put her in harm's way."

Jason and Christian share a look and nod, both visibly relaxing a little. They've obviously been worried that they had been putting Jasmine's life in the hands of the mole, which wouldn't have sat well with any of us.

"Get him in here," Christian tells Terry, who pulls out his phone and holds it to his ear. I hear him giving Layton the order to come down and hangs up.

"What are you going to do?" Jasmine asks next to me.

"I want to see how he reacts when he hears about the mole. The way he responds to being asked if it's him will tell me if we're right to trust him or not," Christian answers, walking over to the coffee pot to pour himself another mug. I don't miss the way he glances at the alcohol on the table beside it. Who can blame him for wanting a drink right now? I know I do. But we need to keep a clear head with the staff meeting fast approaching.

A knock at the door has us all turning to look at it.

"Come in," Terry calls.

I don't have time to register the look between Christian and Jason before the door opens and all hell breaks loose.

The second Layton walks into the room, Jason is in his face, pinning him against the wall and has his gun to his head.

"What the-?" Layton quickly stops talking as he stares at Jason, his eyes wide with fear.

"Jason!" Jasmine jumps to her feet, but I stop her from getting involved.

"What have you been telling people?" Jason growls in his face.

"What? Nothing? I swear!"

"Stop it. I told you I trust him!" Jasmine shouts as she tries to get past me, but I hold her tight.

"I would never put her in danger, you know that!" Layton declares, looking around for someone to help him.

Jason stares at him for a moment, nods once, and lets him go while putting his gun back under his shirt. Layton looks around, shocked, as Jasmine slumps back onto the sofa, her head in her hands.

"Does someone want to tell me what the hell I'm meant to have done?" Layton demands, straightening his T-shirt, his hands shaking. He's brave, I'll give him that. Many men have pissed themselves when held at gunpoint by Jason, but Layton is hiding his fear well. I hear a sniff coming from

Jasmine, and I sit beside her before putting an arm around her shoulders.

"We have a mole in the team," Terry explains as Jason walks over and squats down in front of her.

"Jazzy, I had to be sure. I won't apologise for protecting you, but I'm sorry you had to see it," he whispers as I hear Layton cursing under his breath.

"But I told you I trust him," Jasmine sniffs as she looks at Jason. "Don't you trust me?"

"Jaz, I understand why Jason reacted like that. I would have done the same thing, no matter who it was," Layton says as they look at each other. "It's my job to protect you, but it's also all four of the O'Reillys, and let's face it, no one can do it as well as them," he smiles, trying to reassure her. Jason looks over his shoulder and nods once at Layton before returning to Jasmine.

"Do you understand now, Angel?" His eyes don't leave Jasmine's as she nods and wipes at her face. "I'm sorry for frightening you." He kisses her forehead as he stands and sits on the sofa beside Calvin.

"So, is someone going to fill me in on what's been going on?"

While Terry takes a moment to tell Layton all we've learnt, I pull Jasmine so she is leaning against my side. I run a hand up and down her arm to soothe her. Also to remind myself that she's okay and no one can get to her whilst she's here. They would have to kill everyone in this room, which would never happen, not with us on edge like we are.

Turning my head, I kiss her hair again. Closing my eyes, I take a deep breath, filling my nose with the scent of her shampoo to calm the anxiety cursing through my body. I've never been an anxious person and have never experienced a panic attack first-hand other than seeing Jasmine's. But right now, the way my heart is pounding and tightening at the same time, I feel like I'm on the verge of one.

When I open my eyes, I find Maximus watching me closely. He lifts his eyebrows, checking I'm okay, knowing how I'm feeling without me having to tell him. I nod slightly, signalling I'm fine, before returning to the conversation in the room.

"You know who we have to consider next, right?" Terry's voice brings me back to the conversation happening around us.

"Gordon," Jason answers, nodding. I can see that doesn't sit well with him; he has become close to the man who watches his back daily. "I don't think it's him; he's just as loyal as Layton." He turns to his old bodyguard, who shrugs.

"I only worked with him briefly, but he seemed genuine. From what I have seen and heard, I would be surprised if he was the mole."

Jason nods before looking to Christian, who's a little too quiet. When I turn my attention to my eldest brother, I can see that this is all taking a toll on him. He looks exhausted, physically and mentally. The only other time I have seen him looking this way was when Jasmine was taken, and none of us slept the whole time she was missing.

"Do you want me to get him in here too?" Terry asks. Jason shakes his head before running his fingers through his hair.

"No, I'll deal with him after the meeting." He's on edge, and his patience is running thin. He turns to me, and I know what he's thinking.

"I don't think it's, Mykela. I haven't even told her some of the stuff in that file," I explain.

"I doubt it's her too. She has worked with us for five

years and never taken as much as a sick day; it's why I promoted her to guard Sean when he started managing," Terry adds. Christian and Jason both nod in agreement. Mykela may be quiet, but she has always gone above and beyond for this family. There is no reason for her to have turned on us.

"Layton, do you know who could be giving out information on us?" Christian asks, finally walking back over to where the rest of us have congregated. Layton shakes his head before looking at Terry.

"I can honestly say the team is tight, possibly the tightest since I joined."

"He's right; not a single person comes to mind. Everyone is loyal or acts loyal to you all," Terry adds, looking to Calvin, who nods.

"What about if they are talking to friends or family outside of work and haven't realised what they were doing?" Jasmine asks next to me. I look at Terry, who is watching her.

"It's a possibility," I point out. "Who likes to talk?"

"I can't think of anyone off the top of my head," Terry sighs, looking to Calvin and Layton, who shake their heads.

I take a deep breath and tighten my hold on Jasmine. It feels like we are going around in circles and are no closer to finding out who is selling us out.

The conversation continues around me as the others compare notes on who they think could be behind the information leak. Every name we can think of is thrown out there, but none are a certainty. There is a reason we have the team we do, and that's why this is so unbelievable. The only time we have ever had any issues with turncoats was when Tommy was alive, but since he was cut off and later killed, we haven't had any problems from the staff.

"Let's head to the meeting room; everyone should be there," Terry points out as he stands, pain etched all over his face.

"Should you really be here? You need to rest," Jasmine says, looking at Terry, who looks at her with arched brows.

"You think I can rest with all this going on? If a member of my team has betrayed us, you can be damn sure I will be here to deal with them." God help whoever has let Terry down, as he will make their life a living hell if he doesn't kill them for it.

Jasmine falls into step beside me as we stand and head towards the door.

"You don't have to come, Princess."

Jasmine shakes her head and gives me a small smile.

"I want to be there; I'm tired of being out of the loop."

Christian steps beside her and runs a hand over her head.

"Okay, Sweetheart. But if you want to leave at any point, just let Layton know, and he will step out with you." Christian looks to Layton, who nods.

"Absolutely, just give me the nod, and we'll escape."

"I'll be fine," she replies, holding her head high, determined to show strength. Christian looks at her proudly before kissing the top of her head.

"Then you are more than welcome to come with us. Just remember, no matter what we are like in there …"

"You will never treat me like that, I know," she answers with a smile.

"Good girl," he praises her with pride in his eyes.

We stop outside the dining room, which we use for large team meetings, where we can hear the hushed voices of those inside. Christian and Terry, ensure they are at the front of us before sharing a look.

"Time to remind them who they work for," he sighs, straightening his collar and throwing the door open before storming into the room, his sheer presence demanding everyone's attention. All looking scared, knowing that when Christian is pissed, we all are, and they are in the firing line.

"Which one of you has betrayed us?"

Chapter Twenty-Four

CHRISTIAN

I lean forward, resting my arms on the table and count to ten in my head for the umpteenth time today.

Every one of the men and women in front of me denies sharing any of our secrets, and the biggest problem is that I believe them. One look at my brothers and Terry tells me they do, too. I pretend to be listening to Terry giving them all a formal warning, telling them what will happen if he finds out any of them have been helping the enemy.

There is a new routine for security now, and Calvin has promised to supply armed security for the perimeter. They are trained to be hidden, and that's what we need right now. He will head home and talk to his business partners to determine who will patrol and when. He has told us not to expect anyone to start for the next twenty-four hours as they will need to move things around first.

"For now, I want everyone to act like everything's going on as normal. We pretend that the O'Reillys are none the wiser of the threat out for them other than what happened last night. That especially goes for Jasmine." Terry looks at me, and I bring my attention back to the room. I sense Maximus behind me, placing an arm around Jasmine standing between him and Sean. Jason, as always, is to my right and has had eyes on Gordon the whole time.

"Jasmine is usually kept in the dark about things like this; it's what they'll expect, so we will keep them thinking that. She will pretend she knows nothing about the hit out on me or that we have people gunning for us. She will tell her friends she has no idea what happened this weekend. We want people to think she is still out of the loop to keep her protected." I stand up and look around the people watching me.

"Nearly everyone in this room was present the last time I had to deal with security lying to us. You are all well aware of how that went for them. But here is a reminder. If anything happens to our fiancée, on your watch, your life is forfeit. There will be no second chances. If you fail to report anything suspicious and we find out, you sign your own death warrant. You protect Jasmine with the same commitment as the four of us." Looking around the table, I can see fear in every eye looking back at me. I tell myself I have made my point and sit back down.

"Does anyone else have anything to say?" When I'm met with silence, I nod once and lean back in my seat. "Then follow Terry and receive your new assignments. Take tonight as the only warning you will get." They all turn to look at Terry, who stands from his seat and nods towards the door. Everyone stands and starts to leave the room in silence. Jason joins them, and I see him pulling Gordon in the opposite direction from the others. I know he will be giving him his warning.

I stay in place, counting each of the ten staff members and Calvin out of the door until Terry is the last to leave and closes the door behind him. I relax back into my seat and curse under my breath.

"What a fucking day," Maximus sighs behind me as I pinch the bridge of my nose. I feel two small hands slide over my shoulders before her arms wrap around my neck, her cheek resting against mine.

"Are you okay, Daddy?" she whispers in my ear. I take a deep breath, inhaling her sweet scent.

"Been better, Sweetheart," I sigh. Pushing my chair back a little, I take her hand and pull her around to sit on my lap. I look deep into her eyes as I cup her face. "I am so proud of you and how you are handling everything." Leaning in, I press my lips to hers. "You have been my biggest strength the last twenty-four hours." Jasmine smiles before kissing me again.

"I'm glad I can help."

We all turn our attention to the door as Jason walks in, looking a little murderous.

"Everything okay?" Sean asks behind me.

"Yeah, he says he doesn't speak to anyone, and I believe him. He's been warned, though." Jason walks over to me and places a kiss on Jasmine's lips. "You were amazing; I'm so proud of you, Jazzy."

"We all are," Sean adds as he runs a hand over her head..

"I didn't do anything," she argues as we shake our heads.

"You stood beside us and didn't show one ounce of fear. You held your head high and refused to look away," Maximus explains as he looks deep into our girl's eyes.

"I don't know about anyone else, but I need a drink," Jason announces as he turns and heads back to the door.

"Sounds good to me," Maximus laughs, following him,

quickly followed by Sean. Jasmine looks at me, and I can't help but smile as I help her to her feet and stand beside her.

"I think you deserve one, too."

Jasmine grins as she kisses me on the cheek and skips off to join my brothers. I turn the lights off in the dining room and follow behind them all. Unknown to Jasmine, there is another reason we are all heading for a drink in the sitting room: we plan on talking to her about what she revealed last night.

We discussed it when we were coming home from Mitchell's this afternoon. We need to know so we can help her heal. We have given her time, and if she asks for more, we will give her that, too. The controlling side of me wants to know everything, but like Jason said the other day, she doesn't ask for anything from us. So we have to give her this if it's what she wants.

Walking into the sitting room, I find the twins sitting in their usual spot with Jasmine between them. She's leaning against Sean's side, her legs bent to the side, and her feet resting on Maximus's lap. The three of them talk quietly while Jason watches from the makeshift bar. I can already see five glasses out when I reach him. He's pouring the fourth glass of whiskey as I stop beside him.

"What did you make of it all?" I ask quietly. Jason shrugs as he puts the stopper back in the bottle of whiskey.

"Nobody stood out as lying. I spoke to Calvin very quickly after Gordon, and he said the same. If any of them have shared anything significant, they have no idea they've done it."

There is always the possibility that someone shared information by mistake. Phones can be hacked, software infiltrated, and rooms bugged. Pulling out my phone, I fire off a quick text to Terry.

Christian: I want the whole house and all the cars checked for bugs. I will gather our laptops and phones for you to check as well.

Less than a minute after I click send, there is a knock at the door.

"Come in," I call, picking up the glass of wine I've just poured for Jasmine. Terry enters as I walk over to the sofas and pass her the glass while Jason passes the twins theirs.

"I'm one step ahead of you," Terry announces as he closes the door behind Layton. Both look like they mean business. "I did the dining room before the meeting and also had signal blockers in each corner to ensure that if a phone had been hacked, they wouldn't be able to listen into the meeting." I thank him as I take my seat. "Can you all put your phones on the table?" All five of us immediately oblige and watch as Terry and Layton run something over them, checking for bugs.

"I want an in-depth check done on them all, too," Jason says as he sits in his usual spot.

"I will need to do that in my office. Are you okay with me taking them?" All five of us nod before Terry collects them all up. "I have already run a check on the landlines, and all are safe. We will check each room to ensure they are on the safe side, but I can't imagine how they would have been bugged."

I sip my drink, nodding, thinking the same thing. We are cautious about who we allow in our personal space, especially with Jasmine now living with us. We want our home to be her safe place. The one place she can always come to feel safe.

We all sit quietly as Terry and Layton work together to check the room quickly. Jasmine leans against Sean as she chews on the skin around her thumb, indicating she's anxious. Sean picks up on it as he pulls her hand from her mouth and whispers something in her ear. I'm not sure what he says, but she leans into him further as he presses a kiss to the top of her head.

"I'll be back in a minute," Jason announces as he stands and walks from the room. I'm not the only one that watches him leave. Maximus pays attention to our brother as well.

I sit back for a moment and close my eyes. I'm exhausted and stressed and just want today to be over and done with. We did consider if now was the best time to ask Jasmine about the abuse she suffered, especially with everything else going on, but we came to the conclusion she is probably waiting for us to mention it, which will add extra stress. At least if we ask and she says she isn't ready, she knows we are letting her take the lead with it all.

"Room's clear," Layton announces. Reluctantly, I open my eyes and look at Terry and Layton. "I'm going to check the rest of the house while Terry goes for a lie-down. We will both be sleeping on site for the time being, so we are close if anything happens."

"Thank you. We appreciate it," I say, giving them both a nod.

"Try and get some rest tonight, all of you," Terry orders. I don't miss the fact that he's mainly focusing on me.

"Which one of us is the boss?" I ask, smirking.

"When you are being a stubborn bastard, I am," he replies.

"I'll second that," Jason announces as he walks back into the room with Jasmine's blanket. He drops something behind the sofa as he walks over to her. "Here, Jazzy, you looked cold," he smiles at her as he shakes it out and puts it over her legs.

"Thank you, Daddy," she smiles, pulls it up to her chin, and makes herself comfortable. Jason looks at me and gives me a nod, signalling for us to proceed with the other reason we are here.

"If anything important comes up, let me know; otherwise, we will regroup tomorrow at ten." Both Layton and Terry nod before wishing us a good night and leaving.

Looking over at Jasmine, I see her staring into space while worrying her bottom lip between her teeth. She looks up at me, and I can see she knows why we are here.

"You want to talk about what I remembered, don't you?" Her voice is small and sounds so vulnerable that it breaks my heart. Standing from my seat, I move to sit on the edge of the coffee table so I can take her hand. Jason moves beside me so all four of us are close to our amazing woman.

"We want you to know that we are here to talk when you are ready," I answer, running a thumb over the back of her hand. "You revealed a lot last night, and the last thing we want is for you to think we are sweeping that under the carpet because we aren't. We want to understand so we can help you, but if you're not ready for that yet, all you have to do is say."

Jasmine looks down at our hands as Jason takes her other one.

"We love you so much, Jazzy, you know that. We would never forgive ourselves if we hurt you unintentionally." My brother's words stab me in the chest, because that's exactly what I've been beating myself up about since I grabbed her last night.

Jason moving brings me out of my dark place. I glance as he returns to where he dropped something a moment ago and pulls out her white teddy. The one she clings to when she starts digressing into her younger self. The place she goes when she is feeling vulnerable. She takes it from him and clings, burying her face into the top of its head as Sean's arm tightens around her shoulders. I look to Maximus, who is running his hand up and down her legs. All four of us are giving our woman all the attention she needs.

"I didn't lie to you," she whispers, not lifting her head. "When I said it was only that one time, I thought it was."

Jasmine had told me previously that a man entered her room one night when she was ten. He had inserted his fingers into her, and she had screamed so loud that the neighbours called the police. Jasmine was given to her grandparents, and Carol had to prove she was off the drugs before she could go home.

"Were the memories repressed?" Jason asks softly. Jasmine nods into her teddy, still not looking at any of us. Usually, I would tell her, "*eyes on me*," but this will go however she needs it to. There's a time we are her daddies to guide her; others we are here to give her the love and comfort she needs.

"I have never really remembered much between when my dad left and turning sixteen. After my grandparent's deaths, the only things I remember focusing on were dancing or my friends. I figured it was because nothing much had happened at home as Mum was too out of it to make memories with me. But for a while, the therapist has thought that I may be repressing the memories."

I nod, as he has said as much in a few reports, but he wasn't sure if it was related to abuse from her mother or seeing her in the states she would get into. He believed that one day, they would come back. He expected there to be some sort of trigger.

"What triggered you to remember?" I ask.

"We were talking about seeing Sophia and Amber and how it made me feel," Jasmine looks up from her teddy for the first time and looks to Maximus.

"When did you see them?" Sean asks, frowning. I glance at Jason and see he has no idea, either.

"The day we went to stay at the hotel," Maximus answers, unable to take his eyes off Jasmine. "With everything that happened since, I completely forgot about it," he answers, running his hand up and down her leg.

"What happened?" Sean asks. Jasmine starts to explain how she bumped into them and realised quickly that they had never been real friends to her, not for a long time at least. When I hear it was the same time as Verity went missing, which was only a couple of days before Christmas, I understood why it would have slipped her mind.

"He was asking how our friendship used to be," she sighs, burying her face into the teddy again. "I was talking about how I hid at Amber's once when I was sixteen, and Carol tried to sell my virginity for the first time, and it was like a million memories came back at the same time, and I remembered so many other times she had brought men into my room. How she had stood there and let them touch me, made me touch them, all while she looked on."

"She was in the room?" Maximus growls. Jasmine nods, and I give him a warning look at the same time as Sean and Jason. He nods, acknowledging that he needs to reel it in, and we all go back to giving Jasmine our undivided attention.

"She stayed to ensure they didn't go too far." She looks up at me with her tear-filled eyes, and it breaks my heart.

"She stayed to make sure they didn't rape you," I finish for her. She nods before wiping her cheeks. Maximus reaches for the small table beside him and holds out a box of tissues for her. She takes one with a small thank you and wipes at her face.

"For a short while, I thought maybe it was because she actually cared and that she was protecting me from the worst of it, but then I remembered an argument she had with one guy. She had stopped him at the last second, and when he argued with her, she told him he could place a bid at the auction."

That fucking bitch. She really was going to auction off her daughter's virginity, like the sick fuck she was.

"Did anything happen after that one time you remembered? After you went to live with your grandparents?" Jason asks, tightening his grip on her hand. Jasmine nods, tears flowing freely now.

"The memories are all glitchy and like mini flashes. The therapist believes she started drugging me. Which would explain why there are periods of time I don't remember very well." She looks at me then and bursts into tears. "I'm sorry, I didn't remember, I thought-" Sean doesn't even try to protest when I grab her from his side and pull her onto my lap. She curls up so small and clings to me as she breaks down.

"Don't you dare apologise. You have nothing to be sorry for," I say as I rock her. Holding her so tight, I'm worried I might hurt her, but there is nothing that will make me release her now.

"But I honestly thought you were ... She made me believe I was still a..." My body freezes as what she's saying sinks in. Movement in my peripheral vision makes me look up in time to see Jason jumping up and pulling Maximus from the room with his arm around his shoulders.

"No matter what, you are still ours, Sweetheart. No

one will ever take away how special that afternoon was for all five of us," I whisper into her hair. I had hoped it would calm her, but she starts crying harder instead. I hear her apologise again, and it takes everything in me not to lose it. "Please stop," I whisper as tears fill my own eyes. "You did nothing wrong, Sweetheart. Absolutely nothing."

I look to Sean, only to find him paler than I've ever seen him. He looks like he is on the verge of breaking down. I also don't miss how he looks from Jasmine to the door his twin just left through. The two people he loves more than anything in this world are falling apart, and he's stuck, not knowing what to do for either of them.

"I promise no one will ever touch you again," I whisper as I hold our girl in my arms. "I will hunt down each of them that hurt you and make them pay. Tell me what you need, and it's yours," I whisper as her sobs start to slow.

"Why would she do that? Now her favourite taunt makes sense, and I hate her even more."

"What would she say, Princess?" Sean's voice is rough, and I know he is being held on by a thread.

"Whenever I was confused or couldn't remember what I had done, she would laugh and say, 'What you don't remember doesn't matter.' She could keep selling my virginity because, as far as I was concerned, I was still one." Jasmine rests her head on my chest and cries quietly.

I hear the slightest click and look over my shoulder to where my brothers are walking back in. One look at Maximus's face, and I know he's been crying and raging. His eyes are red and puffy, and his whole body is trembling. They watch Jasmine as they return to sitting in the same positions. I'm unsure if she knows they have returned or even left in the first place.

"Tell me what you need, Sweetheart," I whisper into her hair. "Tell me who they were, and I will kill them for you."

"You already have, I think." Leaning back a little, I can't help but frown at her.

"Who?"

"I heard about the blonde guy who was Hudson's mate. He was there that day when Hudson hurt me."

"He was one of them?" Jason asks, his face expressing the level of shock we are all feeling. Jasmine nods and starts playing with the ears of her bear.

"I always knew I recognised him from somewhere, and when Daddy Max told me about what he said last night, it all clicked into place. I recognised a few faces in that house, and now I know why."

"He's dead; I killed him last night." I had been worried about telling her I had committed murder, but now I wish I could do it again. I wish I could have kept going until there was nothing left of the fucking bastard.

"Did you know Tommy before we met you?"

I look at Sean and frown; surely, he can't be implying what I think he is. But Jasmine looks at him and shakes her head.

"No, but I think Mum knew Taylor or at least a few of his guys."

"When did it stop, Jazzy?" Jason asks, retaking her hand.

"About a year before the wedding, I think. It may have been more like two, as I was hardly home by that point, so she wasn't able to drug me. I think they tried a couple of times, but I would fight them. She stopped then and just resorted to berating me. She was sober for about six months before introducing me to Tommy a few months before the wedding."

I watch Jason's shoulders relax a little and realise he is worried that Hudson has been one of the ones who hurt her. It sounds like the kind of thing he was into. But Hudson started working for Taylor a few months after the wedding. I think if he had been one of them, Jason would have lost it, blaming himself even more for letting the bastard live when he should have killed him.

"I don't remember much more," she admits quietly before wiping her face. When she looks up at me, her blood-shot eyes break my heart. "I really wanted you to be my first." Her bottom lip starts to tremble again as I tighten my arms around her, trying desperately to hold her together as she falls apart on my lap.

"He was, Jazzy," Jason whispers, reaching over to place a finger under her chin and tilting her head up so he can look at her.

"But-"

"But nothing," he cuts her off. "He was the first person you gave yourself willingly to. That makes him your first.

"That afternoon, you gave us all the greatest gift we could have ever asked for. You gave us your heart and trust, and it's something we cherish more than anything else."

"He's right, Sweetheart," I whisper into her hair. "Like I told you a few minutes ago, nothing can take that afternoon away from us. The five of us began something amazing that day, and no one and nothing will ever taint that memory."

She looks at all of us as we try to hide how much our hearts are breaking for our girl.

"Thank you," she whispers, leaning her head back into my chest.

"What for, Shorty?" Maximus asks as he leans forward and takes her hand.

"For being supportive like you always are. For letting me

take those few days to come to terms with everything before telling you all."

"You know better than thanking us for looking after you, Angel," Jason points out, but Jasmine shakes her head.

"I'm thanking you for caring enough to look after me. For always holding me when I feel like I'm breaking apart. I love you all so much, and now and again, I want to show you how much I appreciate you. I do that by saying thank you. So just for once, let me."

"As you wish, Princess." Sean leans in and presses a kiss to the top of her head. "But just know that I am so proud of you and how you have handled all of this."

"I think it's safe to say we all are," I add as Maximus and Jason nod in agreement.

"I'm trying to focus on the future," she whispers as she closes her eyes. "We are going to have a great future together," she adds, her voice sounding heavy.

One thing we have learnt about Jasmine is that crying wears her out physically as well as mentally. Whenever she cries, she curls up against one of us and falls asleep. I like to think it's because she feels genuinely safe with us and knows there is nothing we wouldn't do to protect her.

"Where do you want to sleep tonight, Jazzy?" Jason asks, giving her hand a quick squeeze before she falls into a deep sleep.

"Can I sleep with Daddy?" she asks slowly, not opening her eyes.

"Of course you can, Sweetheart," I respond, lifting her in my arms as I stand.

"You get her upstairs; I'll check in with security before calling it a night," Jason says, looking at me. I nod and leave the sitting room with the twins close behind, as they will want to see her into bed.

Once in our room, I place Jasmine on the bed and step back.

"Let these two help you get ready for bed, Sweetheart. I'll be right back." Kissing the top of her head, I go to the bathroom and take a quick shower. At one point, I notice Maximus's arms around Jasmine as she brushes her teeth. After tonight, I know everyone will want a couple of minutes alone with her, making sure, in their own way, she's okay.

I take my time drying off after my shower and brushing my teeth, giving my brothers as long as they need with Jasmine.

When I finally walk into the bedroom, the twins are gone, and Jason is curled up on the bed with Jasmine. She is almost asleep, clinging to her teddy, which is pressed into her face, to the point I'm worried she can't breathe. Jason is stroking her hair and whispering to her, so I keep my back turned, giving him space, not wanting to intrude on their time together.

When I eventually turn around, he is still curled up, his eyes closed, as he starts to fall asleep. I walk around to the other side and climb in behind our girl.

"Shit, sorry," he curses as he wakes with a jump.

"It's fine to stay there. I think she would want us both here anyway," I whisper, turning on my side so I can lie behind Jasmine.

"No, I need my bed. But come get me if she gets upset."

I nod as he climbs off the bed.

"How is Maximus?" I ask, running my hand over her head.

"He flipped. One of the pictures needs a new frame."

I nod as it's what I had expected. Maximus has always been the one of us who reacts badly to anything Jasmine is put through. His love for her is everything to him, and he can't handle it when he doesn't protect her, even If he hadn't known her when she was hurt.

"Everything else okay?"

Jason nods before yawning.

"Yeah, fine. Try and get some rest, and shout if you need me."

I nod and wish him a good night as he switches the lamp off on her side of the bed and heads to his own room. Leaving me to lie in the dark with my strong, beautiful woman who has proven once again that there is nothing she can't take on and overcome.

Pulling her into my arms, I lie down, burying my nose into her hair as I remind myself that we are here together, safe and sound, even if only for tonight; I'm not going to think about anything other than that.

Tomorrow is another day, and I'm sure it will bring just as much shit as any other, but as always, I know I can face it with this woman by my side, and I am another day closer to tying her to me forever.

Chapter Twenty-Five

JASMINE

I wake with a jump as a loud, high-pitched alarm sounds from all angles.

"Daddy?" I reach for Christian, who should be sleeping beside me, but the bed's empty.

A loud thud sounds from the window as the room descends into complete darkness. Jumping from the bed, I rush to it and throw open the curtains, only to find the bulletproof shutters down.

"Daddy?" I yell this time as I panic, realising it could only mean one thing: we are under attack.

"Daddy!" I scream, rushing for the bathroom to find it empty. "Where are you?" Rushing back into the room, I try the bedroom door, but it's locked. The alarm is still ringing, drowning out all other sounds from outside the room. The only thing I can still hear is my pounding heart. Panic threatens to take over, but I give my head a shake and force myself to focus.

"Christian!" I don't know why I'm still calling him; he's not here. But if he's not here, where is he?

Has he been taken?

Has the house been breached, are all of my men now in danger? What about Mrs Brown, Terry and Layton? Are they safe?

The image of Christian lying in a pool of blood fills my mind. His eyes trained on me as the blood continues to flow from him. The fear consumes me like a cage, trapping me within its bars, tightening until it's all I can feel. In seconds, I see all four of them lying in the same position, all covered in blood and dead. Their images change just as quickly to Mrs Brown and the guys.

With my fingers threaded into the root of my hair, I tug at it, trying to get myself to focus on anything but my vivid imagination. Now is not the time for a panic attack; I need to work through all the steps the guys have drilled into me.

Taking one deep breath in an attempt to force myself to focus, I spin around and rush to the bedside cabinet where I know Christian keeps a gun for emergencies. Grabbing it from its hidden compartment at the back, I check it's loaded and grab some extra bullets just in case. I look down at the gun in my hand, and the image of my mother's face as I killed her is all I can see. I've not held a gun since that day. The guys haven't even attempted to continue my self-defence weapon training; we purely focus on hand-to-hand combat. My hands shake as I check the safety is in place, and the image of the bullet entering my mother's head flashes up again. My breath catches as the guilt threatens to make me vomit where I stand, but I force myself to remember why I did it. I did it to save Christian and will do it again if necessary.

Keeping hold of the strength my men have given me, I rush to the other side of the bed, drop down, and hide as the guys have taught me. The alarm finally cuts off at almost the exact moment I get into position. The memory of the alarm going off when I was locked in that godforsaken hell hole tries to overcome me, but I push it back. I am not there; I'm here in our home and will not be taken again.

I hear voices yelling outside the door, bringing me back to the room. I can't make them out as my ears are ringing from the alarm. I try harder to listen and pick out who I can hear, but it's impossible.

I hear them getting louder, and the sound of the door handle moving has me spinning around and flicking the safety off the gun while aiming at the door.

"Jazzy!" Jason throws open the door, and I instinctively drop the gun onto the bed and rush round to him.

"Daddy!" His name spills from my lips as I cry, throwing my arms around his neck.

"It's okay, I'm here, Angel. I've got you." He holds the back of my head as his other arm holds me around my waist.

"Where are the others?" I demand, pulling back.

"We are all fine. There's no danger. Christian's in his office-" I don't wait to hear anything else. I pull out of Jason's arms and rush out of the room. "Jazzy, wait!" I don't have time to wait. I need to see him. I need to know he's unharmed and that the others are all okay, too.

My throat and eyes are burning as I run down the stairs, nearly losing my balance more than once. I try to push back the images I had of the four of them hurt, but once again, they come to the forefront of my mind, which only forces me to push myself harder to get to him. I need to get there before the panic attack takes hold.

I can hear Jason shouting at me, but I know he's okay; I need to see Christian and the others now.

"Daddy!" Throwing open the door, I run into the room to stop in my tracks.

He's not here.

I scream his name whilst spinning around in a circle, hoping I missed him. But he's nowhere to be seen.

He's meant to be here. Why isn't he here?

Panic hits me like a tidal wave, and I instantly find myself drowning in it. The room spins as I look around for him again. Everything starts to become blurry, and the walls feel like they are closing in as my legs go from underneath me. I need to see that they're okay, but the confinements of the fear prevent me from moving. Panic takes what little breath I have, and a hysterical cry forces its way out of my throat. I can't move; I can't get anything past my constricted throat.

"Jazzy …"

I don't hear what else Jason says as I feel him running a hand over my head. I try to speak, but I don't know if I manage to say the word out loud or if they remain in my head.

"Where?"

Jason pulls me onto his lap and holds me, but as much as I love him, it's not him I want or need.

"Jazzy, he's fine. We are all fine."

All I can do is shake my head because until I see them for myself, I don't trust that someone hasn't taken them from me. Jason must realise as he stands with me still in his arms and carries me from the room. I don't look where he is taking me. The tears stop me from seeing clearly, and I can't stop myself from clinging to his shirt. He holds me tight in his arms as he rushes through the house until I hear him kicking a door with his foot.

"Christian!"

I hear a door open, and Jason charges into a room.

"What's happened?" The sound of his voice causes something to snap inside me, and I turn away from Jason's chest, desperate to see him with my own eyes. I don't have to wait as he pulls me from Jason's arms and holds me. He walks across the room and sits with me on his lap, and I bury my head into his shirt and breathe in his cologne.

"Sweetheart, what's the matter?" He tries to pull away from me, but I grab at his shirt, needing to stay as close as possible to him. I am terrified that if I move just slightly, he will be taken from me. I try to ask where the twins are, but I've lost all ability to speak. Nothing is getting past my constricted throat, not even air.

"Do you really need to ask?" I hear Jason snap. "She was alone when they activated the security system. They triggered it five minutes early, so I was still in my office when we went into lockdown.

"She spent the whole of yesterday listening to us discussing how someone wants you dead and then gets woken up by the house going into lockdown."

Christian curses under his breath as he buries his face into my hair.

"I'm so sorry, Sweetheart. I didn't know you were alone. We are all fine, I promise. They were testing the improved system." I take a deep breath and listen to his heartbeat as he whispers sweet words into my hair. I curl up smaller in his lap, needing the comfort of his arms as they tighten around me.

Even when the tears have slowed and I'm no longer hysterical, I can't face him. I can't bring myself to move, terrified that I will never hear his heart beating again.

"Where are the others?" I whisper. Each word's hurting my throat. Jason appears with an open bottle of water for me. After a couple of sips, I clear my throat and try again. “Where are the others?”

“The twins had gone out to meet with Ryan Donavon. The three of them are training together. They will be back soon,” Christian whispers, running a hand up and down my back.

“I promise we are all fine, Jazzy,” Jason says as he tries to take my hand but stops when he realises it’s in a fist. “What’s in your hand, Angel?” he asks, frowning. I look at it for a moment before remembering. Jason holds out his hand, and I slowly drop three bullets into his palm.

“Shit,” the two of them curse together as Christian’s arms tighten around me again.

“Where’s the gun, Sweetheart?”

I have to think about it for a moment because I don’t remember, but then I remember it falling from my hand.

“On the bed or beside it,” I reply.

“I’m so sorry. I had no idea you were alone. If I had known you were so scared, I would have come to you myself.”

“Of course, she was scared. For fuck’s sake, Christian. She’s terrified of losing you, of losing all of us.”

“I can't lose you,” I whisper into his chest as he runs a hand over my hair repeatedly.

“I’m not going anywhere, Sweetheart. You are stuck with me for the rest of your life, whether you like it or not.” He kisses my head again. “No one will ever take me from you.”

“Don’t make promises you can’t keep, Daddy,” I sigh before yawning, exhausted after my panic attack. They always leave me so drained, and now that I know the guys are all safe, I can tell I’m going to fall asleep.

“It’s not a promise; it’s a vow. I will never leave you.”

I want to believe him wholeheartedly, but I don't think I truly will until we know this threat hanging over our heads has gone. For now, I stay curled up on his lap, listening to his heart as he holds me tight and promises me the world.

Christian

Jasmine sleeps soundly in my arms, her head resting on my chest as she clings to my shirt. She's been asleep for about twenty minutes now after exhausting herself.

When Jason kicked the door, shouting for me, I threw it open, and my heart stopped. I could see her shaking in his arms, crying uncontrollably, and for a second, I thought she had been injured. Even though I was aware we had been locked down, every scenario of someone somehow getting to her rushed through my mind all at the same time. I think I saw twenty ways she could have been hurt in less than ten seconds. My heart broke into a million pieces when Jason pointed out it was my fault she was so broken.

I hadn't even thought to check on her after the security system was checked. I thought Jason was with her, and she would be fine. It never even occurred to me that they had activated the alarm early, let alone that it meant she was probably alone. Jason is right; she has heard over and over again that someone wishes to kill me. It must have been terrifying to be in bed when the alarm sounded, waking up alone.

I'm a fucking idiot.

"How is she?"

I lift my head to see Maximus and Jason walking into

the room. I tuck in the blanket I placed around Jasmine as I look at her sleeping face.

"Worn out," I whisper as Maximus stands before me, looking down at the sleeping Jasmine.

"If she wasn't on your lap, I'd fucking kick your arse," he growls through gritted teeth, staring at me in a way that makes me wonder if he may be the one to kill me in the end. "She went through hell yesterday, as well as having to discuss her abuse with us. Then you leave her alone in bed, knowing full well there will be a lockdown drill. Are you completely stupid? Or just a heartless fuck?"

"Enough!" Jason snaps. "Us fighting is the last thing she needs right now," he warns, stepping between us. Not that he would hit me whilst I have Jasmine asleep in my arms.

Maximus and I continue to stare at each other for a moment before he moves away and takes his usual seat. Jason looks at the two of us for a moment before deciding it's safe to move. He sits in his spot, letting out a deep sigh.

"I need you to take control today," I say, looking at Jason. "We need copies of all security schedules and plans for all situations." I look down at Jasmine as she stirs slightly. "I'm not letting her out of my sight today. I think we both need a day together."

"Any events or meetings you want called off?" Jason asks. I know what he's referring to, and I open my mouth to say yes, but Jasmine chooses that moment to wake up.

"Not my hen party."

I look down to find her looking up at me.

"Or the wedding."

I open my mouth to argue that it may be for the best, but Jasmine sits up on my lap and looks me dead in the eye. "Don't even think about it because if you do, it's not other people you need to be scared of; it's me."

"Sweetheart, you have just been crying to the point you passed out from exhaustion. With everything you have been dealing with, you're physically and emotionally exhausted. If that's not a reason to ensure we all stay safe, then-"

"Stop." Her tone halts me mid-sentence. "I am not cancelling our wedding, the blessing, or my hen party. I refuse to let anyone think that I am still the weak little thing I was when I was kidnapped. I am going to be an O'Reilly, which means I back down to no one, including you."

"Jazzy-"

"No," she snaps, turning to look at Jason. "I will agree to having extra security or changing the plans to ensure we are safe, but I will not hide away and let them ruin this for us." She turns her attention back to me, and I see strength and power in her eyes as she stares deep into my soul. "We have worked so hard to have this happiness and to spend the rest of our lives married. I have spent my whole life with people taking everything from me, and I have had enough. They will not take the excitement and love we all deserve. I will be married to you all, and I dare anyone to try and stop me because they will fail, and that includes you too, Christian O'Reilly."

I look at her for a moment, and my heart swells with pride. Every time I think she couldn't make me prouder; she proves me wrong.

Threading my fingers into the hair at the back of her head, I kiss her hard, crushing her lips with mine. Jasmine kisses me back with just as much passion that when we finally separate, we are both short of breath.

"You are right, Sweetheart. You deserve this, and nobody will stop us from giving it to you." Looking away from my amazing fiancée, I find my brothers watching us, looking as proud of our girl as I am. "Get Layton and Terry in here, and we can ensure she is as safe as possible without ruining her plans."

Jason nods and pulls his phone out as I look deep into my girl's eyes again. I've been on edge about the hen party, especially with how everything ended on her twenty-first. But this time, we already had plenty of security in place. I think with a slight change of venue we will be able to ensure not only hers but everyone's safety.

Chapter Twenty-Six

JASMINE

"I swear my body has never been this relaxed," I hear Danielle sigh from somewhere within the hotel suite we are using to get ready. "We need to go back to that spa as soon as possible so I can have another full body massage."

"Is it the massage you want to go back for? Or that god, Manuel?" Abbi asks.

"Well, if one comes with the other, who am I to say no?" I hear Danielle reply as the girls laugh.

I try not to giggle whilst putting another layer of mascara on my eyelashes. Danielle, Verity and Abbi are all in the main room getting ready while I hide in here.

Giving my makeup one last check, I step back and look at my outfit. Running my hands over my tight white lace dress, which hugs every one of my curves perfectly. I want nothing more than to send a picture to the guys so they can see how sexy I look and feel. But part of me wants to tease them as well. I smile to myself, knowing precisely what Christian would say about that.

"You trying to top from the bottom again, Sweetheart?" Maybe I

am, and why not? As much as I love the guys taking control, I enjoy watching them squirm as I turn it back on them every now and again.

"Jaz, your phone is vibrating!" Verity calls. I give myself one last look in the mirror before walking out of the bathroom.

All three look at me and grin excitedly.

"Oh, Jaz, you look beautiful!" Abbie gushes as Verity fans her face whilst fluttering her eyelids.

"I'm going to ruin my eye makeup by crying!" she sniffs before rushing to me and throwing her arms around my neck. "You look like a real-life bride!"

"But a slutty one who knows how to get what she wants," Danielle teases as I look over Verity's shoulder. "And let's face it: you always get exactly what you want when it comes to the O'Reillys," she winks as Abbi and I laugh while Verity looks shocked.

"Danielle! Jaz does not look like a slut!" she exclaims before looking at me, "But she's not wrong about getting what you want," she smirks before stepping back. She hands me my phone, and I remember her saying it was vibrating. Just as I'm looking at the screen, seeing I have a missed call, Layton knocks on the door and enters with his hand over his eyes.

"You are safe; we are all dressed," I laugh as I pull up Christian's number.

"Better safe than sorry," Layton laughs. "Christian's trying to call you-" he stops when he sees my phone against my ear and me pointing to it. "Well, be sure to point out I still told you," he calls whilst walking out of the room.

"Hey, Sweetheart. You okay?" Christian answers. My heart races as it does every time one of them calls me terrified that something has happened to one of them. Even though they are sure all threats have been taken care of, I still can't help worrying.

"I'm fine. Are you?" I ask, trying to keep the worry from my face and voice.

"I'm okay, Sweetheart, but I have to go deal with something. So, I won't be there when you get back tonight, sorry." Disappointment courses through me. As much as I'm looking forward to tonight, I'm looking forward to the hot sex I have been promised afterwards. As much fun as I will have with the other three, it feels like Christian is missing more and more.

The guys have held back from anything sexual since my memories come back, but I have told them I'm ready and made a point of reminding them of that all day to be sure. I refuse for that psycho bitch to destroy another part of my life. I love sex; my four men make me feel amazing, and that is what I'm focusing on, nothing else.

"When will you be home?" I ask as I listen to Christian's car engine.

"It will only be the one night, I promise. I will be home before you know it tomorrow. This should be the last thing I need to do before the wedding. So you will have my undivided attention until we return from our honeymoon."

"Really?" I ask excitedly.

"Absolutely," I can hear the smile in his voice and find myself squealing excitedly. I don't think we have had more than a few days together without him having to leave for something work-related since we came home from the two weeks at the villa after I was kidnapped.

"I'll hold you to that," I tease as Christian laughs.

"I'm sure you will."

"Who's going with you if Terry is here?"

"Sean's doesn't have anything going on, so Mykela's

with me. Now go and enjoy your evening. I know Verity has put a lot of work into everything."

"I will. Be careful, Daddy, and message me when you get wherever you are going," I order. I hear Christian promise he will before telling me he loves me and ending the call.

For a moment, I hold the phone to my chest and smile, thinking of having him with me for two whole weeks.

"I hope he knows not to call again," Danielle warns with an arched brow when I walk back into the room.

"He just called to tell me he would be away for the night," I reply, placing my phone on the coffee table.

"Is he taking McIntire with him?"

I turn to Abbi and frown.

"He didn't mention anything, why?" I ask as she rolls her eyes and finishes her drink.

"Because that man is a pain in my arse! He's always sniffing around and telling me what to do and where to go. He had the nerve to tell me not to drink much today." She makes a point of filling her wine glass to the brim before taking a big sip. "As if I wasn't going to drink at your hen party."

"Is that why you're on a mission to drink as much as possible?" Danielle laughs as Verity and I share a look.

Abbi has been drinking a lot today. She was started from lunch onwards, even at the health spa, where we spent the better half of the day. It wouldn't have surprised me if she had a few drinks before lunch as she kept sneaking to the changing rooms.

"Hey, I'm just enjoying myself. It's not every day you get to enjoy a wedding like Jasmine's." She declares, grinning at me before taking another deep drink.

"Can you believe it's only a week until the wedding?" I

turn to see Verity grinning at me. "I swear it feels like we started planning everything only yesterday," she adds, filling two glasses.

"Tell me about it," I laugh, taking a glass of champagne from her. "Who would have guessed at the start of this year, the two of us would be in happy, committed relationships with multiple guys," I laugh as we clink glasses.

"Or friends with me," Danielle smiles sheepishly.

"Yeah, I didn't expect that at all!" I laugh as I toast with her. "Nor would I have met you," I add, quickly tapping my glass against Abbi's. "Which brings me to something I need to ask you."

Abbi looks at me nervously.

"What?"

Smiling, I place my glass on the table and turn my full attention to my friend.

"I understand why you pulled out of being a bridesmaid, and I don't want you to feel pressured into anything. Losing your dad the way you did was heartbreaking."

"Why do I feel like there is a *but* on the way?" she asks, looking at the three of us, her eyes wide with worry.

"*But*, I wanted to let you know that the offer is still there if you have changed your mind. I completely understand if you still don't want to, but I wanted you to know that I would still love you by my side if you wanted to be."

Her eyes instantly fill with tears.

"Oh, Jaz, I would. I've regretted pulling out but thought it was too late. You get married in a week, and I don't even have a dress."

"Yes, you do," I answer, passing her glass to Verity so I can take Abbi's hands in mine. "I never cancelled the order; it is still at the shop and ready for you to try on. They will alter it for you the same day we go for the final fittings, and it will be ready for the wedding."

Tears slip through her lashes as she stares at me with a hand over her mouth.

"Are you serious?"

I nod through my own tears whilst smiling.

"Absolutely. You have still been with us every step of the way, and I can't imagine you not standing with these two when I marry my men."

Abbi squeals before throwing her arms around my neck. I hug her back, desperately trying not to cry.

"Thank you, Jaz."

"Don't ruin your makeup!" Danielle laughs behind me. Abbi and I step apart, grabbing tissues from Verity as she waves them at us, giggling as we dab under our eyes.

"I'm so happy right now!" Verity giggles excitedly as she throws her arms around Abbi, who hugs her back. Considering they only met one other time before tonight, they instantly became friends. Danielle and Abbi have known each other for years, thanks to their fathers knowing each other, but they never really talked before we started planning the wedding.

Looking around the room at my three bridesmaids, I realise just how much my life has changed for the better since the O'Reillys made me theirs and as much as I love them for saving me, I love the strength they have given me as well. I would never have had the guts to stand up for myself against Danielle or anyone before them. There really is nothing in this world that would make me give up those four men.

I go to pick up my phone, feeling the need to tell them how much I love them, but Danielle grabs it and places it in her bag.

"That is being confiscated for the night. You can have it when we are on our way home," she declares. Abbi laughs a little too loudly next to her, making me wonder just how much she has had to drink today.

"You know they will freak if they can't get hold of me," I point out.

"They already know you won't have it. None of us will."

"What?" I ask, confused. Danielle smiles at me before turning to Verity.

"You and Christian worked out the rules, so you can explain."

Verity smiles as she turns her attention to me.

"Because the O'Reillys have upped security, there have been a few changes to tonight. But don't panic. I ensured they were all good and wouldn't impact the amazing time we will have."

Taking a deep breath, I sit on the edge of the sofa and try to prepare myself.

"Okay, hit me with them."

"Okay, so rule number one, which you already know, is no social media." I nod, as we had all promised not to share our locations today in case my socials were being watched.

"Rule number two: no phones. I don't think you've noticed, but we haven't had our phones all day, only you. Tonight, no one other than Layton and two other security guards will have their phones. Everyone's meeting us at the club and has already agreed, and we have told them it's due to publicity and the O'Reillys having designated photographers there, which they have organised. Luckily, Layton's sister took photography in college and still does it on the side. So, all moments are still going to be captured."

I look at Danielle, who lives on her phone. She rolls her eyes, shaking her head, and I can't help but laugh.

"FYI, I don't like that rule. But I will do it for you," she sighs, sipping her drink, but I don't miss how one side of her mouth lifts.

"Rule three," Verity announces, returning my attention to her. "The venues for tonight have changed, and no one is to know where until they arrive." I'm not even surprised by that one.

"Let me guess, it's one of their clubs, which they closed for the night to ensure they can control who goes in and out of it."

"Ding. Ding. Ding. We have a winner!" Danielle announces loudly as the rest of us laugh.

"Yes, even I don't know where it is. All I know is a chef is there to make our food for tonight, as well as bar staff, waiters and plenty of security."

"So, how does everyone know where to go if you don't even know?" I ask, frowning. Nearly all the other dancers from the school and a few people who work backstage and costumes are coming.

"I have been busy organising pick-up times from people's houses the last three days. Security is helping to pick people up and deliver them to the club. They also know to hand their phones over to security if they feel the need to bring them. They will all be searched before getting into the cars, so they don't try to sneak any phones in. They have all agreed and know that if they don't comply, then they will be removed."

"Which none of them want because they know they are having a night in an O'Reilly club with a free bar!" Danielle smiles, turning to Abbie as they tap their glasses together.

"I'm sorry you all had to go to so much trouble." I look around at my friends before focusing purely on Verity. "You have so much going on, and you have still organised all of this for me."

"You deserve this, Jaz, more than anyone we know. Your men agree, which is why it's been worth every moment of stress. Plus, it was nice to have something different to focus on." I can only imagine what's been going through her head with everything. I'm about to tell her how much I love her when there is a knock at the door.

"Ten-minute warning, ladies!" Layton calls as he pokes his head through the door.

"Shit! We still need to do the finishing touches!" Danielle snaps as the girls all jump to their feet.

"What do you mean by finishing touches?" I ask, looking around, worried about what they plan next.

"I'll get the stuff!" Verity calls, rushing towards the room where she had got ready.

"I need to pack," I quickly announce, hoping to get out of whatever they have planned.

"Oh no, you don't. The three of us are already packed, and Jason's coming to get your bits, as he knows what is yours better than anyone," Dani smiles.

"Only because he bought it all for me," I laugh. Other than the outfit Verity chose, Jason bought me everything I own, including my makeup and hair accessories.

"Spoilt brat," Danielle winks. I shrug whilst sipping my drink.

"They love it when I'm a brat," I tease as she rolls her eyes and Abbi giggles.

"Oh, I want someone to be a brat for. Eddie isn't into that at all."

My head snaps up as Danielle stares at her too.

"Who?" I ask as Abbi starts chewing on her bottom lip.

"No one, just a hookup." I can tell she's lying, but as I

open my mouth to push further, Verity comes back into the room with something white hanging over her arm.

"Turn around," Danielle demands, grabbing my arms and forcing me to do what I'm told. I feel something slide into my hair and realise what it is.

"Damn it, I thought I had gotten away without having to wear one of these," I laugh.

"Not a chance, you have to wear one, it's the law," she winks as something goes over my head.

"And a sash? Really?"

"Yes, I'm the maid of honour, and I say you have to wear one," Verity declares behind me before walking into view. She moves in front of me and adjusts the sash.

"Oh, Jaz, you look amazing. Here." She shoves a champagne flute into my hand, and the girls all step back and start clapping their hands excitedly. "Quick, get a pic to send to the guys!" Verity says, pointing to Danielle's bag.

"Fine, but only because they will probably turn up if we don't." She pulls out my phone and unlocks it before holding it up. I quickly pose and have fun as she takes a couple of pics before I help her send them to the group the guys and I have.

"Now that's all done. It's time to get this party on the road!" she announces as we all clink glasses and start laughing before finishing our drinks and heading for the door to enjoy the night ahead.

Chapter Twenty-Seven

JASON

Walking into the house, I rub my tired, aching shoulders.

It's been a week since Christian and I beat the shit out of each other, and everything still hurts. Sure, the swelling and bruising is slowly fading, but not as much as I would have liked. The two of us still avoid seeing people, so they don't ask questions. At least we can laugh about it now, well, most of the time. It depends on Christian's behaviour and whether he's snapping at the rest of us.

"You okay now, boss?"

I turn to Gordon and nod.

"Yeah, you turn in for the night. I'll see you Monday." Gordon nods once, disappearing out the back door to grab his car and head home. After spending seven hours stuck with me in a CCTV office, I'm not surprised he ran to get away.

Walking to the fridge, I pull out a beer and drink it in one go. I need to relax and unwind, but I won't do that until Jasmine's home safely.

"Any problems?"

The twins walk into the kitchen, each wearing only a pair of sweatpants. I know they have spent much of this evening at the gym with Ryan, and another fighter Sean is considering possibly signing. He's taking his new role seriously, but that doesn't surprise me. He's always been the brains of the duo, whereas Maximus has been the muscles.

"Nope. She had a great day and hasn't stopped laughing or dancing all night," I reply, smiling to myself as I remember how she spent the whole night on the dance floor with her friends. "It was like she didn't have a care in the world."

"That's such a relief. I was sure something would play on her mind, and she'd miss out on enjoying her day."

I look at Sean and nod. We'd all been worried about it, especially once Christian got called away. I know he would have let her know. But from what I saw in the CCTV room at the club, she didn't let it get her down. Reaching into the fridge, I pull out another bottle of beer and offer one to each of the twins, who take them with a 'thanks'.

"When will she be home?" Maximus asks as he takes a drink.

"Any minute. She's the only one left in the car," I answer. "I followed them until they dropped off the last dancer, then overtook them so I could beat her back. She has no idea I've been following her all day." I didn't think I would get away with it, especially when Verity spotted me at the spa, but she winked when I placed a finger over my lips, and they carried on as if I wasn't there.

"Any word from Christian?" I ask, leaning back against the counter. Both twins shake their heads.

"I'm not expecting to hear from him until tomorrow. He seemed pissed and ready for blood when he stormed out of here," Sean answers, shaking his head. "His temper is starting to get the better of him," he adds, sharing a look with his twin before they both look at me.

"I know," I sigh, rubbing my forehead in an attempt to relax. "He is trying, but he has always done things in his way. He has asked me to deal with a few things, though."

"It's a start, at least," Maximus sighs. "I just wish he would stop taking his shit out on us."

"It's not like you are helping with how you speak to him," Sean adds with raised brows.

"I only speak to him like he speaks to me," Maximus snaps defensively.

"You are both as bad as each other, and you know it. It's always been the same with you two," I sigh as Maximus stares at me, unable to argue.

Maximus and Christian are the most alike out of us all, and it shows by the way they collide at times. I don't think Maximus has completely forgiven Christian for stopping him from going to Jasmine that night or for the fact he has been putting her in danger by not telling us what's been going on. He was livid when he heard about her reaction to the security drill. He's always been extra protective of Jasmine, but he's even worse after hearing about what she remembered from her childhood. We are all very protective of our future wife. But Maximus seems to be trying to protect her from the rest of us, and it's causing a few arguments.

"Do you think he's tracked down Carol's old suppliers?" Sean asks nervously. From the second he woke up the morning after Jaz told us all she'd remembered, he's been in contact with some dodgy ass bastards, asking around about who used to supply her and who was known for having a liking for kids. I have seen a couple of email exchanges on his anonymous email account with information about possible suspects.

"If he has, then I don't think they will be around much longer," I answer, not wanting to say anymore. Sure, we would all like to have a minute with the arseholes, but at this point, we just need them dead and buried so Jaz never has to worry about them ever again.

My phone pings in my pocket, and I know it's the security system telling me there is activity on the driveway.

"She's back," I announce as I watch the limo pull up outside on my screen. Placing my phone and bottle on the side, I head towards the front door with my brothers, eager to see our girl and hear all about her day.

Opening the front door, I watch as Terry climbs out of the front passenger seat, still obviously in a lot of pain from his injuries. We've tried to get him to rest, but knowing that Jasmine is possibly being watched, he's taken it upon himself to be her protection alongside Layton.

"Now that's all finished with. Will you do as you are told and rest tomorrow, knowing we will all be home?" I ask, approaching the car. Terry looks at me and smirks.

"I'll relax once your brother is back. I have a bottle of painkillers and a bed with my name on it ready for his return." Terry isn't used to taking a back seat when it comes to Christian, but they decided that Terry would stay with Jasmine today, and Mykela went with Christian.

I shake my head before walking to the back of the car, where Maximus is holding the door open for Jasmine who climbs out looking radiant in her white dress.

"Princess, you look truly breathtaking," Sean gushes as he takes her hand and kisses her knuckles.

"White certainly suits you, Shorty," Maximus adds as he

pulls her towards him before tipping her back to kiss her. Jasmine yelps before laughing as Maximus rights her again.

"You are both biased." She slaps him on the chest before turning her attention to me. "How do you like my dress? I half expected you to charge onto the dance floor when it kept riding up."

I stare at her for a moment before smiling. Of course, she knew I was watching. She is more observant than we give her credit for.

"How would I have known to charge anywhere?" I tease.

Jasmine walks to me with a swagger in her step. She stops when her body is flush with mine. Taking the collar of my shirt, she started playing with it whilst giving me her come-to-bed eyes.

"I know you've been watching me all day. You aren't as sneaky as you like to think, Daddy."

"Oh really? Tell me, Angel. How did you know I was watching you and not someone else?" I ask, brushing my lips gently across hers as my hand rests on her ass.

"Because I know you. I can feel when you are close, and I know which one of you it is without even seeing your faces," she whispers against my lips.

"I think we need to put that to the test." Without warning, I lift her off her feet and carry her into the house as she laughs in my arms. "We need all three of us to test this theory properly." I look at my brothers, walking behind me, smiling at Jasmine.

"I'm more than happy to see how you plan on testing *this* theory," Sean laughs behind us.

"You are always more than happy to go along with anything if it includes sex," Jasmine laughs in my arms as I carry her through the house.

"Only if that sex is with you, Princess," he answers.

"Right answer," she teases before looking back at me. Her arms are around my neck as I carry her up the stairs. "Just a heads up, you may want to take your time taking the dress off. I may have ordered something a little special."

I stop in the middle and look down at the amazing, beautiful woman in my arms as she chews on her bottom lip seductively.

"How special?"

"You will have to undress me to find out." The wink she gives us at the end is enough to have my brothers and me cursing as we speed up, heading straight for her room.

Placing Jasmine on her feet, I step back and take in how beautiful she looks.

She's wearing a beautiful white lace dress, which hugs her body like she was stitched into it. It stops mid-thigh, where her long legs look perfect in what I can guess are stockings. On her feet, she has beautiful white shoes with a thin stiletto heel at least five inches high. Jasmine is tall even when in trainers, but with her heels, she is almost the same height as us. I might have spent the whole day watching her every move, but now I can admire her up close; she is even more breathtaking.

Maximus steps forward, taking her hand and holding it up.

"Turn around, Shorty. Let us see the whole look."

Jasmine's cheeks become flushed as she smiles, almost sheepishly, before doing as asked. The three of us stare in awe as she turns slowly.

"You are beautiful beyond words every single day, Princess. But tonight, you are truly taking my breath away." Sean steps up as Maximus lets go of her hand. He threads his fingers into the hair at the back of her head, under the veil she is still wearing and kisses her. Jasmine's hands land on his bare chest, and I turn away to give them a second. I'm already making a plan for how tonight is going to go.

Stepping into her wardrobe, I look for a silk scarf I bought for her a few months ago. Luckily, I find it easily, as things could go either way when looking for something of Jasmine's. With her technically having five rooms, she has things in each of them. But this is her main wardrobe where her washing goes.

Walking back into the bedroom with the scarf in my hand, I find Jasmine giggling in Maximus's arms as he whispers something in her ear. From the look on his face, I can only imagine he's teasing her in a way only he can. Jasmine spots me as I move closer, her eyes falling on the scarf in my hands.

"Are you going to tie me up, Daddy?" she asks, her eyes sparkling with eagerness. I shake my head as I stop in front of her. Maximus steps back with a grin.

"As you seem so sure you can tell us apart without seeing us, I thought we could see how accurate your guesses are." Folding the scarf width ways, and then again, I hold it up for her to see.

"I'm going to blindfold you, and the three of us are going to take turns to pleasure you, and you have to see if you can tell who it is."

"Sounds easy enough," she smirks.

"But there will be rewards and consequences if you are right or wrong," I warn. Jasmine doesn't even look phased by this. In fact, she's looking very confident.

"What do I get when I'm right?"

"*If* you are right, we will let you come," I answer, walking behind her slowly. I can see her itching to turn around with me. The way her breasts seem to enlarge as she takes a deep breath signals how excited she is. I know if I reached between her legs now, I would find her soaking wet and ready for us.

"Do you want to know what will happen if you get it wrong?" I ask, gently running a finger over her bare shoulder and down her arm, not missing how her breath catches.

"I won't." I don't think I have ever seen her so confident. There isn't a single doubt in her mind, but she doesn't know that I plan on confusing her, making sure she gets it wrong at least once.

"We will have to see, won't we," I tease, kissing her shoulder gently. Her whole body quivers to the point I'm sure her legs will go from beneath her. But she stays standing as I stand back.

"What are your new safe words, Princess?" Sean asks, looking a little concerned.

"Red, orange and green. Red to stop, orange to ease off and green for everything's fine."

Maximus steps up until he's close enough to cup her cheek. "If it gets too much, you have to tell us. You know everything happens at your pace."

Jasmine nods before leaning into his hand.

"I'm fine, Daddy. I want you, all of you."

We have all been on edge after she remembered her past, but as always, she has gone from strength to strength, proving once again how unbelievably strong she is.

Jasmine has asked that we try not to treat her differently, as it reminds her of why we are being cautious. Jasmine has always been in control of what we do, and even when she is in full subspace, one word and everything stops. This will be no different; if anything, we will check in with her more than usual, simply asking for her colour.

Maximus looks over her shoulder at me and nods, giving me the go-ahead. Stepping forward, I place the blindfold over her eyes and tie it behind the veil.

"I'm leaving this in place," I whisper into her ear. "By the time we are finished with you, the only thing left on your body will be this scarf and veil." This time, when I run my finger lightly over her smooth skin, I slide them towards the zipper at the side of her dress. "Shall we let your other Daddy know what's happening? I'm sure he would love to watch via the security cameras if he's free." A heavenly sigh leaves her as she nods. I kiss her cheek before looking at Sean and giving him the sign to call Christian. Pulling his phone from his pocket, it rings around the quiet room before Christian answers.

"I'm here. But I don't know how long for." The sound of his voice tells me he's been watching since we came up here.

"You got the camera in Jazzy's room up?" I ask.

"I do. But you will have to fill me in on the details I missed."

"Shorty is convinced she can tell us all apart without seeing us. She's so confident that she has agreed for us to blindfold her." Maximus is smiling and seems more relaxed now that he has confirmed to himself that Jasmine is okay with all of this.

"And if she gets it wrong?" Christian asks.

"We edge her for three minutes," Sean answers.

"I will not get anything wrong. I know each of you without having to think about it." She looks up at the camera with a sexy smirk on her face. "Just like I know Daddy will be sitting somewhere, probably a couch, with the laptop on the coffee table in front of him, a glass of bourbon in his hand as he leans his elbows on his knees. His tie will be in his pocket, top shirt buttons undone, sleeves rolled up, and he's already hard." She continues to smile at the camera as Christian clears his throat.

"Is she right?" I ask, smiling at my brothers.

"Yes."

Jasmine looks very proud of herself as well as a little smug. Maybe she does know us better than we realised. That doesn't mean we can't have some fun trying to trick her.

I step back and walk over to my brothers. The three of us standing in front of our girl.

"Can you tell us what order we are standing in?" Sean asks as the three of us stand in a row.

"Daddy Jason, Daddy Max and Daddy Sean," she answers, not even thinking about it.

"Correct," I reply before the three of us move again. This time, I don't even have time to ask the question.

"Daddy Max, Daddy Jason and Daddy Sean."

"She's tracking us," Maximus whispers out the side of his mouth.

"Correct. But let's make it a little harder." I share a smile with my brothers before continuing. "Turn around and face the wall." I might not be able to see her eyes, but I know she just rolled them at me. "Without the attitude, Jazzy," I warn, hoping I get to discipline her a little. It always makes it more fun when she's a brat. I think that's why she and Maximus have so much fun together. I sometimes find myself getting jealous of the way she becomes a complete brat for him.

The three of us start moving positions, purposely swapping and changing a few extra times to ensure she wouldn't have been able to track the sound of feet.

"What order are we in, Princess?" Sean asks, looking confident that she will get it wrong.

"Daddy Maximus, Daddy Sean and Daddy Jason."

"Right again," Christian laughs through the phone. It's time to make this a little harder, I think. I beckon my brothers closer so I can whisper to them.

"One of you go up and get her out of that dress. Don't say a word and see who she thinks it is." The two of them grin at me. The three of us share a look, and Sean slowly creeps up behind her. He slowly takes hold of the zip and starts sliding it down before helping the dress slowly slide from her body. Watching from behind, I'm mesmerised. Everything about this woman is exquisite.

"Daddy Sean," she gasps as his lips brush the skin on her shoulder.

"Correct, Princess," he smirks against her skin as he continues to kiss her skin while the dress falls to the floor.

"Fuck," Maximus and Christian curse at the same time.

I know every set I have ever gifted her. I have to go shopping regularly as my brothers seem to have a thing for ripping her underwear from her body. I rarely buy her white, but after seeing this set on her, I realise that's going to change.

Sean steps away from Jasmine as he holds her hand and encourages her to turn around, ensuring we see the full effect of the white lace bra, thong and suspenders, which hold up the thinnest of stockings.

"Sweetheart do not let anyone rip that set from you. I need to see this in the flesh," Christian's voice comes through the phone. I look over my shoulder to where the camera is and smile. I have no doubt *he* will rip them from her in seconds the moment she stands in front of him in nothing but them.

"Turn her back around," Maximus orders his twin, unable to take his eyes from the goddess before us. Sean nods and ensures her back is to us again. With his eyes set on what he wants, Maximus steps forward and stops inches from her before reaching out and unfastening her bra in one flick of his fingers. A laugh bursts from Jasmine as she slams her hand over her mouth.

"Something funny?" I ask. Jasmine shakes her head, but I can see she's trying desperately not to laugh. "Spill it, Angel."

"I thought you were going to make this difficult?" She turns her head so she is grinning at Maximus. "No one can unclip a bra like Daddy Max." Maximus grabs her face and slams his lips into her, catching her off guard as he devours her mouth. I don't miss how he has to hold her up as he pulls away from her sharply.

"Time to make it harder then," he growls before releasing her and stepping back. "On your knees, Shorty." He takes hold of her elbow as she lowers herself to the floor in nothing but her shoes, thong, suspenders, stockings, blindfold, and veil. Yeah, that's too many items and needs rectifying.

As soon as he's confident she isn't in danger of toppling over, Maximus walks over to Sean and me, grinning.

"Let's see how well she knows our cocks."

"Time to find out how well you know your favourite part of us," I laugh as the three of us walk around each other a few times before stopping in a line in front of her. "If you get all three right, you get your first orgasm," I add, remembering we haven't done anything to her yet. I bet she is soaking that thong; I can tell just from the way her chest swells with each breath she takes. Her cheeks are flushed with arousal. The need to touch her overcomes me; I know it will take all my effort not to do more when I stand before her.

Sean steps forward, his already hard cock in his hand. His eyes close as he swipes the head against her lips before she takes him in deep straight away. Jasmine smirks around his cock, and I'm sure she has guessed who it is. Sean reaches out to grab her hair like he always does when she sucks him off, but he manages to stop himself at the last second. I know he won't be able to stay in control for long as he's already pumping into her mouth, taking control of her the way he always does in their relationship. He's a natural Dom, and Jasmine loves being his sub.

Sean pulls out of her mouth before he comes down her throat, which would ultimately end the game far too quickly. We all want to keep this going for as long as possible. Let's face it: Jasmine is wild at the best of times, but when she has had a drink, she's feral.

"Who was that, Sweetheart?" Christian asks as Jasmine looks toward the camera or at least tries to. She's gotten herself turned around and no longer knows which way she's facing.

"Daddy Sean," she answers, turning back to Sean, who is still standing in front of her, grinning. He thrusts his fingers into her hair and kisses her.

"Correct again, Princess." He continues to kiss her as I move up behind him, desperate for my turn with our girl. I want to tell him to move, but she will know it's me if I speak. Sean eventually releases her and steps back, giving me a playful wink.

Closing the distance between us, she lifts her head as if to look at me, and it takes everything in me not to tell her how much I love the sight of her on her knees with that veil hanging from her hair. I really hope she is wearing one on our wedding day because I plan on fucking her in it and nothing else. At least there's only a week until I can hopefully make that a reality.

Taking my hardening cock in my hand, I do as Sean did and run it over her lips before pushing inside of her mouth. Biting my lip, I close my eyes and force myself to control my breathing so I'm not giving my identity away. However, as I start pulling in and out of her mouth, I look down and see her smirking. Damn it, she knows it's me. I can tell by how she reaches for my hip and traces the angel wings I have tattooed with her name under them. It's a reasonably old tattoo, so she won't be able to feel the difference in the skin. She pulls backwards, letting my now rock-hard cock drop from her mouth as she grins up at me.

"Did you really think I wouldn't know it was you, Daddy Jason?"

"How do you know you're right?" Christian asks through the loudspeaker. Jasmine looks over her shoulder, aiming for the camera.

"Because I know my men, and each of you has a different taste. You might all be around the same size but also feel different." She looks up at me and grins. "You won't be able to trick me like this. Even blindfolded, I know who you are just by being close to you; your cocks and taste are just further confirmations."

Without warning, I grab her under the arms and pull her to her feet. She wobbles slightly on her heels, but I don't give her time to recover as I lift her onto the bed. Leaning over her, purposely nudging her entrance with my cock, I kiss her hard, desperate to taste her mouth before tasting her elsewhere.

"Time for your first reward," I grin against her lips before lifting off her and joining my brothers. Looking at

Maximus, I nod towards Jasmine, who is lying on her back, her ass barely on the mattress.

"I need to make her come," Maximus almost begs, looking to the bed, watching Jasmine as she smiles and waits, her legs open, leaving very little to the imagination as her white lace thong is wet and almost see-through.

"Feel free, but I have a plan which may confuse her a little," Sean says, grinning at his twin. I listen to him as he gives us the details, and there is a chance this might actually work. If any of us are going to try it, they are the best to attempt it.

Maximus walks over to Jasmine and goes to rip her thong from her.

"Do not rip it!" Christian warns through the phone. Maximus flips the camera off but pulls the thong off instead, making a point of holding it up for the camera to show it's still in one piece. This little shit is determined to get a reaction from Christian.

Maximus steps back, and Sean gets into position on the floor. Once settled, he gives Maximus the nod, and I walk away from the bed to sit in the chair and watch for now.

Sean reaches up from the floor and starts to rub Jazmine's plump pussy. It's glistening from her arousal, and I watch as it contracts slightly from Sean's touch. Jasmine's back arches as he slowly pushes one finger into her opening before adding a second a few seconds later.

"Daddy," she gasps as she starts riding his hand.

"Which one?" Christian chuckles.

"Sean," she gasps as he brings her closer to the edge. As another slightly louder moan leaves her, Maximus drops to his knees and thrusts his face between her legs.

"Yes!" She cries out, grabbing the back of his head and keeping him there. For a few minutes, I watch, stroking myself, as Jasmine starts to lose control and screams through her first orgasm of the night. The guys don't let up, though and quickly coax her through a second. Before her second has finished, I signal them to move quickly. The second they release her, I flip Jasmine onto her stomach, tuck her legs underneath her, forcing her ass in the air. I part her ass cheeks and start rimming her sweet ass. Desperate to make her come once more.

"Oh god, yes! Daddy Jason, don't stop!" she starts humping the bed whilst rocking her hips as I lick her asshole over and over again. As predicted, she's wild tonight, thanks to the drinks she's sipped all day. As she pushes her hips down, I slide a finger into her soaking wet pussy at the same time as the tip of another enters her ass.

The scream that leaves her is almost too much. She loves both holes being penetrated, and I know she gets it from all four of us.

She orgasms for a third time tonight, and I know she's reached her foreplay limit. Her whole body shakes as she tries to pull away from me, but I leave my fingers in both her holes for a little longer, enjoying the way it feels as her orgasm threatens to cut off circulation as she squeezes them so tight.

"Red!" she calls, signalling she needs a break. I grin as I stand from her, and Sean places a blanket over her naked, shivering body.

"You okay, Angel?" I ask, lying beside her for a moment, needing to catch my breath.

"You are all going to be the death of me," she gasps, but when she looks up at me, I see a big grin. "I know what you tried to do, but it didn't work."

"What did we try, Shorty?" Maximus asks, lying on the other side of her, placing an arm over her stomach and kissing her shoulder. She turns her head to the side and grins.

"It was Daddy Sean's fingers and your tongue to start with." Her attention turns to me, and I smile.

"But you were all over my ass, Daddy Jason." Leaning in, I press a kiss to her lips, and as much as I want to roll her so I'm able to slide my aching cock into her tight little pussy, I know I need to give her time.

A noise sounds from the phone, and we all turn to look at it as we hear mumbled voices. It sounds like Christian has placed his hand over the phone to muffle them.

"I need to go. I'll be home tomorrow afternoon, Sweetheart."

"Okay, Daddy. I love you," she calls out, lifting her head and trying to work out where to look for the camera.

"I love you too." The line goes dead, and I share a look with my brothers. It's gone one in the morning; there is no reason for him to be called away at this hour. The twins look as confused as I am, and I'm thankful that Jasmine is still blindfolded so she can't see the concern on our faces. I look down and find she's no longer smiling as she was a moment ago.

Reaching round, I untie the blindfold and slowly remove it from her eyes. Blinking a few times as she adjusts to the light, she looks around at the three of us and smiles.

"Hi," she grins at me. Leaning in, I press a kiss on her lips and thread my fingers into her hair.

"So, it seems you were right. You know your men."

Jasmine smiles as she throws her leg over me and straddles my hips. Rocking her hips ever so slightly, spreading her juices all over my aching cock.

"I know how each of you kiss." Leaning down, she grins whilst kissing me and changing positions slightly. Grinding her hips into mine, I realise she's positioning my cock just the way she needs it.

"I know how each of you feels as you fill me." Slowly, she lowers herself onto my cock and takes it all. I breathe in through my teeth as I feel her bottoming out, but she just smiles at me with that devious look in her eyes.

"I know exactly how you like me to fuck myself with your cock." Placing my hands on her hips, I let her take control as she turns her attention to Maximus.

"I know how Daddy Max is desperate to fuck my ass. But he is waiting for me to give him the nod." She nods once with a big grin, and Maximus curses as he jumps from the bed and quickly makes her curse as he fills her with his finger. He slaps her ass with his free hand, causing her to moan, which vibrates through her to my cock.

"Language, Shorty. Don't get too cocky." I catch him rubbing some of her juices onto her back entrance before slowly pushing himself into her ass.

"Yes," she cries, as he fills her completely. I can feel him filling her as she falls forward, burying her face into my neck. She moans deeply as she adjusts to being filled by the two of us. Wrapping my arms around her, I pepper her with kisses and whisper into her ear.

"Good girl, Angel. That's it, take us both. You're such a good girl for your daddies." As I expected, her body relaxes and she starts moving slightly now she's used to us both.

"That's it, Shorty. Use us to get yourself off. You feel so fucking good."

Our girl loves nothing as much as our praise, which we are happy to dish out.

"Daddy." She looks to Sean who moves so he's by my head. "No one can fuck my throat like you." Glancing up, I see a massive grin on Sean's face as he grabs the back of her head and kisses her hard on the mouth.

"No one can suck my cock the way you do," he winks before lifting up on his knees, tightening his hold on her hair and pulling her mouth down on his cock. She lets out a deep moan, and all three of us curse together, each feeling different parts of her vibrate.

Gripping her hip tight, I start lifting my hips to meet hers, Maximus and I follow her lead as we get into a rhythm to ensure we both give our girl the most pleasure possible. Together, the three of us quickly have her moaning through her fourth orgasm of the night; her legs and arms are starting to shake as she starts to tire from her long day and us pushing her a little hard when she got home.

"Colour?" I hear Sean ask as he withdraws himself from her mouth.

"Green … for now." She's tiring fast, and I have no problem stopping, but she smiles at me before looking around at my brothers, who have both stopped and are watching her carefully. "I want each of you to fill me with your cum, making me yours and marking me on the inside as well as out."

Again, the three of us curse under our breath as Jasmine starts taking the lead again, rocking her hips so she's able to get pleasure from Maximus and me. My eyes are closed when I hear her choke slightly, and I know that Sean will be fucking her throat.

Knowing we don't have to hold back anymore, it doesn't take long for Sean and Maximus to find their release. As they move back, giving Jasmine and me a little space, I hold her hips in place and start to lose control. Rolling us so she is underneath me, I get her legs over my shoulders and fuck her hard and fast. I can feel every inch inside of her and listen as she cries out for me not to stop. The first signs of her orgasm are as she spasms around me; I let out a deep roar as I do just as she asked and pump her full of my cum. Her greedy pussy milks me of every last drop, and I don't release her legs until we are both completely spent.

Rolling onto my side, I hold her against my chest as we both gasp for breath and cling to each other like we are never going to let go.

"Open your legs, Princess."

Opening my eyes, I look down at her body to see Sean cleaning her up with a warm cloth, like we always do after we make a mess of her. He dries her off with a towel, and I keep her in my arms as I stand so Maximus can fold down the covers. Laying Jasmine on the sheet, she slides across to the middle of the bed as I pull on my boxers. Maximus walks around to the other side of the bed and holds out a water bottle. He watches over her to ensure she drinks enough before placing it on the nightstand beside the bed.

As I climb into bed beside her, I watch the twins as they do their usual 'rock, paper, scissors' to determine who will be beside Jasmine. They used to try that shit with me, but I beat them every single time, as neither of them have picked up on their tells yet.

"Ha!" Sean laughs as he climbs into bed next to Jasmine, and Maximus gets in beside him.

"Do you think they will ever grow up?" Jasmine asks, looking up at me as she rests her head against my chest. I place one arm behind my head and one around her.

"We've given up hope. If it hasn't happened yet, I don't think it ever will." Jaz lets out a sigh as her eyes drift closed, her body giving in to the exhaustion.

"I'm going to have one baby but three kids eventually, aren't I?"

I laugh, pressing a kiss to the top of her head. "More than likely."

"Hey, don't forget if the dad is a twin, there's a higher chance of the babies being twins," Sean points out. Jasmine's eyes open as she looks up at me, asking for help with her eyes. I laugh, placing another kiss on her head, and hit Sean playfully.

"When we decide to start trying, can you make them wear condoms? I don't want twins."

"Angel, Christian and I could also have the twin gene as our brothers are twins, and so were our mum's brothers."

"I've changed my mind; I don't want kids," she mumbles as she starts drifting off again.

"I'll let you tell Christian, then," I tease as the twins chuckle.

"No, thank you. You can do it."

I'm sure that's what she thinks she said, but it's come out a little mumbled, thanks to the fact she is almost asleep.

"Sweet dreams, Princess," Sean whispers. He presses a kiss to the top of her head, and he lies down, holding her from behind. Maximus turns the lights off, and in minutes, I can hear the three of them breathing in sync as they sleep soundly.

Closing my eyes, I let myself picture Jasmine with a swollen belly, our baby, or babies, growing inside her. I can't wait for the day we get to watch her grow and become the amazing mum we know she will be. Because we might not have had the greatest parents growing up, but the five of us know that we will never turn out like them. There is nothing in this world we wouldn't do for our wife and future kids. God help anyone who tries to hurt them because it will be the last thing they ever do.

Chapter Twenty-Eight

CHRISTIAN

This is pure torture, watching my girl fall apart as my brothers pleasure her over and over again. I want to be there with them. I want to be between my girl's legs as she comes on my cock, fingers or tongue; I want to feel what they're feeling.

Sipping my drink, I hear a knock on the office door. Shutting down the video feed on my laptop, I call out for them to come in as I place a hand over the phone, hoping it's enough to distort what I expect to hear.

One of the security guards, Mykela, walks in; she looks unrecognisable, which is what I needed. She's in a pencil skirt and white blouse, with her hair twisted into a smart updo. Looking every part the secretary she has been playing.

"Mr O'Reilly, they are all downstairs."

"Thank you. Wait outside."

She nods once and slips back out of the office.

"I need to go. I'll be home tomorrow afternoon, Sweetheart," I say into the phone, hoping no one asks any questions. I know they would if they weren't distracted by Jasmine. I hear her call out that she loves me, which stops me in my tracks.

"I love you too," I reply, ending the call before anyone can say anymore.

Standing from the sofa, I reposition my aching hard-on. One thought of who I'm about to face, and my dick softens quicker than it's ever managed before.

Grabbing some leather gloves, I had at the ready. I push them into my trouser pocket and head for the door.

As expected, Mykela and Justin are standing outside the door waiting for me. Justin looks the complete opposite of Mykela's sophisticated look. He is in ripped jeans and an oversized hoodie and seems a little rough around the edges. Both are dressed for the roles they have been playing this evening.

"How many did you find?" I ask as they fall into step beside me.

"Six out of seven, sir. One died two months ago," Mykela explains.

"That's been confirmed?"

"Yes, sir, I saw the grave and autopsy reports myself," she adds.

"How did he die?" I hope it was a long and painful death that made him suffer right up to the end.

"He was killed in a fire when the drug den he was using as a base went up." Mykela glances at Justin, who grins.

"Apparently, they could hear him screaming from outside," he adds.

"Good, I hope the fucker burns for all eternity." Hell is too good for that lowlife and the ones who are about to join him. "Why do they think they are here?" I ask as Justin holds open a door for me.

"They believe you have a business deal for them all, a way for them to make more money. We used the names you gave us to confirm they were who they claimed to be."

"And our people?"

"Still with them all. The druggies think our people have been collected in the same manner," Mykela answers. "They have no idea they are surrounded."

I nod as I prepare myself for what's about to happen. I don't like killing, but sometimes these things need to be done, and these six souls I am happy to hand over to the devil myself.

We come to a stop outside of a door, and I crack my neck, close my eyes for a second and remember everything that has led me to this point and why each of the bastards in there will never see the light of day again.

Pulling my leather gloves out of my pocket, I put one on and then the other.

"Mykela, you know what to do." I don't need to say anymore. I gave her the run down earlier when we had the call to say they had all been found.

"Sir." Stepping up to the door, she enters and clears her throat. "The boss is on their way."

"It's about time. Tell the old bag she needs to hurry up; otherwise-"

"Otherwise, what?" I shout, storming into the room. Every single person freezes, which is precisely what I wanted.

"Fuck!"

Once one person realises they've been had, they all do, and the six arseholes try to make a run for it, but my team is quicker and in less than a minute, all six are kneeling on the concrete floor, with their hands behind their backs held together with cable ties.

"Who the fuck are you?" a guy with tattoos all over his neck and face shouts.

"Shut the fuck up, you idiot," the guy beside him mutters under his breath before looking up at me. "Mr O'Reilly, sir. I don't know these guys. I've not dealt on your territory since you gave me that warning. I know how you feel about-" he stops talking as I stop before him.

"You think I give a shit about your fucking drugs?"

He stops talking and shakes his head.

"I – I don– I don't know, sir."

I squat in front of him, grabbing his hair and pulling it hard so he is forced to look up at me.

"I don't give two fucks about the drugs you are selling now. What I care about is the payments you take for them." Letting go of his hair, I stand so I can see them all.

"Where's Carol? I was told she was waiting for us!" one of the older guys shouts.

"Oh, she's waiting for you," I answer, shrugging off my jacket and holding it out for Justin. Once it's out of the way, I roll up my sleeves. "She is exactly where she belongs." All eyes are on me, and I know they are realising quickly that they are all about to die.

"For those of you who don't know me, I'm Christian O'Reilly. The owner of the O'Reilly Fight Club franchise alongside my brothers. Most people know who we are because they know that we take no shit. If you do us wrong, you die. If you hurt innocents, you die. If you sneeze in the wrong direction on my territory, you die." I walk up and down in front of the six arseholes kneeling on the ground and make sure every one of them looks me in the eyes. Let them see how fucking furious I am and how I have no plans of letting them live.

"What has Carol got to do with you? As I told the prick behind me, I haven't seen her in years."

"If you know Carol, then you will remember her daughter." Each of them pales, which makes my blood boil. "Do you remember her daughter? You should; you used her body as payment for her mother's drugs. My *wife's* body."

All six start arguing, declaring their innocence, but I don't want to hear them.

"SHUT UP!"

They fall deadly silent as they stare at me.

"Do not speak until spoken to!" I roar as my heart rate increases until I can hear it.

"I never touched Jasmine!" my head snaps to the guy with the tattoos on his face. Storming forward, I punch him hard.

"Hold his head!" My guard behind him grabs his head and holds it in place as I pull my flip knife from my pocket. His eyes widen as he tries to fight against my guy, but Justin jumps in to help and the two of them hold him in place.

"You dare say her name!" I growl through gritted teeth. He tries to fight against me, but I hold his jaw open and pull out his tongue. He tries to scream and fight against the three of us. But it is no use. With a few swipes of my knife, I cut through his tongue and throw it onto the ground in front of him. He falls forward as my guys let him go. Blood gushes from his mouth as he groans and cries.

"The next person who even thinks about saying my wife's name will lose more than their fucking tongue!" I yell, making sure they are all paying attention.

"Don't even bother trying to lie your way out of this. I have researched each one of you. I have concrete evidence that you abused my wife, some of you starting when she was only seven years old." I stop in front of a guy I know as

Roger Knox. He had a long history with Carol and even lived with her and Jasmine for a while. He was the one who "won" Jasmine's virginity. He took that from not only her, but also me.

Using the tip of my knife, I press it against his forehead and push it, forcing him to look up at me.

"You lived there for a while. How often did you stand there as she begged to be left alone, wanting it all to end? How many times did you violate her tiny body?" I start sliding the knife across his forehead and down his cheek, leaving a trail of blood in its wake.

"I did some fucked up shit I'm not proud of," he has the nerve to start crying. "I'm sorry; I wish I could take it back." Before he can say anymore, I stab him through the cheek. He screams in pain, which causes the knife to slice through the skin like butter until it exits through the side of his mouth. His scream worsens, and all I can do is smile.

"I'm sorry. I wish I could take it back," I mock before laughing, gripping his hair and pulling his head back. "I can't even pretend. You need to pay for what you did, and I will make sure you do." Throwing his head back, I look at the other five and grin.

"You are all going to pay for hurting my Jasmine."

Chapter Twenty-Nine

JASMINE

"Do you have to do that in here?" I sigh, looking up from the sofa to see Sean working on his laptop.

"What exactly am I doing, Princess?" he smirks, not looking away from the screen.

"You know exactly what you're doing. It sounds like you are hitting each key with a hammer." My head's pounding, and all I want to do is sleep, but the sound of the keys on his keyboard makes it impossible.

"I thought you didn't have a hangover?" he teases. The bastard knows exactly how hungover I am. I might have felt fine when I got home, but when I woke up this morning, my mouth felt like a sand pit, and a brass band had decided to take up residency in my head. Not that I would ever admit it, as I often tease them when they are hungover and don't want the tables turned. I also don't want them to go into Daddy mode and stop me from going out in the future.

"I don't, but I'm so tired it's giving me a headache," I lie. I close my eyes and pull the blanket up to my neck as I snuggle underneath it, desperate to be warm and cosy. I don't open my eyes as I listen to Sean chuckle to himself as he stands and heads over to me.

"Go to bed, Princess. You had a busy day yesterday, and we were up until the early hours of the morning." He runs a hand over my head lovingly, and I sink further into the sofa, wishing he would stay and just play with my hair while I sleep. However, he's already told me how much he needs to do today, so I could never stop him from doing that. No matter how much I want to. So, instead, I shake my head.

"I want to be here when Daddy gets home." Christian won't risk waking me if I'm in bed.

"Okay, I'll work from the office. If you need me, send me a text." He leans in to kiss my head and starts to walk away.

"My head thanks you, Daddy." I grin as he looks over his shoulder, laughing, and leaves the room. Finally, I have the sitting room all to myself, bar Embry curled up beside me.

The second the room falls silent, I regret making him leave. I don't like it here when I'm alone; I prefer to have one of the guys with me whenever I'm home. For some reason, the house feels bigger when I'm alone.

Curling under the blanket, I keep my eyes closed and listen to the sounds of the house outside this room. As usual, there is silence. All I can hear is Embry snoring lightly on the floor in his bed. Sean will have gone to find somewhere else to work, Jason and Maximus have gone to one of their bars to sort out a few things with admin, and Christian won't be home yet.

I missed him when I woke up with the others this morning. I hate it when he has to work away, and I wish he had been here last night when I returned. As amazing as the sex was with the others, I always know when one of them is missing, and lately, it always seems to be Christian.

I know he is the one who deals with most of the shit that gets thrown at them, but just for once, I wish someone else would deal with it so I could have all four guys with me for more than a day at a time. Not that I would ever tell them that. I would never expect them to put me over their work; I know how much they have to put in to ensure that they don't need to work much this week before the wedding or the week after when we are on our honeymoon. I asked them once why they didn't have assistance, and Christian told me he won't pay someone and do most of the work himself. In other words, he is a control freak and doesn't trust someone to do everything to his standard. Maybe it's something I could bring up while on our honeymoon?

The thought of the wedding being so close causes my heart to race and my stomach to come alive excitedly. I can't believe I'm about to get my happily ever after, the thing my mother told me I wasn't worthy of over and over again. She made me feel like no one would ever love me, but here I am about to marry not one but four remarkable men who make me feel like the luckiest woman in the world. The love they show me is unlike anything I thought possible. There is nothing they wouldn't do for me, and I would do absolutely anything for them.

Embry starts to whine beside me, and I look to find him staring at the closed door. He whines and lies back down, his paws under his face as he continues to watch it.

"Who's out there, baby?" I ask, looking at the door, trying to hear who it is. Embry must hear him seconds before me as he jumps to his feet and rushes for the door, just as I hear his voice on the other side.

Embry barks and yelps the second it opens, desperate for Christian's attention.

"Daddy!" Christian looks at me as I rush from the sofa and leap into his arms. He laughs, holding me tight while I wrap my arms and legs around him.

"Anyone would think you missed me, Sweetheart," he grins before I kiss him. I hold his face to mine before leaning back in his arms.

"That's because I have."

Christian smiles as he walks over to the sofa and sits with me on his lap, the puppy still jumping up and down, trying to get his attention. I reach down and pick him up, holding him up for Christian to stroke him. As much as he says he dislikes the dog, I have yet to see any confirmation on the subject. As I lower the pup to the floor, Christian leans his head back against the sofa as he unfastens the top button of his shirt.

"Hard night?" I ask, leaning forward to rest my cheek on his shoulder. He tightens his arms around me and sighs.

"Yeah, but it's dealt with now." He doesn't go into detail, and as much as I want to know what he was dealing with, I know it's best to keep quiet until he tells me. Especially when he is looking this exhausted. Christian buries his nose into my hair and takes a deep breath. "How was your day yesterday?"

I sit up, smiling.

"It was amazing, just what we all needed. Verity did a great job organising it all."

"You have a good friend there," he smiles. Reaching over, he tucks some hair behind my ear.

"She's the best, just like my fiancés." I may be teasing him, but I mean every word.

"Did you enjoy yourself after when your Daddies looked after you?"

"We had fun, but I missed you." Leaning forward, I press my lips to Christian's, wanting him after missing him. For a moment, he kisses me before leaning back. I run my hands up his chest seductively.

"Sweetheart?" There's a question in his voice, which makes me smile at him. I lean in to press kisses to his neck, but he takes my hands and moves so I can't reach him. "Not now, Sweetheart. I'm not in the mood."

Those words hit me in the gut. Christian has never turned me down before. He must see the shock and pain on my face as his eyes change.

"I mean-" Christian gets cut off when there is a knock at the door. I instantly climb off his lap and go to sit next to him, but when he stands, the pain from his rejection hurts deeper. "Come in," he calls, straightening his shirt. I watch him take a deep breath and want to be anywhere but here.

Alasdair McIntire walks into the room, and I see Christian looking concerned about his presence.

"I made it back as soon as you emailed. What's going on?" Christian asks as he walks further away from me and towards the bar to grab a water bottle.

"I need to discuss something with you that came to light this morning," McIntire says, looking from Christian to me. "Morning Jasmine, I hope you had a pleasant day yesterday."

"I did thank you," I reply, forcing a smile. I look at Christian and find him watching me. "I'll leave you to it." I turn to leave, But Christian grabs my hand to stop me.

"We will head to my office, stay here and rest. I'll be back as soon as I can." Placing a kiss on my head, he walks out, followed by McIntire, and I feel the rejection sink into my gut. I want to run to my room and cry, but instead, I sit on the sofa, curl up under my blanket and try to ignore the dread that fills my stomach with rocks.

Christian

Shit, I fucked up. I wasn't able to explain that I was waiting for McIntire. Because I'm exhausted, I didn't word it well, and now I've hurt her. I try to think of any time I've turned her down, but I don't think I ever have. Not in the way I did today. I make a mental note to make it up to her as soon as I find out why McIntire is here.

We walk to my office in silence, and I let him go in first before closing the door. Walking into the room, I round my desk and sit in my chair as he sits in front of me. It's not the first time he has been here. Ever since Geralt Young's murder, McIntire has been working closely with the family, and as I know them well, I have been assisting when needed.

I have spent many years avoiding all dealings with the man before me. He is dangerous, and upsetting him would be a mistake, as I have seen proven on many occasions. But he is also fair, and if you show him respect, then you will receive his respect in return.

"What's going on?" I ask, sitting back in my chair and trying to seem as relaxed as possible.

"I've heard that there are still people trying to take you down, and I thought you should know that they have contacted Nicholson and asked for his input."

"Fuck," I curse, sitting forward. That is the last thing I

expected to hear. "What do you know?" McIntire runs his fingers through his short grey hair and sighs.

"He's been approached and asked if he would consider rising against you. They didn't give him details other than you are overstepping your mark."

When I think things can't get any worse, the hits just keep on coming.

"How do you know this?"

"He called me this morning wanting to know if I was working with you and if I thought you were a threat to him. I told him the truth, that we have a mutual interest in the Youngs, which has been brought around by the morons he hired."

"The bastard is the reason Geralt was killed," I point out, but McIntire shakes his head.

"That whole operation was put together by his brother, who has been missing since. No one has seen hide nor hair of him. When I approached the topic, he told me that he had not sanctioned the retrieval of the drugs and had dealt with the person who had."

"He could be lying, knowing you would have no choice but to go after him if he admitted it," I point out, and McIntire shrugs.

"We both know that, and all I can do is take his word for the time being until I have proof saying otherwise. Why do you think I haven't dealt with him since it occurred." It makes sense that McIntire should have killed whoever was responsible for Young's death, as Young was under his protection, but without any hard proof, it's been difficult to pinpoint who set the wheels in motion with the raid or the murder of Young and kidnapping of Chelsea Hughes.

"So, what do you suggest I do?" I ask, leaning on my desk. McIntire leans back in his chair again and sighs.

"I don't think there is much else you can do for the time being," he answers. "Have you upped security?" I nod in confirmation. "Good, keep it in place and ensure the others are aware of the latest developments so they know to keep an eye out for any danger. Nicholson has no interest in getting involved at the moment, and that could go in your favour, as they may see that it's best to leave you be."

I slump back in my chair and let out a deep sigh.

"The wedding is in less than a week; we are already walking on eggshells, waiting for the bomb to drop after everything that happened at the stag party. I've had to hire extra security as our numbers aren't enough to ensure Jasmine always has at least two guards with her. I nearly had a heart attack last night worrying about her at that bloody hen party. I wanted to get her to cancel it, but she refused, and she was right when she said she deserved it." I rub at my face, feeling defeated once again.

"Don't cancel the wedding; you all deserve this marriage and some happiness. I will do my best to deal with things on the outside whilst you are all dealing with the wedding stuff."

"You don't have to do that," I sigh, but McIntire shakes his head.

"I have become quite fond of young Jasmine, and I think she has dealt with enough. I also dread to think how Abigail would react if I let anything happen to her."

I smile, knowing how close Abbie and Jasmine are.

"I keep telling the others that we need to watch those young women as they will spill our blood if anything else were to happen to their friend." I try to joke about it, but the fear of anything happening to Jasmine terrifies me and haunts me every minute of the day. He pinches the bridge of his nose and lets out a sigh. "Abigail Young hates me enough and is determined to make my life hell. If I let anything happen to her friend, I might as well dig my own grave." He looks lost in thought for a moment before snapping out of it.

"Well, I've come here to do as I wanted. I will leave you in peace if you have just gotten home." McIntire stands from his chair, and I stand and walk around to the other side of the desk.

"Thank you for giving me the heads up; I appreciate it," I say, holding out my hand. McIntire shakes it and gives me half a smile.

"I don't think you have anything to worry about, but it's better to be ready for anything now."

"I couldn't agree more," I answer, walking towards the door to see him out.

"Whilst I'm here, I wondered if you knew how Abigail was yesterday at the spa?"

I turn, frowning as we walk from the office.

"I haven't heard anything, but I haven't had a chance to speak to Jasmine properly about her day. Would you like me to ask? Or would you like to speak to her yourself?" I offer. McIntire seems to think about it for a moment, then nods.

"I'd like to speak to her if that's okay?"

"Of course, follow me." I lead him back to the sitting room, hopping that Jasmine is still there waiting as instructed.

When we enter the room, I find her sitting on the sofa, hugging the puppy. She looks sad, and it hits me that I'm the reason she has lost her smile again.

"Sweetheart, McIntire was asking how Abbie was yesterday," I say, standing beside the sofa she is sitting on and running a hand over her head.

"She was happy considering everything."

"Was she drinking much at the spa?" McIntire asks. I don't miss the concern in his voice, plus it's evident in the way he is frowning.

"Umm, yeah, but she wasn't the only one." Jasmine squirms in her seat, and I can see she's uncomfortable being asked about her friend. "Well, you saw how she was by the end of the evening" she adds quickly as if to prove that her friend did nothing wrong.

Looking back at McIntire, I can see he is deep in thought, as if something isn't sitting right with him.

"Thank you, Jasmine. I hope you had a lovely day. From what I hear, the girls had plenty of surprises planned for you," he smiles. Jasmine seems to relax and nods, smiling back at him.

"They were amazing and went above and beyond what I ever expected."

McIntire looks between the two of us and nods, still smiling.

"That's wonderful to hear. I will leave you in peace now and see myself out. Enjoy the rest of your weekend, and if you need anything before the big day, don't hesitate to call." He nods at me once before walking out of the room, closing the door behind him, and giving me only a brief second to thank him for his kind words.

As soon as the door is closed, Jasmine stands and places the puppy on the floor.

"I'm going to let him out," she says quietly as she goes to walk past me. I take her hand and force her to turn around so she is looking at me.

"I am so sorry, Sweetheart. I didn't mean to upset you before. I am tired and have been awake all night dealing with some pretty nasty stuff. I wasn't turning you down; I just wanted to hold you and relax for a moment before

McIntire was due to arrive." Before I can continue, Jasmine's whole face changes, and I see nothing but concern in her eyes. She steps forward and places a hand over my heart as she looks deep into my eyes.

"You don't need to apologise. I was just so happy to have you home. I didn't think about what you needed at that moment," she whispers, lifting on her tiptoes and lightly kissing my lips. "Why don't I let Embry out? Then I will run you a bath while you have something to eat. Afterwards, we can relax together in bed or down here. Whatever you want."

Running my knuckles down her cheek, I can't help but smile.

"That sounds perfect, Sweetheart, but there is one thing I want to add to that."

"What's that, Daddy?"

"That you join me in the bath, and we relax together before I take you to bed and show you just how much I missed you."

Chapter Thirty

JASMINE

Leaning my head forward, I tighten my arms around Christian's neck, holding him from behind as we lay in the deep, hot bath. Christian relaxes back into me, his hand lazily drifting up and down my arm. We've hardly spoken since we got into the water, but that's okay. My man needs me, and I'm here to help him with whatever he wants. If it's just to hold him as he relaxes and tries to shake off whatever is bugging him, then so be it.

"This is exactly what I needed," Christian sighs contently. "A little time just you and me, pretending the rest of the world doesn't exist."

I kiss his smooth, broad shoulder before leaning my cheek against his.

"Then let's stay in here and let everything else carry on without us," I whisper, smiling.

"I really wish we could, Sweetheart. But we both know that sooner or later, my brothers would come charging in here to drag you away."

"If not the others, then the girls certainly would. We have so much to do to get ready for next weekend."

Christian laughs as he turns his head so I can see his blue eyes.

"I can't wait to marry you. I know I shouldn't want to; I should stay away and keep you safe, but I'm too selfish to give you up." He leans in and kisses me gently before sitting back again.

"I never want to be without you, Daddy." I watch as Christian's face softens, and I can see that there is something on his mind. "What are you thinking?" I ask, worried he's about to tell me something terrible. When he doesn't answer immediately, panic causes my chest to tighten. I know that look; it means whatever he's about to say, I'm not going to like. "What's going on? I can see you want to tell me something," I point out, causing Christian to sigh.

"I want to ask you a question, and I want you to be completely honest with me," he says, turning so he can kneel in front of me. I sit up straight, preparing myself for anything he might throw at me.

"Okay," I answer wearily. He takes a deep breath and cups my hands between his.

"Do you still need us to be your daddies?"

The bath opens and swallows me into a deep black hole. That was the last thing I thought he would ever say to me.

"You don't want to be my daddy anymore?" I ask through the lump in my throat, pulling my hands from his. But he grabs them back and holds them tight, stopping me from removing them again.

"Of course I do, Sweetheart. Being your Daddy is everything to me; I love nothing more than looking after and guiding you."

"Then why do you want to stop?" I ask, a tear sliding down my face.

"Trust me, I don't. I want to be your Daddy forever, even when we are old and grey. But you have grown so much in the last nine months, and I can't help thinking you don't need me or any of us like you did before."

"I do need you; I will always need you," I whisper as my bottom lip quivers. Christian smiles and cups my cheek as he uses his thumb to wipe away my tears.

"Sweetheart, you have become so strong and independent in all the right ways. We could not be prouder of you and how far you come, but you don't need us, not like you used to."

"But I do still need you like that!" I protest, moving my legs to kneel in front of him. "I don't want our dynamic to change; I want you to be my daddy always."

"Unless we are arguing, or more like, you are telling me off?" Christian says with a smile.

"Exactly! But then I will tell you when I want you to go out of Daddy mode like I did the other night. Otherwise, I don't want anything to change with you or the others. I love that you are my daddies; I like being your Baby girl." A sob slips from my lips, and Christian pulls me into his arms.

"You will always be my Baby girl; nothing will ever change that," he whispers into my hair. "I'm sorry, Sweetheart. I never meant to upset you."

"Well, you did," I snap, slapping his chest. "What did you think was going to happen? I would turn around and say, 'Oh no, it's fine. I want to call you Christian,' do you not know me at all?" I exclaim, slapping his chest again.

Christian laughs as he pulls me into his arms and holds me tight. I press my head against his chest and let the tears stream for a moment before pushing them back down.

"Do you forgive me?" he whispers into my hair.

"I haven't decided yet," I sniff as he kisses my head.

"How about I make it up to you?" he asks, leaning back so I can see the mysterious smirk on his face.

"How do you plan to do that?"

In one move, Christian lifts me as he stands from the water. I throw my arms around his neck as he climbs out of the bath.

"Where are you taking me? We're soaking wet!" I laugh as we drip water all over the floor

"To bed so I can show you how sorry I am and make up for upsetting you."

"Mrs Brown only changed the bedding this morning; she will go mad if she has to do it again!" I laugh, envisioning her shouting at Christian. She would never yell at me, I'm her favourite, but she will give him hell.

"I will deal with her," he grins before lowering me onto his bed. He lies over me, his arms resting on either side of my head as he boxes me in.

As I look up into his eyes, I can't wipe the smile off my face. He is so handsome. Even though I know he is a powerful man who is happy to kill for his brothers and me, when he looks at me like he is now, I get to see a side of him, hardly anyone else does. The side that is loving and wants nothing more than to make me smile. When it's just the two of us, I see the vulnerable side of Christian O'Reilly, the side I'm not even sure his brothers have truly seen. It makes me feel special that he chose me to be the one to see him like this.

Leaning down, he presses his lips to mine and kisses me with a softness I often don't see from him.

"It was so hard watching them pleasure you last night," he whispers as his lips leave a trail of light kisses along my jaw and down my throat. "I wanted to be here to make love to you when you got home. I hated that, once again, I was pulled away from you." His lips continue down until he moves over my right breast and takes my nipple in his mouth.

"You can make it up to me now," I sigh as he teases me.

"Oh, I plan on doing more than making it up to you, Sweetheart," he smiles as he moves from one nipple to the other, coaxing a gasp from me as he teases it between his teeth. "I'm going to make love to you until you beg me for a break." He moves from my breasts down my stomach, and I know just where he's heading.

He peppers my skin with soft licks and kisses; my body becomes extra sensitive. His lips leave a trail of goosebumps in their wake as he heads to where I need him the most. When instead of kissing my throbbing pussy, he starts kissing my thigh, I almost cry out with frustration.

"Please, Daddy," I beg as my back arches from the mattress.

"Please, what, Baby girl?" he smirks at me.

"Touch me, lick me, anything but tease me," I'm begging, and I don't care. My body's on fire, and he's the only one who can help me.

"How am I teasing you? By doing this?" He gently blows on the apex of my thighs as I gasp loudly.

"Daddy!" I cry out as he blows again. My stomach tightens as my orgasm starts to build. He hasn't even touched me yet, but I know I'm soaking wet and balancing on the edge.

"Is this teasing?" he asks before running one finger through the middle of my pussy, running from my entrance to my clit, barely touching me the whole time.

"Yes!" I cry out as I nearly fall apart from the slightest touch. "Again, please."

Christian chuckles as he presses his lips to my thigh again and doesn't touch where I need him. When I'm this turned on, I have no problem begging for it, but today, I think I'll brat a little instead.

"Don't think I won't call one of my other daddies in here." It's an empty threat; I would never do that to any of them, but I will happily pretend I would if it gets me what I need.

Christian looks up from between my legs, and I don't miss the way one brow is cocked higher than the others.

"I would like to see you try." He blows on me again, and I moan through the building pressure in my stomach as everything throbs down there.

"Daddy, please. I won't if you touch me again." But instead of doing as I ask, I feel his fingers glide gently over from one hip to another. "Please!" I beg as he continues to laugh quietly.

"I did as you asked, Sweetheart."

"No, you didn't!" I sit up a little to see him, then wish I didn't. The grin on his face is wider than it was a moment ago. "You're being mean!" I pout a little in the hope that he will take pity on me, but of course, this is Christian, and he doesn't.

"And you are acting like a brat," he points out. "What happens when you act this way with me?"

"I get what I want," I try, fluttering my lashes as I do with Maximus whenever I'm playing up for him. That one brow goes higher again as Christian watches me, and I know it won't work.

"That's with Daddy Max. What about when you are a

brat for me?" His voice is going serious again, but that's only bringing out the brat in me more.

"You remind me why you're my Daddy," I answer, thinking of my next response.

"And why am I your Daddy?" he asks, moving up my body until he hovers over me. I can feel the tip of his cock brushing against me as it twitches slightly.

"Because you love me and want me to have the best of everything, including multiple orgasms," I grin as his eyes become slightly darker.

"Part of that is true. Do you want to correct the bit that isn't?"

Chewing on my lip, I shake my head.

"I prefer my answer, so no." A deep sound comes from his chest, and without warning, he rolls away from me before flipping me onto my stomach.

I know what's about to happen, and I'm ready for it when his hand lands on my backside the first time.

"Daddy!" I cry out, trying to hide the smile on my face. From how he spanks me, I know he's in a playful mood, and I make a split decision to keep it that way to give him a reason to smile for a change. He spanks me again before climbing off the bed.

"Don't *Daddy* me. Stay right where you are." I hear him heading to the drawer he keeps some toys in and decide if I'm going to go complete brat, now is the time.

"Or what?" I demand, looking over my shoulder.

"Or you will be taught a lesson." He looks over his shoulder at me, and I can see the slight tic he gets when he forces himself not to smile.

Grinning back at him, I roll and jump off the other side of the bed, keeping it between us.

"Baby girl, are you sure you want to do this? You know the rules; I catch you you are mine to do with as I please."

I smile and shrug casually.

"You will have to catch me first." Spinning on my toes, I rush from the bed to the door and slam it closed before running towards mine. But as I reach the door laughing, Jason steps out, frowning at my naked body.

"Jazzy? What-"

"Grab her!" Christian shouts as he storms from his room. Jason tries to grab me, but I scream and run in the other direction, hoping to get to another room. I reach Maximus's, but he opens the door simultaneously as Sean opens his.

"What the hell?" he curses, staring down at me as I stand before him for a second.

"Fuck!" I scream as he goes to grab me, grinning, but misses as I rush for the stairs.

"The brat's mine," Christian shouts as he takes the stairs two at a time behind me, completely naked. I hear the others laughing together as I make it to head up the second flight of stairs. But Christian is hot on my tail and pulls me down, so I fall onto the stairs on my stomach. He's over me in a heartbeat and pins me to the stairs.

"Seems I caught you, brat. You know what that means." I can hear how happy he is and smile. It's worth any punishment he issues if it makes him forget everything, even for a short while.

"You are going to give me the orgasm you withheld finally?" Looking over my shoulder, I smile at him. "Or do you need one of the others to show you how it's done?" His hand comes down on my ass cheek as I cry out. Spanking is never about the pain. No matter how much I push his buttons, he will never hurt me; none of them would.

"Have you quite finished being a brat? Or do I need to fuck the attitude out of you?" he growls through gritted teeth into my ear.

"At least I might get an orgasm that way if you do."

Christian thrusts his hips forward and impales me in one thrust. I cry out from the shock and slight sting of pain where I wasn't ready for him. But it's the opening he was looking for.

"Are you saying I don't pleasure you?" he asks, wrapping his hand around my throat and lifting my face to look at him. "Do I need to remind you, brat, just what I can do to this gorgeous body of yours?" He pulls almost all the way out, so just the tip is in my entrance before slamming back inside of me. I cry out louder this time, but Christian knows if I wanted him to stop or it was too painful, I would use my safe word.

"I think I need to force orgasm after orgasm from your body until you beg me to stop." He pulls out until it's just the tip again and thrusts back in as I cry out louder.

"You can try," I answer back, unsure why, as I have what I want. He's fucking me hard and dominating me completely.

"The only trying right now is a little brat trying her daddy's patience." He starts pounding into me, fucking me hard against the stairs. His grip on my throat tightens at the same time as he spanks me.

"Daddy!" I cry out as my body comes alive. My skin feels like it's on fire and tightening everywhere. The feel of the carpeted stairs underneath me as Christian fucks me on them adds to the pleasure in a way I never anticipated. His hand comes down on my ass again, and I cry out. He has complete control over my pleasure, so when he reaches round and pinches my clit, I scream through my first orgasm. Christian continues to play with my clit, dragging out my orgasm as long as possible.

"That's right, come on Daddy's cock like the good girl you can be." His teeth sink into my shoulder as he starts fucking me hard again. As he loosens his jaw on my shoulder, the hand on my throat tightens as he spanks me again.

"Did you think I didn't hear you swear downstairs?" he breaths into my ear. He spanks me again, causing me to cry out before he tightens his grip on my throat so much I can't make a sound. "I hear everything, and you need to remember who is in charge in this relationship." He spanks me again before letting go of my throat, and I fall apart again. Screaming through another orgasm as Christian laughs on top of me.

"That's two, how will I give you the third?" he pulls himself out and rolls me onto my back as I gasp for breath, trying to recover from the orgasm that's just nearly destroyed me. He grins down at me before declaring, "I know."

He launches his face to my pussy and has me moaning as his tongue finds my clit. Christian devours me, licking as his fingers thrust into me hard and fast. There's nothing loving about this; he wants to punish me for being a brat, and forcing my orgasms from me does that.

"Oh my god!" I cry out as he nibbles on my clit before sucking it between his teeth.

"No point calling for him; he is of no use to you now," he laughs before he starts fucking me with his tongue.

"Daddy!" I don't know how, but the third orgasm is building quicker than the others, causing my whole body to shake.

"That's right, I'm your daddy and will discipline you when needed." He continues to lick me and finger me until

I'm screaming again and then become overstimulated. I try to back away from his mouth, but he places his hands on my hips and continues playing with my body, dragging out the orgasm as long as possible.

"No more!" I call out as Christian finally lifts his head from between my legs.

"Can your greedy little pussy not take anymore?" he teases as I shake my head, my eyes clamp shut as I try desperately to control my rapid breathing. "Then it's a good thing I know another way to make you scream my name." He flips me onto my front again and places my knees on the step so my ass is in the air. "Colour?"

"Green." I don't know how long it will stay on green, but right now, I don't know how, but I want more.

Christian spreads my ass cheeks, and something warm and wet lands between them. He rubs it into my back entrance before pushing one finger inside. My face is planted on the stairs, and I'm close to being exhausted, but I need to feel him in me again before I use my safe word.

"Daddy," I whisper as he pushes a second finger in, stretching me ready for his cock.

"That's right, Baby, Daddy's going to make you feel good, just one more time," he declares before removing his hand, and I feel his tip pressing into me. A small startled cry leaves me as the head of his cock slips inside of me.

"Fuck. This is going to be quick, so remember your words," he warns before pushing himself fully into my bowels. We call out together as he fills me and holds still, giving me a moment to get used to him. He doesn't give me long, and for that, I'm grateful as the last few orgasms have left my body spent.

Christian takes hold of my hips and starts fucking me hard and fast. The pleasure builds quickly again as I listen to him growling and cursing through gritted teeth, lifting my head and shoulders off the step and holding on while calling out as the orgasm that's been teetering on the edge again.

"Daddy, please," I cry as I start to fall.

"I've got you, Baby. Be a good girl and come one last time for me." My body comes alive, and I call out as I topple over the edge and come so hard I think I squirt on the carpet below us.

"Fuck," Christian roars as he pushes into me forcibly, and I can feel him falling apart as well. He doesn't loosen up for a few minutes as I feel him filling me with his release before he slumps forward and rests his cheek on my back as we both gasp for breath.

Without saying a word, Christian leans off my back and removes his now softened dick from my ass.

"Are you okay, Sweetheart?" he asks, helping me sit on the stairs.

"Yes, Daddy," I whisper, looking up at him through heavy eyelids. Christian brushes some hair from my face before placing an arm around my back and one under my knees.

"Put your arms around my neck," he orders softly. I do as instructed, and he lifts me as he stands and starts walking down the stairs. We reach the landing, where the other three had laughed at us. Now, they are nowhere in sight, and I'm grateful, as I'm not ready to be shared between them. I want to give Christian my undivided attention.

He walks us to his room and kicks the door closed behind us. Leaning into his bare chest, I smile contently as he holds me tight before placing me softly on the bed.

"Does anywhere hurt?" he asks, checking down my body.

"No, I'm fine," I reply, unable to wipe the grin off my face or take my eyes off him.

"Are you sure I didn't hurt you?" he asks, running his fingers gently over my knees, which look a little red and have the indentation of the carpet on them. Sitting up, I place a hand on his face and give him a big, satisfied smile.

"I'm fine, Daddy. Nothing hurts. Come and lie down with me." He looks me in the eye before nodding and holding the blankets back for me. As soon as I'm settled and have some of the water he offers me, he climbs in and pulls me into his arms, holding me as I rest my head on his bare chest, listening to his heartbeat. I can feel his eyes on me, and he smiles as I look up.

"I love you so much, Sweetheart," the words barely a whisper from his lips as his eyes don't leave mine. "There is nothing I wouldn't do to keep you safe and happy." Rolling so I'm lying more on my stomach, I smile at my man. Placing a hand on his cheek, he leans into my touch.

"I know, Daddy. That's why I love you so much." Christian closes his eyes whilst remaining leaning into my hand.

"I've done some terrible things in my life," he whispers, keeping his eyes closed. "I've stolen, destroyed families, beaten people, and killed to get us where we are today, but I would give it all up for you." Opening his eyes, he looks deep into mine again. "If I thought you would be safer by us walking away from everything I have worked to build, I would do it without hesitation. It's a life I never wanted you dragged into." He takes a deep breath before continuing. "But I think I'm in too deep. I can't find a safe escape, and I don't want that for you or my brothers."

"Whatever happens, whatever you want to do, we will face the consequences together," I try to reassure him. "We are all here for whatever you need us for."

"I don't want you hurt because of me, and it's not only me that thinks it's a possibility." He closes his eyes for a second as if blinking back tears. "My brothers have made it clear that if what I am is putting you in danger, they will take you and protect you."

My eyes open wide at the thought of them moving us and leaving Christian here. "I would like to see them try."

"I will make them, Sweetheart." The words shock me so much that I have no idea how to respond. "I will let them take you from me if it means you have the life you deserve."

"It won't be a life without you," I point out. I know what he's trying to do; this is his attempt to clarify his plans. He wants me to lie here and do as I'm told. I'm not having it, though.

"In five days, you will be my husband, my *legal* husband. You wanted the traditional vows, so for richer or poorer, in sickness and in health, nothing can separate us apart from death, which is not going to happen for a very long time. Or have you already forgotten the vow you promised me the other day?"

Christian shakes his head and tightens his arms around me, holding me tight against his naked body.

"You are stuck with me for the rest of your life, whether you like it or not," he whispers into my hair as he kisses my head.

"That's right. So, you are as stuck with me as I am with you." I roll back on my side and snuggle up to my man in the safest place I know, in his arms, where nothing will ever get to me because he won't let it.

"Now that's sorted. Can we spend a few hours like this, please? I'm tired." Christian laughs as he kisses the top of my head again.

"We can do whatever you want, Sweetheart."

"Good," I smile into his chest. "Then, put a film on because I want a day in bed with tons of snacks."

Christian laughs as he reaches for the remote to turn on his giant TV.

"That sounds perfect."

Chapter Thirty-One

JASMINE

"Are you sure you're okay there on your own?" Verity asks as I check the temperature of my bath water.

"Ver, I'm never alone. Security is on site twenty-four seven now. No one is getting into this house without them knowing." I wish I could have some time alone, but the guys have forbidden me from being left unprotected until we know for sure the threat against Christian has been eradicated. Since they killed Mitchell, there haven't been any more buildings damaged, and things have quietened down. But it's too early to know if that is the end of that whole shitstorm.

"I guess so. I just worry about you."

"I know and appreciate it, but honestly, I'm fine. Abbi has already offered to come round and stay, and I told her no." I had been on the phone with her when Sean had a message from Maximus to go meet him at the gym. Sean wasn't too happy about it, but Christian and Jason were also picking up the wedding suits. They aren't meant to be getting them until tomorrow, but the shop owner called to say they had a family emergency and asked if they could pick them up tonight to be on the safe side.

Jason was heading to a club to pick up some paperwork; they decided to go together, with the club only being a few streets away from the tailor.

"Have you managed to get any more out of her about her new boyfriend?" Verity asks as I shut off the taps. The bath filled to the level I like it.

"Only his name is Eddie, and he pulled out of a date they were meant to be going on tonight at the last minute." Shrugging off my robe, I hang it on the back of my bathroom door, which I leave open so I can hear the music playing lightly in my bedroom.

"I think we should try to get more out of her tomorrow when we collect the dresses."

"Oh, I plan on it," I laugh, heading for the bath. "Now, leave me alone. I have a deep bubble bath with my name on it and a book about a billionaire mafia boss to read."

Verity starts laughing as I light a couple of candles and place my Kindle by the bath on a stall with a towel and a glass of wine.

"I can't believe you still read those. You have four of your own billionaire mafia bosses."

"They aren't billionaires; at least, I don't think they are," I laugh as I climb into the water.

"Well, I'll leave you to it. Bear is dropping me off at yours in the morning around eleven," she explains as I hear someone calling her in the background.

"Sounds like you are wanted, so I'll see you tomorrow. Have fun, and don't do anything I wouldn't do," I tease.

"That really doesn't leave much," she laughs before we

both say goodbye and end the call. Placing my phone on the small stall with everything else. I settle into the water and close my eyes for a moment. Taking a deep breath, I inhale the scent of vanilla and roses from the bubble bath Sean gave me for Christmas. It's beautiful and so relaxing.

This is what I needed: a little time to relax before everything starts going at a million miles an hour in the lead-up to the weekend.

A smile creeps on my lips as I think about the wedding. In three short days, I will be Mrs Jasmine Rose O'Reilly and married to four remarkable men who show me every single day how much I mean to them.

I never dreamt we would ever get to this point. When I first met the O'Reillys, I was a scared seventeen-year-old who fell desperately in love with her new stepbrothers. It never crossed my mind that they would fall in love with me, too, let alone that I could have all four of them. Sure, there have been times when the five of us in this together have been difficult, but the issues tend to be out of the house rather than in it.

When it became common knowledge at school that I was in a relationship with four different guys who all knew about each other, I was called every name imaginable. I had people refuse to work with me on group projects, and I was kicked out of a study group for being a 'money-grabbing whore'. It was tough, and as much as I wanted to confide in the guys about all that was happening, I couldn't because I was so worried they would decide I wasn't worth the hassle, or the most likely outcome, Christian would charge into the school and demand everyone apologise to me, whilst getting the teachers involved. I couldn't let that happen, as it would only make matters worse. But that's when the most unlikely of friendships formed. The same girl who had bullied me for years stood beside me and had my back.

Danielle and I hated each other; there was no other word for it. She loved to make my life a misery, and nothing brought her pleasure other than trying to break me. I lost count of how many times I left that school in tears because of how she treated me. There was even a time or two that Layton wanted to get involved, and I had to stop him. But things started to change when she found me hurt and bleeding after being attacked by Hudson. When Danielle found me, she got help and stayed until Layton arrived and brought me home. The following day, she visited, and our relationship has never been the same since. Now, she is one of my best friends and never stands for anyone attacking me verbally or otherwise.

Remembering I haven't replied to her message about tomorrow, I open my eyes and retrieve my phone from where I had left it. Just as I open it, I hear a strange noise from the bedroom. I stop and listen to see if I can hear it again. But then the music changes, and I relax, realising it was just the previous song finishing. Sitting back in the bath, I pull up Danielle's message and type out the reply.

Jaz: Sorry, I forgot to reply. Be ready for 11:30; we will pick you up.

A loud, high-pitched alarm sounds, making me jump and drop my phone in the water.

"Fuck," I curse, pulling it out and grabbing a towel to dry it. If this is another lockdown drill, I'm going to kick Terry's ass for not giving me a heads-up.

I reluctantly climb out of the bath, pulling a towel from the stall and wrapping it around my body. The alarm continues to sound as I hear a weird clunking sound coming from my bedroom. Slowly, I make my way to the door and grab my robe, wanting to be as covered as possible. If it were anything else, I would think it was one of the guys trying to scare me, but none of them would ever mess around with this.

Slowly walking into the room, I listen to the sound again and realise it's coming from the window. Turning, I expect to see the shutter down, but instead, it's less than a quarter of the way and seems to be jammed. The sound is it fighting to drop the rest of the way.

"What the?" I walk closer to the window, trying to determine what's going on when something moves across the glass. Jumping back, I rush for the bedroom door and try to open it, but it won't move. Realising we have gone into complete lockdown I uncover the keypad and type in the code, but nothing happens.

"Come on," I mutter to myself as I try the code again, but it still doesn't do anything. "Shit." Turning back to the window slowly, I can't see anything there now other than the broken shutter still trying to close. Rushing to the bathroom where I left my phone, I lock the door and pull up the security number. In the last couple of days, the guys have drilled in the protocol for any situation I may encounter. One thing they all had in common was that I didn't call any of them or answer my phone in case someone was looking for me, and the sound of my voice led them to me. I'm only meant to message security with any issues and tell them where I am.

Backing away from the bathroom door and hiding behind the bath as I pull up the number for security; it's a group chat linked to the phone security will be using.

Jasmine: Is this a drill? My bedroom shutter didn't close, and I'm locked in as my security code doesn't work on the door.

I await the reply, but it's not security who replies first.

Jason: Has the security system been activated? No notification has come to Christian's or my phone.

Sean: Mine neither. Security, confirm what's going on!

I open our personal group chat, and the five of us share and send a message.

Jasmine: The house has gone into lockdown. My shutter is broken and hasn't shut. My door won't unlock, so I've hidden myself away.

Jason: We are on our way. Get in the panic room and stay there until one of us, Layton or Terry, comes to get you.

Jumping to my feet, I head over to the bathroom door and listen to see if I can hear anything from inside my room. The alarm is so loud that it's impossible to hear anything else with the door closed. Slowly, I open the door, inch by inch, listening for anything that may mean someone is in my room. With the door open a tiny amount, I look through the gap and am confident that the room is clear before taking a chance and running to the wardrobe where the panic room is located.

As I run across the room, my phone vibrates in my hand, but I don't risk looking at it. Something moves out of the corner of my eye as I pass the window, but I don't let myself look. I continue to run until I reach the back of the wardrobe, where a panic room is hidden. Moving the clothes out of the way, I find the hidden compartment and open it to type in the code, praying it will work. Thankfully, the door opens, and I jump in before slamming it and locking it from the inside. I take a deep breath and try to calm my breathing. I'm safe now; no one can unlock it from the outside now that I've activated the lock inside.

Leaning against the door, I take a deep breath and try to calm my racing heart. I look at the small room around me and try to focus on it, not what could be happening in the house.

The room is tiny and situated between mine and Jason's room. They had it built before I moved in, knowing there was always a chance I would need it. It consists of four walls, all sound and bulletproof, and a door. On one of the walls, there is a TV, which I turn on, knowing it's linked to the CCTV, but it only connects to the camera in my room. There is also a phone beside it where I can contact the security hub. I pick up the phone and wait for it to connect, but when it continues to ring without being answered, my anxiety starts to grow.

Where the hell is everyone? Why are they not answering? There should be two members of the team in the hub and checking the grounds, as well as two of Calvin's armed guards. Surely, this must be a technical fault because there is no way someone could possibly get close enough to activate the alarm. The lockdown system has to be activated manually unless someone tries to force access into the property. Is that what I saw at my window? Was someone trying to get in? Why has my window shutter malfunctioned? I need to know what's going on.

Lifting my phone to send a message, I realise there is

one from Layton on the security group. It must have been why my phone vibrated when I was rushing into the wardrobe.

Layton: The lockdown programme was activated at 20:24. I'm unable to make contact with the team, and the notification system failed. As far as I know, Jaz, Mrs Brown, and two security guards are at the premises. I'm en route and will be there in less than 10 minutes. Terry will get there after me but is also en route. DO NOT enter the premises before I get there. Jaz and Mrs Brown, get in the panic rooms; you will be safe there. Only message via this thread to ensure everyone's safety.

Knowing the guys and Layton and Terry, are on the way helps put my mind at ease a little. Whilst I'm locked in here, nothing can get to me. I freeze as I realise I might be safe, but what about Embry?

He's locked in the conservatory, ready for bed. I never have him with me when I shower or have a bath, as he loves the water and keeps trying to join me, which makes a huge mess, so I locked him in there before coming upstairs. Tears fill my eyes as I worry he's in danger. Do the conservatory doors and windows lock like the rest of the house?

Lifting my phone, I plan on asking someone to check on him when I realise I have no signal in here, so I have no way of contacting the others. Sitting back against the wall, I bring my knees up to my chest as I shake, feeling the cold from my wet towel. I should have known better and grabbed some clothes before coming in here. I make a mental note to place a few items of clothing in here. That's when I notice a blanket tucked away in the corner and grab it before wrapping it around myself.

Sitting back, I try to keep calm and warm as I wait for someone to get home, let me know what the hell is going on, and check on my baby. If anything happens to him, I will make whoever hurt him pay, and I won't be hiding behind my guys; it will be me they need to fear.

Chapter Thirty-Two

MAXIMUS

My car comes to a screeching stop just down the road from the house. The way has been blocked off by cars and people. Spotting Christian's and Sean's cars and a few of the security members, I jump out and head to my brothers. Everyone turns to look as I reach them: Terry, Layton, and Logan, all obviously anxious and stressed as they huddle around a tablet in Logan's hands.

"What the fuck is going on?" I yell as I approach. I glimpse the house through the trees surrounding our property; all the windows are covered, and there is no sign of life anywhere inside.

"Someone has completely overridden the system. No one can get in or out," Sean answers.

"So, how did you get out?" I demand. "You were meant to be in there with Shorty!"

"Because I was on my way to you, dumb ass!" he snaps, throwing his arms up in the air.

"Why were you coming to me? I told you I was going to train and then come home."

Sean stares at me like I've gone mad.

"You texted me to meet you at the gym to sort out some machine issues."

"No, I never did. I didn't even have my phone; it was in my car the whole time." I hear a few curse words thrown around as Sean pulls out his phone.

"Are you telling me this wasn't you?" Holding up his phone, I read the message and frown. It's there for everyone to see. It's even under a message I sent him this morning.

"What the fuck? I didn't send that!"

"Where is your phone?" Christian asks. I turn around and head back to retrieve it. I know it's there, as I read Jasmine's last message saying she was heading to the panic room.

Pulling my phone from the stand it's been sitting in; I open it and head back to the others. After retrieving the messages, I quickly confirm there is no message on my phone.

"See, I told you I never sent it!" I point out, showing my phone to the others.

"This whole night is just getting more and more fucked up," Jason sighs, rubbing his face. He looks at Logan and nods towards the house. "Are we any closer to working out how to get in?"

Logan shakes his head as he starts clicking on the tablet in his hand.

"I need to find a way to override it from the hub. They have managed to lock it down so no one can access anything without being on the network." He frowns at his screen whilst swiping angrily across it.

Storming away from us, he heads to the black van I recognise as one of his, throws open the back door and jumps inside.

The four of us stand at the open door and see Calvin working on the computers they have in there. I can see various viewpoints of the property; all seem to be from drones they must have flying around.

"Area is clear. Our guys have searched every inch, and they haven't found anyone," Calvin explains before taking off some overhead headphones and turning his attention to us. "Someone has definitely been here, though; they left tracks on the west side of the building."

"That's the same side as Jasmine's room," Christian adds, his fists tightening. Calvin nods before continuing.

"Her shutter is open, as she said. We think they planned to get in through them. From what we can see, no one is inside except Mrs Brown and Jaz."

"Have any of you heard from Shorty?" I ask, looking back at the house through the trees.

"The only way is for her to call the security hub number, but they are locked out of there as well. They were doing their rounds when the alarm was activated," Christian sighs, rubbing the back of his neck as he looks up at the house all barricaded.

"Could we get in through Shorty's window? Isn't there a huge ladder in the garden shed?" I ask, looking at Calvin.

"It's gone. It looks like they took it to make life even more difficult for us," Christian sighs, pinching the bridge of his nose.

"We're trying to get hold of one of our guards to come out and try. I don't think there is anything that woman can't climb." Logan explains, turning his head to Calvin, who is watching me. I know what he's thinking, and it gives me an idea.

"The perimeter is completely clear?" I ask.

"Yeah, they are long gone. They must have realised they

had failed and run for it," he answers. I think about it for a second before walking around the van.

"Let me see what I can do."

I used to be a damn good climber. I often climbed in and out of our old house where we lived with Tommy. He would try and control me, so I would escape to get pissed, knowing how much he hated it. When I wasn't in the ring, I would be at a climbing centre near there. It's been a good few years, but I'm willing to try. "Sean, come with me," I snap, heading to the house.

"What are you going to do?" Christian calls as we head away from them.

"Give me a second, will you!" I yell back. "He's just worried I'll work out how to get in without him," I mutter under my breath.

"Pack it in. The last thing we need is you winding him up. He's already stressed as it is," Sean sighs beside me. Always the diplomat, looking to keep the peace. Sometimes, I wish he would just take my side without trying to keep everyone happy.

"Whatever," I sigh, stopping at the back of the house. Taking a few steps back, I look at Shorty's room and see the shutter pushing against something. "What the fuck is that?" I ask, trying to get a clear view of what is stopping it from closing.

"We don't know. Layton tried to climb up to have a look, but he couldn't get close enough," Sean answers, looking up at the window. The light is still on, and we know she is safely in her panic room. I never thought I would be grateful for Christian insisting we had it installed. There is no way anyone can get into it. There again, they weren't meant to be able to get near the house, but here we are.

Walking up to the wall, I check out the drainpipe, brickwork, and exterior cladding.

"Could you climb it using the cladding and the pipe?" Sean asks beside me.

"Maybe," I answer trying to work out the best route. I know my upper body strength isn't what it was when I climbed a few times a week. But the thought of my Shorty up there alone is enough to give me the push to attempt it.

Taking a few steps back, I look to the first area I plan on placing my hands and feet before taking a run and jump. I get a grip on the cladding and look to the next place to position my hands and feet to climb a little higher.

"What the fuck?" I hear Logan curse below, but I'm too busy concentrating to respond.

"For fuck's sake, please don't break anything, the house or yourself," Jason sighs. I look down and flip him off before making my way up the wall a little further.

"Should we get something to break his fall, just in case?" Layton asks.

"He won't fall. If anyone can get up the side of the house to Jasmine, it's Maximus."

"That's the nicest thing you've said about me in a while, Christian," I call back as I adjust my grip and lift myself a little higher.

"Don't make me take it back," I hear him sigh as I laugh before cursing as I lose my grip for a second.

"Fuck."

All humour is lost for a few minutes as I manage to get a little higher and closer to the window. It's not easy-going, and there are times I'm literally hanging on by my fingertips. If I stop for too long, people below start shouting out where they can see a gap I can use. It pains me when I realise I need to move away from Jasmine's window and head to Jason's because the way isn't safe to keep going straight up.

"You've got this, Maximus, just a few more meters," I hear Terry call up.

"Easy for you to say; your feet are planted firmly on the ground, old man!" I call back at the exact moment as my left hand slips from the gap in the wall. I hear a few people cry out as I hang from the wall quite literally by the fingertips of one hand. Taking a deep breath, I swing myself up and grab on with both hands again.

I manage to get to a ledge I can rest on while working out a game plan. I probably should have done that before climbing up here, but all I could think about was getting to my girl.

"What's the plan, Maximus?" Jason calls up.

"I'm thinking," I yell back as I find my feet. Leaning back as far as I dare, I look at the shutter to see if I can determine why it didn't close. When I look, a piece of fabric and two car jacks catch my eye.

"This wasn't a malfunction," I call back as I try to think of how to get in that room without the shutter slamming down on me. "It's been propped open. But I can't see any sign that they got in." Once I'm sure I'm safe from falling to my death, I look down at those below. "Are we sure there is no one inside?"

"I've managed to access the inside cameras; the place is clear. The puppy is in the conservatory; Jasmine and Mrs Brown are both in their panic rooms," Logan calls up.

"Are you armed?" Christian calls. I reach behind my back, where I usually keep my gun and stop. Looking down, I realise I'm still in my gym gear.

"I only have my knife. My gun's in the car." I look over to the window and put a plan together. "In the garden shed, there should be a bucket. Grab that and put the gun, a couple of screwdrivers and a hammer into it. We can get it to me using a rope. I'm sure there's one in the shed or somewhere." I watch as people all rush off to grab what I asked for.

"Logan, are the doors inside unlocked yet?" I remember Shorty saying something about the code on her door not working.

"No, but I've almost managed to reset them so that you can use a new code for now, and I will change them all once the building is safe." I hold up my thumb to show I heard him before looking to the window again. If I hit the corner of the glass, the whole thing should shatter, and I'll be able to knock it out so I can get inside.

"Maximus, Jazzy is the only one who can unlock the panic room. It's done from the inside," Jason calls. "When you enter her room, stand in front of the camera, and she should see you."

"Will do. Are we one hundred percent certain that no one is hiding in the house?" I call down.

"Yes, Logan has been able to keep an eye since getting access to the cameras inside," Calvin replies. Thank fuck for that; the last thing I need is to worry about getting ambushed in there. I hear the others discussing how to throw the rope to me so I can pull the bucket to the ledge. I spend a little time trying to find the best route from here to her room and how I will break the window. There is nothing for me to safely stand on to look at the wall, which is why I've asked for the screwdrivers. If I can force them into the wall, I may be able to use them as supports to stop me from falling. Is there a way I can use them to support me while I smash the window? That in itself isn't going to be easy. We have reinforced glass on all windows, making them virtually bulletproof. Nothing about this will be easy; there are many things that could go wrong, but the thought of my girl in there alone and scared has me determined to get to her, no matter what I need to do to do it.

"Maximus!" I look down and see the guys all looking up at me. "We've tied something to the end of the rope. Jason will throw it up to you. Once you catch it, you should be able to pull it up. No problem," Sean shouts. I hold up a thumb and squat down, ready.

"Okay, this may take a few warm up throws," Jason calls before spinning the rope, and everyone steps back to avoid getting hit. The first throw doesn't even get halfway up the house, and I can't miss the opportunity to mock him.

"Calvin, can Luna come and give her Uncle Jason some help?"

"Fuck off prick, I'd like to see you try this!"

"I don't need to; I just climbed up the side of a building, jackass," I yell, smirking at my brother, who's shaking his head and muttering to himself. I can't hear him up here, but from the way Sean starts laughing, I know it was taking the piss out of me. Jason smiles at him before he tries again to throw the rope up. It gets much higher this time, but it is still not enough to reach me. Jason curses under his breath and takes a step back before lengthening the amount of rope he's holding and starts to swing it again. This time, when he lets go, it flies straight for me, and I manage to catch it, even if only just.

"Got it!" I call out as I start pulling the bucket up to me. I have to stop a few times as I nearly lose the contents as the wind picks up and makes the bucket swing. Eventually, though, I have it up with me.

I pull everything out and work out the best way to carry

it all. My pockets are only small in my sweatpants, and I will need both hands to climb to the window.

I look down at my brothers once I'm confident I have everything in place and won't drop it all.

"Stand back; I don't want to fall on any of you."

"You won't fall," Jason calls up.

"Christian, I hope you've replaced my bourbon because I will need a drink after this!" I call down as I start to get my fingertips into the holes in the bricks.

"There is a brand new bottle that was delivered today," he laughs as I lift myself higher.

"Why didn't you start with that? I would be in there already!" I stop and look down at my brothers, who all look small as they shield their eyes from bright outdoor lights. "Don't tell Shorty I would have saved the bottle before her. I like my balls where they are and don't want to give her a reason to pour this one away." They all start laughing as I get closer to the window.

My arms are killing me, and my fingers are bleeding, but nothing is going to stop me from getting to my girl. I know she will be putting on a brave face, but inside, she will be terrified. That's the type of woman she is. She would rather everyone thought she was fearless and strong than admit she was scared.

When I finally get underneath the window, I take my time to examine the shutter.

"There's a car jack holding the shutter open," I call out. "One on each side."

"Blood is going to be spilt when I get my hands on the fuckers that did this," I hear Christian curse. I will happily help him. I don't know what we need to do to clarify that our Jasmine is not to be touched. I will kill every fucker if it means she will be safe.

Looking at the jacks, I notice some material hanging from one of them.

"How the fuck did they get up there? That's what I want to know," I hear Jason asks below. I am about to tell them to shut up so I can think, and then something flashes in my peripheral vision. Looking in that direction, I notice a hook sticking into the wall above the window, answering the question. It's climbing equipment. They must have used the ladder and attached themselves with rope while getting everything in place. How the fuck weren't they seen?

I try to get a feel for where to put my feet next, but there's nothing. This is what I was scared of; I would have to rely on my upper body strength. It's also why I asked them to send up extra screwdrivers.

"If you can't do it, turn around. You've got a damn sight higher than any of us could have," Jason calls.

"I can do it; it's just …" I stop partway through and decide to just go for it. Taking hold of a screwdriver in one hand, I let go and swing my body, using the momentum to get higher. Slamming the screwdriver into the concrete between bricks, I test it; thankfully, it stays in place. Once one screwdriver is secure, I do the same with the next. Once that one is secure, I go back a little and start climbing until I'm able to grab hold of the drainpipe that runs down past the window. Praying it doesn't come away from the wall; I climb up it until I'm at the same level as the windowsill. Taking a deep breath, I grab hold of the wooden sill with one hand and pull myself onto it.

"You clever bastard!" I hear Jason shout below, but I'm too focused to reply. I use the screwdrivers I shoved into the wall to take some of my weight as I stand on them while keeping as much weight as possible on the windowsill, knowing the screwdrivers won't hold for long.

I move until both feet are on them and I'm in the best position underneath the window. With difficulty, I shuffle another screwdriver out of the sleeve on my hoodie where I had hidden it. As soon as it's in my hand, I know I only have a few seconds to make a real difference.

Everyone is deadly silent below. I can feel all their eyes on me as I close mine for a second, let out a deep breath, swing one arm up over my head and slam the point of the screwdriver into the corner of the window. The whole pane shatters but remains in place as I expected.

By now, my arms are screaming as I hold on with both of them, trying to keep as much weight off the supports at my feet, knowing they will bend. The screwdriver is lodged into the glass, and I know I still need to remove the broken pane and break the second. With one hand, I reach up and put some of my weight onto the windowsill, but instantly, I know it won't hold much longer.

"Go back, and we will work something else out!" Sean calls.

"No, I can do this!" I call back as I manage to press my feet against the wall to take some of the pressure off my arms. It's not much, but it may buy me a little time, even if it's only seconds. Acting quickly, I grab the hammer from the side of my sweats and hit the window as hard as I can from this angle. It's not great, but some of the glass falls out, which makes it easier to get to the next pane.

Not giving my body time to give up, I swing the hammer again, shattering the second sheet of glass, but the next blow does nothing. Reaching up, I knock as much of the glass from the window frame as possible before using it to hold on to. As soon as I hold the plastic frame, I know I have a better grip and will be able to do more damage now. I'm still at risk of falling, but the likelihood has dropped.

Gripping the window frame and cutting my hand in the process, I pull myself up higher so I can use my left arm as an anchor while throwing as much force as possible into my right. I hit the window with the hammer again. This time, the glass shatters and falls into the room. There is still a lot of broken glass in the window frame, and I quickly hit it out of the way before pulling myself through it, still cutting myself all over.

I hear the others shouting and cheering below, but I'm not acknowledging them. I look to the camera on the ceiling and wave before heading to the panic room in the wardrobe. The door opens as I reach it, and Jasmine throws herself into my arms.

"You're okay, Shorty, I've got you." Burying my nose into her hair, I take a deep breath and let myself hold her for a minute.

"Did you just climb through my window?" she demands, leaning back in my arms.

"All part of the rescue mission, ma'am," I wink before noticing that she's shivering. I grab the blanket from the floor and wrap it around her before lifting her up.

"Can we get out now?" she asks as I carry her from the wardrobe and sit her on the bed after checking there is no glass on it.

"Not yet; Logan is working on it." I walk back over to the window and look down at the others. "I've got her. She's cold, but other than that, she's unharmed." The others all seem to let out a sigh of relief together. "Any chance we can get out of here yet?" I ask.

"Passwords, Mum," Christian calls up. I head over to the control panel before typing in our family code: the date of Mother's Day, the year she died.

Almost instantly, the lock clicks, and I walk over to

Jasmine to pick her up, not wanting to leave her for a moment.

"Let's go and see how many doors we can unlock. Hopefully, we can get the others in the less exciting way," I wink at her as I carry her from her room and head down the stairs.

A few hours later, I'm lying in bed with Shorty in the middle and Sean on the other side of her. Neither of us wanted to be away from her tonight. The other two are still up, trying to find out what the hell happened and how things escalated so quickly.

As soon as I unlocked all the main doors, the shutters lifted, and everyone was able to get in. Shorty had been more worried about the puppy than she was about someone trying to get into her room.

"Do you think we will ever get a couple of months where someone isn't either trying to kill one of you or kidnap me?" she asks from where she is resting her head on Sean's shoulder.

"We can only hope, Princess," he smiles.

"I don't think we have to worry about anyone taking you, Shorty," I point out. Jasmine turns around, frowning at me.

"How did you work that out?"

"Because if they do, they will realise you are too much of a handful and bring you back within the first few hours."

Sean bursts out laughing as Jasmine turns and slaps me across the chest.

"What are you trying to say?" she demands as I wrap my arms around her to keep her from hitting me again.

"That you are a complete brat, and you know how to push everyone's buttons without even trying."

"You make it sound like a bad thing." She leans forward until her lips are brushing against mine. "You love it when I'm a brat because you love nothing more than taking me over your knee. Isn't that right, *Maximus*?" My eyes widen as I feel myself hardening.

"What did you call me?"

Jasmine smiles seductively as she wiggles against my cock, now solid in my boxers.

"Maximus." Her voice is seductive, and when I glance at my brother, I find him smirking.

Not giving her any warning, I lift her with me and throw her back onto the bed so she is flat on her stomach. Gripping her hips, I lift her ass before slapping it once.

"You are pushing your luck, brat. Last warning. What's my name?"

She looks up at Sean, who shakes his head.

"Don't expect me to help you. You do it to yourself," he smiles.

"You are meant to love me, *Sean*."

His eyes widen before a grin spreads across his face.

"Now you've done it, Shorty." I spank her again, causing her to moan out loud. I look at my brother, who has moved closer to her. "Do you want to choose the punishment, or can I?"

"Tell me what you think, and then I'll decide," he answers.

"I'm thinking I fuck her pretty little pussy, hard, whilst spanking her. You can have her naughty little mouth, as we both know you love fucking her tight throat." Sean looks down at Jasmine and grins.

"Sounds perfect to me." He places a finger under her

chin as I pull down her underwear. She's already soaking wet. "Anything you want to say before I take away your ability to speak?" he asks her. Jasmine shakes her head, and I catch a glimpse of a smile.

"Then let us give you a reminder of who we are and what you are meant to call us," I add before thrusting forward and filling her as Sean grabs her hair and fills her mouth, leaving her utterly helpless against us, just the way she likes it.

Chapter Thirty-Three

SEAN

Something wakes me, and I'm unsure what until Jasmine groans in her sleep. She's leaning into me, her arm over my stomach. I press a kiss to the top of her head and slide an arm underneath her before closing my eyes and hoping to fall back to sleep.

A shout rings through the house at the same time as a loud alarm clock ringtone sounds in the room.

"Fuck!" Maximus is out of bed as quick as me. Both of us scrambling to pull on our boxers.

"Who set the alarm?" Jasmine asks, looking around. Before we get a chance to answer, the door flies open and two people in uniform pile into the room. Jasmine screams, pulling the sheet up to cover her naked body as Maximus sees red.

"Get the fuck out!"

"We have a warrant!" one of the officers answers, crossing his arms over his chest with a smug grin on his fucking face.

"I don't give a shit! My fiancée is naked, and I will not

let you stand there while she gets dressed!" he yells, pointing towards the door. Jason charges into the room and stands beside me as I'm the closest. Together, we block their view of Jasmine, still sitting in bed. Maximus stays on the other side of the bed, ready to protect her if needed.

"Your warrant doesn't allow you to be present in a room with people who are getting dressed. Now get out before I contact the police station myself." Jason stares at the cockier of the two officers, who looks younger than me. For a moment, I don't think either one of them is going to back down, but eventually, Jason wins as the officers turn to walk from the room.

"You have two minutes; I will be timing you," the cocky bastard calls as he closes the door. Jason turns around and looks at Jasmine.

"Get dressed and come down to Christian's office. Do not say a word to or in front of them. We will get this sorted." He leans over and presses a kiss to the top of her head as she nods silently.

"What the fuck do they want?" Maximus growls as he pulls on his sweatpants and grabs a t-shirt.

"Our relationship has been reported," Jason answers.

"What for? We aren't doing anything wrong!" Jasmine protests.

"No, we're not, and once they see that, they will have no choice but to leave with their tail between their legs," I reassure her as I go to the drawer of clothes she has in here and grab some underwear, leggings and a vest top for her to put on. "Get dressed, Princess; I don't trust them not to storm back in."

Jasmine gets out of bed, and Maximus helps her get dressed as I pull on my sweatpants. Jason gives me a nod before walking out of the room, no doubt to buy us a little time to get Jasmine covered.

I turn around to check on her, but Maximus has her attention while pulling one of his hoodies over her head.

"Don't worry, Shorty, we have planned for this." He takes her face in his hands and presses a kiss to her lips. Jasmine nods as the door opens, and the officers walk back in.

"Time's up," he smirks, looking from me to Maximus and Jasmine. I don't miss the way he checks Jasmine out. I'm sure he was hoping she wouldn't be completely covered. I step back from the door and signal for Maximus to take Jasmine ahead of me. With his arm around her shoulder, holding her protectively, he leads her past the police and onto the landing. I step to follow them but stop when I'm in front of the cocky prick.

"Officer ...?" I ask, wanting his name.

"Davies," he answers with that smug smirk as he puffs his chest out. He's skinny and probably never thrown a real punch in his life, but he loves to hide behind the badge. I keep my voice calm and collected as I address him.

"Officer Davies. I'm not sure how long you have been in the police or if your mother taught you any manners, but it's rude to check out another man's fiancée in front of him. Especially when you are trying to scare said fiancée in their own home. Just a word of the wise, do not look at our future wife like that again."

"What are you actually going to do about it if I do?" he grins smugly. I make a mental note to check out his history once all of this is handled because I bet he has a long list of victims who are too scared to speak out.

"All I will do is make a call to the right people. How they decide to handle your blatant disrespect is up to them. But

I'm sure I won't be the first to complain or the last." I walk away from him and follow my brother and Jasmine.

"It's not like she's really your fiancée. Unless reports are right, and you are going to break the law by all marrying your little whore."

Anger boils in my gut, and I take a step forward to have a word with this gobby piece of shit, but his colleague jumps in front of him, looking outraged.

"Wow, Guy, that was out of line!" the officer next to him protests before looking at me. "I am so sorry for what my colleague just said, sir. I assure you we do not all act this way."

"Thank you, Officer…?"

"Jones, sir." He steps forward and holds out his hand. "I can assure you that you will have no further issues with Officer Davies, and I will happily speak to anyone you decide to discuss this interaction with." He looks genuinely appalled by Guy's actions. I shake his hand and give him a nod of thanks.

"Sean, your brother wants you downstairs. I'll deal with these two." I turn to Terry's voice and see how angry he is. I bet he crashed here last night, if he slept at all.

"Okay, but watch Officer Davies here; I don't trust his intentions," I tell him. Terry looks from me to the officers.

"Why do you think I'm here." He points to his chest, and I realise he is wearing his own body cam, except his is better hidden. A small smile spreads across my face as Terry winks. He's good, I'll give him that. Leaving the landing, I head downstairs to find out what the hell is going on.

Maximus and Jasmine are standing outside the office, talking to Mrs Brown.

"Mr O'Reilly, I'm fetching some tea and coffee. Would you like anything?" she asks as I reach them. She also reverts back to calling us Mr O'Reilly when we have unfamiliar guests.

"Just a coffee, please, Mrs Brown." She smiles and walks away from me as I take a step so I'm on one side of Jasmine and Maximus on the other.

"Remember, Shorty, we've done nothing wrong. Let Christian do the talking and only answer questions you are happy to. They cannot force you to talk." Jasmine looks up at Maximus and nods before taking a deep breath. I lean in and press a kiss to the top of her head.

"We are right here, Princess. We aren't going anywhere." When Jasmine turns to me, I see just how amazing our woman is. I give her a wink, hoping to encourage her, as I open the door and step back to let them walk in holding hands.

Entering the office behind the others, I see Christian sitting behind his desk, with Jason beside him. Of course, he's dressed in a suit, and his whole body screams dominance. He has never backed down to the police before, and I know he won't over this. He turns to Jasmine and gives her a smile before nodding at us. He holds out a hand, and Jasmine walks to his side before leaning in and kissing him. Christian goes to stand for her to sit in his chair, but she places a hand on his shoulders.

"I wish to stand but thank you."

"Are you okay, Sweetheart? I hear the officers upstairs gave you a bit of a fright." He places an arm around her waist, and she leans against the chair.

"They were rather rude." She turns her attention to the sergeant in front of the desk and lifts one brow. "I didn't appreciate the wake-up call or the fact they were reluctant to let me get dressed without an audience."

"I've been made aware, and the officer will be dealt

with. All I can do for now is apologise to you, Miss Connors." Jasmine nods once as she continues looking ahead with her back poker straight and head held high. I don't miss the way Christian looks up at her, and my own pride is reflected on his face.

"You might want to add a couple of other indiscretions when dealing with Officer Guy Davies's attitude," I add, walking over to the sofa where Maximus is and sitting beside him.

"What happened?" Christian asks, turning his attention to me.

"I had to have a word with him about how it is considered bad manners to check out another man's fiancée in front of him." I sit back on the sofa and try to ignore how Maximus stiffens beside me. "He obviously disagreed as he proceeded to point out a few incorrect facts and then resorted to name-calling." I ensure I have the sergeant's full attention when I add. "I will not tolerate anyone disrespecting Miss Connors or making her feel uncomfortable in her own home. I know his colleague Officer Jones will vouch for Davies's behaviour as he encouraged me to complain."

I watch the sergeant and notice his jaw ticking slightly, obviously unhappy with his officer's actions.

"I would like to know what he said." Jasmine stares at me, and I can see she's not happy. "I ignored the way he tried to throw his authority around, but I will not have him calling anyone in my household names." She crosses her arms over her chest and turns her attention to the sergeant.

"I am happy to take a statement from Mr O'Reilly so you are not bothered by the off-"

"I think our fiancée has a right to know what was said," Jason interrupts. "Plus, she is not the only one who wishes to hear this." He turns his attention to me at the same time as Christian and Jasmine.

"He pointed out what we are all very much aware of, which is Miss Connors is legally not my fiancée. He enjoyed saying that it would be against the law for us all to marry her, which, again, we are all well aware of. He then proceeded to say, and I quote, 'Unless reports are right and you are going to break the law by all marrying your little whore'." All three of my brothers' backs straighten further as they turn their attention to the sergeant, who has lost quite a bit of colour from his face.

"I want his badge," Christian says from the desk as he removes his arm from around Jasmine and leans his elbows on the desk in front of him, interlocking his fingers. "I want your word, Sergeant Myles, that this *Officer Davies* will be dealt with and not given the chance to disrespect anyone else again." The way he stares at the sergeant tells me all I need to know. He will ensure the arrogant prick is fired, and he can never work as an officer of the law again. Then, Christian will take his life, and no one will even notice he's missing.

Sergeant Myles turns his attention away from us and to the officer standing in the room. Myles looks like he's ready to blow his top. It seems like I was right, and Officer Davies has made a habit of trying to act bigger than he is.

"Go and tell him he's to get his arse here now!" The officer nods at his sergeant and leaves the room.

"While we wait for your officers, would you like to finally explain to my brothers and Miss Connors what it was you so rudely dragged them out of bed for," Christian says as he sits back in his chair, looking annoyed as Jasmine places a reassuring hand on his shoulder. It works as he reaches up to put a hand over hers.

"We had a report that there was a polygamous relationship which was about to change and break the law by becoming bigamous. There was also the belief that Miss Connors was being forced into this relationship against her will, as well as reports of incest."

"Incest?" Maximus and Jasmine call out at the same time.

"I hope that you are referring to the fact that our fiancée was once our stepsister and not accusing my brothers and I of such acts," Christian warns, leaning forward again.

"Of course, there was no mention of you and your brothers taking part in such relations." Sergeant Myles pulls a handkerchief out of his pocket and wipes his brow. It takes everything in me not to smile at how nervous he is.

"That's what I thought." Christian opens a drawer in his desk and pulls out a folder before sliding it in front of the sergeant. "All documentation is in there, as well as a letter of consent to check these with the relevant authorities." He sits back again and places a hand on Jasmine's, which is back on his shoulder, both looking calm and at ease.

"Inside, you will find a copy of our father's marriage certificate to Miss Connor's mother, Carol Connors. It is dated, and if you do the maths, you will see that Miss Connors was one month from her eighteenth birthday when we met at the wedding. The four of us are of no blood relation to her, which makes the claims of incest ridiculous." We watch as Sergeant Myles flicks through the papers in the file.

"There is a copy of our notice of marriage. Only Miss Connors and myself are named on it, as we are the only ones getting legally married. My brothers and Miss Connors then have a blessing, where they exchange promises to each other rather than any formal ceremony, but it will not be legally binding, meaning they will be husband and wife by name, not by law."

"We are all well aware that she is not our fiancée nor will she be our wife legally; that does not change our love for her," Jason adds, stepping closer to Jasmine and placing a hand on the bottom of her back.

"There is no law to stop us from calling her our wife, same as there is nothing stopping her from referring to us as her husbands," Maximus adds.

"And how do you feel about all of this, Miss Connors?" Sergeant Myles asks. Jasmine smiles at him as she shrugs.

"I don't need a piece of paper to tell me they are mine, same as they don't need one to claim me as theirs. Society may not classify our relationship as normal, but I don't care. I will always love all four of the O'Reilly brothers equally, and although they may have once been my stepbrothers, I never saw them as such.

"The three years they were in my life before we started this relationship, they did nothing but protect me and show me how strong I am. I'm not ashamed of our relationship, nor feel it worthy of this invasion of our privacy. Whoever told all these lies should be charged with wasting valuable police time." She leans on the table and stares Sergeant Myles in the eye.

"As for me being forced into this relationship, that is just laughable. If anything, I've forced them, as they had to accept I could never choose just one of them. The only reason I am legally marrying Christian is for my own protection, should anything happen to one of my husbands. I will legally be an O'Reilly and will be treated as such by being able to be their advocate when they cannot represent themselves." She stands back up and leans into Jason rather than Christian. Jason places his arm around her waist and holds her close, proving she does not love one over the other.

"If you need me to give a formal statement and confirm all I have said, I will happily do so with our solicitor present."

Sergeant Myles wipes at his face again, and we can see he knows there is nothing illegal about any of our relationships.

A knock comes from the door, and Christian shouts for them to enter. The officer sent to retrieve the others walks in ahead of Davies and Jones with Terry on their tail. Terry looks like he's ready to commit murder, and I can only assume he has heard all that Davies said about Jasmine.

"Officer Davies, I believe you have something to say to the O'Reillys and Miss Connors," the sergeant snaps. Davies looks around at us all and tries to fake sincerity as his eyes land on Jasmine.

"Sorry, I called you a whore."

Maximus twitches next to me, and I quickly grab his arm and shake my head, reminding him he can't risk jumping the prick, yet.

"Apology not accepted." All of our heads snap to Jasmine as Officer Davies looks shocked. "You came into my home, barged into my room whilst I was in bed and tried to intimidate me before calling me a whore."

"Well, in my defence, Miss Connors, from what I could see on my search, every room is yours. I do believe I've never met a woman who sleeps in five different beds and isn't paid."

This time, it takes all my strength to keep Maximus under control as Officer Jones, Sergeant Myles, and my brothers yell out in protest.

"Sergeant Myles, if you do not deal with his lack of

respect, I will take this as high as I need to," Christian warns as his temper gets dangerously close to boiling point. Jasmine steps next to him and places a hand on his cheek, forcing him to look at her.

"He doesn't matter. He is obviously a spoilt kid with a narcissistic personality disorder. His comments do not affect me. As I said a moment ago, I am proud of our family."

Christian takes a deep breath before looking at the sergeant who is watching Jasmine.

"Miss Connors, I am extremely sorry for his lack of respect, and I can assure you he will be dealt with." He turns his attention to the officer before adding, "Starting with his immediate suspension." Officer Davies goes to argue, but the sergeant has had enough. "Officer Jones, escort him to the police car, please. I will be there shortly."

"Yes, sarge," Officer Jones replies before looking at Jasmine. "I am sorry for the way my colleague spoke to you. That kind of treatment was unnecessary and cruel."

"Thank you," Jasmine replies, giving him a small smile.

"It's the least I can do," he smiles before nodding in the direction of Jason and Christian, followed by the two of us on the sofa. Turning his attention to his soon-to-be former colleague, he nudges him towards the door, and I can hear them arguing as soon as they think they are out of earshot.

"Again, I am sorry for the inconvenience of our visit. I can assure you everything will be documented, so if anyone tries this again, all the paperwork is available."

"You can keep those copies on file; I have the originals," Christian says as he straightens his jacket and walks around to the front of his desk. "I understand why you had to visit; that was never the issue. You believed a young woman was being forced to be in a relationship with four men, which is something that should never be taken lightly. However, I want Officer Davies dealt with, and I will be sending my solicitor to ensure he is."

"As you should. Its officers like that who give our forces a bad name." Sergeant Myles holds out his hand, and Christian shakes it. Turning his attention to Jasmine, he gives her a warm smile.

"I wish you and your fiancés all the best on your special day, and I have a feeling you will all live a very happy life together."

Jasmine steps forward with her hand out, which he takes with a fond smile.

"Thank you, that means a lot." She looks around the room at the four of us with a big smile. "I know we will all have a life filled with happiness and love."

The sergeant smiles at her fondly before saying one last goodbye and leaving the five of us alone together.

I swear we all count to ten before launching ourselves at Jasmine. Jason gets there first, picks her up and twirls her around in a circle as she squeals laughing.

"You were outstanding, Jazzy!" he lowers her enough to kiss her hard before placing her back on her feet.

"Outstanding doesn't cover it! I don't think I have ever been so proud of you, Princess," I grin, pulling her into my arms so I can kiss her. I feel her being pulled away from me to see Maximus grab her face and smash his lips into hers.

"I know I said not to worry, but you controlled the whole room!" he laughs, picking her up and squeezing her tight before putting her back down. She turns in his arms, grinning as she faces Christian. I don't think I have ever seen so much pride and love on his face as he has right now.

"I know you were meant to do all the talking, but I needed to have my say," she says, smiling at him.

"You were amazing, Sweetheart. You were calm and in

control of everything, and I, for one, am so proud of you." Stepping forward, he places a hand on her cheek and kisses her. Jasmine throws her arms around his neck and kisses him back before pulling back, looking worried.

"What time is it?" she demands, grabbing his wrist to check the time. "Shit. Verity will be here in an hour." Spinning around, she rushes out the door without even saying goodbye, only to return thirty seconds later to give each of us a kiss on the cheek before rushing back out of the room. The four of us laugh as we look around at each other.

"Well, that was a fun morning," Mrs Brown laughs, walking into the office with a tray of coffee and mugs. I take them from her and place them on the desk to begin making up everyone's drinks.

"You can say that again, but we always knew it would happen sooner or later," Jason sighs, walking over to the sofa and taking a seat. Looking around at my brothers as I start handing out the coffees, I don't miss the huge smiles on their faces. Our girl stood there this morning, held her head high and laid her claim on us. She didn't seem embarrassed or scared. Instead, she was proud and showed us how far she has come.

"I said I would take young Jasmine's coffee to her," Mrs Brown says as she picks up Jasmine's favourite mug and walks out.

"Can I just say our woman is fucking amazing! She was so brave and took no shit from any of them," Maximus grins. "When she refused to accept that prick's apology, I nearly cheered."

"I thought he was going to explode," Jason laughs, taking his mug from me.

"I honestly thought she would accept his apology to avoid a scene, but she was so mad she didn't care what happened," Christian grins. "After everything last night and now this, I thought she would struggle, but she is getting stronger and stronger with each issue that gets thrown at us."

"That's because she is far stronger than she ever gave herself credit for," I point out, sitting on the sofa by Jason.

"It just confirms she was made to be ours. She may not be an O'Reilly by name yet, but she proved, once again, that she is in spirit. I, for one, can't wait to marry her," Jason adds before holding up his mug. "Cheers to the most amazing fiancée any four men could ever ask for."

"Cheers!" we call together before taking a sip of our coffee and thinking about how lucky we are to have this amazing woman in our lives.

Chapter Thirty-Four

CHRISTIAN

"Officer Davies has been suspended immediately following further investigation into his behaviour, not only today, but it seems he has a bit of a reputation for being a smug arsehole."

I sit back in my desk chair as I pinch the bridge of my nose.

"It's a start, at least. I want him struck off the force with a permanent black mark on his record," I order my solicitor.

"Trust me, he won't be working again any time soon. I should have his personal information to you by the end of the day."

I thank him and end the call before a deep yawn escapes. After a very late night, I'm exhausted trying to work out who was trying to get into Jasmine's room. She remembers seeing something out the corner of her eye at some point but isn't sure if it was possibly the jacks that held up the shutters or a person. Some ripped fabric was also stuck in one of the jacks so it could have been that. There was also the question of how they got up there and fitted the two jacks without setting off the alarms or being spotted.

Maximus found what he believes is a climbing hook in the wall above Jasmine's window, which adds more questions than answers. He will go back up safely with the ladder he will purchase later when he gets back from dropping off the new security details at the hotel where the wedding and reception are being held.

Terry and I were up until five this morning going over the footage and trying to find some kind of time stamp for when the jacks were put into place, but there was nothing. It looks like the footage has been corrupted, so it's been picked up by Logan, who will review it and see what he can dig up.

At this rate, Calvin and his team will be paying Jason for the manor they purchased from him with the money they are making from us alone. We have some of their guys surrounding the house, and we hired extra security for the wedding. Jasmine will now have Jason's security, Gordon, with her and Layton. Calvin has stepped up to be Jason's security if he needs it, but hopefully, with the wedding being so close, the only time he will be leaving the house is with me, or I will be here so Terry can go wherever he's needed.

"Daddy?"

Her sweet voice brings me out of the constant worry as I look up and see her standing at the door. She's wearing a beautiful white blouse with a black pencil skirt. Her hair's pulled back from her face but hangs loosely over her shoulders. As gorgeous as she has always been, there are times like now when her beauty truly leaves me speechless, and I wonder what I have done to deserve this fantastic woman in my life.

"Are you okay?" she asks, walking into the room and

heading to me as I hold out an arm, desperate to hold her, if only for a moment.

Pulling her onto my lap as I push my chair back a little, I capture her lips with mine, not caring if her lipstick transfers over to me.

"I will be better when you are safely away from this house next week," I answer. Jasmine smiles sweetly whilst wiping her thumb over my lips to remove the lipstick.

"At least no one will get to us if we spend the week of our honeymoon in bed." Wrapping her arms around my neck, she leans to the side, brushing her lips over my ear. "I can't think of any better way to celebrate our marriage than with a constant stream of orgasms." Her teeth graze over my earlobe, and I'm unable to hold in the moan that leaves me as my cock hardens underneath her.

"What time is your appointment?" I ask as she kisses the side of my neck. My hand slides up her thigh and to her hip so I can grip hold of anything, anchoring her to me.

Jasmine giggles and lifts her head, smiling at me, telling me I'm not going to like her answer.

"I'm leaving in a minute, so no time for what you're thinking," she winks before standing up as I groan with frustration.

"You are turning into a tease, Baby girl," I sigh, rubbing my face as she kisses my cheek.

"I will make it up to you later." She leans on the arm of my desk chair and grins. "I will let you put me in any position and use any hole you want."

Standing up, I force her to step back and trap her against the desk, just like I did the very first time I told her how I felt. Placing my hands on the wood behind her, caging her in, I lean in, so I am looking deep into her eyes.

"How am I meant to concentrate today when all I can

think about is bending you over and making you come on my cock until neither of us can think or see clearly?" Unlike the timid little thing my girl once was, she doesn't look shocked; instead, she places her arms over my shoulders and closes the little distance between us.

"I think you will be just fine, Daddy. Just think about how wet I will be as I try on the dress I will marry you in on Saturday," she grins as I wrap an arm around her waist. "But first," she whispers against my lips, "I have to go and meet my maid of honour who is probably here." She kisses me and tries to step away from me, but I tighten my hold and kiss her with everything I've got until she's gasping for breath and limp in my arm.

Stepping back from her with a grin as she tries to get control over herself, I sit back in my chair.

"Have a lovely time with your friends, Sweetheart. I will be here waiting for you."

She stares at me for a moment before turning around and strutting towards the door, purposely swinging her hips as she goes.

"While I'm out, try to decide which one of us will be on our knees later." Turning around, she looks back at me and slowly closes the door. "FYI, it won't be me," she winks, closing the door behind her.

"Carry on, and you will be *over* my knee!" I call out, hearing her giggle from the other side of the door. Then, the click of her heels becomes quieter as she walks away from my office.

That woman is going to be the death of me. If it's not because of the constant worry of keeping her safe, it will be due to the way she makes my heart race and my mind forget I don't have the stamina of a twenty-one-year-old anymore.

My phone pings on the desk, signalling the security cameras have been activated. Looking at the screen, I spot Travis pulling up outside before escorting Verity out of the car, where Jasmine and her two security guards are waiting for her. Closing the screen, not needing to see any more, I lean back in my chair and attempt to control the urge to stop Jasmine from leaving the safety of this house. Only to remember it's not as safe as I would like it to be.

My office door flies open, hitting the wall as Travis Donavon storms into the room, slamming the door closed behind him. I'm straight up onto my feet, ready for whatever this prick wants to throw at me now.

"One month, O'Reilly!" he yells, slamming his hands on my desk and leaning forward as I stand behind it, already working out all the ways I can get to him to kick his ass. "One fucking month of having you back in my life, and you are bringing shit to my door!"

"What are you throwing a hissy fit over now, Donavon?" I demand, leaning forward on my desk and refusing to back down to this arsehole.

"Why the hell is Nicholson contacting me asking about you and your brothers?"

Shit. Why didn't I even consider he would ask Travis about me? He's trying desperately to get Travis working for him and will use any reason to contact him.

"What's he said?" I demand.

"He wanted to know if you are a threat to him and what you deal in." Travis stands up and crosses his arms over his chest. "I swear to god, O'Reilly, I will not let you put my girl in danger; she has been through enough shit without you dragging her down."

"You think I want *my girl* in danger? Do you really believe I would endanger Verity or any of Jasmine's friends?" Stepping back from the desk, sending my chair flying backwards, I storm around to the front of it and stand inches from Travis, who uncrosses his arms, looking as ready to fight as I am.

"I need to know what he said, and then I will know what action to take. If I thought Verity was in danger just by being around Jasmine, I would ask you to take *both of them* and run. To hide Jasmine away from me and my brothers until we could take care of things." Travis stares at me as what I said sinks in.

"I've done all I can to keep that man and his shit away from my family for the last month. I don't need another reason for him to be contacting me. I will keep Verity from Jasmine if it's for her own safety."

My anger explodes, the red mist starts to descend, and I act before I think. Grabbing him by his jacket, I pin him to the wall, taking him by surprise.

"You have no fucking idea how much shit is going down here right now, so you coming in here throwing a tantrum is not fucking helping!" I snarl in his face. Travis attempts to push me away, but I'm stuck tight as I stare at him.

"I will fucking kill you if anything happens to my fiancée because of you lot!" Getting in my face as he grabs my top and spins us around so I'm pinned to the wall. He goes to swing at me, but I'm quicker and punch him in the stomach, winding him and giving me a chance to knock him to his knees. "You stupid fucking piece of shit!" he snarls, jumping back to his feet before we throw ourselves at each other and end up on the wooden floor.

"Enough!"

Someone grabs me from behind at the same time as someone else pulls Travis to his feet. Jason steps between us with his hands out, trying to keep as much distance between us as possible.

"For fuck's sake! I thought we were past this shit!" he yells as I shrug off whoever is holding me. Travis shrugs off Terry but doesn't stop staring at me. "What the hell are you fighting about now?"

"Ask your arsehole of a brother," Travis snarls. "He's the one who has pissed off Nicholson!"

"What the fuck is he talking about?" Jason yells, turning his full attention to me.

"I don't know, ask him! He's the one that came in here shouting about it!" I point to Travis as he crosses his arms over his chest. Jason turns around to face Travis as I walk away and grab a bottle of water from the side. Needing to do something, anything to distract myself.

"Tell me what's going on?" Jason asks calmly. I can feel Travis's eyes following me, but I don't allow myself to look back at him.

"I had a call today from him, asking questions about you guys. What you are into? Are you a threat to him? Did I know anything about the uprising against you? He also asked if you were the type to kill dealers?"

"What did you tell him?" I ask, sitting behind my desk chair and opening the bottle, desperate to hide how much my hands are shaking.

"Fuck all. I told him we hardly speak, and as far as I'm concerned, you don't deal with anything that would be considered a threat to him. As for killing dealers, I told him you only would if they were dealing on your properties, but even then, you would give a warning first."

"Thank you," I sigh, sitting back in my seat.

"I didn't do it for you, arsehole. I did it for Jaz. I don't give two shits what happens to you." Travis walks up to my desk and leans on it again. "But like I said, there is nothing I wouldn't do to protect my fiancée."

"Fiancée?" Jason asks as I look up at Travis, the question in my eye. "Jazzy never said anything."

"Because Verity isn't telling her until you return from the honeymoon. She doesn't want to take any focus off Jaz," Travis explains, looking at Jason before turning his attention back to me.

"Congratulations," I say, surprising myself how genuinely happy I am for him. He may be a pain in my arse, but I know he loves Jasmine's best friend and makes her happy; that's something I will always be happy for. That girl struggled with her life, but I know the Donavons will always protect her.

"Fuck off," he growls, pulling a seat in front of the desk and falling into it. I can't help but smile, knowing that's his way of thanking me.

"We would never knowingly put Verity in danger," I point out. Travis nods as he knows that deep down. "But lots has been happening in a short space of time, and we are doing all we can to keep the girls and ourselves safe."

"What's been going on?" he asks as Jason approaches us, grabbing a second chair. "Did you really kill six dealers in one night?"

"Yes, I had a very good reason, and that's all I'm saying on the matter." Jason looks at me and mouths, "Carol." I nod once, watching his shoulders relax a little.

"As for what's been going on? How long have you got?" I sigh, rubbing the bridge of my nose.

"Not long, so stop stalling and tell me what the fuck you've gotten yourself into this time, O'Reilly."

Chapter Thirty-Five

JASMINE

"So what? They just barged into your room, no warning at all?" Danielle frowns as we all climb out of the Mercedes Christian purchased for days like this when a five-seater wouldn't be enough.

"Yep. The arsehole even wanted to stay while I got dressed," I answer, shaking my head. "I thought Maximus was going to lose his shit. He probably would have if Jason hadn't come in when he did."

Verity comes and stands beside me from the other side of the car and links her arm with mine.

"I hadn't even thought about the police and how they may see our types of relationships. I'm sorry you were put through that." She gives my arm a little squeeze while giving me a reassuring look. I smile before leaning my head on her shoulder.

"I hadn't either, to be honest. But it looks like the guys always knew it was a possibility and had everything ready to prove we were doing nothing wrong." I had no idea Christian had everything to hand like that. I want to know how he has a copy of Carol and Tommy's marriage certificate. Is there anything that man can't get hold of?

"Maybe I need to get Travis to put together a folder like that. At least if it's to hand, we don't have to worry about being caught out." She glances at the distance momentarily as she gets lost in her thoughts. She has had so many reasons to be on edge the last few months that I know a simple thing like this will worry her.

Maybe I shouldn't have said anything. But then I know I couldn't have hidden it either. At least now she knows it's possible so she can be prepared like Christian was. Her daddies and Ethan will always do everything they can to help give her peace of mind.

I tighten the hold on her arm, meaning she has no choice but to lean into me. For a moment, we smile together, knowing we are both finally doing okay after having so much shit thrown at us by our pathetic excuse of parents. I look at Danielle and Abbi chatting as we walk down the street. Layton and Gordon are close by. I will be back to having extra security for a while, but I'm okay with that. I've tried to put a brave face on, but last night scared me.

There was a moment when I was alone in the panic room, and I had no idea what was happening outside of it. I hated not knowing if the guys were safe or if people had managed to get into the house. I plan on talking to the guys tonight and telling them how hard it was and that I need to be able to reach someone in that kind of situation. The room is completely soundproof, so even if I were to call someone, I wouldn't be heard from the outside.

I look around at my friends and realise how lucky I am that I don't have to hide much from the girls. Okay, they have no idea how bad the threat is and how much I know, but I can talk to them about the basics. They all know what kind of lives the O'Reillys live as their parents are all part of the same world. It makes everything much easier, as I have never been very good at lying. I will never know how I hid how desperate my life had gotten before the guys saved me.

"Is Luna going to be there this morning?" Verity asks, dragging me from my thoughts.

Today is not a day to think about the past. Today is another day closer to the wedding, and even with everything going on, I can't wait to be Mrs O'Reilly. I'm determined to make it down the aisle. I refuse to let anyone ruin this wedding for any of us. We deserve to be married and together; no one can take that away from us.

"Her and Chelsea are meeting us half an hour after our appointment starts," I answer with a smile. "She is so excited to try on her dress again. She has had Chelsea or Calvin send me a picture daily so we can count down together." That little girl has become my little shadow, and I love her.

With everything going on, Calvin and the guys decided to keep her from the house, which I understand entirely. Chelsea and Luna, like the rest of us, have been through so much that I would do anything to protect them from anything else. One of the guys will drop them off at the appointment today and then pick them up after, just to be on the safe side. Logan had initially wanted to pull Luna from the wedding party, so she and Chelsea wouldn't have to be there. But Calvin pointed out that as they are providing the security, it doesn't look good that they won't risk their own family being there. I think it helped that Christian and Jason assured him that they would have cancelled it if there were a real threat of anything happening, and we would elope. It's an option that crossed my mind a few times last night.

"Has she forgiven her mum for not letting her join us at the club yet?" Abbi asks. The four of us burst out laughing, remembering her trying to tell her mum we could get her into any nightclub.

"I think it may have taken her a few days, but she seems to have forgotten about it all now."

We all turn the corner and look to the bottom of the street where the large bridal shop is situated. Every time I see the shop, my heart bursts with excitement, and tears burn my eyes. I love the dress I've picked out. I never understood how people said they *knew* when they tried on their dream dress, but I burst into tears when I saw my reflection as I stood in that long white dress. It is perfect in every way, and I know the guys will love it. Am I hoping at least one of them cries? Absolutely! I want them to experience all the feels as I walk down that aisle. Am I betting the one to cry will be Maximus? Of course I am!

"I can't believe you are finally picking up the dress to take home!" Abbi exclaims as she grabs the arm Verity isn't still holding.

"Do the guys have any idea what kind of dress it is?" Danielle asks next to her.

"Do they shite? It's driving Maximus mad, not knowing," Layton laughs from behind.

"I nearly died when you called Jason and told him it was black. The poor guy was trying so hard to be supportive and excited for you, but there was no hiding the sheer panic," Gordon adds as I look over my shoulder at him, grinning.

"I honestly thought he was okay with it. I was disappointed that he didn't react at all."

I had been sure he would have had some sort of panic

attack. If there is anything Jason loves more than his family, it's shopping for us, especially me. I don't think he can go longer than a few days without buying me something. He knows my style better than I do, so when I decided to tease him and say I had a black dress and was worried about what Christian would say, he was so supportive and told me not to worry about Christian if I could look as hot as I do in a little black dress he knows I would look like a hot princess in a black bridal one.

"Jaz, I think I can speak for all of us when I say those guys wouldn't care what you wore. All they want is you and for you to be their wife," Verity says, smiling. I can't help smiling back as I know she's right. Plus, I'm just as excited about the wedding as they are. I just wish people would stop causing so much drama for us and let us enjoy this special occasion.

We come to a stop outside of the shop and look up at the beautiful building. It is so luxurious and stands out from the rest of the street. It's definitely high-end, but that's not surprising, given that they have designed dresses for some of the wealthiest people. Celebrities and even royalty come here for wedding dresses, ballgowns, cocktail dresses and, some, for their fancy cruises and special occasions. There is a long waiting list even to get an initial appointment, which, of course, Jason managed to get them to forget. Apparently, a few of my cocktail dresses came from here, and they couldn't wait to meet the girl Jason had been shopping for.

"You ready?" Verity asks as she lets go of my arm and steps back so I can press the bell. I look around at my three best friends and two security guards, who are all grinning broadly at me. The excitement I'm feeling echoed on their faces.

"Let's do this."

Pressing the bell, we giggle excitedly while waiting for someone to call through the intercom to check who we are.

"Yes?" I hear Penelope ask, taking me a little by surprise with her sharp tone.

"Oh, hi. It's Jasmine of the O'Reilly wedding." I look around at the group and notice they all picked up on her initial tone. There are some muffled voices through the intercom before Penelope speaks again, sounding a little cheerier, but there's still something like panic in her voice.

"Of course, Jasmine. I'll come down to let you in now." The intercom goes dead, and I look around at the others, who are frowning.

"She's usually just buzzed us in," Layton points out, his body language instantly changing as he and Gordon share a look before going into guard dog mode.

"I'm sure she just has another party in. Or something is going on; let's face it, they are always busy," Abbi points out. But I don't miss the warning look she gives Layton.

"I'm sure that's it," I reply, trying to push back the worry that something else is about to go wrong.

"Still, I would like to speak to her first and check the building out," Layton says before turning to Gordon. "You stay with the girls in the entrance hall; I know the building better."

Gordon nods as Danielle rolls her eyes.

"Oh please, it's probably that the order of champagne hasn't chilled to the right temperature. I know these ladies, things like that cause them to go into a panic." I look at her and know she's probably right. I'm about to say just as much when the sound of the door opening stops me. We all turn to look at the door as Penelope stands there.

"Sorry for the delay. Come on in."

No hello or friendly smile and warm welcome. Penelope

doesn't even look at me. I also don't miss the way Gordon takes hold of my wrist, a sign he is ready to get me out of here if he needs to.

"Ma'am, is everything okay?" Layton asks as he steps in front of me because even I can see that everything is *not* okay.

Chapter Thirty-Six

JASON

I walk through the house, enjoying the peace and quiet for a moment. Everyone has a million and one things to do right now. If it's not trying to find out who attempted to break into our home last night or who is trying to bring us down, it's to do with the wedding.

The closer we get to the weekend, the busier everyone seems to be. There always seem to be calls to make or things to pick up, and that's before we even include all the shit that's been going down.

Christian and I filled Travis in on what's been going on. It turns out Christian had once again tried to hide shit from me. McIntire told him two days ago that Nicholson was asking about us. Travis assured us that it didn't sound like Nicholson was looking to rise against us, but that doesn't mean it won't happen eventually.

As soon as Travis left, I demanded to know about the dealers. As I suspected, Christian managed to track down anyone Carol was associated with through other contacts. The six he killed the other night were all who were left.

Dealers don't have the longest life span, as they usually piss someone off or use their own drugs and end up overdosing. Either way, he believes everyone who ever touched Jasmine is dead.

I have spent the last half an hour training in the sparring room, trying to work out what the hell we are going to do. We discussed cancelling the wedding and developing a new plan, but it may be too late. Plus, I can't see Jasmine agreeing to cancel it; we don't want to ask her to.

As much as I'm looking forward to the wedding itself, I'm now looking even more forward to the honeymoon—two whole weeks of just the five of us in the villa. We have no plans but just to take some time to relax and enjoy the start of our new lives with our wife.

What Jasmine doesn't know is that after the initial two weeks, we are taking turns to take her away for a week. Maximus is taking her to Italy—Sean, to Spain. Christian has opted for Paris, and I'm taking her to the Maldives. Christian has cleared everything with her school, and I'm sure he donated a large sum of money to ensure it doesn't affect her attempts to take on a lead role in the next production.

"What do you mean they are all dead?"

I look towards Christian's office, where the door is a jar. I rush in, desperate to know what the hell has happened now and who the fuck is dead.

The first thing I see when I open the office door is Christian pacing with his mobile to his ear.

"How is that even possible? What could have killed every single one of them like that?" he spots me when he turns and holds up a finger as he continues to listen to whoever is on the other end of the call.

My first thought is that something's happened to Jazzy

or the twins, but I know Christian would never shush me like that if there were a problem with them. Of course, that means it could be about anything.

What the fuck is going on? We have come under fire a few times in the past, but this is getting out of control now. I can't remember the last time I slept for more than an hour at a time. Even when I do, it's only because I'm exhausted or Jazzy is in my arms, so I know she's safe.

"Is there anything we can do to fix this? I don't care about the cost; money is no object."

I look back at my brother, frowning. If people are dead, what the hell can money do to fix the situation? What could he be referring to if not people? We don't own any animals other than the puppy, and I know he's fine as he's curled up on his bed in the corner watching Christian. That dog wants to be wherever he is, and it seems my brother has given up fighting it.

Christian's shoulders sag as he lets out a long, defeated sigh. "Okay, see what you can come up with, but I understand what you're saying. If I don't hear any different in the next twenty-four hours, I will take it as all is lost … No, don't worry about that; it wasn't your fault; keep it, and I hope you get to the bottom of it all before anything else goes wrong for you … You too. Thank you again for all you have done, goodbye." Christian hangs up the phone and curses under his breath before running his fingers through his hair.

"What's going on now?" I ask, unable to take the suspense anymore.

"That was the florist. They've just gone to their warehouse, where they keep all their flowers, and they are all dead. Thousands of pounds worth of plants withering and unrepairable."

"The flowers for the wedding?" I ask, already having guessed the answer.

"Gone. They don't think they can get anything replaced in time. They have lost everything."

I know I should feel sorry for them, and I do. But all I can concentrate on is how much this will devastate Jazzy. She loved the flowers she picked out for the bouquets and centrepieces. She dragged us all along and spent hours going back and forth with ideas. She has designed them all herself, and the florist was so excited about putting her pieces together. They even tried to encourage Jazzy to work for them, as they loved her designs so much.

"Do you think it is a coincidence? Or was this done because someone discovered the florist we are using?" I ask, knowing what my brother will be thinking and will have come to the same conclusion as me.

"You know my view on coincidences. There are none," he replies as he walks around his desk and switches on his laptop. "The florist thinks there must have been some sort of pesticide used locally which has gotten into the air vents or water." He looks up at me, and I see the disbelief in his tired eyes. "It must have been put in there on purpose. The florist knew it too, but she didn't want to admit someone could do something that evil on purpose."

"Oh, if only they knew how evil people can be," I sigh, taking my usual seat in front of his desk. "I was going to ask what the plan was to deal with everything from last night, but I think you are a little preoccupied now."

Christian sighs as he sits back in his chair and rubs his face. "Any chance you can grab me a coffee? I need to try and sort this shitstorm out whilst finding other options before I have to tell Jasmine what's happened." It's written all over his face how much he dreads that conversation. He's not the only one.

"No problem. I'll be back with it now." Standing from the chair, I head out of the room, wanting to give him a little time to clear his head.

When I find out who was responsible for this, I will be the one to end them. It's one thing to go after my brothers & me; let's face it, we've done plenty in the past to probably deserve it and more. But Jazzy has done nothing wrong, yet here she is being victimised purely because of her association with us again. It infuriates my brothers and me. There have been times we have all wondered if we are doing the right thing by marrying her. But Jaz has made it clear she would never let us walk away, even if we tried.

Reflecting on how well she handled herself in the last twenty-four hours shows how far she has come. She is handling everything so well, but we are waiting for the situation that will be what starts the avalanche of emotions she must be bottling up. Maybe this will be it.

It looks like we were all called away last night to ensure she was on her own. Drew suggested that it may have been a trial run, a way for the perpetrators to see if they could control the security system and get us away from the house. Logan doesn't think they are that clever, and they had hoped to trap Jazzy last night. To do what, I have no idea.

Until last night, they seemed to have left her alone. They didn't do anything at her hen party or try to get to her when she's out of the house. Nothing is adding up, and it's infuriating me. We are all stressed and being pushed to the breaking point, and I honestly think Jazzy is the only reason none of us has gone on a rampage and started killing people until we get answers.

I walk into the kitchen to find Mrs Brown humming as she makes up salad for dinner.

"Afternoon, Mrs Brown." I don't manage to hide the sigh that follows.

"Well, that doesn't sound like someone about to get married in a few days. What's happened now?" she asks, looking at me.

"Just things going wrong that shouldn't be. I'm sure everything will be okay," I smile, hoping to reassure her. She watches me momentarily and nods, knowing better than to ask too many questions.

"Well, one thing that will go right is that you will be happily married in just a few short days," she winks before returning to her salad. I smile, realising that it's one thing guaranteed to make me happy.

Everything aside, my Jazzy is about to be my wife, and that one thought alone is enough to lift any mood. That is until I hear the back door slam as someone charges into the kitchen.

"Where is he?"

Terry stands with his phone in his hand and looks furious.

"His office. What's happened?" I ask as Terry looks to the kitchen door, and Christian appears.

"What the fucks with the SOS message? I was on the phone," he demands, looking at our head of security.

"I know because I tried to call your phone. We are leaving now," Terry demands, heading to the garage door before looking at me. "That includes you."

"What the hell is going on?" Christian and I say in unison, never expecting the words that leave Terry's mouth.

"There's been an incident at the dress shop."

Chapter Thirty-Seven

CHRISTIAN

For the last twenty minutes, as Terry drives Jason and me to the shop where we know Jasmine and the girls are waiting for us, my mind has thought of everything that could be wrong. We have tried to talk to the guards and Jasmine, but the signal in the shop has been a real issue. I tried to call the shop, but the call just rang out.

Terry explained that he had a few calls where Layton would answer, but the line was too distorted for either of them to hear the other. In the end, he messaged with a brief explanation.

Layton: There has been an incident here, and I have taken control of the building. All girls are safe and will remain here with Gordon and me until you send back up or get here yourself. Someone has possibly hacked the system, and I don't trust using their phone line or internet, and the signal is terrible. The important facts are that the building is secure physically, and the girls are safe and in no immediate danger.

I wanted to message him back and demand to know what was happening, but Terry insisted on letting him concentrate on everything there and to be patient. Usually, I'm the most patient out of all of us, but after everything that happened with the florists and yesterday's possible kidnapping attempt, I need to know what the fuck has happened now.

"Messages still aren't going through to Jazzy. I haven't bothered trying to call."

I don't bother turning to look at my brother behind me. I know he will be just as on edge as me. Neither of us likes not knowing what's happening when Jasmine is involved.

I'm so glad he decided to have Gordon go with her today. Two members of security are better than one, especially when there are other people involved. Plus, we both trust Gordon and Layton to do everything they can to protect our girl.

I hear Jason's phone ring and turn, hoping it's Jasmine.

"It's Calvin." He answers the call as I wait to see if he knows anything, as I know Luna and Chelsea are meant to be with Jasmine.

"What's going on?" Calvin asks, and I realise Jason has put him on loudspeaker.

"Where are Chels and Luna?" Jason asks

"We are in a coffee shop around the corner from the dress shop. There is a sign on the door saying they are closed with no explanation, and Chelsea can't get hold of Jasmine, and neither can I." Calvin knows Jasmine would never purposely let Luna down; she has taken the big sister role with his girl and loves her dearly.

"Take them home, and Jazzy will be in touch when she can," Jason answers, visibly relaxing. That little girl has been through so much in the last few months; the last thing we or her three fathers would want is for her to be caught up in whatever this is.

"So, something is going on? Need backup?" Calvin asks, having Jason's back as always. I don't think that man will ever stop being his bodyguard. They built such a close relationship in the years they worked together and went through so much that they will forever be bonded like brothers. Luna even refers to Jason as Uncle Jason, which he loves.

"I'll let you know. We don't know anything other than that Layton has locked down the building with Jazzy and the girl inside. The systems have possibly been hacked, so he can't risk using the landlines or the internet; the signal is nearly non-existent. We will be there in a minute."

"Okay, let me know what you need, and I will take my two home, keeping them out of the way."

"Thanks, Cal; I will keep in touch."

The two say goodbye before ending the call. Jason sighs and I look at him over my shoulder.

"At least the pregnant lady and young child aren't in there," Terry points out as he drives through town to the bridal shop. I can only imagine the carnage if Chelsea and Luna were in danger. Logan would be there kicking the door down before we ended the phone call. He has proven to be more protective of his girls than I am of Jasmine, and that's saying something.

"I will rest when I know the others are too, especially Jasmine," I answer. It makes me sound like a dick, but I don't care. Yes, I care if the others are safe or not, but the need to see with my own eyes that Jasmine is safe and unharmed will always be my priority.

"When we arrive, is there any point in asking you to stay out of the way until I know it's safe?" Terry asks, looking at me and then Jason in the rearview mirror. We both just look at him and tell him all he needs to know. Nothing is going to stand between us and getting to Jasmine.

In less than five minutes, we park and arrive at the shop. From the outside, everything looks no different than at any other time I've been here. Jason and I have been to get Jasmine dresses, shoes, and accessories for events a few times over the last year. Jason has been here a lot more than I have over the years, and it seems his shopping addiction has come in handy when they managed to fit Jasmine in for her first dress consultation with only a week's notice.

Jason rings the intercom bell and stands back so the three of us can be seen on the camera. Only to realise there is no indication that it's on.

"Hello?" a woman's voice comes over the intercom.

"Penelope, it's Jason and Christian O'Reilly. We've been told Jasmine's here." He looks at me and nods to the intercom. He has picked up on the woman's tone as well. She sounds upset and scared.

"Password?" Layton's voice comes over the intercom, all business.

"And so the lion fell in love with the lamb," I answer, looking at Jason, who's smirking. "We need to stop her from picking the passphrases."

"Coming now," Layton answers, but I don't miss the giggle in the background. At least it doesn't sound like anyone is hurt.

As soon as the curtain on the front door flicks and we see Layton look out, we all jump to attention. He opens the door and steps back as the three of us enter.

"What's going on?" I ask as Layton locks the door and rubs a hand down his face. He physically relaxes a little now that he's no longer the one in charge. Terry will always take over when present.

"No one is hurt, physically anyway. I'll explain as we head up the stairs; everyone is on the top floor." We all fall into step behind him as he starts talking.

"As soon as we arrived, we knew something wasn't right. Penelope sounded stressed when she answered through the intercom. I wasn't the only one who noticed; Jaz did as well. An issue was confirmed when we were ushered onto the top floor." Layton stops and turns to look at us. "Penelope and two of her assistants finally admitted what was going on, which included being locked out of their system, their security and internet was lagging, which it never had before. We realised there was a major security issue, but I was worried about leaving with the four girls and only two of us, so I decided to wait for backup and lock down the building." He stops at the door and takes a deep breath. "It's easier to show you than explain the last bit." Opening the door, I walk in ahead of Jason as we look around for Jasmine.

I see her sitting in a chair surrounded by her friends. All of them look a little red-eyed, but whatever is going on doesn't seem to be affecting Jasmine as much as the others.

"Sweetheart, are you okay?" I ask as I squat down in front of her. Jasmine looks me in the eye and nods whilst forcing a smile.

"I'm fine, just a little shocked someone would do this," she answers, showing me the smile she hid her pain behind for years.

"What's happened, Jazzy?" Jason asks softly behind me. Jasmine looks up at him as she tightens her hold on my hands.

"Someone's ruined her dress, that's what's happened!"

I look up to see Danielle looking murderous.

"What?" Turning my attention to Jasmine, I watch as she blinks back tears whilst nodding.

"All the dresses have been covered in red dye or something. None of them can be salvaged," Verity explains behind Jasmine. I turn to Jason and can see he's struggling with his temper. I look to the ladies who own the shop as I stand, straightening my suit.

"Mr O'Reilly, we are so sorry. We have no idea what happened. They only arrived last night," Penelope looks ready to burst into tears. I don't miss how she's shaking.

"Did you check them when they came in? Could it have happened when being transported?" Jason asks. Penelope shakes her head, looking between the two of us.

"I always check them. They were fine on arrival, so I signed them off with the delivery driver."

"Did you notice anything suspicious yesterday or this morning?" Terry asks. Penelope looks to Layton, who nods.

"They told me a lady came in yesterday to book a consultation, and was being very difficult, causing a few issues before she finally left." Layton turns his attention to Terry. "I have already checked the CCTV, and that's when we realised it had somehow been turned off, and nothing was recorded from an hour after the dresses were delivered."

"She was a distraction so someone could get in and ruin the dresses or make it easier for them to get in once everyone had gone home," Terry sighs, rubbing his face.

Jason looks at me, and I close my eyes for a moment before turning back to look at Jasmine.

"Do you mind if I look at them, Sweetheart?"

She shrugs whilst her jaw clenches for a moment before that fake-ass smile appears again.

"Doesn't make any difference now; I won't be able to wear it." I know she's trying to lighten the mood, but I can also see she is close to her breaking point. My girl is heartbroken on what should have been a wonderful day she should remembered fondly forever. Now, she will remember it for all the wrong reasons. Leaning in, I kiss her head, wishing I could stop all this from happening to our sweet, big-hearted girl.

"We will get to the bottom of this, I promise," I whisper into her hair. She looks up at me through her eyelashes and nods.

"I know, Daddy."

Turning to Jason, I see him talking to Layton and Gordon. All look sombre as the girls surround Jasmine, giving her the support she needs.

Turning to Penelope, who looks just as upset as Jasmine's friends, I realise everyone needs to get out of here and have time to breathe, especially Jasmine, who is getting closer and closer to losing the fantastic control over her emotions she has right now.

"Penelope, can you show me these dresses? Then we will decide what the next steps will be."

Chapter Thirty-Eight

JASON

With my arm around Jasmine, I hold her close as we quickly get her to the car. She'd been so strong when inside, but now that everyone has left, she's starting to lose the last control she's been hiding behind.

"I'm so sorry, Sweetheart. I can't even imagine how devastated you are right now; I know how much you loved that dress," Christian whispers as he holds the back door of his car open for her.

"I'll ride back here with her," I whisper, helping her into the car. Christian looks at her for a second, like he wants to argue, and I know he does, but we also know what she needs right now.

Climbing into the car as Jaz slides across to the other side, I try to ignore my anger. I glance at Christian, who nods once, signalling he gets it before closing the door. In no time, he's in the passenger seat while Terry drives. Layton has taken the other girls home, leaving us to focus on our girl.

Each of them is devastated for their friend. They love

her so much, and to see someone hurt her in this way was too much for them. I've messaged Travis to give him a heads-up, as I'm sure Verity will need someone with her when she gets home. I'm waiting for the day he tells us he's keeping Verity away from Jasmine for her protection. He was close to it this morning, so this may be the thing that seals that fate. Would I blame him if he did? No. I wouldn't think twice if the roles were reversed, and Jasmine was in danger because of Verity and her guys. It's the role we play as their daddies and protectors.

For a short while, we travel in silence. Jasmine stares out of the car window with her arms wrapped around herself the whole time, a sign she feels vulnerable, and who can blame her? I want to reach across, wrap my arms around her, and reposition us both so she's sitting on my lap so I can hold her like I know she needs. But I also know that there are times she needs to process her feelings in her own way. So, instead of doing what I long to, I leave her in peace and wait for when she needs me.

"It wasn't dye on the dress, was it?" Jasmine's attention doesn't move from the window, but she knows the answer to her own question. I glance at Christian, who's watching our girl intently.

"No, Sweetheart. I don't think it was."

As soon as I got Layton on his own, while Christian was still seeing to Jasmine, he told me he believed it was blood. Whose blood, I don't think I want to know.

"I knew it wasn't the moment I saw it, but I didn't want to freak poor Penelope out any more than she already was," she whispers. One of her hands goes beside her, and I take the opportunity to wrap my pinkie around hers, needing any sort of contact she will allow. But the second she feels my hand beside her, she grabs hold and looks at it for a moment before her tear-filled eyes find me. "At least if they've ruined the dresses, they should leave everything else alone, right?"

Before I can stop myself, I look at Christian, who looks at me as if asking for help with his eyes.

"Daddy?" We both look at Jasmine as she glances between the two of us. "What aren't you telling me?" she demands, looking from me to Christian. "You both said no more secrets, so what else has happened?"

I hear Christian sigh, and I apply a little pressure to our girl's hand, showing her she's not alone.

"We had a call just before Layton made contact. There is an issue with the flowers," he explains. Even with me holding her hand, I can feel it starting to shake as I swear she stops breathing.

"What kind of problem?"

"They are all dead, Angel. They have all been destroyed." Jazzy looks at me for a moment as if waiting for the punchline, but when all I can do is offer her a small smile in the hope of giving her some hope, I can see the defeat taking over.

"Sweetheart? It will be okay; we will sort something," Christian starts, but when she turns her head and looks out of the window, ignoring him, he stops and, for once, doesn't force her to use her words. Because what words could she possibly have to say right now? What is there other than shit.

"Okay." Her voice is so quiet that for a moment, I think I must have dreamt the reply. But slowly, she turns to look at us as the first tear slips down her cheek.

"Jazzy," I whisper as I cup her face. But the second my hand touches her cheek, she leans into it with her eyes closed and strength breaks.

Not giving a shit about laws or the risk of an accident, I unbuckle her seatbelt and pull her onto my lap as she starts to cry uncontrollably. I hold her tight as her heart breaks, and all I can think is we are to blame for this. We did this to her because of the type of people we were forced to become, thanks to our father. So much of the pain she has felt in the last year has been because of that bastard, and I would love nothing more than to find his body so that I can set it alight and fucking piss on it.

Jasmine lifts her arm, and Christian reaches around the seat and takes her hand. I don't know who needs to contact more right now, him or her.

"We will fix this, Sweetheart. I promise we will get to the bottom of it all, and you will still have the wedding you deserve."

I nod whilst kissing the top of her head.

"He's right, Angel. We will all work together to make sure nothing else can go wrong."

"You know those are the famous last words, don't you," Jasmine sniffs, looking up at me, and I can't help smiling down at her.

"Yeah, but we all know I'm the best person to have around in this kind of disaster," I reply. When Jasmine frowns, I can't help grinning at her.

"Jaz, that man was born to shop. He will have you girls fitted and stunning with time to spare," Terry says from the driving seat as he pulls up outside the house.

"Well, he's not wrong, and let's face it, he's going to love every minute of shopping for you all. He was a nightmare when shopping for our suits," Christian adds, smiling at Jasmine, attempting to cheer her up. She looks at me, and for the first time since we arrived at the dress shop, she has a glimmer of hope in her eyes.

"Okay, Daddy. Let's see how good your shopping skills are."

I wink at her once as Christian climbs out of the car, opens our door and helps Jasmine out of the vehicle. I watch him wipe the tears from her face with a hanky he pulls out of his pocket before leaning in and kissing her softly on the lips.

"The only important thing on that day is that we *will* get married. The four of us get to share you as our wife every day for the rest of our lives."

"That's what I kept telling the girls as they were crying," Jasmine agrees before leaning into him so he can hold her close. "As long as I can marry you all on Saturday, nothing else matters."

"We don't deserve you, Sweetheart," Christian whispers into her hair before looking over her head to me. I couldn't agree more.

"There you are! Why was no one answering their fucking phones?" Maximus yells as he storms out of the house.

"We were dealing with something," I sigh, turning to give him my full attention.

"Yeah, well, so was I, and it was an issue I needed help with."

"What's happened?" Christian sighs as he holds Jasmine against his side and leads her towards the house. "Can it wait until I get Jasmine settled? She's had a bad day."

"Sorry, Shorty, but whatever happened is going to get brushed under the carpet when you hear this."

All three of us turn to Maximus as he rubs the back of his neck.

"Well, that doesn't sound good," I sigh, taking Jasmine's

hand and ensuring she has support from both sides, Christian and me.

"It's not. I've just gotten back from the venue. They're closed, effective immediately, due to burst water mains. The whole function room and the ceremony room have been destroyed."

"You mean?" Jasmine whispers as I stare at my brother in disbelief.

"Yeah, we don't have anywhere to get married."

Chapter Thirty-Nine

SEAN

Leaning against the door frame, I watch Ryan as he goes against the trainer in a practice fight. His form has improved so much in the last month. He's lighter on his toes; his breathing and speed are stronger. I always thought he could be a great fighter one day, and he's proved time and time again that I still underestimated him.

"Mr O'Reilly, sir." Turning to my head to look over my shoulder, I find the receptionist standing timidly behind me. She hasn't been here long and is still very nervous around me.

"What's up?" I ask, returning my attention to the ring where I hear Toby, the trainer, groan in pain. He's bent over, clutching his stomach as Ryan laughs.

"There is a woman at the desk demanding to see you. I explained that you weren't to be disturbed when with Mr Donavon, but she isn't taking no for an answer."

"What's her name?" I ask, frowning. I know it can't be Jasmine, as she's gone to pick up the dresses for the weekend.

"Mykela, sir."

"Shit." Pushing myself from the door frame, I rush towards the reception area, entering the security code. "She can come and go whenever she needs to," I sigh, rushing for the reception, where I spot Mykela pacing.

"I'm sorry, I didn't know," Tammy stutters behind me. Usually, I would offer her a smile or something to help put her at ease, but if Mykela wants me, it's not good. She usually spends the time in the car when I'm here or reading in my office. She would only interrupt if something was wrong.

"What's happened?" I ask as soon as I'm within earshot.

"Maximus just said to get home," she tells me before looking me up and down. "Do you have everything?"

"Anything of importance is in the car; let's go." I turn to look at Tammy and point to the door we just exited through. "Can you tell them I've had to leave and to continue with today's plan. I will contact them tonight to see how it went." I don't wait to hear her response, as my priority is getting home.

"Do you know anything?" I ask, pulling my phone from the side of the door where I stashed it before heading into the new gym I've set up. I start searching through my messages, looking for anything from Jasmine or my brothers, but the only message I find is from Maximus. For a split second, I wonder if it's another hoax, but I have no choice but to trust it.

Maximus: Get home as soon as possible. Everything has gone to shit, and Shorty needs us all.

I quickly type out a message and wait to see if he gets back to me.

Sean: What's happened? Is Jaz okay? Has she been hurt?

Maximus: Too much to explain over text. Physically, she's fine and safe; we all are. But emotionally, she needs us.

Sean: I'm less than five minutes away.

I put my phone on my lap and try to take some calming breaths. No matter what I'm doing, I will always be there if my girl needs me. I don't have to worry about Ryan, as I have employed the best trainer I could find. I only need to be there to check how he's getting on and his skill level to know who to pair him with for fights. Today was meant to be the last time I was there when he trained until I get back from our honeymoon anyway.

"Have you heard anything?" Mykela asks as she turns down the road that takes us home.

"Just that there's too much to explain via text, but everyone is safe." I pinch the bridge of my nose and try to prepare myself for whatever's happened now.

"Do you think you guys will get a break soon?" Mykela asks next to me.

"I think we have more chance of hell freezing over," I chuckle under my breath.

"Your dad will be down there, so anything's possible."

I laugh, looking at my bodyguard grinning whilst we pull into the property. The two of us have formed a good working relationship, which has developed over time. When Mykela started, she was all business, but slowly, she has begun to relax a little, and when together, the banter is fun.

Looking up at the house, nothing looks any different than when I left it this morning. The two guards outside the front are in full view, and I know two are in the trees. No unrecognisable cars are parked up front, which signifies that whatever has happened may not have happened here.

"Want me to come in with you?" Mykela offers as she pulls around the back of the house, next to a white van. Looking up at the ladder beside the house, I can see where they are fixing Jasmine's window after last night.

"Nah, you go to the security hub and see if Terry needs you for anything. If I'm going to be here for the rest of the day, I'll let you know so you can shoot off." I catch her nodding as I climb out of the car and head to the back door.

"Call me if you need anything, though," she calls as her window opens. "Even if just to talk."

"Thanks, will do!" I call back as I let myself in.

The first thing I notice is how quiet the house is. Mrs Brown isn't in the kitchen, and I don't see anyone walking through the house. I have no idea where everyone is, but I head to the sitting room first, knowing that's the most likely place where everyone will gather.

Walking into the room, I'm greeted by four sombre faces. Jason is pacing around with his phone in his hand, Christian is behind Jasmine's desk on the phone, and Jasmine is curled up on Maximus's lap with her teddy and blanket. It's a sure sign that she's overwhelmed and struggling with her emotions.

"Are you okay, Princess?" I ask, walking over to her. She shakes her head as Maximus kisses her hair.

"Sit with Sean, Shorty," he whispers into her hair before looking at me. "I'll get you a drink."

Maximus leans back, allowing me to scoop her into my arms and sit with her on my lap, holding her close as she leans into me. Running my hand up and down her thigh, I can feel her shaking slightly. Her hold on her teddy is tight, and her breathing is ragged, like she's on the verge of tears or is recovering from them. Pressing soft kisses to her head, I remind myself that whatever's happened, she's here in my arms, where I can protect her from whatever is trying to hurt her. I just wish I was able to protect her psychologically as well.

"Does someone want to tell me what's going on?" I ask, looking around at my brothers as Maximus walks over with two fingers worth of bourbon for me. "Is it that bad?" I ask, taking it.

"Worse," Jasmine whispers.

"The wedding's off."

As the words leave my eldest brother's mouth, Jasmine shakes in my arms again, and I hold her as she starts to cry silently.

"Wish to elaborate?" I ask, watching Christian and Jason sit on the opposite sofa from me and Maximus sit on the other.

"Today alone, the florist, dress shop and hotel have been attacked," Maximus answers, sipping his drink.

"What? How?"

"The florist called first to say that their warehouse's air purifier had been contaminated, which resulted in all the flowers for the wedding being destroyed," Christian explains, placing his right ankle on his left knee and sitting back on the sofa. He looks exhausted, and so does Jason when I turn my attention to him.

"Jazzy went to the boutique to pick up the dresses with the girls, but Layton had to lock the whole place down. The dresses had been covered in what we believe is blood."

"What the fuck?" Why would anyone do something like

that? It's one thing to destroy the dresses, but a complete other to cover them in blood.

"It was horrible; the dresses are ruined, and the poor women who work there were traumatised," Jasmine whispers, her voice wobbling through the tears.

"Did they know it was blood?" I ask, but Jasmine shakes her head.

"I told them it must be dye that looks like blood, but I could tell. I think the others could as well."

"I'm so sorry, Princess; I know you loved your dress," I whisper into her hair, kissing the top of her head.

"It was a beautiful choice and I can see why you were so excited because of it," Jason adds from across the room.

"So, what's happened at the hotel?" I ask, not missing how Christian, Jasmine and Jason all turn their attention to Maximus.

"I went to give them the heads up about extra security and that Logan and Drew would pop in to see what was needed. But when I arrived, there were workmen everywhere. The manager explained there had been a burst pipe overnight. The whole area we have booked for the wedding, blessing and reception has been damaged, and there is no way they can have it ready for the weekend."

"What about the gardens? They offered them to us before," I point out, but Maximus shakes his head.

"They are like a swamp. The sprinkler system had been activated, and with all the rain we've had the last month, the ground has flooded. There must be at least two inches of water sitting on top of the grass. With more rain forecasted, there is nothing we can do to drain and dry it enough to be useable."

"And there is nowhere else? Not even a village hall somewhere?" I ask, but Christian shakes his head.

"I've been calling around. We all have, and nothing is available at such short notice." That makes sense, especially with a wedding as big as ours. There are one hundred and sixty guests invited; it was hard enough finding somewhere to house us all in the first place. Finding somewhere else with less than four days to go will be impossible.

"So that's it then? We aren't getting married," I sigh, burying my face into Jasmine's hair as my brothers remain silent.

Everything has been going perfectly. Sure, there were blips along the way, as is to be expected when planning any normal wedding, let alone one with four grooms. Still, I really believed that even though people were constantly trying to attack us at the moment, there was nothing they could do to stop the wedding. I guess I was wrong.

"It's not fair," Jasmine whispers as she leans her head against my chest.

"I know, Princess, but there isn't much we can do about it," I point out, tightening my arms around her.

"I've tried everything, Sweetheart. Nowhere is available on Saturday," Christian sighs, not taking his eyes off our girl. He looks as devastated as I feel.

"So, we get married another day instead," she points out.

"Of course we will, Jazzy. We will marry you as soon as we can. Once things calm down, we know you are safe, and this won't happen again. We will get everything rebooked and get married." Jason leans forward, cupping his glass between two hands, as he leans his elbows on his knees.

"Nothing is going to stop us from making you our wife, Shorty," Maximus adds, watching Jasmine as she sits up on my lap.

"But they are stopping us. We are letting them win," she argues.

"If they were winning, they would have separated us, Princess. But the five of us are too strong for that. We will be married, and it will be as soon as possible, just not this Saturday."

"What about Sunday then?" she asks, looking around at us all. I can see from the look of my brothers that they are thinking the same thing as I am.

"Sweetheart, I know you are upset, but you need to be realistic here. Nowhere is going to be able to house all our guests or put together a wedding of that size in such a short space of time," Christian sighs, shaking his head.

"How many guests do we have?" she asks, standing up from my lap and walking over to her desk.

"One hundred and sixty-three," Jason and Christian answer in unison as we watch Jasmine sit in her chair and pull forward her laptop.

"How many of them actually matter?" she asks, pulling a pad of paper and pen beside the laptop.

"What do you mean?" I ask, confused.

"I mean, if you could only invite those who matter, how many would it be?"

"I don't know, why?" Jason answers, looking at the rest of us as we shrug.

"Sweetheart, what are you thinking?" Christian asks, standing from the sofa and walking over to her. She notices him coming and taps a few keys before I hear the printer spring to life.

"Just humour me for a minute, please, Daddy." When she looks up at him, I can see he's going to. If there's one thing we all know about Christian, it's that he may be

Jasmine's Daddy, but she is the one with the real control. If there is a way he can make her happy, he will do it.

"Okay, Sweetheart. But please think about everything logically," he says, running a hand over her head. "You could have been kidnapped only last night. People are targeting us and the wedding, so the likelihood of us being able to hold it anywhere any time soon is improbable."

"What about if we had it here?"

"What? As in the house?" Maximus asks, leaning further forward.

"Yes, or even one of your clubs," Jasmine starts before standing from her chair and walking around the front of the desk. "Just hear me out before you tell me no," she adds, looking at each of us.

"We're listening," Christian says, walking back over to the sofa giving her the floor. She smiles, thanking him without words before turning her attention to the rest of us.

"What if we send out emails to all guests and tell them that the wedding has been cancelled due to unforeseen circumstances and will be rearranged at a later date."

I look at my brothers and can tell they are all hanging on her every word like I am. She pushes herself away from the desk and picks up the papers which have finished printing. Carrying them over to us, she separates them into piles and places one in front of each of us, keeping one herself.

"I don't know about you, but I don't care if most of these people come or not. Other than our close friends and family, i.e. Terry, Layton, Calvin and his family, Verity and the guys, Abbi, Danielle and, of course, Mrs Brown. The rest I wouldn't miss."

Looking down at the list in front of me, I realise I feel the same way.

"We only invited most of these people because we felt we had to," Jason points out as the rest of us nod.

"So, what are you suggesting? We cancel the big wedding and have a smaller one here?" Christian asks. Jasmine nods before sitting next to me.

"What's the most important thing about this weekend?" she asks.

"That we will all be your husbands," I answer, running a hand down her back. She turns to me and smiles.

"Exactly. I don't need a fancy dress or thousands of pounds worth of flowers; I just need you four."

"And we only need you, Jazzy. But hosting a wedding here is a lot of work, and there is still the chance of someone finding out and trying to get to you," Jason points out. He looks to Christian as if to provide a backup, but he's looking at our girl.

"That's why we tell everyone it's off, so we only invite those we trust to a ceremony on a different day," he answers, as Jasmine nods. "It might just work." He stands from the sofa and starts pacing, rubbing his chin as he thinks it all through. "Jason's right, though, Sweetheart. It's a lot of work, and I'm not sure how much help the four of us would be," he adds, looking at Jasmine.

"Daddy, you do realise I have spent the majority of my life in the world of production, don't you? Danielle, Verity and I could organise this in our sleep. The only thing the four of you will have to worry about is doing as you are told for once," she grins, causing Maximus, Jason and I to laugh, and Christian's brow disappears under his hairline.

"Baby girl," he sighs without the usual warning tone.

"I know. Don't top from the bottom," she sighs, smiling at him. "But you know I can do this. Plus, with the girls' help and Mrs Brown's, we could have a small intermate ceremony, which we would probably enjoy more than the one we had already organised."

All eyes are on Christian now as we wait for him to agree or not.

"You really think we can keep it quiet?" he asks; Jasmine nods quickly. "And you will be safe?" Again, Jasmine nods.

"I will have Terry and Calvin included in everything so they can determine what security is needed and when."

"What will you need from us?" he asks as Jasmine smiles further, knowing she has got him where she wanted him, on her side.

"Your bank card," she smiles whilst fluttering her eyelashes, "and for you to go through the list and cross out anyone who doesn't need to be here."

Christian smirks as he reaches over, picks up the sheets and rips them in half.

"All I need are those in this room and those you have already mentioned."

"Does that mean we can do it?" she asks, bouncing in her seat. Christian looks to Jason, who is smiling.

"I'm happy to try, at least, if you are."

Christian looks back at Jasmine and sighs.

"Fine, you can try to rearrange everything for Sunday."

Jasmine squeals, jumps up from the sofa and throws herself at him.

"Thank you, Daddy." Kissing him on the cheek as his face becomes serious.

"But, if I think you are in danger at any point, I will pull the plug, even if it's right before the ceremony," he warns, and Jasmine's face becomes serious again.

"I know; that's what I expected."

"I mean it, Jasmine," the fact he uses her name shows

his seriousness. "No matter how much I want to marry you, I will put your safety before a piece of paper."

"I know, Christian, same as I will put yours over it as well." They stare at each other for a moment, but Christian's face is the first to relax.

"Okay, get the girls here and see what you can get sorted while I send the emails."

Jasmine grins from ear to ear and kisses his cheek before rushing from the room.

"Was this the right move?" I ask, sitting back in my seat. Christian sighs deeply as he downs the rest of his drink.

"I don't know. It could work if we manage to do it right, but we still don't know who is giving out all our secrets, so it might all blow up in our faces." He looks at the picture we have on the far wall of the five of us, taken the night we asked her to marry us, and I can see the worry on his face. "I had to give her the chance to have what she wants more than anything, though," he says to no one in particular. "She wants to be ours, but she also wants to get rid of the name her mother chose for her. It's not her birth name, and it's a constant reminder of her bitch of a mother and what she put her through. I think marrying us and becoming O'Reilly by law is a way for her to shed the pain of the past and start afresh with us."

The four of us sit silently as we let that sink in. To us, O'Reilly is just a name we share, but to Jasmine, it's her future; it will be her children's surname, and more importantly, it will be a way of putting the past far behind her and moving forward.

"Hey, where is she?"

We all turn to see Terry and Layton standing at the door, looking around.

"Jasmine? No idea why, what's up?" Christian asks, the worry back on his face.

"Not a clue. She just messaged me asking the two of us to come and talk to her about something before she calls the girls," Layton shrugs as he looks at each of us.

"We are cancelling the wedding on Saturday and holding a very private one here, if possible, on Sunday. We don't want many people to know," Jason explains quickly.

"I want your help deciding who knows what," we hear Jasmine call from somewhere outside the room. "I'll be in Daddy's office."

"I need my office, Sweetheart," Christian calls out.

"Fine. I will be in Daddy Jason's then," she sighs dramatically.

"What if I need *my* office?" Jason laughs. We hear her huff before she storms into the sitting room and stops in front of us with her hands on her hips.

"Then, as that is my desk, this is technically my office, and you can all get out!" she orders, pointing to the door forcibly.

"Why have we got to get out?" Maximus laughs.

"Because this is top secret, and I don't trust you to keep your big trap shut!" she snaps. We all turn to Maximus slowly and wait to see if he blows up. He stares at her momentarily, his mouth gaping open, and his eyebrows lifted so high we can't see them. Slowly, he closes his mouth and stands from the sofa.

He walks up to Jasmine, who refuses to back down, with a stern look on his face.

"I think a brat may be pushing her luck," I hear Jason mutter under his breath as Christian and I try desperately not to laugh.

Maximus stops in front of her and looks down, forcing her to tip her head back to look him in the eye.

"Because you have had a bad couple of days, I will let that one slide. However," he warns, holding his finger up for emphasis. "Just remember which one of us risked their lives and climbed up the side of a building to get to you last night." Jasmine's eyes widen for a moment before her face softens ever so slightly. "You can use this as your office, but only because I am saying you can. If you backchat me again, I don't care what you have been through; you will find yourself over my knee. Is that understood, Shorty?"

"Yes, Daddy," she replies sheepishly, giving him the biggest puppy dog eyes I have ever seen from her. "Sorry," she whispers before lifting on her toes to kiss his cheek. "And thank you for rescuing me," she adds for good measure. Maximus looks down at her and hums deep in his throat before leaving the room. The rest of us take that as our cue to go as well.

"Let us know if you need anything," I smile, leaning in and kissing her cheek.

"Use this for anything you need," Christian adds behind me as he holds out a bank card.

"Thank you," she replies, smiling at all three of us.

"We love you so much," Jason smiles at her. She kisses him on the lips before stepping back.

"I love you all more. Now out, times ticking, and I have things to do."

The three of us laugh as we walk out of the sitting room and head to where Maximus is leaning against the wall, smirking.

"You were calmer than I thought you would be," Christian laughs as Maximus grins triumphantly.

"I know for a fact she will now be soaking wet and

desperate for me by the time she goes to bed," he winks as we all laugh.

"Let's head to my office and see if we can make a start on these phone calls and emails," Christian sighs as we all start following him.

"Anyone else think she's going to throw us the best wedding ever?" Maximus asks, smiling at us all.

"I have no doubt. I also know if Danielle King is involved, I need to consider re-mortgaging the house," Christian sighs, rubbing his face as the rest of us laugh, all trying to push back the worry that something may still come along and ruin this for our girl.

Chapter Forty

JASMINE

Sitting on the floor, with my back resting against the sofa behind me, I re-read through my notes.

"Are you okay with all of this, Terry?" I ask, looking up to where he's sitting in the seat behind me.

"Of course I am. The most important thing to me, other than all your safety, is that you are happy, Jaz." He places a hand on my shoulder and gives it a slight squeeze. "You are all important to me, not just because of my job. You have brought so much happiness to the guys' lives."

"They have to mine as well," I point out, smiling.

"I know, honey, which is why I know how important this is to you all." He leans forward and wraps an arm around my shoulders, hugging me. "You all deserve this, which is why I will do everything in my power to ensure you get it."

I lean into his hold, resting my cheek against him.

"Thank you. You mean just as much to us as well." I feel him kiss the top of my head and smile as I close my eyes and enjoy the feeling I always get around him.

The guys are my daddies; their love for me is unconditional and obviously also sexual. But Terry reminds me so much of my father before I lost him, from how he gives me little hugs now and again or makes me laugh when I need it. There is nothing sexual there, and there never will be, not like with the guys. But Terry always has a shoulder to lean on when I need one.

Like every time I think of my father, I feel my eyes welling up. I wish he could be here to walk me down the aisle. It's something I have thought about a few times recently, and it has made me miss him even more.

A knock on the door makes me blink back the tears.

"Yeah," Terry calls out, sitting back in his seat. The door opens, and Layton sticks his head in.

"Hey, the girls have started arriving. Where do you want them?" he asks.

"Everything sorted on the top floor?" Terry asks. Layton nods and walks into the room a little more so he can close the door.

"Yeah, all cameras are off. I've told the team that everyone in the house wants some privacy for the time being. No one will question it with everything else that is going on."

"Can you take them up there and let them know I will be there in a minute? I just need to talk to the guys about something first." I stand a little wobbly after being cross-legged on the floor for so long. "Can you stay with them and make them aware of the no mobile rule for the time being?" I ask. Terry nods as he smiles at me.

"I'm on it. Go and see the guys and call me if they have any questions."

I take him by surprise when I lean in and press a kiss on his cheek.

"They are all still in Christian's office."

"Thank you," I whisper with a smile before leaving the room and heading to Christian's office, where I know the guys have been since they left the sitting room an hour ago.

As I approach the door, I can hear Jason talking. From the sounds of it, he is speaking to a wedding guest.

"No, there is nothing anyone can do now, but we appreciate the offer. Our main priority is keeping our fiancée safe, which unfortunately means postponing the wedding for the foreseeable future. We will be in touch as soon as we know the new date." I have to remind myself that the wedding has not been cancelled, and we will be getting married on Sunday.

I have already called the registrar and explained the situation. They have agreed to all the changes and promise to keep everything under wraps. They are also filing the paperwork on Monday, as their boss will be away and we will have left for the honeymoon, so no one will know where we are by then, and it will all be too late. We will be married, and that's all that matters.

Taking a deep breath, I walk in and smile when all four guys turn their attention to me. Jason quickly ends the call he was on, and Christian stands from his desk.

"Is everything okay, Shorty?" Maximus asks from the sofa where he is sitting with Sean; both have laptops in front of them with the list of wedding guests between them.

"I wanted to give you all an update before I go and see the girls." I look at them all and smile, hoping to ease the worry on their faces. "I'm okay, I promise," I add, hoping to reassure them. Jason takes my hand and guides me towards the seats around the sofa and coffee table.

"Have you managed to sort anything out?" Christian asks, holding the chair out for me. I nod as I sit and allow myself to breathe for a moment to calm my racing heart.

"Jazzy, if it's not possible, it's okay. We can come up with something else," Jason says softly, placing a hand on my knee as he sits on the coffee table in front of me.

"It's more than possible," I answer, smiling. "The three of us haven't stopped since you left, and I just need a second to breathe," I laugh, closing my eyes and leaning back in the chair so my head rests against Christian's stomach. I feel his hands start rubbing my shoulders and open my eyes to find him looking down at me as his hands work their magic on my tight muscles.

"Take all the time you need, Sweetheart. We aren't going anywhere."

"You better not; Terry may track you down himself and kick your arse after this," I joke, glad to see the first signs of a smile on his gorgeous face. I wink at him before looking forward to the others as his hands tighten on my shoulders playfully. When I finally pay attention to the others, I can see they have relaxed a little and even have slight smiles on their faces.

"So what's the plan, Princess?" Sean asks, sitting back in his chair.

"There's a lot to go through and not much time as the girls have started to arrive, so this will be quick."

"Christians used to hearing you say things are quick," Maximus winks as Sean and Jason roar, laughing.

"Fuck you, prick face," Christian yells behind me as I cover my face and try not to laugh out loud. "You can pack it in as well, Sweetheart," Christian warns, tickling me so I jump from the seat and sit between Maximus and Sean for protection.

"Pay attention, I don't have much time!" I point out again, spinning my attention to Maximus and holding up a finger to stop him as he opens his mouth to no doubt insult his brother again. “Stop it.” He makes a show of rolling his eyes and shutting his mouth. “Thank you,” I sigh, rolling my eyes whilst trying not to smirk.

“Okay, so the main thing is that the registrar will be here Sunday at one PM. They understand the situation and aren’t putting it on their work calendars or contacting anyone via their system. Nothing will go on until twenty-four hours later when we will already be out of the country.” I glance around at the guys and see they are all paying attention.

“The main details you need to know is that the only security team members who will be in the know are Terry and Layton. Everyone else will be told that we are devastated about cancelling the wedding and will be going away Saturday morning to get away for a while. They are also being fed false details on where we are flying from and where we are going. The hope is that *if* any of them are giving away our secrets, someone will try something on Friday night to prevent us from leaving, and we will be ready for it, deal with everything and are still okay to go ahead with Sunday’s plans.” I look to Jason before continuing. “That does include Gordon, but we agreed that if you want him there, we will sort it so he is kept in the loop.”

“Don’t worry about him, Jazzy. Yes, he is a friend, but he was invited because I felt I had to. My relationship with him isn’t like it was with Calvin. So, if he has a problem with being kept out of the loop, I will deal with him when we return from the honeymoon.” He offers me a smile, and I relax before turning to Sean, who is already smiling at me.

“Same goes for me, Princess. If Mykela doesn’t like it, I will deal with her when we return.”

“Thank you,” I smile at each of them before taking a deep breath and carrying on.

"As you can imagine, keeping it quiet while the girls and I sort everything will be hard, so the cameras have been turned off," I explain. "Security has been told that we have shut it off for now. They will be told that we require our privacy at the moment. Terry and Layton will still be able to access them, though."

"Makes sense," Christian nods, looking slightly impressed.

"Just to be clear, this includes all cameras, not just on the top floor where the girls will be staying, but the whole house," I continue. "They are all off when security is on site. We don't want to risk people seeing things they shouldn't and getting suspicious."

"Jazzy, that's a lot of areas without coverage. What if something happens when the cameras are off?" Jason asks. But I just smirk at him.

"This is why Terry is going to be moving into my room until we leave for our honeymoon," I announce proudly. "That way, we are protected from the inside and out."

"Who will be guarding outside?" Christian asks. But again, I have it covered.

"Calvin and Drew are on their way around. He already has the low down, and they will pick eight people they trust from their team. The eight will make two teams, and they will be doing twelve-hour shifts. These people will not be inside; they will keep the outside covered. Basically, everyone will think we are on lockdown until further notice and on skeleton staff."

The guys all stare at me for a moment, obviously shocked that we have organised so much in less than an hour.

"Terry's on the ball; I'll give him that," Jason laughs as I lean forward and slap his leg.

"Hey, most of this was me! He's just helping me put the plans into place!" I yell, slapping his leg again for emphasis.

"Seriously?" I hear more than one voice say in unison.

"Yes, seriously! When will you learn? I'm the brains of this family!" I protest, sitting back, folding my arms over my chest as I stick my bottom lip out.

"You're right, Sweetheart. You really are the brains of this family most of the time," Christian smiles at me.

"Better," I sigh, trying not to smile. Sean nudges me with his shoulder and winks, knowing it gets me every time. Git.

"So, is there anything else we need to be made aware of?" Christian asks.

"Not at the moment; I will have more for you later when I've had a chance to put things in place." I chew on my lips and decide to voice something I've been thinking about.

"I want your honest opinion on something," I say, looking at Christian more than the others.

"I'm always honest with you, Sweetheart." The four of us all share a look before laughing, knowing that he's been anything but recently. "Hey, lesson learnt, okay!" he protests, looking slightly hurt.

"You're right; we're sorry," I say, standing and sitting on his knee to put my arms around his neck and kiss him on the cheek.

"What did you want to talk to me about?" he continues ignoring his brothers as he wraps his arms around my waist.

"I've been thinking about asking Terry to walk me down the aisle." I'm not even surprised when Christian's eyes bulge from his head as his jaw drops.

"Do you mind me asking why, Jazzy?"

I turn to Jason and smile.

"I've been thinking about it for a while," I admit.

"There have been times he has been so supportive and cares about us so much."

"He's like a father figure," Sean adds. I nod, smiling at him.

"You guys are my daddies and are the best Daddies a girl could ever ask for. But Terry, he …" I try to think of a way to word it without upsetting Christian, but as always, he knows how my mind works. He cups my cheek and turns my head so I'm looking at him. He smiles as his eyes are nothing but loving.

"He reminds you of your father. It's okay, Sweetheart, you can say it," he says softly, as he runs his knuckles over my cheek. I nod as tears fill my eyes. "If you want to ask him, I think you should."

"He will probably turn me down anyway," I giggle nervously. I feel a hand on my knee and turn to find Jason smiling at me.

"You don't know if you don't ask."

I know he's right, and when I look at the twins, I find them smiling.

"I think you should ask him," Sean says.

"Me too. You might give the old man a heart attack, but I think you will be surprised by his reaction."

"You do remember he is only four years older than me, right?" Christian sighs, shaking his head at Maximus.

"Yep, your time on this Earth is ticking, old man," Maximus winks as I lean into Christian.

"Stop it; no one is old or dying soon!" I protest. After the last few weeks, it's not a topic I find funny in the slightest.

"Thank you, Sweetheart," Christian praises as he kisses the top of my head. "So, do you want to ask him?" he asks.

I think about it for a second and realise I already know the answer.

"Yeah, I do. Can you call him in?"

Christian smiles as he pats my leg to stand and get to his desk. He picks up the main phone and presses Terry's extension.

"Hey, can you come here a minute?" I don't hear what Terry replies, and Christian doesn't bother saying anymore before ending the call. "He's on his way," he says, standing back behind me as I sit in the chair he just vacated. He places his hands on my shoulders and rubs them again.

"That feels so nice," I sigh, leaning my head to the side and closing my eyes for a moment.

"Say the word, Baby, and I will massage any part of your body you want." He leans down and kisses my exposed neck. "Play your cards right, and the four of us will join forces and not stop until you are a wet, floppy mess." Opening my eyes, I find the other three smiling at me, already planning all the ways they will pleasure me.

A knock sounds from the door, making me groan as the others laugh.

"Later," Christian whispers into my ear before calling for Terry to enter.

"You rang?" he announces as he enters the room.

"Yeah, come here a moment. Jasmine wants to talk to you about something," Christian explains. Terry walks over to join us whilst frowning.

"What's up? Have you thought of an issue?"

"No," I answer, shaking my head. My mouth is suddenly dry, and I'm nervous about asking. Christian gives my shoulder a quick squeeze, and I know I need to ask; otherwise, I will always regret it.

"I was wondering if you would walk me down the aisle on Sunday."

Terry's eyes widen at the same time as his jaw drops. Suddenly, I'm very aware that it's probably the weirdest request for me to make.

"You don't have to," I blurt out. "I know it's probably something you only want to do for your daughter, but-" I get tongue-tied, and a squeeze of Christian's hands on my shoulders stops me mid-rant.

"You want me to walk down the aisle?" Terry asks, his eyes still as wide as saucers. I nod as my eyes fill with tears. "Why me and not Layton?"

"Because Layton is my friend, and I love the annoying git dearly, but you are our family and someone who is always there whenever I need them, no matter what's going on. You are more of a father to me than my dad ever had the chance to be, and it feels right to ask you." The tears are overflowing now, and I'm terrified I made a mistake asking him, but it also feels right. Terry smiles as he squats down before me and takes my hands.

"Honey, you are so special to me, like a daughter." He reaches up and wipes the tears from my cheeks. "I am so proud of you, and it has been a pleasure to watch you become the strong, powerful woman we all knew you could be. I can't think of any greater honour than walking you down the aisle." The moment I see his eyes filling with tears as he smiles at me lovingly, the dam breaks, and I burst into tears as I throw my arms around his neck. Terry laughs as he hugs me back.

"I take it you're okay with this?" Terry asks, looking over my shoulder as I pull away. I turn to see Christian smiling at him.

"More than okay," he answers, walking around the chair

and holding out his hand. Terry stands and takes it before pulling him in for a hug. Jason steps up to them as Christian steps back and embraces Terry before the twins come forward and hug him, too.

"Okay, I'm leaving before you all make me fucking cry. Some of us are meant to be big scary security guards," he laughs, taking a deep breath as the rest of us laugh.

"The three girls are upstairs waiting for you. I wouldn't make them wait much longer; they may come looking for you," he winks at me before stepping towards the door. "I'm going to an emergency security meeting. Do you want to come as well?" He asks, looking to Christian, who nods before turning to the others.

"You okay to carry on making your way through the guest list?"

"We've got it. Go and sort this out, and then we can work out what's left to do," Jason answers.

"Thank you," I smile at them before rushing around and kissing each of them. "If you want me, I will be with the girls in the spare rooms on the top floor," I call, rushing from the room as they tell me to contact them if I need anything.

As I make my way upstairs, I smile, thinking how much happier I am than when I left to see the dresses this morning. Even on the way there, the visit from the police was playing on my mind, and something still felt off. But for the next few days, I don't have to go anywhere or see anyone I don't want to. I can just plan what will be the happiest day of our lives. I will ensure it is, and I know the girls waiting for me will help me make my dreams a reality and have my back like they always do.

Chapter Forty-One

CHRISTIAN

Sitting back in my chair, leaning to one side as I rest my chin on my forefinger, I watch the last few security team members enter the meeting room and find their seats. I'm furious and want them all to see it. I want them to be on edge and scared because they fucking should be. I'm past angry; I'm fucking murderous. Judging by the way they are all avoiding eye contact with me, they know it, too. We don't know who knows what at the moment. Some will know more than others, but by the end of this meeting, they will see that we have been pushed too far.

I look at Terry, standing on the other side of the room. He nods, signalling everyone is here, and closes the door before standing beside me. For once, he's not sitting, as we want to show that this is not our usual meeting.

We agreed that I would do most of the talking today, as I want everyone to see that even though my brothers and Jasmine are not with me, as they usually would be, we are still in this together and a united front. Terry and Jasmine have filled me in on all they agreed on and what we want people to know.

"I'm sure you are all wondering why you have been called in here today." I sit forward and make a point of looking at each individual as they watch me nervously, all too scared to look away, scared it will make them look guilty. They should know better by now. If I thought they were guilty, they would already be dead. I just need the proof, and I will end them right here.

"It's been a rough few weeks, to say the least, and what should have been the happiest day for everyone in this household's lives so far has become a disaster." I make a point of sitting back and giving the room a moment's pause so I can watch everyone's reactions.

"Today, after the events that transpired last night, things have become a complete shitshow. This morning, we were awoken by the police with a warrant after someone reported that we were breaking the law with our relationship, which was a poor attempt to get us arrested. Luckily, the police realised quickly that all claims were untrue, and it's now on record that we are doing nothing illegal.

"We then discovered that the flowers and wedding venue had been targeted. Neither will be available for the wedding on Saturday. To top that off, Jasmine and her bridesmaids went to collect their dresses, and they had all been covered in blood. The girls are absolutely devastated, to say the least. The women in the boutique are terrified in their own store and traumatised. It was not a pretty sight." Looking around, I can see many people seem shocked and appalled. I don't bother looking at Terry; I know he will be focused on watching everyone else, too.

"Because of this, as I'm sure you have all now guessed, the wedding is off. It was a heartbreaking decision for us to make and for Jasmine to accept. In the space of a few hours, she has taken several steps back in the healing process she has been working through after years of abandonment issues and abuse." A few people's faces are saddened at the news. As many have told me, the whole team loves Jasmine; they all seem more protective of her than we are. *Seem* being the main word there.

"You have all been called in because we will be going into complete lockdown. We have never used this protocol before but feel we have no choice. This will hopefully give us all the time, especially Jasmine, to come to terms with everything. *No one* will be allowed on or off the premises, and you will all be on leave until we return from what should have been our honeymoon. We will be leaving very early on Saturday morning and will return when Jasmine is ready." Sitting back in my chair, I refuse to look anywhere but at those in front of me.

These should be the people we trust more than anyone else; they literally hold our lives in their hands on a daily basis. But, right now, we can't trust any of them, and it's infuriating. This is a situation I never thought I would have to deal with, but here we are.

"You will no doubt be approached by people wanting to know what's been happening and where we are, and all I ask is that you simply reply, 'no comment', until told otherwise. If you are unsure of anything or need to report anything suspicious, don't hesitate to get in touch with Terry. He'll be here for the whole period we are in lockdown and coming to the villa with us, so he will be kept in the loop the whole time." I look around at all the faces in front of me again and decide to get them out of here as quickly as possible. Otherwise, I run the risk of firing every single one of them without warning.

"Are there any questions?"

Looking around them, I don't miss the exchange of glances and a few chewing on their lips. Mykela is the first to put her hand up. I nod at her once to signal for her to go ahead.

"Will you require us personal guards at all? Or are we also on leave?" She glances at Gordon and Layton sitting on the opposite side of the table.

"You will be on leave as well," Terry answers, stepping forward and leaning on the table. "The O'Reillys and Jaz will not be leaving these premises, so you will not need to be here. I will stay in the security hub to ensure they are safe, especially after everything in the last forty-eight hours, but they want space to help young Jasmine." He looks at each member of the team, and I don't miss how a few look genuinely upset it has come to this.

Gordon lifts his hand a little, and I nod for him to continue.

"Will we get to speak to the others before we leave?" Knowing that although they don't have the relationship Jason and Calvin have, Gordon is still protective of Jason and thinks highly of him.

"I'm sure Jason will be happy to speak to you before you leave. I already know Jasmine doesn't want to see anyone other than Layton who will see her before he heads off." That's not true; Layton is going nowhere and moving into one of the spare rooms in the security hub. But again, it's a lie we will uphold for as long as possible.

"What will happen with pay?" I hear someone ask, and I see Justin looking at me. "I hate to be the one to ask, sir. But I have a baby on the way and-"

"I completely understand," I interrupt, surprised it's taken this long for anyone to ask. "You will all receive full pay until you return to work full-time. You will not be using any of your holiday time either. This lockdown is a decision we made as a family, and we would never leave any of you out of pocket because of our choices."

"That being said," I add, leaning forward on the table again. "If I find out any of you are the reason all of this has occurred, and you have been giving others our personal information, I don't care whether you have family or not; you will die for what you have put our fiancée through. She is completely heartbroken, and it is purely down to those who have betrayed us and, more importantly, her.

"Jasmine has suffered her whole life thanks to those who have used and abused her. Some of you present even helped me to make some of those abusers pay. But there are still things about her past that no one, other than the four of us, knows and she wants to keep it that way. To say she suffered at the hands of those who should have loved her is an understatement. She finally had her own way of getting away from the years of pain, a way of starting afresh, losing the name of those who abused her, and having the name of the family who love her for who she is. To the four of us, it was just a wedding, a piece of paper that told us what we already knew: Jasmine is ours. But to her, it was shedding the past and starting afresh with a family who worship the ground she walks on. *That* is what someone has taken away by doing this, not the wedding, or the dress, flowers or celebration, but the thing that was to be the turning point in Jasmine's healing. For that, I will not rest until the person is found and made to pay."

Call me overdramatic; I don't care. I want whoever has done this to know what they have done, and I will not rest until they pay for it. I'm done pretending that someone in here isn't betraying us. I want them to hear what they have truly done to someone they all claim to care for.

"Is there anything else you wish to mention?" I ask Terry. He shakes his head and looks at everyone.

"You all know the protocol for a complete lockdown and what is expected of you. The cabinet in the office is unlocked; leave your work mobile and firearm in your slot and sign them in, as well as anything personal guards have, tablets and so on. If anyone doesn't, I will be knocking on your door to find out why. I will email you all when I know what it will look like once the O'Reillys and Jaz are coming home. All passwords and emails on the server have been changed, and phones are locked. You will not have access to anything until you return to work and a new password is chosen, as explained in the lockdown protocol you have all signed at the beginning of your employment.

"Also, so you are all aware, if I find out anyone has been involved in this attack against any member of this household, I will see to it personally that you pay. Do not assume you have gotten away with it because you have not." He looks at each of his people, and I know this is far from the end. Terry will be going through everyone's emails and phones with a fine-tooth comb to hopefully find who is responsible.

"Everyone has finished for the day and can go home as soon as everything is signed in. If you have a question, I will be in the office in five minutes to answer them." He turns his attention to me and signals that he's done.

"You are all dismissed," I announce, pushing back my chair and standing.

For a few minutes, it's chaos as everyone wants to shake my hand and ask me to pass on their love to Jasmine. They ask that if we find anything out, I let them know. It's tough, as I'm sure they all know that someone on this team is the one to let us down. I'm sure everyone has their suspicions about who it is, but there isn't enough evidence to confirm it. Other than Gordon and Layton, the rest have worked with us for years. They all watched as we became who we are today, and there were so many ways they could have taken us down; I will never understand why they have waited until now.

"You okay?"

I look to Layton and nod.

"I am so ready to lock down and have a strong drink," I sigh as I watch the last few people leave.

"Yeah, I can imagine," he nods, watching the others disappear, leaving the three of us alone. "Everything is going well upstairs, and I will be heading off in a bit before coming back in an hour," he adds quietly, hoping no one is listening.

"Thank you," I reply before looking to Terry.

"You really think it's one of them, don't you?" he asks. I nod whilst forcing myself to relax my jaw.

"I can't think of any other explanation. How else would the bastards know which dress shop Jasmine had used or the florists? Sure, anyone can find out about the hotel, but I've received notification that the suit shop was also broken into during the early hours of this morning. If the owner hadn't called us to pick them up early, I have no doubt they would have also been vandalised." Both Terry and Layton curse under their breath.

"What about what I found at the dress shop? How many of the others know?"

My jaw clenches as I look at Layton.

"My brothers and I are the only ones other than the two of you that know," I answer as I feel the piece of paper burning in my back pocket. I need to put it somewhere before Jasmine sees it.

Layton had discovered it in the dress bag, which held Jasmine's wedding dress. He made the decision not to tell anyone until Terry arrived. It's something we've decided she doesn't need to know, as it's more of a scare tactic than a threat.

Run before they spill your blood too.

"We will get to the bottom of it, but in the meantime, it will be harder for anything to happen while we are all locked in here," Terry says, rubbing his face. He looks as tired as I feel.

"We can only hope," I sigh as I head towards the door. "I'll be in my office if you want me," I call, heading away, needing a moment to myself.

As I walk through the house, I see Jason and Gordon talking quietly. I need to speak to my brother and see how he feels about Gordon not being here if Sunday goes ahead. I don't think he was lying to Jasmine, but I also want to see if there is a reason he's keeping the guard at arm's length.

"The twins are in the gym for the next hour; Mykela has gone down to speak to Sean," Jason calls as I walk past. "The girls will be leaving as soon as they are happy Jasmine is going to be okay," he adds. I nod and say goodbye to Gordon before entering my office and closing the door behind me.

I finally find myself alone and can breathe for the first time without needing to act as expected. Making it impossible to ignore the pain.

No matter what I do, there is always someone or something around the corner ready to destroy me or those I love.

Nothing about what I do should have any bearing on Jasmine. But that message, sent through her wedding dress, was personal. It just proves that, once again, I was unable to protect her. Once again, I am failing her.

Walking to the bar, I pour myself a strong drink and throw it back in one gulp. The liquor burns its way down my throat, and I enjoy the pain it leaves in its wake. It's a way of reminding myself that I cause pain for so many people I love, yet there seems to be nothing I can do about it. Not that I don't want to, that I just can't. It seems that the harder I try, the more I fail, and failure has never been an option for me, but now, for the first time, I can't see a way of winning this one.

After pouring another drink, I head over to the sofa and sit down for a moment, with my head resting against the back as I close my eyes, desperate for peace.

Chapter Forty-Two

CHRISTIAN

When I open them again, the room is much darker. Blinking back the heaviness of the sleep I hadn't planned, I look around. Jasmine's blanket is draped over me, and the glass I held is on the table beside a glass of water. Quickly, I glance at the clock and realise it's been over two hours since the meeting finished.

Rubbing my face, I force myself to sit up and clear my head. I can't remember the last time I slept that heavily. Especially as it seems I didn't even wake when someone, no doubt Jasmine, came in and put the blanket over me. She loves this blanket and waking up like this makes me smile, as I know it will be her way of showing that she loves me. She would have gone out of her way to find it when she couldn't be the one to hold me.

I hear a couple of hushed voices outside the room and frown, trying to figure out who it is.

"You can tell him from me; if *my* daddy is still sleeping, he will have to wait because I am not waking him up because *your* daddy is having a tantrum."

Chuckling to myself at her overprotectiveness, I stand and fold the blanket. I'm just placing it on the back of the sofa when the door opens slowly.

"It's okay, he's a wake. I'll let you deal with this one while I go back to Mrs Brown," Jasmine says to Verity before she smiles at me, letting a slightly annoyed Verity enter.

"Everything okay?" I ask, offering her a warm smile. She is usually still a little nervous around me, but today, she seems downright annoyed, and for a moment, I think it may be aimed at me.

"No. Daddy is just being unreasonable and won't listen to me. He's demanding to talk to you," she replies, thrusting her phone towards me. I smile as I roll my eyes.

"Yeah, us Daddies can be unreasonable like that," I wink before lifting her phone to my ear as she giggles and relaxes. "What's up, Donavon?"

"Do you want to explain how you feel it's acceptable to keep my girl at yours without her phone for four days?" He is as pissed as I am confused.

"I would if I had any idea what you are talking about," I reply, rubbing the bridge of my nose. I turn to look at Verity and smile. "Can you get Jasmine for me, please?" Verity nods before rushing out of the room. "What have you been told?" I ask, already knowing the three Donavons are on the approved list of wedding guests.

"Verity was vague about the wedding being off, but not off. Something about it's been moved, but she can't tell me anything. All I know was she was asking to stay there but won't have her phone the whole time," he sighs, and I can tell he's relaxed a little now he knows I can put some context to it all.

"Yeah, I'd be confused as well," I laugh, sitting back on

the sofa and taking a sip of water. "I'll be honest. I have no idea what the girls are up to and how they plan on spending the next few days," I admit, relaxing on the sofa.

"So, is the wedding off?"

"Yes and no. It's been moved to Sunday, and we are only inviting a handful of people who are important to us."

"So that explains why Verity acted like there wasn't a wedding."

"There's no reason for her to hide anything from you three, as you are still invited. Other than Calvin and his tribe, you are the only ones from outside the family that are." I take a second to register how important that is to me. I think he's as shocked as I am by the way he replies.

"Wow, I thought I'd have been the first one crossed off the list."

"Yeah, me too," I laugh. "Guess things really have changed between us."

"Think that will depend on whether you decide to keep my girl from me." I can hear the teasing in his voice, and I can't help but laugh.

When we were younger, Travis was my best friend, the only person I was ever around other than Terry and my brothers. I never realised how much I missed him and that friendship until he came back into my life before Christmas.

"I wouldn't dream of it. I know there is no way I would let Jasmine stay out that long without at least one of us with her." I look up as Jasmine walks into the room, whispering to Verity. "Speak of the devils, and they shall appear," I add before beckoning Jasmine to me with a finger. "Want to explain what's been going on?" I ask as she sits on my lap and smiles at me sweetly.

"I came in earlier to tell you everything, but you were asleep."

"I'm awake now, Sweetheart, so please fill me and Travis in." I place the phone on the coffee table whilst activating the loudspeaker.

"Okay, so to ensure no one finds out the plans, I have asked the girls to hand their phones to Terry and tell anyone outside of the house that they will be staying with me until Friday night. You know, because I'm devastated and all that," she grins, rolling her eyes.

"And they've agreed to it?"

"Of course they have; they're my best friends," she declares, shocked I would ever doubt they would.

"How do Verity's Daddies and Ethan feel about it?" I ask, raising a brow.

"They don't agree," Verity sighs, sitting in one of the chairs that still sits by the coffee table.

"No, we do not, and you know why," Travis warns.

"Abbi's boyfriend is fine with it," Verity whines. "Why can't you be?"

"Because I'm not your boyfriend." He could just be referring to the fact he is her Daddy, as I would never allow Jasmine to refer to any of us as her boyfriends when we first got together. Or he could mean that he's her fiancé, which Jasmine is completely in the dark about. I look to Verity, who looks at Jasmine sheepishly, but she seems oblivious to the underlying meaning behind it.

"I understand why they are reluctant to let you stay without contact," I explain, looking to Verity. "If it were the other way around, I wouldn't feel comfortable with Jasmine staying away that long without contact either."

"But why?" the two girls whine together.

"Because you have both been through a lot recently, and as your daddies, we wouldn't be doing our jobs if we didn't make sure someone was close on the off chance you needed them." The girls share a look, and I know they will argue, but there's no point. I've already come up with a plan.

"Travis, would you all feel better if you stayed with her?"

"I would relax a bit if one of us were there, yes," he answers, and I get it. Only this morning, he was worried about Verity being hurt because of her association with Jasmine. Since then, she has been offhandedly attacked by her bridesmaid dress being destroyed. I still wouldn't be surprised if he followed through on his threat and kept Verity away.

"How about all of you?" I ask, already working out sleeping arrangements.

"All of them? But Verity only has one room upstairs, and the bed isn't big enough for them all," Jasmine points out.

"If Terry is staying in your room, the guys can run the security quarters. There are three rooms, plus a kitchen and sitting area. They wouldn't even have to come into the main house if they didn't want to." Let's face it: I don't think having Travis and me under one roof for four days is a good idea. We will end up killing each other before Sunday comes around.

"But where will Layton sleep?" Jasmine asks.

"There will be a spare room on the top floor with Verity not needing it. I'm sure he will be fine sleeping up there," I shrug. "What do you think, Travis?" Verity and Jasmine stare at the phone as we hear Travis and other muffled voices. I can tell he has his hand or something over the speaker. I'm sure the twins will be happy to have them here as they can drink the days away with Ethan and Ryan.

"If they stay, will you be able to control your temper

around Travis?" Jasmine asks quietly. I haven't told her about this morning, and I doubt Verity knows either.

"We will be fine. If he gets on my nerves, I will use your body as a form of stress relief," I whisper, nibbling at her ear as she squeaks.

"Okay, we would like to take you up on your offer," Travis finally answers. "As long as you are happy with it?" he adds.

"Me or Verity?" I ask, smiling at Verity.

"I don't give a fuck about you, O'Reilly. I only tolerate you because your Jasmine scares me, and I like her."

"Awww, I like you too," Jasmine gushes as Verity giggles behind her hand.

"Don't worry, Donavon, the feeling is mutual," I sigh, rolling my eyes. I lean in so my lips are by Jasmine's ear. "Until they leave, you had better avoid wearing underwear because I may be using your body a lot." I smile as her whole body tenses, and I feel her vibrating.

"Verity, why don't you take your phone and you and the guys can devise a plan of what you need while I talk to Jasmine for a moment."

Verity smiles as she picks up her phone and walks out of the room, talking excitedly.

"I'll meet you back upstairs," Jasmine calls after her.

The second the door is closed, Jasmine spins around and kisses me, thrusting her fingers into my hair.

"Do you need something, Baby girl?" I smirk as she stands slightly so she can pull up the pencil skirt she is still wearing, making it easier for her to straddle my lap.

"You know exactly what I need, Daddy," she smiles before squealing as I stand, holding her against me as I walk over to my desk to place her on it.

"Lie back and show me that pussy like a good girl," I

order, my mouth already watering with the need to taste her. I watch her smile as she lays down on the desk so I can push her skirt up further and reveal the white thong she has on.

"Is this the one from the weekend?" I ask, playing with the material, ensuring my finger brushes over her. The way that her breathing hitches now and again tells me she feels it all.

"You told me to keep them for you, so I did. I was going to surprise you after picking up the dresses." I know the reminder of the dresses is painful for her, so I make a point of sticking one finger out as I play with the material so it slips between her plump pussy lips.

"You really are my good girl, aren't you, Baby," I whisper, feeling how wet she is.

"I will always be your good girl, Daddy," she cries out as I slip one finger into her.

"Yes, you will, Baby girl. Just like I will always be your daddy." Not giving her any warning, I pull the fabric to one side and start to eat her like I've longed to all fucking day.

She is so wet and ready for me that it doesn't take long until she is crying out, begging me not to stop, as if I ever would. Between her legs is my favourite place to be. Whether it's my mouth, hand or cock. Nothing compares to the way her body responds to me and my touch.

"Daddy, I …" her breath catches before she has a chance to finish what she was about to say. Her whole body comes alive as she cries out almost silently through her orgasm.

"I love the way you flood my mouth as you come on my tongue," I growl as I undo my trousers, desperate to feel her pussy clamping around my cock.

I don't give her any warning before thrusting into her.

She screams with pleasure as I fill her oversensitive pussy, just the way she likes it. She's still recovering from the orgasm, and I know just how to get her there again.

"Fuck you are so perfect," I growl through gritted teeth as I grind into her while rubbing her exposed, swollen clit with one finger. As she comes again, I tighten my grip on her hips as I start using her body to chase my own release, knowing if I time it right, I will be able to give her one more at the same time.

"Daddy, use me," she calls out as her eyes become heavy again, and she meets me thrust for thrust. For a second, she opens her eyes and looks at me with a devious smile. "Fuck me, Daddy."

A deep growl bubbles from my chest as I pull out of her and turn her onto her front.

"Did you just swear at your Daddy?" I ask, rubbing the tip of my cock through her wet pussy, from her clit to her back passage and back again. When she doesn't answer me, I pull back a little. "Answer me, Baby girl," I demand as she moans with frustration.

"Yes, Daddy," she answers as I thrust into her pussy and spank her ass at the same time.

"I don't hear you counting," I warn as I spank her again.

"Two," she cries out as I do as she asked and start fucking her hard as she's bent over my desk. As my hand collides with her ass cheek again, she moans loudly before shouting three.

"I don't think spanking is a punishment for you anymore," I point out as my teeth clench tighter as I try desperately to control my need to release. I spank her a fourth time, and she cries out as her pussy squeezes me so tight I lose all control and fill her with my release. I manage to spank her one last time, pushing her over the edge with me.

Leaning over her, I sink my teeth into her shoulder, dragging out her orgasm so her pussy squeezes my cock, dragging out my own at the same time. I love this after-sex connection, where we are completely spent and undone together. As I slide out of her, I pull her back with me as I sit in my chair and hold her on my lap, cradling her against my chest as she curls up small.

"I love you," I whisper into her hair. "No matter what happens this weekend, I will always love you."

"Everything will be fine, Daddy. Nothing will stop us from being married," she whispers, running a finger around my chest through the gaps between my shirt. Glancing down, I watch her eyes close, and she smiles.

"What's got you smiling?" I ask, tucking some hair away from her face. I hate when anything gets in the way of me watching her. Whether it's her hair or something far bigger, my heart aches when I can't see her. Being in her presence is what has gotten me through everything. She once told me I'm her safe space, but she is mine and so much more. She anchors me when I feel like I'm losing control of everything in my life. She grounds me and makes me see the bigger picture, even when she doesn't even realise she is doing it.

"I think you might be right that spanking isn't a punishment anymore," she whispers, looking at me through her lashes.

"I've known that for a while," I answer, shaking my head while trying to stop myself from smiling. "It's okay. I have other punishment ideas."

"Like what?" she asks as I turn the chair so I can reach for the aloe cream I keep in one of the drawers. I have them scattered all over the house because the woman on my lap has a habit of pushing her luck.

"Stand up," I order, ensuring I make enough room for her. She sees the cream and smiles as she does as she's told.

Standing before me, I push a little on her back so she bends over the desk again. Showing me the way her ass has reddened under my hand. I fucking love the way she looks like this. I love seeing my mark on her, showing the world she is mine. I gently kiss each hand mark before slowly massaging a little cream into her skin.

When I am done, I reach for a box of tissues and use them to dry her wet pussy, before slowly lowering her skirt back down, ensuring it's in place. Jasmine straightens up as I stand and put my bottom half back together again. Trying to look a little presentable.

"You didn't answer my question," she points out as I tighten my belt.

"I know." Hooking a finger under her chin, I tilt her head back, ensuring she can see I've gone into Daddy mode. "And I won't until I decide you need to know." Her jaw drops as she stares up at me wide-eyed.

"That's not fair!" she pouts, but I just cock a brow at her, letting her see I'm not messing this time.

"Who am I?" I demand, secretly only doing it because I love the sound of it on my lips.

"My Daddy," she answers, throwing in a little sass.

"Which means I do not need to justify everything to you. Everything I do is for your good and protection. So, lose the attitude and try not to be a brat unless you want to learn your new punishments the hard way." Caging her against the desk by leaning against it, with an arm on either side, I ensure I have her full attention. "Now, be a good girl and go and see your friends. You have a lot to get on with, and I have taken up enough of your time."

"Okay, Daddy," she answers, smiling before kissing me softly as I stand back, giving her room to leave.

"I expect to see you all for dinner at the usual time unless told otherwise," I add as she heads towards the door.

"Already planned on it. I'll make sure Verity's Daddies join us, too." She turns to look at me as she slowly pulls the door closed. "I'll make sure your favourite stress release is available," she winks before disappearing with a giggle.

Chapter Forty-Three

JASMINE

I look around me and smile. It's Thursday afternoon, and I think we might actually pull off the impossible.

From one side of my dance studio to the other, there are tables filled with boxes of fake flowers, decorations we have made to hang around the wedding tent that will be put up Sunday morning, as well as a few for the tables.

Today, we are finishing the table decorations, and then Abbi and Verity will make the buttonholes, leaving Danielle and me to make the bouquets. The three of us have made these types of things before for props. Personally, I think we are doing a damn good job. I send a silent thank you to our dance teacher, Mrs Florence, for being a stickler for perfection and making us redo everything until it was perfect. It seems we would need these skills again after all.

For the tenth time in the last hour, I glance over to the rack where all our dresses are hanging in dress bags. They arrived last night and are already altered and ready for Sunday. My dress may not be the one I had designed especially for me, but there is something about this one that makes me well up every time I see it. Poor Mrs Brown has gotten sucked into all the planning. She not only spent last night doing any alterations needed with the dresses but is also making the food for our little gathering after the wedding. She is fantastic, and I've already told Christian we need to do something special for her as a thank you, even if I know she will have a fit.

"Jasmine, dear. What's your favourite type of cake?"

I look up from the flowers I'm working on and frown.

"What do you mean? For dessert?"

"Don't be silly, dear, I know that's hot chocolate fudge cake with ice cream," she chuckles, flipping a page on her notepad. "No, I mean as in sponge cake. I know you like lemon and wanted it in the original cake, but is it your favourite?"

"I love your lemon cake, but why are you asking?" She can't seriously think she still needs to make our wedding cake.

"For your wedding cake, of course, I was going to be making it anyway."

Damn it, I should have seen this coming. There is no way I can let her take on a big job like that when she is already doing so much.

"Don't worry about the cake, Mrs. Brown. That was before you were doing everything else. You've got enough going on with the food and the dresses now." The second the words leave my mouth and I see the look on her face, I know I have a fight on my hands.

"You need to have a cake! You can't have a wedding without one!" she exclaims.

"We don't need one, honestly. I promise we will be fine

without one. I couldn't let you take on even more than you have already."

She looks at me like I've completely lost it, and she wants to throw me into an asylum. Looking at the grand scale of things, a cake is the least of our worries. There's only going to be nineteen of us anyway.

"No family of mine is getting married without a cake. So, do as you are told and tell me what flavours you want." I try to argue again, but she storms off, leaving me feeling guilty. She's never been cross with me before, and I think I may have hurt her feelings.

"Do you think I was out of order?" I ask, looking at the girls.

"No. She has a lot to do already," Verity says, glancing at Danielle with a warning.

"Sorry, but yeah, you should have just accepted it with a thank you," Danielle shrugs, never being one to sugarcoat anything. Looking around, I can tell the girls are divided over what I should do, which doesn't help me.

"I'll see if she brings it up again. If she does, I'll tell her to ask Christian." I go back to the flowers before me when Abbi chuckles under her breath.

"Think she's decided the same thing."

I turn and see Mrs Brown has come back with not one, but all four O'Reillys, who look like they are trying desperately not to laugh in front of Mrs Brown.

"Will you explain to this girl what happens if you are in my bad books?" she demands, placing her hands on her hips.

"What did you do?" Sean sighed, looking at me.

"Nothing! I just said she didn't need to go through all the trouble of making us a cake because we didn't need one!" I expect the guys to agree with me, but all four hiss through their teeth as they recoil from me in unison.

"Shorty, I love you, but you're on your own with this one," Maximus grimaces, looking between me and Mrs Brown.

"Sweetheart, if Mrs Brown says she is making you a cake, you accept the cake," Christian adds, glancing at Mrs Brown, who nods.

"Jazzy, I told her she didn't need to make me a cake for my twenty-first, as I had no intention of being home for it." Jason looks to Christian, who looks like he's about to burst; his lips are sucked into his mouth as he tries desperately not to laugh or smile

"Guess where he spent his birthday," Sean says with a smile.

"It wasn't in the strip joint he wanted it to be. But at least there was cake," Maximus laughs as Jason slaps him around the back of the head.

I look to Mrs Brown, who has her hands back on her hips, looking like she is daring me to continue arguing with her.

"I love your lemon cake; it's my favourite. Thank you, Mrs Brown," I answer quietly, playing with the bottom of my jumper, feeling bad for upsetting her. I can't even bring myself to look at her as I mumble an apology. All four O'Reillys are struck down with coughing fits until Mrs. Brown turns and looks at them all.

"Are the four of you ever going to grow up?" she asks, rolling her eyes before turning back to me.

"Thank you, dear. See, it wasn't that hard." She walks up to me and cups my cheek lovingly. "The boys mother, bless her heart, loved making them cakes for their birthdays or any celebration. It's a tradition, and she asked me to carry on when she knew she wouldn't be able to. She would have loved nothing more than being the one to make your wedding cake, so it's my honour to do it for her." She kisses my cheek and walks away, leaving us all staring at her speechless.

"Well, now I feel like a giant bitch," I gasp under my breath, throwing my hands up in the air. "You could have warned me!" I snap, still whispering. I glare at the guys, but one look at the shock on their faces, and I realise; they never knew.

"Is that true?" Maximus asks, turning to Christian and Jason.

"I'd forgotten she always made our cakes," Christian whispers, looking at Jason, who's watching him nodding.

"It all makes sense now. Mrs Brown has never missed a birthday or celebration," Jason answers to no one in particular as he shakes his head.

The guys don't talk about their mother much; I know very little about her other than that her name was Helena, and she loved her boys, who loved her too. I've always wanted to learn more about her, but I know what it's like to talk about someone you miss, so I never ask. I'm not sure if they speak to each other about her; they never have around me anyway.

"Are you okay, Daddy?" I ask Christian as I step up next to him. I take his hand, and he looks down at me momentarily before forcing a smile.

"I'm fine, Sweetheart." He kisses the top of my head and walks out of the room, leaving the rest of us to watch as he goes. Not liking how unhappy he is, I go to chase after him, but Jason stops me by taking my hand.

"Leave him, Jazzy. He's okay, he just needs a minute." He looks back to the door before pulling me into his arms.

"He's been missing her more than usual lately. He wishes she had met you and seen how happy you make us all."

"Has he said something?" I ask. Jason leans down and kisses my lips before looking deep into my eyes I notice the way his are sparkling as they fill with tears.

"She would have loved you," he smiles as he tucks some hair behind my ear. "You would have been the best of friends and caused so much trouble together." He looks to where Christian left and sighs deeply before a single tear escapes down his cheek. "He didn't need to say anything for me to know he's missing her more because I am too." Without looking back, he walks from the room. The twins share a look as they watch their brothers leave.

Sean wraps an arm around my shoulder and kisses my head.

"Mum has always been a challenging subject for them. It's easier for us; we had each other to get through losing her, but Christian and Jason didn't. Tommy made sure they didn't get to grieve for her and pushed Christian harder once she was gone. With her not being there to remind him of what good he had in his life, Tommy could use Christian's grief and turn him into the ruthless man he became. He was taught how to turn his anger and hurt into a weapon, and it took him a long time to see that's what Tommy was doing; by then, Tommy had what he wanted. He could get his hands on anything he wanted without getting them getting dirty. That's what he had Christian for." He looks to Maximus, who seems a little lost in his own head. He takes a deep breath before grinning, and I know he's pushing all his feelings down.

"Can I go back to stripping the Donavons of their cash now, Shorty? I had a blinder of a hand when we got dragged away." He turns and winks at Verity, who stands with her hands on her hips and points between the two brothers.

"Leave my men alone. If you think Jaz is scary, you haven't seen me protect them yet!" we all stare at her for a moment before bursting out laughing. Verity looks shocked and then furious as we all try to stop.

"Oh, Ver, honey. I love you, but you are scary as a church mouse," Danielle smirks as

Verity stares at her.

"Bitch," Verity mutters, sitting back down and going back to the flowers in front of her.

"Don't worry, sweetie, we won't take all their money. We will leave enough for them to at least buy you a nice diamond ring," Maximus winks as Verity's cheek flush as she mutters something about "too soon."

"Is that to go with the new ring on her hand?" I tease. Verity's head snaps up as I grin at her. "You forgot to swap it to the other hand yesterday after lunch. And whenever you take it off, you automatically put it on your ring finger," I point out.

"Yeah, but that doesn't mean she's engaged!" Danielle snaps, turning to Verity. "You aren't engaged, right? You would have at least told me if you were!" Danielle stares at her, and all I can do is laugh.

"Danielle, stop trying to scare her into saying she's not," Abbi giggles, shaking her head. "She's probably just wearing it on that finger at times because she wonders what it will be like to be engaged. We've all done it!"

The three of us stare at Verity, who looks like a deer stuck in the headlights.

"I need some fresh air," she declares, jumping to her feet and rushing from the room.

"Hey! Don't run from us!" I yell, racing after her while the others jump to their feet and chase after her, too.

"Verity, they are in the sitting room!" Sean shouts after her as he tries to stop us from chasing after her. "Leave the poor girl alone!" he laughs as Danielle violently moves him out of the way. "Fuck she is vicious when she wants to be," he curses, rubbing his side.

"She has a lot riding on this," I laugh, walking up the stairs with the guys. They both start asking questions, but I refuse to explain further. Telling them to wait as we listen to the commotion coming from the sitting room.

We walk in to find Verity curled up on Ryan's lap as Danielle stands in front of her.

"See, she has nothing to say on the subject. *Nothing!*"

"Danielle, enough," I sigh, shaking my head. "I'm sure she will tell us everything once Sunday is out of the way," I wink at Verity as Ryan and Ethan laugh. "FYI," I add, smiling as she looks up at me sheepishly, "I hope I'm right because I would love nothing more than knowing my fellow brat was going to marry her daddies too."

"Really?" Verity asks nervously.

"Absolutely! *If* you are hiding it, I know it will be because you are worried it will take attention away from me. But that would mean you have forgotten how much you mean to me and how your happiness *is* my happiness. Nothing will ever be more important than that."

Verity and I look at each other for a moment before she jumps up from Ryan's lap and launches herself at me. I hold her tight as she sobs into my shoulder.

"It's been so hard not telling you!"

I laugh, hugging her even tighter.

"It's been so hard not letting you know I had guessed."

Danielle starts cursing loudly as Abbi bursts out laughing.

"What the hell is going on?"

I look behind me to see Travis, Christian and Jason looking confused as they walk into the room together.

"Are you okay, Sweetheart?" Travis asks, walking over to us as I release Verity, and she quickly wipes her eyes, grinning.

"I'm fine, Daddy," she replies, laughing as she leans against him while still holding my hand. "Jasmine and the girls just worked out the secret," she grins up at him as his face comes alive, and he smiles at her.

"Is that so?" he teases. She nods, squeezing my hand.

"So, just to confirm," Danielle says, stepping right in front of us. "You are …."

"Engaged," Verity answers before moving her ring back onto the left ring finger.

"Son of a bitch!"

"Danielle!" Christian snaps, staring at her. Everyone else turns their attention to the woman, and she throws her arms up dramatically. This is followed by a string of curse words that turn the air blue.

"What?" she yells at him before facing Verity. "Love this for you, seriously, you deserve it," she adds with a smile. "But could you have waited until she was on honeymoon? Do you have any idea what you have cost me!"

"What?" Verity asks, looking around. I lean in and press a kiss on her cheek.

"I'm personally over the moon you spilt the tea *before* the wedding," I wink before turning to Danielle and Abbi, grinning. Walking away from the others, I pick up the internal phone and press Layton's call button.

"Can you bring my winnings to the sitting room, please?

Thanks." I hear Layton laughing as I hang up. Turning my attention back to the room, I find the others watching me.

"Did you all bet on me?" Verity demands, stepping away from Travis.

"Yes, and because you can't hold your own piss, I'm down a thousand pounds!" Danielle exclaims.

"You were the one who was so sure she would spill *after* the wedding, but before the end of the honeymoon, you demanded that we up the stakes, twice!" Abbi laughs, taking a seat on one of the sofas.

"You bet a grand each?" Christian asks, looking at me with disappointed eyes.

"No. Five hundred each," I shake my head. "It started at fifty, but she upped it to two fifty after the hen party. She went for double or nothing the night before the dress disaster." I turn to Verity and smile. "Once we get back from the honeymoon, I have a hen party to plan." Turning so I can lean my back against Christian's front, I turn my attention back to Verity and smile, smiling at the way all three guys are now surrounding her.

"That should cover our drinks for the night," I wink as Christian pinches my hip playfully.

"Well, now the cat's out of the bag, how about we celebrate?" Christian announces, surprising the hell out of all of us. He's been so much more relaxed since going into lockdown. I guess knowing no one can get in or out, or even contact him is a weight off his shoulders.

Verity thanks him before heading over to me and threading her arm through mine.

"Who would have thought the Donavon's and O'Reilly's would be like this?" I ask, chuckling.

"Yeah, it's a lot to take in, but it makes our lives a little easier," she giggles.

"I'm so happy for you, not just because I'm richer for it, but because you deserve this."

"We both do, Jaz. We are finally getting our happily ever after," she replies before turning back to laugh at Travis as he opens a bottle of champagne he takes from Christian. Both of them grinning like kids as they start filling the flutes Christian places on the table in front of them.

"We really are, Verity, and it's going to be great."

Chapter Forty-Four

CHRISTIAN

The day is finally here, our wedding day.

The sun shines as the four of us walk out of the house to the large tent. Our wedding suits look great as we walk to the front of the aisle, where the registrar, Lucinda, is waiting for us.

"How are you all feeling?" she asks, smiling at us all.

"I'm ready to get this show on the road," Maximus laughs. He's been a ball of energy all morning. I had hoped the two bourbons we shared in the sitting room would calm him down, but I think it's made him worse.

"I promise this will feel like it's over in a heartbeat, and you will wish it could have been dragged out a little longer," Lucinda giggles. I don't miss how her eyes linger on Jason a little longer than the rest of us. Sean and I share a look, and I know he's noticed it as well.

"So, you all remember the plan? Christian," she turns her attention to me and smiles. "You will be at the front when Jasmine arrives, and we will begin the legal wedding ceremony." She glances down at her notes, obviously checking everything. "You and Jasmine have chosen the traditional vows for the marriage, which I will prompt you through. And we will have you both sign the marriage register." She looks up, still smiling. "Will you want pictures of just the two of you before going to the next bit?"

"No, we will each have individual ones done after the blessing," I answer.

"And you have here that Verity Stevenson and Terry Peters are signing the register as witnesses. Is that still correct with the smaller wedding?"

"Yes, nothing with the ceremonies has changed except the missing one hundred-odd guests." What the hell had we been thinking, inviting all those people? This is what we wanted, small and intimate.

"Great, so as soon as the register is signed and I pronounce you husband and wife, the rest of you will stand from your seats and step forward."

"They will already be standing. They are all my best men; they were always going to be beside me when I got married, whether it was to our girl or not." I give them all a smile as Jason places a hand on my shoulder and gives it a squeeze.

"You've had our backs long enough; it's time we had yours for a change."

"It's obvious you are all close, and not just because you all love the same girl," Lucinda smiles before sniffing and looking back to the notes. "So as soon as you are all in front of me, I will say a few words about the five of you being here to have your relationship blessed in the eyes of those you hold dear, then ..." she runs a finger down the page. "Ah, yes. You will all say a few words, as there are no traditional vows. Sean, you will go first, followed by Maximus, Jason and then Christian." She looks up at us again. I can't help wondering if her face hurts from smiling so much. "Jaz is then going to say a few words before the maid of honour does a short reading. Then you are all free to enjoy the rest of your day. Are there any questions?" We shake our heads, looking around at each other, smiling as we relax and let ourselves enjoy the moment we've waited so long for.

Lucinda looks up to the front of the tent, where I spot Mrs Brown smiling; she gives us a little thumbs up before waving towards the house and rushing to her seat. Music starts in the background, coming from somewhere, and I take my place at the front of the aisle.

I don't remember the last time I felt so sick from excitement and nerves. I know if I held my hand out in front of me it would be shaking like a leaf in the breeze. I look to my right at my three brothers, who all look as I feel. The four of us don't look away from each other until Lucinda clears her throat. We all turn together to watch as little Luna comes into view with a big smile, looking beautiful, followed by the three bridesmaids. All of them look amazing as they smile and wipe at their eyes. I can't help but give the three of them a wink as I smile, but then the music changes and we all turn further around as the love of our life comes into view at the top of the aisle.

There she is, our world, our Jasmine, walking towards us in the most beautiful white dress and looking like an angel. No, an honest-to-god goddess. Any other word is an insult. Everyone ceases to exist; all I can see is my Baby girl. Her smile lights up her whole face as she walks gracefully towards us. I hold out my hand for hers, desperate to touch any part of her, feeling the happiest I ever had. But as she reached out and placed her hand in mine, somebody else's hand appears and stops her from touching me.

"Terry?" Turning my attention to my friend, sure, he

must be trying to wind me up. But when I look at his face, I see it's not Terry but Connor Grant, Jasmine's father.

For a brief second, he looks like the smiling, happy version of the man in the pictures Jasmine has in her room, but his face quickly morphs into the version which I saw before I put a bullet through his brain.

He looks at me with the eyes I now realise his daughter inherited from him; they don't look scared or even reassuring like they did that night all those years ago. No, he looks at me the same way he looked at Tommy and Hardy, with pure hatred.

"Did you really think I would let this happen?" His lip turns up in disgust as I stare at him open-mouthed. "Did you really think I would allow you to marry my daughter? You, the man who killed me!"

"I didn't want to do it," I sputter, but Connor just shakes his head at me.

"And that makes everything okay? Everything that happened to my little girl was your fault." He lets go of Jasmine's hand and takes a step towards me.

"All the years of her mother abusing her."

He steps forward again as I step back from him. His eyes burning into mine as I'm unable to look away.

"All those men that went into her room. Each of them touching her, inserting themselves into her tiny body. It's all because of you."

Every step he takes towards me, I try to keep the distance between us, but he doesn't stop advancing.

"Every scream, tear, and ounce of pain is your doing."

My back hits the side of the tent, which has morphed into a brick wall, stopping me from putting any more distance between us.

"You took her one protector away, giving her mother all

the freedom she needed to abuse *my* baby girl. So, give me one reason why I should let you marry her."

"I love her; she is everything to me." Tears fill my eyes, and I look over his shoulder and see her standing there surrounded by a bright light, which makes her look even more like a goddess. "You know I never wanted to kill you, but I had no choice. But there is nothing I wouldn't do to protect her."

"Prove it." The venom in his voice has my attention snapping back to him.

"Wh _ what?" I ask, stumbling over the single word, which is lodged in my throat, threatening to choke me through the fear. It's the same two words Hardy said after he asked me what I was willing to do to protect my brother.

Connor's head tilts to the side as he grins at me, looking more evil than I ever thought he could.

"Prove it." It's Connor in front of me, but all I can hear is Hardy, the humour and demand in his tone.

"Ask anything of me, and I will do it," my whole body starts to shake as I look back at my sweet girl. I know the answer before I once again hear Hardy's voice coming from Connor's mouth.

"Choose."

Closing my eyes, I know what I'll see when I open them, but even knowing doesn't save me from the pain of what's in front of me.

Where my three brothers had been stood watching only moments ago, I find them now on their knees, hands tied behind their backs, all shaking and crying quietly. Behind each of them are people I never wanted to see again, each holding a gun to my brothers' heads.

Standing behind Jason is Hardy, grinning like he did that night he held a gun to his head when I was fifteen.

"What's it going to be, Christian? Time's ticking," he smirks, placing a hand on Jason's shoulder, holding him in place.

"He won't choose; he's not got the balls," Hudson laughs from behind Sean. He pulls a knife from his pocket and holds it to Sean's neck. "I wonder if he will bleed like she did." Sliding the knife around the side of Sean's neck, Hudson grins. "I love the way she screamed and bled for me. He lifts his hand, suddenly knifeless, as I see blood on his fingers. There's so much of it, and I know it's hers. He lifts his fingers to his lips and licks the blood from them, grinning at me the whole time. "Does she always taste so sweet?"

I go to jump forward, needing to kill him, when Connor places a hand on my shoulder, stopping me.

"Choose."

The word is barely a whisper, but as it leaves his mouth, I hear another voice that causes every muscle in my body to tighten as my blood runs cold.

"He's too weak to have any real balls. His Mama made him that way." I turn to Tommy's voice as he stands over Maximus. He leans forward so he can talk straight into Maximus's ear. "You want to be like him? Do you really think your big brother can teach and prepare you for life? You are even weaker than he is."

"Who's it going to be, Christian?" Again, Connor's lips move, but it's Hardy I hear. "Who lives and who dies?"

Looking at each of my brothers, my eyes burn from the tears; I'm shaking now for a completely different reason. The excitement and joy have evaporated; all that's left is fear and despair.

"I can't," my fifteen-year-old voice whispers. Every second of that night flashes through my mind. None of us are in the tent anymore. We are all in that warehouse where it all began.

"This is the easy bit; you simply decide who lives and who dies," Connor points out as a sick laugh fills the air and my stomach drops. He takes my hand and places my gun into it. It feels heavier than ever, and I want to drop it as it shakes with my hands.

"Please! He thinks he's all that, but he's worthless." I turn to her voice as my heart crumbles. Carol stands behind Jasmine, who is kneeling with her hands behind her head, her mother holding a gun to it. "You left her to kill her own mother; that's how weak you are, O'Reilly."

"Daddy," the word on Jasmine's lips brings me to my knees as I stare at the four people I love more than anything in this world, all surrounded by people from our past once again, threatening to take them from me.

"Time's almost up, Christian. Who do you choose?" Hardy squats down at me as he did that night. He pushes a gun into my hand and grins. "Only one can live, so who will it be? Your brothers? Or the daughter of the man you killed?"

I look back up towards Jasmine, whose father is now standing beside her, his arms crossed over his chest as he glares at me.

"Save her, Christian!" I turn to Maximus to find him staring at me. "You always make out you love her more than anything; prove it! You think you love her more than the rest of us do, so prove it!"

"I don't love her more; we all love her the same!" I argue back.

"That's bullshit, and you know it!" he yells. "You've had no problem defending the way you control us and our relationships with her. So why argue that now? Save her!"

His words hit me like a blow to the chest, and it hurt so bad I check I haven't been shot.

"I'm sorry." I look at all three of my brothers, each with a ghost of our pasts behind them.

"We know. It's okay, Christian." I look at Sean as he gives me one of his reassuring smiles. "Save her for us."

"Give Jazzy the best life," Jason adds, giving me a small nod. "Save her."

"No."

All our heads snap to Jasmine as she looks at me, smiling even as Carol pokes her with the gun. "No, Daddy. Save them; you need them more than me," a single tear slides down her cheek as she tries to reassure me. "Save them, Daddy."

"I can't lose you," I cry, staring at my poor girl as she tries to protect me as she always does. I turn to my brothers to find them all watching me. "Any of you. I've failed."

Taking a deep breath, I lift the gun and place it against my temple. I won't kill them; I won't let any of them suffer, not when there is a simple answer. Everything that has gone wrong in their lives is because of one person. Me.

"I've failed you, and I'm sorry." Closing my eyes, not wanting to cause them any more pain. Seeing a person's soul leave their body through their eyes is always the worst part; I won't let them see it with me. I take a deep breath, thinking of the four people in front of me as I try to pull the trigger, but a warm hand touches my face as the gun is forced away from my head. Startled, I open my eyes wide to see the eyes I never thought I would see again.

"Ma?"

"My sweet boy," my mum smiles, and my heart stops. "My poor, sweet Blackbird."

I'm frozen as she leans in and kisses the top of my head,

as she always would when she found me upset or hurting from something Tommy had put me through.

"I'm sorry, Ma." The tears flow easily now as I look into her sweet, bright eyes. "I failed you."

"No, you didn't. You could never fail me." Lifting her other hand, she cups my face whilst wiping away my tears with her thumb. "You broke your own wings so your brothers could fly. I am so unbelievably proud of you. You have done so much for them, but now it's your turn to be happy." She leans forward to kiss the top of my head again.

"Now, mend your broken wings and learn to fly."

Chapter Forty-Five

CHRISTIAN

I wake with a jump, my body slick with sweat, and the bed feels like it's soaking wet. Wiping at my face, I realise it's not just sweat; tears are streaming from my eyes. The need to see my brothers and Jasmine consumes me as I jump from the bed, pulling the sheets from my semi-naked body as I nearly trip on the way to the door.

Last night, we all went to Jason's room to make love to our girl. We were all a little tipsy and very much in love. He hasn't got the biggest bed, so I left them all to sleep while I went back to mine. Now, I regret it more than anything because I need to see they are all okay.

Even though I know it was a dream, it felt so real. My heart's racing as I throw open his bedroom door and charge in.

"Shit!" Jason jumps from where he's sitting up in bed alone.

"Where are they?" I demand, looking around in a panic.

"Who? What the hell is going on?" Jason rushes to get out of bed so he is beside me.

"The others!" I turn to rush out of the room when I hear her voice coming from the bathroom.

"Blackbirds singing in the dead of night. Take these broken wings and learn to fly all your life." Her voice draws me to her.

"That's it," I hear Jason say quietly, and I know he remembers it too.

"All your life." I hear her sing as I open the door. Jasmine is standing in the shower, her head lifted as she washes the soap from her hair. "You were only waiting for this moment to arise."

Hearing the words again brings every emotion I felt in the dream rushing forward. I must make a sound as Jasmine looks towards me and smiles. That smile, the light to my dark. As my eyes lock with hers, my legs turn to jelly underneath me as I remember her kneeling there, Carol, with a gun to her head, as she pleaded with me to kill her instead of my brothers.

"Daddy!" she rushes towards me, still soaking wet from the shower as I crumble to the floor. She lands beside me and grabs my face with both hands, just as Mum did in the dream.

"Daddy, what's wrong?"

Unable to speak due to the thickness of my throat, I pull her into my arms as I burst into tears. Burying my face into her shoulder, I cling to her, desperate to never lose her.

"Fuck, Christian!" Jason snaps as I hear Jasmine panicking. "Speak to me," he places a hand on my shoulder, but all I can do in return is grab his hand and hold it tight. I open my mouth to speak, but all I can do is desperately gulp down air as I try desperately to catch my breath.

"Shush, Daddy, it's okay." Her sweet voice gives me something to focus on as she cups my head and runs a hand over my hair from where she sits with my head now on her chest.

I'm vaguely aware of her whispering to Jason as she continues to run a hand over my head.

"I've got you, Daddy. I'm right here," she whispers into my hair while leaning her head against my head. I don't remember the last time I cried like this. Even after the stag party and all that happened when we got home, I didn't break like this.

At some point, Jason pulls his hand from my grasp and walks away, promising to be right back. When he returns, he places something around Jasmine, and I realise she is freezing, wet, and shivering. It's the trigger I need to drag myself back to her.

Without saying a word, I pull myself out of her grasp and pick her up as I stand.

"Daddy?" she asks, placing a hand on my cheek.

"I'm okay," I reply in a raspy voice. I still feel like my chest is being crushed in a vice. I can't catch my breath, but I try to take slow, long ones as I sit on the chair by Jason's window; pulling a blanket from the bottom of his bed, I wrap it around her, ensuring she's warming up. I pull her tightly against me as she curls up and places a hand on my cheek.

"Where are the others?" I ask Jason, who's sitting on the edge of his bed, watching me with bloodshot eyes.

"In the gym with Ryan, Ethan and Layton." He leans forward and places a hand on my arm, looking concerned. "What freaked you out? Has something happened?"

I shake my head before looking down at Jasmine, who is looking up at me with tears sliding down her cheek.

"I'm sorry," I whisper, wiping her tears away.

"What for?" she asks, frowning.

"I didn't mean to scare you." I look up from her blue eyes and straight into Jason's grey ones. "Neither of you."

"What happened? I don't think I have ever seen you like that," he asks. I open my mouth to lie; it's instinct to tell them I'm fine, even when I'm not.

"The worst nightmare I have ever had," I reply, tightening my arms around Jasmine.

"You're safe; we all are," Jasmine whispers, cupping my cheek as she forces me to look at her, and both of us still cry silently. "You are okay, Daddy. None of us are going anywhere."

"Has he woken up at all?" The sound of Maximus's voice pulls me from the deep sleep. Not long after I curled up on the chair with Jasmine, Jason insisted I lay on the bed while Jasmine got dry and into something warmer than a wet towel. Knowing it was to help Jasmine, I did as I was told. As soon as she was dressed, she sat next to me as I placed my head on her lap and held her legs to me as she ran her hand over my head. Promising whatever had happened wasn't real, and they were alright.

"No, he curled up and hasn't moved," Jasmine whispers, still running a hand over my head.

"Do you have much to do today?" Sean asks, "Or are the girls taking over so you can stay with him?"

I hear Jasmine laugh with no humour under her breath.

"You think I would leave him, or any of you, like this? I don't care if the wedding doesn't go ahead at this point; I just want him to be okay."

"I'm fine," I answer, feeling Jasmine jump underneath me.

"Christ, Christian, you nearly gave me a heart attack!" Sean snaps, placing a hand over his chest as Maximus and Jason laugh.

Sitting up, I rub the sleep from my stinging eyes and sit next to Jasmine, who instantly leans into me. Wrapping my arms around her, I use the scent of her shampoo and warmth to ground myself.

"You good?" Maximus asks, watching me as Jason reaches for a water bottle and passes it to me.

"Yeah, it was just a messed-up dream, but it felt so fucking real it took me a while to realise that's all it was," I mumble before taking a deep drink from the bottle.

"Want to talk about it?" Jason asks. I look at Jasmine and the others before letting out a deep sigh. I want to say no and hide it all from them. It was just a stupid dream, after all. But even when I remind myself of that, it is still difficult to grasp as it felt so real. Busing myself by sipping my water, I quickly think about how much I want them to know.

"It started as Sunday morning. We were dressed and in the wedding tent, talking to the registrar. Nothing stood out; we were just there laughing and waiting for Jasmine. But when she walked down the aisle to me, and I went to take her hand from Terry, but he changed to her father." Closing my eyes, I look up at the ceiling as I start to shake. I swallow back the sick that threatens to come up as I picture him glaring at me. I hear Jasmine gasp and take her hand in mine, unable to bring myself to look at her or the others.

"He was pissed?" Maximus asks, and I can't help chuckling under my breath.

"Understatement of a lifetime." I shake my head and

continue to focus on the ceiling. "He refused to let me marry her, which was when all hell broke loose."

I don't look at any of them as I continue the play-by-play. When I get to the part about being forced to choose, I look at Maximus as tears fill my eyes again.

"I don't think my relationship with Jasmine is more important than yours. If I've made you ever feel like that, I'm sorry."

Maximus just stares at me for a moment with his arms crossed over his chest. The way his eyes widen, even if just a little, tells me there was some truth in that bit. It would explain why we've been butting heads so much recently.

"I know." For a moment, I think he means he doesn't forgive me, but then a tiny smile lifts one side of his mouth. "You can just be such a controlling arsehole!"

I laugh as the others snap at him. "He's not wrong," I point out as we smile at each other.

"I'm never wrong," he winks before his smile fades. "So, who did you shoot?"

I shake my head as I remember how I felt lifting the gun and holding it to my head.

"I turned the gun on myself."

Jasmine gasps next to me as Jason hisses through his teeth. I shrug as they all look like they are about to be sick.

"I'm not suicidal," I point out, trying to get that point across. "I have no plans on ever going down that route." I pinch the bridge of my nose as I lean my head against Jasmine's, resting on my shoulder. "I would never choose between you guys. I will always take a bullet for you all." I take time to look at each of them, the four people I love more than anything and know I would do it if I had to. I will always look after them.

"Is that it? That's when you wake up?" Sean asks. I

consider telling them about Mum but, for some reason, decide against it. I will one day, but not yet.

We stay silent for a moment; they give me the time to breathe, which I need right now. Before I get a chance to be asked any more questions, I climb off the bed and stand in front of my brothers, promising with one look that I have their backs and that I always will, before walking out of the door.

Chapter Forty-Six

JASMINE

"Shit."

Looking away from the door, Jason sits on the edge of the bed and puts his head in his hands.

"Did you have any idea he was so bad?" Sean asks as I move to kneel behind Jason, wrap my arms around him, and lean my cheek against his back. I think we both need some sort of comfort right now.

"No," Jason replies, placing a hand over mine resting on his stomach.

"Have you seen him this bad before?" Maximus asks. I don't think he has looked away from the door since Christian left.

"Only once. He didn't sleep for a month after Mum died, because of nightmares. Tommy was fucking vicious with him when it started affecting his fights and everything else."

The twins both curse under their breath; Maximus pinches the bridge of his nose as Sean rubs the back of his neck.

"What do we do to help?"

"So now you fucking care?" Sean spins around and stares at his twin as Jason and I look on in surprise.

"What the fuck is that meant to mean?" Maximus snaps, turning his attention to Sean, who looks angrier than I have ever seen him towards his brother.

"You know what it fucking means. You have made it your mission to give him shit for months. From the sly comments to throwing downright nasty insults, don't forget Christmas when you only got the bloody puppy for Jaz to piss him off!"

"Enough," Jason snaps as I stare at Maximus, my mouth hanging open. Did he really use a gift for me to get at his brother? I think I know the answer from how he refuses to look in my direction.

"He goes harder on me than anyone else, don't try and say he doesn't because he fucking does," Maximus yells, pointing towards the door, which is thankfully closed. "So yes, I make comments and digs and do things just to push his buttons; what does he expect when he bitches at me all the time!" He closes the distance between him and Sean, so they are nose to nose. The two-inch height difference between them means Maximus is looking down at him. "But not once, not for a second, have I not loved my brother. He's not the only one who would take a bullet for each of you because I would, too. Without a second thought, I would jump in front of that prick. Because as much as we rile each other up, there is nothing I wouldn't do for that man. He may be a prick, but he's our fucking prick, and he's been the best father we could have ever asked for, which says it all as he's only meant to be our brother."

I don't miss the way Sean doesn't look away from his

brother, but his eyes soften as he realises there is so much love between them under the looks, digs, and everything else.

"He only goes harder on you because you have always reminded him of himself." The twins finally stop staring at each other and turn to Jason, who takes my hand and pulls me around him, so I'm curled up on his lap. Jason holds me tightly for comfort, and I'm okay with that.

"You have always strived to be like Christian, it's why you went into boxing in the first place. You jumped at every chance you could to be just like him, and as you got older, that didn't change, and you know it." Jason tightens his arms around me as I relax into him, letting him know I'm here for him.

"Most would take that as a compliment, but he doesn't," Maximus mumbles.

"Of course he doesn't, you absolute dickhead!" All three guys watch me climb off Jason's lap and stand before Maximus.

"Excuse me?" Maximus stares down at me, but I've had enough of the bickering and snide comments, like everyone else.

"I called you a dickhead, and no, I'm not taking it back." I don't give him a chance to answer again before I finally snap. "One of these days, you are going to realise how much that man hates himself." I stare at him while pointing towards the door. "I know each of you hates having to kill people. We are all well aware that Christian will try to be the one to do it rather than any of you. Have you ever seen him after he's killed someone? I don't mean when he knows you are around, but when he is in the shower, alone and broken. Because I have. Have you heard him crying out in his sleep because he's reliving what he's done? No, but I have. Why do you think he gets up before the rest of us every morning and very rarely sleeps in whatever bed we end up in? Because he doesn't want us to know he's suffering.

"That man in there wouldn't only kill others to save you, but he would kill himself before letting you turn out like him. That's why he's tough on you; he doesn't want you to follow in his footsteps. He blames himself for every single thing that has gone wrong in all our lives. But most of all, he blames himself for the fact you have to do the things you do." I turn away from a shocked-looking Maximus, not caring what he has to say on the matter. We are all sick of the way he can be with Christian, and it needs to stop.

"Why did he react so badly when he walked into the bathroom? That wasn't just because I was in there."

Jason shakes his head before looking at the others.

"You were singing the song Mum used to sing all the time. She loved the Beatles, but something about 'Blackbird' made her sing it more than any other," he sighs, looking at the door.

"Why didn't you tell me? I would have stopped," I point out, devastated that I've been walking around for weeks unknowingly singing a song that upsets them all. But when Jason turns back to me, he's smiling.

"Because I love hearing it. It's like she's here again."

"I forgot about that," Maximus whispers, looking at the door. "She would sing it more around Christian than anyone else."

"That's because he was her Blackbird," Jason answers with a sad smile. "For years, he was her Little Blackbird." He gives his head a little shake. "Tommy would give her hell for it, claiming she was 'making him weak,' so she stopped to protect him. I'd forgotten all about that."

"It doesn't look like he has, though," Sean whispers. The four of us look at the door, all thinking of the broken man who just walked through it.

Walking back over to Jason, I press a kiss on his cheek.

"Can you tell the girls to lay off what we were going to tackle today? If they want to go home, they can." I turn to walk out of the door, but Jason grabs my hand and stops me.

"You want to call off the wedding?"

"I don't know," I answer honestly. "I'm going to spend the morning with him and see what he wants." I look around at the others and offer them a small smile. "Could you honestly enjoy the day if you know one of us is hanging on by a thread?" I'm surprised when Maximus is the first to shake his head. Stepping up in front of him, I kiss his cheek. "You are a dickhead, but you're my dickhead."

He chuckles under his breath, shaking his head.

"You're lucky you're so damn cute."

"I'm your brat, and you love it."

"Yeah, I do."

"But a word to the wise," I say, letting him see I'm serious. "If you *ever* use me to get at any of the others, you won't like my response. Whether through a gift or by making comments regarding any of our relationships; I am not a pawn in any of your games." I look around at the others to make a point. "That goes for you all. There are enough people willing to use one of us against the others; I won't have any of us acting the same."

"Yes, ma'am," they say in unison. I used to think this was them all being sarcastic, but apparently, it's because I can be quite scary when I want to be.

Not saying another word, I walk out of the room and head straight to Christian's, terrified of what I will find. Do

I think he would do something stupid? No, he'd never want to leave us unprotected, but that doesn't mean he's not suffering. We all knew it was bad, but after seeing the way he broke this morning, I think it's time he got some help.

Standing outside the room for a moment, I take a second to prepare myself for whatever I find there. Taking a deep breath, I slowly open the door. Trying to be quiet in case he has fallen back to sleep. But he hasn't.

Christian is sitting on the far side of the bed where I sleep, still in nothing but his boxers, holding his head in his hands. He's breathing heavily as he fights his inner demons.

There have been times since moving in that I have woken to find him in the same position, but the second he thinks I'm awake, he heads to the bathroom, shutting himself away and promising he's fine. But after today, he's not going to suffer alone. He has helped me heal since everything has come to light; it's time for me to carry some of the burden.

Walking into the room, I quietly shut the door and head to his side. He doesn't realise I'm there until I climb onto the bed beside him. Placing an arm around his shoulders, I gently pull him down so he can rest his head on my lap as he did before falling asleep. This time, he doesn't cry or say anything. He just stares at the window as I run a hand over his head.

"I love you," I whisper, leaning over to kiss his head. "I know you love me and want to protect me, but that doesn't mean you have to struggle on your own." I hug him the best I can from this position. "You need to start talking, whether to me, your brothers or even a therapist. But you need to talk to someone."

"I know," his voice barely a whisper. "I'm too tired to keep doing this."

"Then tell me what I can do," I whisper in his ear, holding him tighter. "Tell me what you need, and I will make it happen."

"I don't know." Those three words wreck me as this man in my arms always knows what to do. He fixes everything and everyone but himself. It's my turn to fix him.

"I'm sorry," the words are out before I can stop them.

"You haven't done anything wrong, Sweetheart. It's all on me."

"I'm apologising because I didn't know your mum liked the song I've been singing for weeks. If I had known, I would have stopped."

"I wouldn't have asked you to," he replies, rolling onto his back as I sit up so he can look at me.

"Do you ever talk about her?" As I expected, he shakes his head. "Can you tell me about her?" I want to get him talking and opening up, and for some reason, I think talking about his mum might work.

"She would have loved you," he says, his eyes finding mine for the first time. "You remind me of her so much. She was always singing and dancing around and just … happy. She never shouted, but we still knew when she was fed up with our shit. She would rather spend all day in the garden or the kitchen with Mrs Brown than anything else." He smiles, looking up at the ceiling. "I wish she could be here when we have kids. She would have been the best grandmother. They would have been spoilt rotten, and she would have been so hands-on. She loved being a mother, even if not so much a wife. Tommy was always an arsehole, but she never let him break her."

"She sounds like she was strong and amazing," I point out, brushing some hair from his forehead.

"She was so strong; even when the twins were born

three months early, she was still there for Jason and me, as well as at the hospital for them." He seems lost in thought for a moment, and I wait, giving him time to process. "Has anyone ever told you how we nearly lost Sean?"

"No!" I snap, my whole body tensing. Why has no one told me this?

"You wouldn't know it, looking at how he is now, but he was the weaker of the two. He was so tiny, his lungs hadn't fully developed, so he was on all kinds of machines; he didn't stand much of a chance of survival. But Mum saved him; she realised that he deteriorated every time they separated the two of them. Maximus would whine whenever he wasn't next to Sean, who would struggle with his breathing. The nurses didn't believe her, but Mum told them she knew her babies, and they weren't to be separated. Just three days later, Sean was improving, and Maximus was the most content baby the nurses knew."

"They say mothers know more about their babies than anyone, no matter how old they get." I smile, ignoring the fact that my mother was the complete opposite. She was a first-class evil bitch.

"She knew everything; no matter how much I tried to hide from her, she knew." The way his smile slips tells me she knew things he really didn't want her to.

"Did she know about that night?" I ask, knowing she would have still been alive when Christian killed my father to protect Jason.

"I think so," he says as his eyes fill up. "She found me in the woods at the back of the house. I was crying, hugging my knees to my chest. Tommy wouldn't tell her what was wrong, and Jason was so scared by the event that he didn't speak for nearly a month. We were worried he had become mute. I used to sneak into his room after Tommy had gone to bed and sleep with him to stop the nightmares. They were the only thing that made him make a noise."

"So how did she find out?" I ask, confused.

"She could have guessed; I think the fact that I was covered in blood, with busted knuckles and sitting in trousers soaked in my own piss was a giveaway."

I gasp as tears fill my eyes at the same time as Christian's widen.

"Shit, Baby, I wasn't thinking. I'm so sorry." He sits up and cups my cheeks as I burst into tears. "I can't believe I said that. I'm so sorry. Sometimes I forget it was your dad."

"That's not why I'm crying," I snap, taking him by surprise. "I'm crying 'cause I'm fucking furious at that arse-hole, Tommy!" I yell, jumping to my feet as I start pacing around the room. "You were fifteen! Fucking fifteen, and he allowed you to get so scared you .... You pissed yourself!" I turn to Christian, surprised to see him smiling. "How are you smiling? I am on the verge of going looking for his body so I can piss on him! Before I set him alight!"

Christian laughs aloud before sucking his lips between his teeth.

"It's times like these you remind me of her the most."

"Well, that makes me like her even more. Sounds like we would have gotten along just fine," I snap, rolling my eyes before sitting beside him again.

Christian moves up the bed and holds an arm out for me once he's sitting against the headboard. I sit beside him and curl up against his side.

"You two would have been a terrible combination. I dread thinking how many punishments you would add up in just one day together," he says into my hair as I roll my eyes again.

"She sounds like she wouldn't have let you punish me."

Christian laughs as I feel him shaking his head.

"Not a chance, but then again, what goes on in our bedroom is no one's business." He kisses the top of my head as I place a hand over his heart, glad to feel it beating normally. "She was in the dream."

I move a little to look up at him, but he's staring at the ceiling.

"I've always believed she would be so disappointed in me. I've felt like I have failed her every day since she died." His eyes close as he takes a deep breath.

"She died of breast cancer; it was so quick. She went from running around, cooking, and cleaning to sleeping twenty hours a day in six months. She still tried to make time for us, though. Every second she was awake, she would be with at least one of us, ensuring we knew how much she loved us.

"I didn't handle it well. I was falling apart on the inside, but on the outside, I was the loving brother and son. I helped the twins with their homework and picked flowers daily for her room. She loved being outside, so I brought the outside to her when she couldn't go out there anymore." He goes quiet for a moment, and I let him have the time to remember her.

"The night she died, I was with her," he says quietly after a few silent minutes to himself. "Tommy was out, nothing new, so I was reading *Pride and Prejudice* to her. It was one of her favourites. She tried to smile at me, but her eyes looked so heavy, and I remember thinking, 'It's going to be tonight.'

"Just before ten PM, she opened her eyes and smiled while holding her hand out to me. She called me something she hadn't called me for years and asked me to climb on the bed with her, so I did." Christian lets out a deep breath as he blinks back tears.

"She was so tiny in my arms. I held her just like this," he looks down, giving me a small smile. "She reached up, cupped my cheek, and whispered that she needed me to be brave and look after my brothers. She told me that no one could protect them like I could, and I was to make sure Tommy couldn't hurt them like he had me. It was then I knew she was aware of what was going on. So I promised her I would, because how could I not? I love my brothers more than anything other than you. There is nothing I wouldn't do for them.

"I still remember the last words she said to me, and I will never forget. She started humming 'Blackbird', and with her last conscious breath, she whispered, 'Fly, Blackbird, fly.' She took her last breath less than five minutes later."

"Why did she call you Blackbird?" I ask, curiosity getting the better of me. Christian frowns, probably wondering how I know. "Jason told me earlier."

"Of course he did," he chuckles. "She loved the Beatles. I think if she had gotten her way, we all would have been named after them, but Tommy hated them. When I was born, my hair was jet black; it reminded her of a blackbird. She would sing it to me whenever I would cry. Apparently, it was the only thing that would make me stop. I was her Little Blackbird for years until Tommy put a stop to it.

"When I was seven or eight, he started forcing me to box, determined to 'man me up.' One day, Mum and I were in the kitchen doing something, and he flipped, that it was her fault I was so soft, and she was babying me by calling me by a stupid nickname. He also hated that I called her Ma. So, from that night, I was just to be called Christian, and she was my mother or Mum. We tried to keep it behind his back, but I slipped up and called her Ma in front of him, and he beat the shit out of me. So, from then on, she made us stick to his rules. Even though we both hated them."

"Did he ever hit her?" I ask, and I'm surprised when he shakes his head.

"Tommy was many things and a complete shit, but he never touched a woman. He had no issues belittling her and gaslighting her until she nearly lost herself for a while. But sometimes I think he did love her, in his own way."

"I wish I had gotten to meet her." I smile as I reach up and wipe away a stray tear from his cheek.

"Me too, but if she had lived, we may have never met you, Sweetheart." Christian cups my cheek before pressing a soft kiss to my lips. "I don't even want to imagine a world where you aren't in our lives." He looks back to the window and appears to be deep in thought.

"This isn't the life Mum would have wanted for us. When she appeared in the dream, I remember crying and apologising for failing her and not protecting my brothers. I had the gun to my head, but she lowered it and called me Blackbird and told me she was so proud of me." Christian swallows deeply as he watches out of the window. "She told me that I had broken my wings to ensure my brothers kept theirs, but it was my time to fix my wings and fly." Christian looks down at me, and my heart stops. "I want to move on and live life the way we should."

"Do you still want to go ahead with Sunday?" I ask. Christian frowns as he stares at me.

"Of course I do. Why do you ask?"

"You had a nightmare about the wedding; I wasn't sure if it was your way of realising it's not what you want."

"Sweetheart, if anything, after speaking to you, I want it

more than ever! Is that why you are sitting here? Because you have stopped getting everything ready?"

"No, I'm here because you were hurting, and nothing is more important to me than you four. If you're hurting, so am I!"

"Well, I'm fine now, so get out there and make sure everything is ready for Sunday!" he declares, pushing me until I'm off the bed. "Go; see the girls and get shit done while I have a an hour in the gym." He is back to being playful Christian, and the spark slowly returns to his eyes. But I know he still has a long way to go, and I will be there every step of the way with him.

"You are only pushing for it because you don't want to be the one to tell Mrs Brown we wouldn't need a cake." I laugh as he gives me a well, duh, face. "Fine, everything is still going ahead, and I'm going to see the girls." Before I get a chance to walk away from the bed, Christian grabs me around the waist and pulls me in for a hard, passionate kiss.

"Thank you," he whispers as he leans his forehead against mine. "I know I don't need to say it, but I want to. You have no idea how much you help just by being you and distracting me when I need to be distracted or showing me love when I need it the most. You just make everything better, and I can't wait till Sunday."

Tears well up in my eyes as I throw my arms around his neck and hug him.

"I'm always here for you, Daddy. Even when you think you don't need me." I press a kiss to his cheek and rush from the room before I do something I will regret, like burst into tears and become an emotional wreck.

Chapter Forty-Seven

CHRISTIAN

It's been three hours since I woke up, and I still can't shake off that fucking dream. I'm on edge, and although I know there is no way any of those particular people can get to my family, there are still people who can. I can't let that happen; I won't let it happen.

There is only one thing, other than losing myself in Jasmine, that helps me clear my head and work out what I need to do: hit something.

Within ten minutes of Jasmine leaving our room, I was in my gym shorts and walking down to our gym. I was so glad I didn't bump into anyone, whether family or friends; I wasn't ready to speak to anyone other than Jasmine. I have never been very good when it comes to talking about feelings. Tommy drilled it into me from a very young age that feelings will get you killed. *"It's best to shut that shit off and stop focusing on the past. It's behind you for a reason."* Even though I have pushed my brothers and Jasmine to accept their emotions and talk about them, I've never been able to follow my own advice until today.

When Jasmine sat on our bed and encouraged me to talk, I felt a little lighter than I had in a long time. Could I be like that with someone other than my girl? Probably not. Jasmine has this way of making me comfortable enough to talk without even realising it. How did I, of all people, get lucky enough to have such an amazing woman by my side? I will never understand it.

I will never understand how Jasmine has grown into the big-hearted, considerate, selfless woman who always puts everyone before herself. She was brought up by such an evil, manipulative excuse of a mother who never showed her any love, yet that's all Jasmine does. It's why everyone who meets her loves her.

Jasmine and Carol Connors couldn't be more different if they tried. Carol thought of no one but herself; the only time she ever wanted to admit she was a mother was so she could use her daughter to get what she wanted: drugs and money. Yet Jasmine was the perfect daughter in so many ways. Even when her mother was using drugs and abusing her, Jasmine still believed that there had to be some good in her somewhere.

The morning Jason and I took Jasmine to the house to get her things, I realised just how bad things had gotten and how evil Carol could be. Jasmine had told us several times what Carol was like when she was using, but seeing it first-hand made me realise just how strong Jasmine had been all those years. How she lived in those conditions with a mother that vile, I'll never be able to comprehend. Tommy was an arsehole, violent and controlling, but my brothers and I had each other, as well as Mum, Mrs Brown, and a handful of friends, such as Terry and Geralt Young, who always looked out for us the best he could, it's why he put up with Tommy's shit. But poor Jasmine had no one in her corner once her grandparents died.

Thinking of Carol and Tommy, my nightmare flashes before my eyes again. Instead of letting it pull me under, I envision Hardy standing before me with that smug smile I took great pleasure in removing from his face. After all the pain he had caused my brother, there was no way I was going to let him live. I put everything I had into getting harder and stronger. I took out anyone who dared to look at me the wrong way. But the main plan was to make Hardy pay, and I did.

I've never taken pleasure in causing death. Every single one was a necessity to ensure that no one even considered attempting to hurt my brothers again. Even if I made myself the primary target, I didn't care as long as those three were safe.

The whole time I've been trying desperately to push back all the memories of how I got to this point, I attack the punch bag like it is every single person who attacked me in one way or another. With Guns N' Roses blaring in my ears, I don't hold back, desperately trying to find some sort of release because then I may be able to think of a way to get this latest threat away from my family. My mum told me to mend my broken wings and fly, but how can I do that when it will leave us all vulnerable? I will never take that risk, not now that we have Jasmine.

Every nerve in my body comes alive as I sense someone approaching me from behind. I don't stop to think; I spin around whilst dropping to the floor, taking out their legs in the process. Before they've even hit the deck, they flip forward so they can get their balance before jumping back.

"What the fuck?" I yell, pulling my earbuds out. "Are

you trying to get yourself killed?" I stare at Terry, who looks a little shaken.

"I called your name four times, O'Reilly!" he snaps as I hear someone laugh from the door.

"I had these in!" I thrust my hand out to show the two earbuds now resting on it. "If I had heard you, I would have fucking answered."

"I tried to warn him," Jason announces as he walks into view. As soon as our eyes meet, he gives me a look, checking to see if I'm okay. I nod subtly before turning my attention back to Terry.

"I was going to come and see you after I finished in here anyway," I sigh, turning back to the punching bag.

Getting my feet in the right position, I start jabbing at the bag. Terry stands behind it, far enough that if it swings, it won't hit him, but close enough that I will hear him over the sound of my fists hitting the stiff leather.

"I've managed to unscramble the footage from the night before the attempted break-in."

I grab the bag as it swings back towards me so I can give him my full attention. He holds out a small stack of papers, which I notice all have pictures on them.

"Do you recognise any of them?" I ask, taking them from him and flicking through the pile. Each one is time-stamped. It looks like it took them a grand total of five minutes to get the jacks in position. After all, they had a ladder, which conveniently disappeared so Maximus was forced to climb up the wall.

"No, I have run them through our databases, and they don't match any old employees. I'm going to ask Calvin to give it a go on his system."

I nod, knowing it's likely he will be able to match them

to a name, and if he can't use his system, then Logan will be able to by hacking the CCTV database or something.

"Chuck me my phone," I nod towards the ring where I placed it when coming in. Jason throws it to me, and I quickly take a picture of the prints. "Are these on the system?" I ask, flicking through the images to photograph each one.

"No, thought it was best to just keep a paper trail for now until we can clear our people."

"Good, that's what I was thinking." I pull up a contact number and click call. I listen to it ring three times before he answers.

"McIntire." His voice comes through sharp and stressed.

"It's me. Have you got a minute?" I listen to mumbled voices on the other end of the line and wait to be addressed.

After a few moments, I hear what sounds like a door closing and footsteps echoing before the squeak of McIntire's office chair sounds out, signalling he's sitting down.

"Hey, how's it all going?"

"It's okay. Been better, but that's to be expected."

"I can imagine," he sighs. "What can I do for you, Christian?"

"How well do you know Nicholson's men?" I ask nervously. McIntire and Nicholson are not friends, but they do respect each other to a point. If anyone knows who these guys works for, it is the man on the other end of this call.

"I make it a point to know all who pose a threat."

"Do you have your laptop to hand? We have some stills from our security footage. I would like you to look at it and tell me how worried I should be."

"Send them over."

I explain I'm putting him on loudspeaker and hold my phone in my hand as I pull up my encrypted email app.

"You should get them any second." I click send and wait patiently to hear if he knows who it is. If it is Nicholson, the wedding will be off, and I'll send everyone home. My brothers and Jasmine will be on a plane within the hour. I'm already planning where to send them when I hear McIntire curse.

"They don't work for Nicholson." That should be a relief, but his reaction has me doing anything but relax.

"How worried should I be?" I ask, looking at Terry and Jason, who are ready to follow orders.

"You still on lockdown at the house?"

"Yes," I answer nervously.

"Is Abigail still there?"

I look to Jason, who frowns, nodding.

"She's here, as are Verity and Danielle King."

"Send them all home and wait for my call. I will collect this bastard myself and bring him to you." I can hear him walking around again through the phone as I look at Jason, who is staring at me wide-eyed.

"Do I need to get Jasmine to a safe house?" I ask, looking at Terry, who is already tapping on his phone.

"No, she will be perfectly safe. You all will. But everyone else needs to leave, and don't tell them why. I'll be in touch." He ends the call as I look at Terry and Jason, hoping they have some kind of idea of what the fuck is going on.

"I'll go get the girls out of here; you shower and get dressed. We will all meet in the sitting room in thirty minutes," Jason orders before turning to Terry. "Can you fill Layton and the twins in?"

"What will you tell everyone to make them leave?" I ask, making sure everyone knows the story.

"I'll explain that we need some time as a family before the wedding. They know something is up, as Jazzy nearly called everything off this morning. We can just play along with whatever she told them."

"Sounds good to me. Send Jasmine to my room, and I will tell her, so she isn't blindsided or panicking that something is wrong with me," I say, grabbing my shit and heading towards the stairs leading up to the main house.

"I'll send her as soon as her friends go to pack."

I nod once and take the stairs three at a time, praying that whoever McIntire is collecting to bring here isn't another major threat to my family.

Chapter Forty-Eight

CHRISTIAN

Walking out of my bathroom with a towel around my waist as I dry my hair with another, I focus on the tasks at hand.

Get dressed.

Destroy whoever is threatening my family.

Make sure Jasmine and my brothers are safe.

The only thing that will ever be important to me is keeping our family safe.

Heading into the walk-in closet, I try to focus on the first task: getting dressed.

"Daddy?" I can hear the worry in her voice and once again hope that by the end of the day, it will be a thing of the past, for now, at least.

"In here, Sweetheart." Jasmine appears in the doorway, looking panicked, before rushing forward to throw her arms around my neck.

"What's going on? Are you okay?"

"I'm fine, Sweetheart," I reply, pressing a kiss to her head before stepping back from her arms. Letting go of her is the last thing I want to do, which is why I have no choice but to do it; otherwise, nothing will get done. "What has Jason told you?" I ask, heading over to where my shirts are all hanging.

"Just that we needed everyone to leave and for us to meet in the office in twenty minutes." Slowly, Jasmine steps closer and places a hand on my arm. "What's happening?"

Grabbing my deodorant, I quickly spray myself before shrugging on a shirt.

"Terry managed to get some images from the security cameras, which show who broke the shutters on your window."

"Who was it?" she asks, her eyes widening.

"I don't know," I answer honestly as I fasten my buttons. "Because I know McIntire makes a point of knowing everything about his competition, including who works for them, I sent him the photos." Pulling the towel from around my waist, I chuck it into the washing basket and grab some boxers.

"I take it he knows who it is?" Jasmine asks. I don't miss the way her eyes keep looking down at my cock, until it's hidden away inside my underwear, semi-hard just from her looking at it.

"Like something you see, Baby?" I tease, unable to stop myself from laughing when she realises she's been caught.

I love it when she looks at me like she knows she's meant to be paying attention, but all she wants is my dick buried deep inside one of her holes. Smiling at the warm blush on her cheeks, I quickly carry on before I make us late by taking her against a wall.

"McIntire knows who they are, and he wasn't happy. He has gone to collect them himself and will bring them here. He told me to ensure the others had left before he arrived."

Jasmine frowns as I pull on some trousers and tuck my shirt into them.

"Do you think it's one of his guys?"

I stop mid-action and stare at her for a moment.

"I hadn't even thought of that," I admit before continuing to get dressed. "You really are becoming the brains of the family, Sweetheart." I give a teasing smile, but my heart is swelling with pride. She surprises us every single day with how much attention she is paying and how she finally has the confidence to voice her suggestions and observations.

"But why would he want the others gone?" she asks. I think back at the conversation and realise something.

"He asked if Abigail was still here; I think he wanted her gone before he arrived; the others were more of an afterthought."

"Well, that makes sense; she would know if it was someone who worked for him," Jasmine points out as she turns around and selects a tie for me as I turn up my collar. "There again," she loops the tie around my neck before tying it. "It could be that he just didn't want to see her. Abigail hates McIntire; she has no problem telling him that to his face, either."

"She's braver than most of the men I know then." I smile as Jasmine tightens the knot on my tie, ensuring it's in place. It's a little thing she's been doing for the last few months, and I love it. I love how she concentrates to ensure it's perfect every time.

"She's stupid, and I've told her so. He's powerful for a reason."

"She doesn't need to fear him," I say, hoping to put her at ease.

"I know that; she is just in self-destruct mode and not looking at the bigger picture," Jasmine sighs, running her hand over the tie to ensure it hangs flat. "I think he cares and wants to help her, and she knows it. But she wants to blame him for her dad's death, even though he wasn't at fault. So, she's pushing every one of his buttons to get a reaction. Looking for a way to keep him as the bad guy." Finally looking up, she places her hand on my chest and lifts to press a light kiss to my lips. Pulling away with a smile, she looks up at me with so much love my heart aches as I place my hands on her hips.

"You have come a long way since you went through something similar, Sweetheart, and we are all very proud of you for it." I tuck some hair behind Jasmine's ear, which is hanging in her natural curls because she didn't blow dry it his morning. Once again, she put my needs before her own, showing how big her heart is, even after everything she has been through.

"I had four great men in my corner to help me come to the realisation," Jasmine smiles. Running my fingers across her cheek, I thread them into the hair at the back of her head and lean in to kiss her, a smile on both our faces as we get lost in each other's eyes.

My phone rings in the bedroom, and I sigh reluctantly, releasing Jasmine's hair. Taking her hand, I pull her into the bedroom, reaching for my phone charging on the side. My stomach drops a little when I see the name on the screen.

"Did you find them?"

"Yeah, we will be with you in ten minutes. Where do you want him?"

Ten minutes later, I'm pacing around the basement, which is situated under the gym. It was specially built to ensure people never found what we hide or do down here. If people attack our home, this is where they come before they die. No one we bring here ever leaves alive; we can't take that risk. The entrance to it is also our means of escape if we need to in a hurry. It's a feature we added when we were trying to make the house as safe as possible for Jasmine, knowing people may use her as a way to control us.

As much as I hate killing, there are certain things that make it a little easier; one of those is if I'm killing someone who hurt our girl or attempted to. I have no issue making those people disappear, so they are never seen or heard of again.

Looking around, I see Jason and Maximus are just as tense as I am; neither of them is saying anything, just watching the door and waiting for Terry's signal. I needed as many hands as possible, but I left Sean with Jasmine upstairs, so she wasn't alone in case anyone comes looking for her. They are staying in the sitting room with Mrs Brown, ready to go if necessary.

"Do you have any idea who it could be?" Maximus asks, walking over to me. I shake my head, looking at the door, not wanting to miss the signal.

"Jasmine thinks it might be one of McIntire's men, which would explain why he is bringing them in himself."

"Fuck, I hadn't even thought of that," Jason curses as he joins us.

"I didn't either; she makes a good point, too, as it would explain why he wanted Abigail gone." I continue trying to decide what to do if she's right.

"She would be able to identify him," Maximus mumbles more to himself than any of us, but I nod anyway.

"Jasmine said that, too."

"Shorty really is becoming the brains of the family." Maximus grins as Layton laughs.

"Or you lot have taken one too many blows to the head."

"That's more likely it," Jason winks. I shake my head, but I can't hold back my smile. We like to tease her, but Jasmine has always been an intelligent woman; she just didn't have the discipline to put it to any use. But now she's coming out of her shell; she is surprising not only us but others as well. Her teachers are full of praise, giving her the boost to continue working hard and exceeding everyone's expectations.

Seeing her artistic side while organising the wedding was an eye-opener. I have a feeling that if being a professional dancer doesn't work out, she won't be short of options. The florist would snatch her up in a second if she ever went there to ask for a job.

A red light flashes above the door, catching everyone's attention, signalling they are close. Terry had left to meet McIntire and escort him and his prisoner down the tunnel.

"I know I say this a lot, but don't you think we give McIntire a little too much information? He knows our businesses, our relationships, and now our one route to escape if we were to come under attack."

Turning to Maximus, I try to keep a straight face and not show how conflicted I am right now.

"Trust me, I know, but the alliance we have formed benefits others, and he knows that I never ask him to do things for me; he is offering without expectations."

"At the end of the day, he's been more than happy to help and obviously thinks highly of Christian. Otherwise, he wouldn't do all he does," Jason adds.

"What are we going to do if it is one of his guys who's

been causing all this shit?" Maximus asks. I don't miss the way Jason and Layton turn their attention to me, as I have no doubt they've been trying to work out the same thing.

"I don't know," I admit, shaking my head. "It's something that we will have to decide when the information is presented to us." I look back to the door and watch as the green light flickers. "Let's just hope this helps us put an end to this shit," I sigh, walking over to the centre of the room as the others step beside me, and Layton heads to the door to open it.

I hold my breath and wait for the door to open, unsure of what to expect on the other side. Before the door opens halfway, a person with a sack over his head, dressed in a yellow t-shirt and ripped jeans, flies into the room, landing on the concrete floor. I hear a muffled yelp, sounding like he's been gagged. A furious McIntire storms into the room and grabs the guy's arms, which are tied behind his back and yanks him up so he's kneeling on the ground.

"His name's Edward Grey, but he goes by Eddy. He's a fucking waste of space with no job, lives in a shithole, and likes to think he's smarter than he is." I have seen McIntire angry before, but nothing like this. He grabs the sack and rips it from his head. Eddy already looks like he's taken a beating. Judging by the way he flinches away from McIntire, he's the one who dished it out.

"Don't fucking look at me, you piece of shit. Look at the ground, and if I see you looking up at me again, I will carve your eyes out."

I look at him with an arched brow, but McIntire doesn't see me; all he focuses on is the arsehole in front of him.

"How do you know him?" I ask, wanting to see if someone will come looking for the shit.

"I've been watching him for a couple of months, waiting for him to fuck up and give me an excuse to take him out."

"I told you, I don't know-" he gets cut off mid-sentence by McIntire grabbing a fist full of hair and slamming Eddy's face into his knee. Eddy screams out in pain as blood gushes from his broken nose.

"I already have all the reasons I need to finish you, but first, you are going to have a little chat with the O'Reillys here and explain what your intentions were when you attempted to climb into their fiancée's bedroom." McIntire looks up and gives me a nod.

"He's all yours; if you decide you don't want to kill him, don't worry; I will be more than happy to."

"What's he done to piss you off?" Maximus asks behind me. McIntire glares down at Eddy, who is still kneeling on the ground, holding his bleeding nose.

"He has been seeing someone who doesn't belong to him," McIntire answers.

"Who?" I ask, almost sure I know the answer. When he turns his attention to me, I can see why people are so scared of him with one look. I have to stop myself from stepping back, wanting to put as much distance between us as possible.

"Abigail Young."

Chapter Forty-Nine

CHRISTIAN

My eyes shoot up to McIntire. Abigail, was the leak? Surely, she wouldn't do that to Jasmine; the girls are very close. From their first meeting long before Geralt was killed, they became inseparable. Jasmine has called her every single day since Geralt was murdered. Abigail has even told me herself that Jasmine has been the one to keep her going.

I turn to Jason and Maximus and can see the sheer shock and disbelief on their faces.

"No. There's no way Abbi would betray Jasmine," Maximus declares, shaking his head.

"That's because she hasn't, not knowingly anyway. She is as much a victim here as Jasmine," McIntire answers. "This prick has used her to listen in to conversations and probably gone through her phone at times as well."

"I haven't done anything; I love Abbi!"

McIntire punches Eddie in the face, growling.

"Enough of the bullshit! I warned you what would happen if you didn't back off, and now I have even more of a reason to end you. How long and painful your death will be depends on what you tell us now." McIntire turns to me, and I see why he is so feared. "What have you got down here? I left my stuff in the rush to get him here."

"Jason, can you show him while I speak to our friend here?" I don't need to look at Jason to know he will do as I asked.

Stepping in front of Eddie, I squat down, ensuring I'm still a little taller than him.

"Do you know who I am?"

Eddie nods as blood runs from his nose.

"So you are aware of what happens to people who come for my family?"

Again, Eddie nods, only looking at me for a millisecond at a time. I look at him cowering on the concrete floor and can't believe Abigail would lower herself to something so pathetic.

"Head up." Eddie looks up at me, and I take in an inventory of his injuries that I can see. His nose is broken, and his lip and cheek are split, and I think his eye socket may be broken. McIntire doesn't mess around that's for sure.

Eddie looks around, no doubt checking where McIntire is before whispering to me.

"He's mad. I haven't done anything. He has been trying to scare me off for a while, so now I think he wants to kill me."

"Too right, I'm going to kill you, you little shit. I'm going to enjoy every second of it," McIntire shouts, walking back over to us. "Here." I barely manage to catch a phone as it's thrown at me. "See if you can get into that; otherwise, I will have to do this the messy way."

I stand and look down at Eddie.

"Do you want to make this easy?" I arch one brow in

question and don't miss the way he starts to sweat. "Am I taking that as a no? What have you got on here that you don't want us to see? Proof of your recent activities? Names of people you know? Accomplices, maybe." Touching the phone, I can see it is fingerprint-protected. They are difficult to unlock without said fingers, but when I see McIntire leaning over our guest, I realise he has already thought of a solution.

"I don't have all day, so last warning before I let him take over. What is on this phone?"

"Just pictures," he mumbles, going back to looking at the floor. "Pictures Abbi wouldn't want you seeing."

I look over to McIntire; if possible, he looks even angrier. Fuck, this man is going to lose his shit. He stalks forward, grabs Eddie's hands, which are still tied to his back, and brings down a butcher's knife.

Eddie's screams fill the room, echoing off the walls as his blood splatters onto the ground. McIntire throws the hand onto the floor in front of me as Eddie brings the two arms in front of him, one with blood spraying from where his hand was only seconds ago.

"Jason," McIntire bellows over the screams. Jason walks forward with a handheld blow torch, which McIntire takes as he points to Layton. "Hold him down." Layton looks at me, and I nod, giving him the go-ahead to follow someone else's orders. Layton and Jason pin Eddie down, and McIntire starts the blow torch.

The smell of roasted skin fills the air as he cauterises the wound. It takes everything in me not to gag. Maximus moves as far away as possible; he has never had a strong stomach for this kind of torture. Show him blood, broken bones, even internal organs, and you would think he didn't even notice. Add the smell of burning flesh, and he's a goner.

Looking over my shoulder, I nod, giving him the go-ahead to leave if he needs to, but he shakes his head. This is too personal; I know he will need to be here to discover why everything has come to this.

McIntire moves away and turns off the flame as the others release Eddie, who curls up in the foetal position and cries loudly.

"He's all yours. Do what you want, but I will be the one to kill him." McIntire doesn't wait for my response; he grabs the severed hand from the ground, holds out his hand for the phone, and heads to a seat in the far corner, no doubt to search the phone.

Turning back to Maximus, I nod to the other side of the room. "Get the other chair." He does as I ask without a word. Placing it beside the withering Eddie, my brothers grab him under the arms and heave him into the chair. Judging by his colour, I'm pretty sure he's about to pass out.

"Here's what's going to happen." I unbutton my cuffs and slowly start folding up my sleeves. "I'm going to ask you some questions, and if you take too long to answer, you will get punched. However, if I think you are lying…" I pull my flip knife out of my pocket and open it in front of him. "I will stab you."

"Why should I bother? That psycho is going to kill me anyway!" Eddie shouts, drool and snot hanging from his mouth as he lifts his arm to wipe it away; he sees the burnt stump and cries harder.

"How did you think this was going to go?" I ask, frowning. "When you joined this little crusade, how did you see it ending?"

"I haven't done anything. I swear!" He starts to sway,

but Jason grabs his shoulder and holds him in the chair. There's nothing gentle about the gesture; I can see his knuckles turning white where he's gripping him hard.

"He's lying. It's all here on his phone. The locations and times of the girls' meetings, the vendors, everything," McIntire's face darkens, but I know better than to ask what he has found. I trust him to tell me if it concerned Jasmine.

Turning back to Eddie, I sigh.

"Who have you been working for?"

"No one." The wind is taken out of him as Maximus punches him. He falls to the floor, crying out as he lands on his burnt stump.

"I warned you not to lie to me, Eddie." Maximus stabs him, before kicking him so he rolls onto his back, and I look down at him. "Let's try something a little easier." Placing a foot just above his wrist, I apply the smallest amount of pressure. Eddie howls and tries to move away from me as soon as I lift my foot. "Pin him." I don't speak to anyone in particular as I know Jason and Maximus want in on this.

"Please, I don't know anything!" he wails, trying to escape my brothers, but Jason backhands him across the face. I watch his eyes as he stares at us all. He's a fighter, and I'll give him that.

"I'm going to tell you what I know, and you will fill in the gaps. Understood?" Eddie opens his mouth to speak, and Maximus punches him. He's gunning for blood, and there is nothing Eddie can do to prevent the beating he's going to get.

"This is what I know; stop me if I'm wrong," I declare, getting the chair he was just sitting in and placing it backwards over his torso, the legs on either side of his stomach, leaving me with the back to rest on as I straddle it, keeping a foot near his burnt arm.

Looking down at him, he tries to look away to avoid eye contact, but he is met by Jason's angry face on one side and Maximus's murderous face on the other. Eddie attempts to close his eyes, so he isn't looking at any of us, but that won't help him. "Look at me when I'm speaking to you, or I will let McIntire carve your eyes out like he threatened to."

"Oh, he will lose his eyes, that's for sure," I hear McIntire answer, but don't look to him for an explanation.

"I don't think the person you are working for is the one who started this whole mess," I start. "I think they saw that I was a target and used that to their advantage, hoping it would deter me from discovering what they are up to." Leaving a pause, I watch Eddie, noticing a small tick in his cheek.

"The person who has been vandalising wedding dresses, flowers, hotels and trying to get to our fiancée is not the same person who organised the coup at our stag party. However, they did give Mitchell all the information he needed and ensured they got into the building without being spotted." The tick in his cheek appears again, which tells me I'm on the right track.

"Who was selling our information to the competition?" I ask, leaning forward a little, and see the tick again.

"I don't know." A scream fills the air as I apply a little pressure onto his arm. "I don't know! I would say if I did!" he screams.

Flipping my knife in my hand as I lift my foot, I flick it downwards and watch as it sticks into the top of his arm. He screams again, and for a second, I think he's about to pass out. But he somehow manages to stay conscious.

"You're lying to me, Eddie. I don't like being lied to," I point out, leaving the knife in his arm. When he opens his mouth to argue, I shake my head slowly. "Don't bother lying; I know your tell, so I can tell when I say something you didn't think I knew." Slowly, I make a show of placing my foot just above his wrist again.

"So, if the person you are working with isn't associated with Mitchell, I think they are trying to get Jasmine out of the picture somehow." I watch as the muscle in his cheek twitches, confirming my suspicions. If I thought I was angry before, that's nothing compared to how I feel now.

"Who the fuck wants to kill our woman?" Maximus screams, grabbing the knife and twisting it. Eddie screams as Maximus twists it further.

"No one! No one wants her dead! Please!"

I turn my attention to Maximus, but he still glares at Eddie.

"If they don't want her dead, then why are they trying to destroy her?" he asks through gritted teeth. Eddie stares at him momentarily, his cheek ticking as he tries to stop himself from talking. While he's distracted, I hold out my hand, and Jason drops his knife.

"Last chance," I warn as Maximus finally looks up at me and sees the knife. Eddie follows his line of sight as his eyes widen, and he starts to cry.

"Just kill me. I won't turn them in!"

"Are they worth your life? Do they deserve your loyalty if they are leaving you high and dry like this?" I point out, shaking my head. "Are you really willing to die to protect them?"

"YES!" he screams as I bring my foot down onto his burnt wrist. "I would rather die than turn them in. Wouldn't you do the same for your brothers?" His face slips when he realises he's given us something huge to work with. Eddie starts to lose it, realising what he's done. Screaming and trying to fight against Jason and Maximus.

"Somebody shut him up!" I snap as Maximus looks for something to gag him with. Jason, as usual, is one step ahead, grabs my knee, and pushes down so my foot presses against Eddie's wrist. Eddie lets out a blood-curdling scream as I apply more pressure before he passes out from the pain.

"Well, that's one way to do it," I sigh, running my fingers through my hair. "Gag him and tie him up somehow. I don't want him screaming when he wakes up."

"McIntire, what do you know about his family?" I ask, heading over to where he is sitting, the amputated hand lying on the table beside him.

"He has one brother, but he's stateside and has been for years," he answers. "He does have a sister, but I've not bothered looking into her, as she's never around, and Abigail hasn't met her or doesn't plan to." McIntire opens Eddie's phone and starts scrolling through his contracts. "The kid is a moron; it seems he tried to get close to Danielle King, but she wasn't interested, so he turned to Abigail. Looking through messages, he always made excuses for not being able to meet her friends."

"But it was probably so Danielle didn't recognise him," I finish. McIntire nods before turning Eddie's phone around.

"See if you recognise any of these numbers."

Taking the phone from him, I walk over to Terry, who is locking the chains around Eddie.

"See if any names stand out or have the same number as any of our guys."

"Yeah, no problem, give me two-" the phone beeps as a message pops up.

M: I can't take this anymore. I need to find out what's happening; I'll call you when I leave theirs.

Terry snatches the phone from me as we open the messages from "M" There's hardly anything there, but Terry knows what he's doing. He passes the phone to Layton, who looks at the message and curses while Terry sets up his computer.

"Wait, I know this number!" Layton calls out. We all turn to watch as he pulls his own phone out of his pocket and starts scrolling on it. "Shit! The fucking bitch!" he curses, showing Terry the screen. Terry's eyes widen as he grabs the phone on the wall and presses a button.

"Answer, goddamn it!" he curses, almost bouncing on the balls of his feet.

"O'Reilly." I hear Sean's voice and stare at my brothers, who are all watching the scene unfold.

"Sean, we know who it is. You need to get down here."

"Sounds serious. Okay, I'll head down now."

"Bring Jasmine and Mrs Brown with you, but don't bring them into the basement," I say, looking to Terry, who nods.

"They will be fine up here. Mykela's just arrived."

The colour drains from Layton's face as Terry curses.

"Sean, we are on our way, so do not let her know. Keep her occupied."

"Why?" Sean asks as it all starts to click into place.

"Because she's the mole."

Chapter Fifty

SEAN

There has to be some mistake. Mykela can't be the mole; she's been with us for years.

I'm running on autopilot as I head to the front door, where I know Mykela is waiting. I don't want to open that door, not now that I know she's selling our information, putting my Princess in danger. I've never wanted to hit a woman before, but right now, I could kill her.

Guess the numbness has been burnt away by the fire of rage flowing through my body.

"Let her in and take her to Christian's office," Terry had instructed. *"Keep her away from Jaz. We are coming up."* For the plan to work, I need to let her in. Taking a deep breath, I plaster on a smile and open the door.

"Hey! What are you doing here?" I ask, stepping back so she can enter.

Mykela walks in wearing light blue skinny jeans and a thick, warm jumper. Considering I can count on my hand the number of times I've seen her in any makeup, it's strange seeing her in with a full face of it. Her light red hair, usually in a messy bun, has been straightened and now hangs down to the middle of her back.

“I wanted to pop up and check everything is going okay,” she smiles as I close the door.

“Well, it's good to see you. Come through to Christian's office. He’s down in the gym, so we can talk there.” I lead her through the house and to the office and signal for her to take a seat on the sofa.

Pulling my phone out of my pocket, I send a quick message to my brothers.

Sean: We are in the office. I will see how much I can get out of her, so listen at the door.

I put my phone on the desk with the screen down in case they message back. I quickly busy myself making two glasses of water whilst trying to remain calm. The last thing I need is for her to get her back up, thanks to the alcohol.

“You been enjoying your downtime?” I ask, placing a glass in her hand.

“Meh, it's been boring, to be honest. I’ve missed everyone, so I thought I would pop up.” She looks down at the glass; it's almost as if she's nervous. “I know it's against protocol and shouldn’t be here. But I've been worried. I guess I can’t stop worrying about you, even when I know you are locked in.” Looking up at me through her lashes, she smiles sadly. “How is Jasmine doing?”

Hearing Jasmine's name on her lips makes me want to reach out and grab her by the throat. I don’t know what the guys have learnt, but for Terry to sound so worried when I said she’d arrived, it must be something bad.

“She’s distraught and is struggling with everything. She doesn’t know what to do with herself,” I lie. When I left her and Mrs Brown in the sitting room, Jasmine was laughing as the two of them played with the dog.

"Can I ask you something?"

Looking back to Mykela, I force myself to relax back into my seat.

"You know you can," I smile.

"I don't know how to word this without it sounding shitty, but bear with me," she starts, fidgeting nervously. "But is this really what you all want?" I open my mouth to argue, but she puts her hand up to stop me. "Hang on, let me finish." I nod my head but continue to watch her closely.

"I've known all of you for what? Four years?" I nod as she continues. "In that time, your biggest issues were due to your relationship with her. People are using her to get to you or your wedding. I just worry that none of you are going to end up happy. You deserve better, Sean." I don't miss the way she says my name at the end, singling me out from the others.

"I hope you're not blaming Jasmine," I warn. Mykela shakes her head.

"No, I like Jasmine; she's a sweetheart; she's just … misled. I don't think she truly knows what she wants, which is understandable considering the abuse she suffered. But I worry the five of you will end up miserable."

"How do you know about her past?" I ask, frowning.

"I helped Christian track down the ones who abused her. He killed them all." Before I can say anymore, she continues. "Let's face it, she has a stronger relationship with Christian. What if they decide one day to keep things just between them? What happens to you?"

"If Jasmine ever picks one of us over the others, we will step back and let them be together without interference. It's something we have talked about as a family." I never thought I would have to defend our relationship like this, especially not with our staff.

"Look, I know I'm being out of line, but I care about you, Sean. You are different from your brothers, and I can't stand by and let them bully you into being in something that just doesn't suit you." She moves closer on the sofa, making me want to put more distance between us, but if I get up, she may become insulted.

"My brothers have never forced me to do anything I don't want to." I have to stop myself from saying more, knowing I need her to speak to me openly.

Mykela sighs as she places a hand on my leg; for a second, I think it's a reassuring touch, but then I look into her eyes and realise what she's really up to.

"Sean, you can't be happy, I mean truly happy. You deserve someone who treats you as well as you treat Jasmine. Someone who would never leave your side, not some girl who would never choose you, and is happy going from one of you to the other, not giving a shit if you may need her or not."

This time, there is no hiding the shock on my face as I jump to my feet.

"So what do you suggest I do, Mykela? Leave? Who am I leaving? Jasmine? My brothers? Or both?"

"Personally, I think the best thing that could happen is for you to get away from this place, from their *business,* because you are too good to be caught up in all the shit they deal in. They bring you down, and you deserve better. You aren't a thug like them. You hate violence and need to do all you can to distance yourself from them." She moves closer until she's right up in my face, and I can't believe I didn't see it sooner.

"Think about it, Sean. Think about how much easier life would be if Jasmine stayed with your brothers and you were free to love who you want to love." I need to keep this going because if I play my cards right, I will get a full confession from her. "Tell me you've never considered it, and I'll back off."

I haven't, not for one moment, but I stay silent in the hope she will think that I have. I purposely look away from her, but she cups my face between her hands and encourages me to look at her.

"I can see you have, and I have seen it for a while. Don't think I haven't seen your shoulders slump when you hear Jaz is with one of the others. Or how you force that smile every time you walk into the room and she sits on one of the others' laps. I hate seeing you so miserable. You deserve so much more than she's willing to give you."

Please God, if you ever listen to anything from me, please make sure Jasmine is not outside this door listening.

"You're right; I hate seeing her with my brothers," I reply quietly. "I have thought about leaving a few times, and even more so with the wedding being off, I feel like she should leave with the others, and I could just go off on my own."

"Then do it. We could leave tonight."

"We?" I ask, playing dumb, knowing precisely what she hopes will happen.

"Of course; you can't go anywhere without me." Mykela grins as she rests her hands on my chest. "I know you need time to get over Jasmine, and I understand completely. But maybe one day you will realise that I've always been here since the moment we met."

"You have?" I'm not acting, as I had no idea.

"Of course. Why do you think I worked so hard to become your personal guard?"

"I had no idea." Again, I realise just how blind I've been.

"It's okay, you do now, and maybe one day you will return my feelings." She continues to smile at me, and I feel sick to my stomach. Even though I know all this is a lie, it feels wrong. "What do you say? Shall we run tonight?" She looks so hopeful, but I need to get more out of her.

"We can't," I sigh, turning away. "I can't leave with everything going on. I need to know they are all at least safe. They are still my family."

"They will be fine," Mykela says behind me, touching my shoulder.

"No, they won't. Someone is after each of us, and I can't leave them in danger."

"No one is after any of you. You sorted it when you sorted Mitchell." I turn to argue, but Mykela smiles and nods. "Trust me."

"But the dress, the flowers, and the security system, so many things have happened, and I can't leave until we know the threat has gone."

"Babe, it will be fine," she smiles, cupping my face again, as I try desperately not to recoil from her touch. "I think you will find they weren't trying to hurt anyone, just get the wedding postponed, giving them time to scare Jasmine away."

I pretend to think about it for a second before making my eyes bulge from my head.

"Did you…?"

"I did what was needed to buy us more time," she smiles. "I knew if the wedding was cancelled, and Jasmine disappeared, I could get you to realise what's right in front of you."

The woman is a fucking psychopath.

"It can't have all been you?"

"It was," she smiles smugly. "It wasn't easy, but with a little help from my brother, I taught myself how to hack the system, which helped me get into the dress shop, florist and the hotel. Slipping the night staff some sleeping pills helped with the hotel. He thought I was just a friendly guest and still has no idea he fell asleep, which gave me time to cause the damage needed to the ceremony room."

"But how did you get into Maximus's phone to message me the night of the lockdown?" It's something we haven't been able to work out.

"That was easy; he always leaves his phone in his car. All I had to do was unlock it with the spare key I borrowed from the office, send the message and then delete it from his phone but not yours." Of course she would know everything we do; she has watched us for years.

"But why the dresses? That was aimed purely at Jasmine, even though you claim to like her."

"I do like her, which is why I don't want her to marry your brothers." She takes a step forward and cups my cheek. "Babe, your brothers are evil. They kill without a second thought of who they leave behind. I will never understand how sweet and caring you are when you're related to them and Tommy."

"My brothers do what they need for us to survive," I argue instinctively. "Everything they do is for our family."

"Normal people don't live like this, babe. They don't kill and steal. They don't hunt people down because of their past. Christian could have just reported them to the police; they didn't need to die."

I open my mouth to tell her they did deserve it, and I hope he made their deaths painful. But I need to keep her on my side.

"The stag do?" I ask quietly. "I could have been killed." Mykela's eyes darken as she shakes her head. "That was Mitchell and his men getting out of control. He was the only main threat. After that night, you were safe. I made sure of it."

"So if I leave, are my brothers and Jasmine free? No one will turn up to hurt them if they lower security?" Mykela shakes her head and smiles.

"So, we can leave and never come back if you want. You can stay with me until you get on your feet. Or we could move into a temporary home until we find somewhere else? Whatever you need, I'm here for you."

I nod, causing her to squeal and throw her arms around my neck.

"What do you want to do?" she asks, releasing me.

"You head off, and I will pack a bag. We can meet up somewhere, or give me your address, and I will come round."

Mykela nods excitedly before heading to the desk and writing down her address. When she hands it to me, I can't miss the huge smile on her face. How long has she had these feelings for me?

"Before you leave, try to persuade Jasmine to run. Your brothers will bring her down like they have done to you, and I do like her. You are just too good for her."

"Jasmine would never leave my brothers. Nor will they ever let her." Neither will I, and I need to make sure she knows that if she has heard any of this.

Mykela watches me for a moment before leaning in and kissing my cheek. I jump back on instinct, not wanting her to touch me. I'm disgusted with her and all she has done. Just as I think she has seen how repelled by her I am, she smiles and cups my face again.

"You take all the time you need. I have waited this long for you; I can wait a little longer until you realise how much you love me, too."

I can't bring myself to answer, so I just nod and head to the door. Stepping back, I run my fingers through my hair.

"You go out first. I've got to at least leave them a note, so they don't try to find me."

"Good thinking. Message me when you are on your way. I let her open the door and stand to the side. I'm so glad that I did, as the first thing Mykela saw was a furious Jasmine as her arm swung out and punched Mykela in the temple, knocking her clean out.

Chapter Fifty-One

SEAN

Walking away from the basement, I hold my head high even as I hear Mykela screaming my name. Calvin and a couple of his female guards have come to collect her and her brother's body. They are going to take her to do what needs to be done. We have no choice; she needs to die.

Mykela knows every single one of our secrets, locations and protocols. We can't trust her to keep her mouth shut, especially as she's becoming crazier by the hour. She needs to go, but none of us could do it. Killing her brother was one thing, but a woman is a low even Christian will avoid at all costs.

McIntire has already killed her brother, he took great pleasure in it, and we can't help wondering what exactly Eddie did to Abigail because McIntire's reaction to the piece of shit was extreme, considering they weren't trying to get to him personally.

McIntire and Christian are upstairs with Jasmine to find out what she wants them to tell Abigail about the whole mess.

Fuck, this is not how this week was meant to go at all, and I feel solely to blame.

Exiting the tunnel, I walk through the sparring room and, for a moment, consider forgetting everything and spending an hour in here to release some of the pent-up anger. But I know I can't hide from her any longer. I need to face Jaz and check that she's okay.

"Sean, wait a minute."

I look over my shoulder just in time to see Jason exit the secret entrance to the tunnel. He looks as tired as I feel.

"You okay?" he asks, shoving his hands in his pockets as he approaches.

"No, not really," I answer, desperate to get the hell away from all of this and clear my head.

"You didn't do anything wrong. Even Terry had no idea how obsessed she had become with you. There was no way you would have foreseen the extent she was willing to go."

I nod, not trusting myself to speak, as I hold the door open for him, which leads to the stairs into the house.

"How much did she hear?"

Jason looks at me, and I know I won't like the answer.

"All of it. But she knows you were just saying it to get information from Mykela."

I nod, wishing I could believe him, but I can't. I know it will be playing on Jasmine's mind as I used every insecurity she has ever voiced.

"Even pretending made me feel like shit," I admit as we walk into the hallway. "I honestly had no idea. If I have done anything to lead her on, I'd-"

"You'd what?" Jason asks, coming to a stop. "Sean, you wear your love for Jazzy on your sleeve. Anyone who has known you in the last four years knows you have waited for her. You didn't even try to fuck her out of your system like the rest of us. You knew she was yours from that moment in the hotel, and no one can say otherwise." I know he's right, but it doesn't help. Just the thought of Jasmine questioning my love for her has me wanting to fall to my knees and beg her until she knows how much I love her.

"Come on, she will be wondering where we are." Jason pats me on the shoulder before we head to the sitting room, knowing that's where the others will be.

Jason walks in ahead of me; I swear the pressure in my chest is enough to floor me. Slowly entering the room, I eventually force myself to look at her, only to find her already on her feet and rushing towards me. Jasmine throws herself at me, and I only just manage to keep us from falling. She wraps her arms around my neck and squeezes me to the point I laugh.

That's what this woman does for us. She always has been the light to our dark, and how Mykela ever thought I would give up my Princess is beyond me.

"I love you," I whisper into her ear. "There hasn't been anyone since we met, and there never will be. It's always been you, Princess."

"I know." Lowering her feet to the floor, I reluctantly let her go. But Jasmine has other ideas as she takes my hand and leads me to my usual spot. I sit down, and she curls up on my lap.

"Here you go, Shorty," Maximus smiles when he passes over her blanket. Thanking him quietly, I help her get comfortable before holding her close to me as she rests her head against my shoulder, looking at the others.

"Everything okay?"

Looking at Christian, I nod and let out a deep breath.

"They've gone." Jason hands me a glass of bourbon as he sits with his own.

"Good, then I will leave you in peace. Hopefully, that will be the last of the drama for a little while." McIntire announces as he stands. He turns to Jasmine, and his smile softens. "Thank you for all you have done for Abigail; I know she will understand when the time comes to tell her what happened here today."

"Be gentle with her; she's not as strong as she tries to make out. She is still very vulnerable," Jasmine says, looking him straight in the eye.

"I know, and that's why I've been trying to help." A look is shared between them before Jasmine relaxes back against me.

"Just remember, I will always protect her, even if that means from herself," Jasmine adds, staring at one of the most dangerous men in the UK. He stares right back at her before laughing.

"Jasmine, darling, I saw you knock out a woman with one punch. I have no intentions of ever being on the receiving end of that fist."

"Then don't upset or hurt my friend, and we will be fine."

I see the others tense out of the corner of my eye as I wait and mentally prepare myself to get Jasmine out of the way if he pounces, but instead, he gives her a short nod and smiles.

"Message heard, Miss Connors."

"It's O'Reilly," she announces, looking away from him. "I don't need a piece of paper to tell me what I already know." Our eyes meet, and her stare floors me. "I belong to my men as much as they belong to me." Just like that, when I thought I couldn't love her anymore, I fall even deeper in love with her.

"You are absolutely right, Mrs O'Reilly."

I can't tear my eyes away from hers as I hear McIntire take his leave. Lifting my hand, I run my knuckles down her cheek.

"Are you okay?" I ask, needing to hear it from her. A small smile appears as she nods her head.

"I really am."

"I'm glad to hear it," I whisper against her lips.

"So, what's the plan then?" Maximus announces as he climbs to his feet and heads to the minibar.

"With what, exactly?" Christian asks, sipping his drink.

"Well, the bad people have been taken care of, and we can safely leave the house again. So is Sunday still going ahead?"

I look to Jasmine, who is looking around at the others.

"What do you want to do, Princess?" I ask, holding her close.

"I want to get married," she smiles at me before turning to Christian. "Unless you can think of any reason, we can't."

"Sweetheart, I can't think of a single reason not to. But can you still get everything done in time?" he asks.

"Everything is done. All the girls and I have to do is get things sorted on Sunday morning. Like putting up the decorations once the tents are up."

The five of us all look around at each other and smile.

"Message the girls and tell them everything is going ahead." Jasmine bounces excitedly on my lap, to the point I have to protect my balls. "But …!" Christian adds, which has her stopping in her tracks.

"But what?" her face drops, and I can't help smiling. She is so adorable when she pouts with her sad eyes.

"But … I want them here in the morning for ten AM and to have everything they need to stay overnight. I will organise everything with Verity's Daddy, so don't worry about that. Just talk to her." I can tell from the grin on his face that Christian is planning something special for our girl.

"Okay, Daddy, thank you." She kisses me on the cheek before jumping off my lap, picking up her puppy and rushing around to kiss everyone else before leaving the room to call the girls.

"What are you up to?" Jason asks, smiling as we all turn our attention to Christian. He's sitting back with his left ankle resting on his right knee, sipping his drink, unable to hide the smirk on his face.

"I think she has done enough for this wedding, don't you?" We all nod in agreement as he grins. "Tomorrow, we will get the girls to show us what goes where and then ask the tent people to come early. They were only coming Sunday morning because we didn't want anyone seeing them the night before and guessing what we were up to. But now we can do things properly, which includes spoiling our girl.

"As soon as we know what's what, the girls can go and spend a day in a spa and sleep in a hotel before getting ready there for the wedding." Christian smiles as he seems to relax on the sofa. "The wedding of her dreams may have been ruined, but we can still ensure she has the best day of her life."

"I can agree with that," I smile, holding up my glass.

"I think we all can," Jason adds, lifting his own glass at the same time as the others. Taking a sip of our drinks, we plan and book a few extras to make our girl's wedding even better.

Chapter Fifty-Two

SEAN

Walking up the stairs, I rub my face, longing for a long, hot shower before bed. I listen out for Jasmine but can't hear her anywhere. She didn't come back to the sitting room after disappearing to call the girls. I expect she will still be organising everything with them.

Christian informed us that McIntire isn't planning to tell Abbi about Eddie- not the whole truth. He wants to try to make it seem like Eddie has lost interest. Jasmine doesn't want her to know that she was giving out details, which is why the original wedding was ruined. She worries Abbi will stop talking to her because she's ashamed of what she's done, even though not one of us blames her.

When the others filled me in on how he got access to Eddie's phone, I was glad to be upstairs. We have heard many horror stories about what that man is capable of, but to see it first-hand has shaken Maximus up. He's determined to stay on McIntire's good side now, so he never finds himself at the receiving end of his rage.

Glancing at all the closed bedroom doors as I pass, I

wonder which room Jasmine is in. Unfortunately, that thought causes Mykela's voice to play back in my head.

"She has a stronger relationship with Christian. What if they decide one day to keep things just between them? What happens to you?"

I can't deny that it hit a little too close to home. This is something that's not only played on my mind from time to time but Maximus's and Jason's too. Sure, we all have different relationships with her, and she will seek each of us out depending on what she needs, but that doesn't stop the worry that one day, this will all be too much, and she will pick him. But we try not to dwell on it, as that would cause problems in itself. What do they call it? A self-fulfilling prophecy? When you believe something so much, you incidentally make it come true. Yeah, no thanks, I'm not losing my girl because of my own insecurities.

Opening the bedroom door, I walk inside and stop in my tracks. There, curled up on the bed, fast asleep, wearing one of my T-shirts, is Jasmine. Her Kindle is beside her, as she's fallen asleep whilst reading. It's not the first time any of us have found her like this. She is forever reading on the bed and falling asleep, still on top of the covers. What shocked me was that she was here. After everything this morning with Christian, I was sure she would be sleeping in his room.

Walking over to her side of the bed, I grab a blanket I keep on the chair for times like this. I place it over her gently. Unable to resist the urge, I kiss her forehead softly while picking up her Kindle and placing it on the bedside table next to her.

She stirs ever so slightly and snuggles under the blanket with a little sigh before settling again. I watch her sleep for a moment, as she's looking so peaceful and beautiful. I want nothing more than to curl up and hold her all night, but I need to shower first. I can still feel the phantom of Mykela's touch, and I want to wash her away before I hold the love of my life. Jason is right; from the moment I saw Jasmine in the hotel lobby standing with Carol and Tommy on their wedding day, I knew she was mine. There wasn't anything I wasn't willing to do to have her in my life forever.

Turning around, I walk to the bathroom, quietly closing the door behind me. Jasmine can sleep like the dead, but that doesn't stop me from ensuring I don't accidentally wake her. She probably hasn't had a sound sleep in weeks. Only last night, the five of us, all a little tipsy, were up until two in the morning, making love. The four of us made her scream so many times she lost her voice. It's my second favourite way to spend my time. The first, of course, is when I get her to myself, and the only name she screams is mine.

As I wait for the shower to heat up, I strip from my clothes and throw them in a pile to be thrown out or burned. I don't want anything to remind me of today, and I know I would think of Mykela every time I see that polo shirt if I were to keep it. I want to forget the way she looked at me with hope in her eyes when I lied to her. Or the way she screamed my name when she realised I wasn't going to run away with her.

When she woke up chained beside her brother, she begged me to save her, telling me over and over again that we were meant to be together. Jasmine had stood behind me, not saying a word. I hadn't been able to look at her for fear she believed what she had heard. Luckily, she only stayed long enough to realise Mykela was unstable before turning around and walking out of the basement without so much as a word to me. I was thankful in a strange way as I couldn't get my head around Mykela and her betrayal.

Having Jasmine close to the woman screaming that she loved me and would do anything to prove to me we belonged together was challenging, to say the least.

Pushing myself away from the sink, I walk into the shower and stand under the hot water. Tipping my head back so the spray hits my face, I let a few tears run free. I hate it when it's someone close to us who does the unthinkable and betrays our trust. It's so much harder to deal with afterward. I'm not saying any time is easy; every death has left its mark on us. But I've had Mykela by my side for four years. Sure, she was just a member of the team for the first four years, but this last six months, when she has been my guard, we have grown close. She had become a friend.

Taking a deep breath, I force back my grief. I have no right to feel anything; Mykela is dead because of me. In what world should I feel any sort of loss for her when I didn't prevent her death?

"She knows too much, Sean; you know this needs to be dealt with. She has shown she is willing to do anything to have you to herself; what if she uses her knowledge of our home and lives to seek revenge? She could bring anyone to our door, and we wouldn't be able to protect ourselves or, more importantly, Jasmine." I know Christian was right; if anything happened to Jasmine or my brothers because of me protecting someone, I would never forgive myself. No, I need to do what we always do in these situations and bury it.

Taking a deep breath, I force myself to wash my hair and body, reminding myself that Jasmine is in our bed, waiting for me to join her. Even though I have no doubt she will stay asleep all night, being able to hold her is more than I expected tonight.

Turning off the shower, I grab a towel and give myself a quick rub down before tying it around my waist and grabbing a second to use on my hair. As I throw that one into the washing basket, I leave the bathroom to find Jasmine sitting up in bed.

"Hey, sorry, did I wake you, Princess?" I ask softly. Jasmine shakes her head and gives me a small smile.

"No, I wanted to stay awake to check on you." Climbing off the bed, she walks to where I'm looking for clean boxers. "Do you want to talk about it?"

"I'm okay." It's a lie; I'm sure she sees straight through it. But I wrap an arm around her waist, closing the distance between us. "I'm so sorry you had to hear all of that," I whisper, looking deep into her blue eyes. "I had no idea how she felt, I swear, Princess. If I had any inkling, I would have-" She stops me by putting a finger over my lips.

"I know, Daddy," she whispers, reaching up to brush some damp hair from my forehead. "I trust you completely and know you would never have purposely led her on. You're not the type of person who purposely hurts someone that way. Which is probably why it was so easy for her to fall in love with you." A smile spreads across her face as her eyes sparkle in the dim light. "It's one of the reasons I fell for you the hardest to start with."

My eyes widen as I stare, amazed.

"I always assumed it was Jason," I chuckle as Jasmine shakes her head.

"I fell for all of you that night, but there was something about the way you smiled at me that made me feel seen for the first time. Like somehow you saw the real me behind the mask I wore quicker than the others." Jasmine looks at her hand, which is now resting on my bare chest, and her smile slips. "I don't care about Christian more than you, more than any of you."

"I know, Princess, we don't-"

"I wasn't finished," she interrupts, lifting one brow. I can tell she's trying to say something. So I stop and nod for her to continue. "I have always told you all I don't have a favourite, and I really don't. But I know I have been spending a lot of time with Christian recently, and I feel like I should explain."

"Shall we get comfortable first?" I suggest, desperate to hold her in my arms.

Jasmine nods, so I tell her to get into bed. As she does, I quickly run the towel over myself again before climbing beside her. Jasmine curls up against me as I place an arm around her, as she rests her head on my chest.

"You know you don't have to explain anything to me, Princess." Running a hand over her head, I wait to see if she will continue or change the subject. Either is fine with me as long as she is here, in our bed.

"I want to talk to you about this. I don't think I will rest properly until I do."

"Then talk to me. I will always listen to you." Kissing the top of her head to encourage her, I listen to her taking a deep breath before continuing.

"As I said, I never have and never will have favourites. But I'm not stupid, and I know you have all noticed I've been spending a lot of time with Christian when he's home. Not just the last few months while everything has been going on, but since you all rescued me. It wasn't that I felt safer with him or that I loved him more. It was because I knew he needed me just as much as I needed you all at that time."

I still underneath her as she starts tracing the tattoos on my chest.

"I haven't said anything because it's not been my place, and he asked me not to." She lifts her head and looks at me.

"Believe it or not, I won't share things any of you tell me in private. First of all, I'm not like that, and secondly, we all have secrets and deserve to keep them from those we don't want to share them with."

I had never considered that she must carry so much weight on her shoulders just by listening to each of us. Maximus doesn't think twice about having a rant about Christian in front of her, and it never crossed my mind that she would go running back to Christian and repeat it all. She is right; she isn't the type to share things with others who wouldn't want her to. I want to tell her how amazing she is, but she continues before I have a chance.

"You heard about how he was this morning and what I said after he had left. I wish I could say it's the first time he's woken up shaking and crying, but it's not. He has never been that bad before, but he's still suffered. He has been struggling to sleep, and when he does, he is plagued with nightmares. I've tried to get him to talk to me or anyone, but he wouldn't. So, instead, I've been making a point of sleeping with him so I can hold him when the nightmares start, which usually helps him settle enough so he doesn't wake up. But some nights, I don't hear him. I wake up to him sitting on the edge of the bed with his head in his hands or standing in the shower leaning against the wall with his head down; the water's so hot I'm scared it will scald him.

"I'm only telling you this as I know you have all been worried I would pick him over you or that our marriage will mean more because it's legal, but you couldn't be more wrong." Jasmine sits up in front of me, tucking her legs to her right.

"Don't try to deny it; I have heard the little comments, and let's face it, Daddy Max doesn't have the ability to filter his thoughts before they come out of his big mouth." I can't help the laugh that bursts from my chest as she has hit the nail on the head. Judging from the smile on her face, she's proud of that one. But her smile slips slightly as she looks towards the door. "Maybe don't repeat that last bit to him, though. My butt needs a break after swearing four times last night." It takes everything in me not to laugh out loud again, so instead, I take her hand and press a kiss to her knuckles.

"Your secret is safe with me," I throw in a wink for good measure.

"Thank you, Daddy. My butt and I appreciate it."

She lays back beside me, using my chest as a pillow, and goes back to tracing my tattoo.

"Just to confirm, in my eyes, there is no difference between my marriage to you or the others. I love you all, and that will never change. It's just that sometimes one of you needs me more than the others." Jasmine turns slightly so she's more on her stomach, making it easier to look me in the eye.

"Is that why you are here tonight?" I ask, tucking some hair behind her ear as she nods.

"You've had a rough day, and I knew you would be beating yourself up about it all. I wanted to ensure you knew I didn't think differently about you or us. I understand why you said what you did, and I know you love me just as much as I love you, which is a lot." Her playful smile is back, and I can't help flipping us over, startling a scream from her before she bursts out laughing.

Nudging her legs with mine, she opens for me eagerly as I use my arms to cage her head, making it easier to stare into her eyes.

"Thank you, Princess. I will never understand what we

did to deserve you, but I'm grateful you're ours." Softly and slowly, I kiss her lips, savouring the feel of them against mine. "I never thought about how much you help us all, not just by being our light but our loving, supportive and selfless fiancée. Who I cannot wait to make our wife." As I brush my lips against hers, she wraps her arms around my neck and pulls me in closer. So I get to show her a whole other way, how much she means to me.

Chapter Fifty-Three

JASMINE

I love it when I wake up before the guys. There is no better way to start the day than lying in their arms as they sleep soundly underneath me. After all the drama the last few days, I am more than happy to lie here and listen to Sean's heart beating in my ear as I use his chest as a pillow.

Don't get me wrong, if he woke up now and flipped us over before fucking me into next week, I would be more than happy with that outcome as well. That's my second favourite way to start a day.

Slowly, I lift my head and look at the clock on the bedside table. It's just after eight, and I need to get up, shower and get everything prepared before the girls' arrival.

Tomorrow, I'm marrying my four men, and I am willing to pray to every single God, Goddess, Demon and so on so that everything will finally be okay. Because we fucking deserve this, we deal with so much shit that not a single one of us asked for, and I've just about had enough of it, in all honesty.

Careful not to wake Sean, I slide out of his arms and

head for the bathroom to start getting ready. Once inside, I turn the shower on to warm up before grabbing my hairbrush and giving my hair a quick once-over. It's one big giant mess after Sean gave me multiple orgasms last night as we made love. Usually, Sean is dominating and loves to take complete control when in the bedroom, but last night, he was gentle and loving, which was what we needed after all that happened yesterday.

Stepping into the shower, I stand under the water and lift my face, letting the water wash over it, and try to wash away the emotions left from yesterday.

Whenever I think about how Mykela spoke about me and the guys, especially Christian, anger consumes me like no other. There are a few people I can honestly say I hate, and all for good reason, but as much as I try to hate her, I can't. I understand why she fell for Sean; he is funny, caring, thoughtful and absolutely gorgeous. There is nothing he wouldn't do for those he loves; when he looks at you in a certain way, he makes you feel like you can do or achieve anything you put your mind to. He makes you feel alive with just one smile. I can't blame her for falling for him; he's too perfect not to love. But I can hate her for trying to take him away from me.

People assume that because I have four men, I would be okay if one or two left me, but that's far from the truth. The thought of losing any of them is enough to bring me to my knees. If Sean had left with Mykela, I don't think I could have carried on like others expect me to. I have separate relationships with all the guys, and they all love me in different ways. To lose one would change everything and break me in a million ways.

Grabbing my shampoo from the shelf, I pour some onto my hand and start working it into my scalp. My chest tightens as I think of how much Sean will be hurting. He didn't just see Mykela as a member of his staff; she was a friend. Things are going to be different around here with her gone. It will have a rolling effect on Terry's team for a long time. It will also take a long time for the guys and me to truly trust anyone. If someone who was part of the team for four years can turn against us, how do we know the others won't as well?

The thought of Sean having to pick another guard has me worried. Would it be wrong of me to insist he doesn't have another female guard? I have never been the type to tell any of the guys what to do or how to work; it's not who I am. But I think I might have to put my foot down this time.

Turning my back to the water so it rinses the shampoo from my hair, I open my eyes to find Sean leaning against the door frame, his arms and legs crossed. The look in his eyes tells me he's been watching for a while. The fact his cock is standing to attention gives it away too.

"Take a picture, Daddy; it will last longer." Grinning, I turn back around, showing him my back. I smile to myself as I sense him getting closer, knowing he will join me. Even though I'm expecting it, I still jump a little, giggling when his arms wrap around me from behind.

"I don't need to take a picture; I can see you naked whenever I want," he whispers against my neck as he kisses his way across my shoulder. "Because tomorrow, you will become my wife, and no one will ever be able to stop me from having you whenever I want." Sean turns me in his arms, so our fronts are pressed together, the hot water still flowing over us.

"What were you thinking about when I came in?" he whispers, cupping my cheek as he tightens his arm around my waist, making sure there is no space between us.

"Nothing," I lie, not wanting to bring up the elephant in the room. Sean turns me around so he is standing at my back and reaches for the bottle of shampoo.

"You're lying to me, Princess. Tell me the truth; I'm a big boy and can take whatever it is." I know he can, but that doesn't make me want to protect him any less.

Sean starts massaging the shampoo into my hair, and I find myself closing my eyes and relaxing into his touch.

"I was thinking about yesterday," I admit. "I know you are hurting, and I wish there were something I could do." I should leave it at that; I know I should, but I can't help adding. "I was also wondering if I would be a typical nagging girlfriend if I insisted you never have a female personal guard again."

Sean bursts out laughing, as I had hoped he would. Like me, the guys get stuck in their own heads sometimes, and that's not what I want for my man right now.

"First of all, Princess, you are not my girlfriend. Tomorrow, you will be my wife, which means you will get extra nagging privileges." I can't hold in the excited squeak that leaves me as I bounce on the balls of my feet slightly. Sean laughs behind me before telling me to turn around so he can rinse out the shampoo.

"Secondly," he starts, washing all the shampoo. "I had already decided I wouldn't have another female on my team." I listen as Sean squirts something and feel him running his fingers through my long hair again as the scent of my conditioner fills the space around us. "I'm sure people will call me sexist for it, but the fact is, you were hurt by Mykela's actions and her feelings towards me. That is not something I will tolerate, and I know Christian will say the same thing at the team meeting today." He braids my hair to allow the conditioner to sit briefly before picking up the shower gel and rubbing it onto his palms.

"I don't even know if I will have a guard again."

"Why?" I ask as he washes my shoulders and back, massaging them as he goes. "Is that safe?"

Sean smiles as he nods.

"Perfectly safe. I don't deal with the illegal shit like Christian and Jason. I only had a guard in the first place, as Christian sometimes worries about me a little too much." He stops washing me for a moment as he looks into my eyes.

"No one will ever take me from you. You know that, right? No one could ever make me feel the way you do."

"No one else can have you. They will have to go through me first," I smile.

"After seeing you punch Mykela yesterday, I don't think they will be brave enough to try." Leaning forward, he presses a kiss on my lips, and I wrap my arms around his neck.

"I'm very protective of those I love."

"And we are very grateful for your love, Princess," Sean whispers against my lips before stepping back a little.

"Now, be a good girl and let me finish taking care of you." He lowers himself to his knees, maintaining eye contact the whole time.

Tipping my head back, I wash the conditioner from my hair as Sean washes my belly and hips. Lifting my foot, he places it on one of his knees and slowly begins to massage his way up, starting from my toes and all the way up my thigh. Keeping my head back, I moan as his fingers slightly brush against the throbbing apex of my thighs before moving down the other leg.

"Daddy." I don't mean to moan his name, but my body is becoming more and more alive with his teasing touch.

"I'm only trying to look after all your needs, Princess." The sound of his teasing tone makes my body react to everything. The water flowing over me leaves goosebumps all over, even though it's still hot.

"I still have one place to clean," I hear before he grabs my hips and buries his face between my legs.

"Oh my god," I cry out as his tongue swipes over my clit.

"I need better access," Sean grins up at me as he takes the foot that's on his knee and places it on his shoulder before his tongue laps at my clit again. I can't hold back; the need to cum throws caution to the wind as I start rubbing against his face. The thought that I might slip lasts about one second before it is ignored, and I go back to chasing my orgasm through his mouth.

Sean slowly inserts one, then two fingers inside of me, moving them in and out, pushing me closer and closer to the edge. Threading my fingers into his hair, I lose control and thrust against his face as he continues to finger fuck me and lick my pussy just the way I like it.

"Daddy, I'm … Oh my god!" My orgasm crashes into me like a tsunami. I scream as my body comes alive, but Sean's not finished with me yet.

Before my orgasm has even shown signs of ending, Sean jumps to his feet, grabbing my ass as he lifts me so I can wrap my legs around his waist. His cock is buried in me before I realise what he's doing. I cry out as he fills me, stretching me with the perfect mixture of pleasure and pain.

"Daddy!" I cry out as he slams my back against the cold tiles and starts fucking me hard and fast.

"You are mine, Princess," I hear him declare through gritted teeth. "No one is ever separating us. Do you hear me?" I try to speak, but I'm unable to do more than cry out with pleasure. "Say it," he growls. "Who do you belong to?"

"You, Daddy! Always you!" I cry as he pushes me to my limits, and I cry through another orgasm.

"Fuck!" Sean curses before both of us lose the ability to form words as he brutally fucks me against the tiled wall. We both cry out in grunts and moans as we forget about everyone and everything else because there is no one, just the two of us, and nothing else matters.

An hour later, the two of us, now fully dressed, walk through the house hand in hand, heading to the sitting room to find the others.

"Will I be the last one to fuck you as Jasmine Connors?" Sean asks as he turns me and pulls me against his front, holding me tight.

"It depends on who will be sleeping in my bed tonight," I answer, smirking.

"No one, as seeing the bride before the wedding is bad luck." Sean winks before leading me into the sitting room.

"We will all be under one roof; I'm not sure we will be able to stick to the no seeing each other rule," I laugh, stopping when I see who's in front of me.

Sitting on the sofas are the three girls, Jason and Maximus. Christian is standing beside Terry, who is grinning at me.

Seeing Abigail causes my heart to stop. How am I meant to keep everything from her? She is one of my best friends, and I want to be honest with her, but I also worry that she isn't strong enough to handle the truth right now.

"You've got this, Princess," Sean whispers in my ear as he turns me in his arms and holds me, no doubt to hide the fact I've frozen. "She needs you to pretend. It's for her own good." Stepping back, he hooks a finger under my chin, tipping my head up. "Now stop panicking. We are getting married tomorrow." He winks for encouragement, but I know he's helping me hide my discomfort. God, I love this man. I smile at him before turning my attention back to the girls.

"It's not ten yet!" I exclaim. "Why are you here already?"

"Ask your Daddy. He insisted we were here at the crack of dawn instead of sleeping in our cosy beds," Danielle sighs, rolling her eyes. Verity elbows her in the side and tells her to stop whining through gritted teeth before smiling at me.

Sean steps back, giving me over to Christian, who takes my hand and pulls me further into the room.

"After everything you have been through the last few weeks, we decided to ensure you had time to prepare and enjoy your last twenty-four hours before becoming our wife." He lifts my hand to kiss my knuckles. "So, I rang the hotel and asked if the bridal suite was still available. It is, so you are going to spend today in the hotel spa getting as many treatments as you want. Then, the six of you will have a leisurely dinner in your room this evening. As you all get your nails done, so you will be relaxed and refreshed for tomorrow."

"Six?" I ask.

"Chelsea and Luna will be joining you for dinner and

then staying in the hotel as was originally planned," Jason answers from his seat.

"But there's still so much to do; we have to put everything up in the morning when the tent people arrive."

"It's all been taken care of, Jazzy." Jason stands and walks over to stand next to Christian. "You have done so much for our special day; let us take over now."

"Yeah, now the hard work is done!"

"Danielle!" Verity snaps, slapping her shoulder. Abbi and I share a look. We try not to laugh as the guys all watch with raised eyebrows.

"But are you all sure it's not going to be too much, and you don't even know-"

"Jasmine, dear, I will be here to oversee everything." Mrs Brown walks into the room holding a travel mug in one hand and a croissant in the other. "I know what goes where and what the others don't need to worry about." She gives me a cheeky wink, and I know exactly what she's referring to.

"See, everything will be perfect, we promise." Sean steps behind me, wrapping his arms around my waist from behind as the others stand in front of me.

"Go and relax, have some fun with the girls and don't worry about anything here." Maximus points out, standing next to Christian.

"You have been our pillar of strength the last few months, especially the last week. This is our way of showing you that we appreciate everything you have done. Not just recently, but ever since we met you," Jason smiles. Looking at the four of them, my eyes start to burn.

"You've done more for me," I point out, but Sean steps around and shakes his head.

"Princess, you made me realise last night that there are four of us to look after you, but you look after all four of us, and we know that's no easy task."

"It's really not," I giggle, crying a few happy tears.

"So, take the girls and have a relaxing day and night, and we will see you tomorrow at the altar," Christian smiles, stepping forward. "Danielle is more than happy to drag you out, kicking and screaming, if she has to," he adds, glancing over at her. She gives me a little finger wave.

"Okay, let me go and pack," I announce excitedly, but as I turn to leave, Jason grabs my hand and pulls me back.

"It's all done. Your suitcase is in the car with everything the girls said you need. You don't need much as a makeup artist and hairdresser will arrive at the hotel in the morning as previously arranged."

"Really?" I ask, looking around at the four of them before me. All are smiling as they nod.

"Really. Now go on; Layton is waiting in the car. Verity has full control for the next twenty-eight hours until the wedding. What she says goes." Maximus says, looking to Verity and then back to me, seeming a little scared. "She's gone into scary mode, Shorty, so good luck."

Jumping forward, I throw my arms around him tightly.

"Will you save me if she gets too bossy?" I whisper in his ear before letting go.

"You know I will always save you," he winks before stepping back so I can hug the others before leaving.

"Have a lovely time, relax and get pampered. There is nothing left to worry about." Jason hugs me before kissing my lips.

"Look after them for me?" I whisper into his ear as I hold him tight once more before letting go.

"Always," he smiles, and I feel a little better, leaving them all after everything in the last few weeks.

Sean pulls me into his arms as I hold him tight.

"See, I was the last to fuck you before you became an official O'Reilly," he smirks as the others sigh dramatically.

"Trust me, the whole house knows it," Maximus sighs. "You two were anything but quiet."

"Hey, at least it was in our room, unlike some!" Sean looks at Christian as I bury my face into his chest.

"Wasn't my fault she ran. The stairs just happened to be where I caught her," he shrugs, grabbing my hand and pulling me from Sean so he can kiss me passionately whilst tipping me back.

When he looks into my eyes, there's a sparkle in them that I haven't seen for a while. I hope this means he is finally relaxing enough to start looking out for himself, not just us.

"You look happier," I whisper without meaning to. Christian's smile drops for a moment as his eyes widen, but just as I'm about to apologise, he places me back upright and takes my face in his hands.

"How could I not be? We are all okay for now, and tomorrow, I get to marry the love of my life with my brothers standing beside me. What more could I want?"

"Sex," Maximus offers with a shrug.

"A blow job," Sean adds

"Jazzy going a whole day without causing trouble," Jason suggests.

"Jaz going a full *hour* without getting into trouble." Terry pipes in.

"I'm not that bad!" I protest as the girls laugh from their seats. Sticking my bottom lip out, I turn to Christian. "Tell them, Daddy." I flutter my eyelashes at him. Christian tips me back again and kisses me until I'm breathless.

"You are perfect just the way you are, brat and all." He straightens us up before releasing his hold on my waist. "Now go, some of us have a wedding to organise." He slaps my ass playfully as the girls jump up and start dragging me out of the sitting room.

"Wait, the puppy!" I call.

"It's okay, Shorty, I've got him, now go." Maximus points as I turn to Mrs Brown, who is following behind.

"I need to tell you something," I whisper, hoping the guys won't hear.

"Why do you think I'm following you?" she winks.

As soon as we are by the front door, the girls come to a stop, knowing what I have to say to Mrs Brown is important.

"I have a delivery coming today. It's important the guys don't see it. But you will have to do something with it." Leaning forward, I whisper everything into her ear in case anyone is listening in. When Mrs Brown steps back, she has tears in her eyes.

"You are so kind and have the biggest heart," she whispers. "I promise it will all be done." She passes me the coffee and croissant before cupping my cheek. "I love those boys as if they were my own, and I have come to love you as the daughter I never had. I know Helena would have loved you and the care you take of her boys." She kisses my cheek and wipes a tear away with her apron. "Now go, have a lovely time, and I will have everything ready for the morning."

"Love you, Mrs Brown." I've never said it to her before, but I love her more than I ever loved my mum. I realise I have for a long time.

"I love you, too, Jasmine dear." Without another word, she turns around and walks into the kitchen.

"Come on, we have a bottle of champagne with our name on it," Danielle announces as she opens the front door, revealing Layton standing beside the limo.

Looking back at the house as I wait to get into the back, I realise I won't be here again until tomorrow when I officially become an O'Reilly, and I can't think of a better family to marry into.

Chapter Fifty-Four

CHRISTIAN

"Is that everything, sir?"

"I have no idea, but I'm sure it will all be perfect." I smile, signing the invoice. "Thank you for organising everything on such short notice," I add, handing back the clipboard.

"You are more than welcome, sir. I hope you all have a wonderful wedding day," the young man says before turning around and leaving out of the back door.

Embry starts whining in his cage, and I feel guilty about keeping him locked up. Considering I didn't want a dog, the mutt has wormed his way into my heart.

"I know you want out, but there are too many people coming and going. Your mummy would kill me if anything happened to you." Reaching through the bars, I give him a quick scratch behind the ear before heading back towards the sitting room, where we have all agreed to meet for a drink before heading down to the wedding tent.

Walking through the house, I can't wipe the smile off my face. After months of planning and years of waiting, our woman is about to be legally bound to us forever. I may have referred to her for years as mine, but today, I will have a marriage certificate to back me up. After everything that's happened, it feels like something is going right for us. Even though a small part of me is still waiting to hear that she's run away or something has happened. Let's face it: nothing has ever been simple for us.

Walking into the sitting room, I spot Jason already there, his hands shoved in his pockets, as he looks out over the garden.

"Everything done?" he asks, not looking away from the window.

"Seems to be. If it's not done now, then it's tough." I walk up beside him and look out where I can see the Donavons talking to McIntire.

"Did you know he was invited?" Jason asks.

"Not until this morning. Verity called and said Jasmine wanted to invite him to say thanks for all his help. But I think there was an alternative motive," I admit.

"Abbi?"

I nod, looking at my brother. We all noticed she was drinking a lot when staying here and not looking after herself in many ways. McIntire saw in a message between Eddie and Mykela that it was easy to get info from Abbi; all they had to do was let her have a few drinks, and she was easy to manipulate. I know Jasmine has felt uncomfortable around her at times because of how much she drinks. But she would never say anything to her as she also knows she is grieving her father.

"Who's stupid idea was it to wear fucking bow ties?" Maximas storms in, fiddling with the material around his neck.

"Told you we should have got him a clip-on," Jason laughs.

"Fuck you, prick. I know you mean that as an insult, but next time, do it!" Maximus snaps, pointing at a smirking Jason. I smile, stepping forward and slapping his hands out of the way.

"I wear a tie nearly every single day; I wanted something different for today," I explain as I go about tying it.

"Fair enough, I guess. I still hate the things."

Stepping back, I take in Maximus's suit. We are all matching today, probably for the first time in many, many years, as we always make a point of looking different. But today, we stand as one to promise our girl the world and more.

Jasmine hasn't seen the suits. Jason decided that he wanted to surprise her. As usual, I left him to organise them, as the three of us can't understand why he enjoys clothes shopping as much as he does. He had us try on nine different suits before deciding on this one. It probably would have been more, but Maximus threatened to stab him, with Sean offering to help. We settled on a navy blue suit with a waistcoat, white shirt, light pink handkerchief in the jacket pocket, and bow tie. Light pink is part of the colour scheme that Jasmine picked. The bridesmaids are wearing pink, except Luna, who is wearing a white dress with a pink sash around her waist, and Verity, who, as maid of honour, is wearing a slightly different shade of pink. Because the dresses have all been purchased online in the last few days, we have no idea what they are like. Not that we knew much about the last ones, other than the colours. I can't help wondering if Jasmine managed to get a white dress on such short notice. I know I speak for all of us when I say she could walk down the aisle in nothing but a black bag, she would still look beautiful.

"Mrs Brown is on her way down. She wants to speak to us," Sean announces as he walks in, tugging at his shirt sleeves under the jacket.

"Who tied your tie?" Maximus asks, looking at his twin in shock.

"I did; it's not like they're hard."

Jason and I burst out laughing as Maximus glares at his twin.

"Fuck off, you're all pricks," he mutters, heading to the bar as the rest of us laugh. A knock cuts us off as we turn to see Gordon standing at the door.

"Hope I'm not interrupting."

"What are you doing here?" Jason asks, walking up to him and pulling him in for a one-arm hug.

"Jaz called me last night and told me what's been going on. She thought that now the situation has been dealt with, you would like me here."

"Too right I do; thank you so much for coming."

I hadn't realised how much Jason wanted him here until now. I should have seen through the lies and that he was just trying to keep everything as quiet as possible.

"Are you okay with this?" Maximus asks Sean while Jason and Gordon speak together for a moment.

"Yeah. Jaz called me yesterday to check before calling Gordon," he replies, smiling. It seems our girl has once again outdone herself with how thoughtful she is. She really thinks of everyone before herself, and I can only hope that any children we have will take after her because I couldn't be prouder of her.

I hear Jason saying goodbye to Gordon and look up to see him walking back over. The four of us each pick up a glass from the table where Maximus has poured us four reasonably small ones. I'm glad he hasn't gone for his usual triple measure, as the last thing we need is for one of us to be tipsy and say the wrong thing.

"Can you believe we are actually doing this?" Sean asks, looking at us all.

"No, I thought there was no way she would ever marry us," I laugh.

"Whatever, I knew Shorty would marry me, even without you three," Maximus smirks, winking at us as we shake our heads.

"I'm still waiting for Terry or Layton to call and say she has run," Jason laughs.

"The only place my girl is running, is down the aisle to marry you lot."

We all turn to see Mrs Brown walking into the room.

"You look beautiful, Mrs Brown." Sean smiles as he leans in and kisses her cheek.

"I love the hat, Mrs B. pink's your colour," Maximus smirks as she gives him the side eye.

"I'm sure it would look better on you, though; it would hide that big head."

The rest of us laugh as Maximus places a hand over his heart.

"Not cool, Mrs B. Not cool at all."

"You're right, you all look very handsome," she smiles, cupping my cheek lovingly. "But something is missing." She walks over to Jasmine's desk and opens the bottom drawer. "Right, here we go." Mrs Brown stands up with two medium gift boxes in her hand before retrieving two more.

"What are those? And why are they hidden?" Jason asks, laughing nervously.

"These, young man, are gifts from your very thoughtful and beautiful bride."

"What?" we all say in unison as we stand in front of the desk. Mrs Brown smiles, before pointing to us all.

"Line up in age order; it's easier."

We all do as she says, and she places a box in front of each of us after checking the tags.

"Everything in those boxes are gifts from Jasmine, things she has put together for each of you. I promised I would deliver them to you myself, as obviously she can't." We all look from Mrs Brown to each other before looking at the box.

"Can we open them?" I ask carefully.

"Of course you can."

The four of us open the boxes and look inside.

A pink and white buttonhole is on the top of light pink tissue paper.

"Is that…?" I ask, picking it up carefully and looking at the added details.

"It's a blackbird feather," Mrs Brown confirms. "She had them delivered as soon as she heard about your mother and her singing that song for you."

Looking at my brothers, I see we all have matching flowers and feathers. I can't stop looking at the beautiful, touching tribute to our mum.

Forcing myself to put it on the side, I lift the tissue paper to find a wooden gift box and letter.

Opening the box first, I find a beautiful pocket watch. It's engraved on the front and reads.

Daddy and his Baby girl

Glancing at the others, I can see them all holding similar watches.

"What does yours say?" I ask Jason, who smiles as he runs a finger over it.

"Daddy and his Jazzy."

"Daddy and his Shorty," Maximus adds

"Daddy and his Princess," Sean says, blinking back tears.

"Open them," Mrs Brown says softly. We open our pocket watches, and my heart stops. There, smiling up from the inside of the front, is a picture of Mum and me. It was taken a few months before she was diagnosed. Again, I look at my brothers and see them all barely holding it together.

"They were originally designed to hold pictures of Jasmine with each of you. But she decided you needed your mum here with you today. She spent hours searching the photo albums for the right ones."

Blinking back the tears, I let out a slow, deep breath, desperate to regain some control over my emotions. Once again, I look at my brothers and know they are just as touched by our sweet girl as I am.

"Okay, one last thing from Jasmine," Mrs Brown declares before pulling out a laptop and turning it around to face us. "Jason, be a dear and open my email from Jasmine, please." Jason glances at us all, and we watch as he pulls up the email and opens a video.

Jasmine comes onto the screen, and I realise it must have been filmed yesterday at the hotel.

"Hey," she giggles nervously. "Hopefully, you have your gifts now and like them; if it's too much, please don't feel like you have to wear them. I just wanted to include your mum somehow and thought this may be a great way to do it." How could she possibly think we wouldn't love her thoughtful gifts?

"I originally wrote you all letters, which are still in the boxes, but things have happened since, so this is an appendix to the letters you can read later." Even though I know it's not live, I can't help smiling with her. She's so nervous that it's adorable to watch.

"I wanted to take this chance before the day really starts because it's going to fly by, and it's something I want to say before tonight, and that's thank you.

"Thank you for supporting me, helping me grow, and showing me what it's like to be wanted.

"Thank you for choosing me and loving me in such a way I learnt to love myself too. Everything I am is because the four of you showed me that I haven't been the problem; other people have." She takes a small, deep breath before smiling at us.

"I love you so much and know that no matter what direction my life takes me, you will protect me from losing myself again. You will do what you always have and protect me from harm, even if that means protecting me from myself." Jasmine is silent for a second, and I'm grateful I need that second to catch my breath. I am so thankful for this woman and all she has brought into not only my life but my brothers' lives, too.

"I hope none of you mind, but I have asked a few more people to attend today. The first is Gordon. I know, Daddy Jason, you would have preferred it if he had come and were only being polite when you said you didn't.

"The second is Molly Young. I know how much Geralt meant to you all, and if he had been alive today, there would have been nothing that would have stopped him from attending. Molly was over the moon when I asked her, and it was nice seeing her cry happy tears for once." This woman has thought of everything, and I couldn't be more thankful for her.

"I've always promised I don't have a favourite, and I've meant it," Jasmine continues as I struggle to watch through the tears which have filled my eyes. "I love all four of you so much, and I can't wait to start the next chapter of our lives together.

"We have so many plans, and if the last few months have taught us anything, it's that we are stronger together. You are the loves of my life, my biggest supporters, the reason I laugh freely and love feisty. Nothing in this world could ever take me from you, and I can't wait to see what the future holds.

"From the bottom of my heart, I love you all, and I'll see you soon."

The screen goes blank, and no one says a word for a moment. We stare at the screen and try to process everything our girl just said.

"Well, now I wish I'd gotten her a present," Maximus sighs as we all burst out laughing.

"You have already given her everything she has ever needed: a home and a family who loves her." Mrs Brown steps from behind the desk, coming to a stop in front of me and picking up my buttonhole.

"You all have something very special in that girl. She has put so much love into everything she has created for today, and it will all be perfect, just as you all deserve." She pats me on the chest and starts walking around my brothers, fixing their buttonholes, too.

"When she mentioned honouring your mother, I was speechless. She told me she understands why your mother sang that song before she died. It wasn't just because of your nickname, Christian; it was because she knew that you would all be broken when she died, like the blackbirds in the song." Mrs Brown pats Sean on the cheek before heading towards the door.

"You have all come so far and dealt with so much since her death, but I couldn't be prouder of my four boys, and I will honour your mother myself today by being here watching the four of you marry that amazing woman who your mother would have adored."

"Thank you, Mrs Brown," I whisper, stepping forward to kiss her cheek. "For everything you have ever done for us," I add as my brothers all kiss her on the cheek as well. "I'm sorry I was such a miserable, bossy arse, until recently. You have always been more than an employee to us. You have been our family for as long as I can remember and a mother to us since Ma died. We love you." Mrs Brown blinks back the tears, whilst pushing her shoulders back. She looks around and smiles.

"It has been my pleasure," she whispers. Taking her hand, I place it in the crook of my arm and smile at her.

"Let us see you to your seat; we need to ensure you have the best one in the house."

After seeing Mrs Brown in her seat and saying a quick hello to everyone, including an emotional Molly, the four of us make our way to the front of the aisle, where the registrar, Lucinda, awaits us.

"I am so excited for this wedding; everything looks beautiful. How ever did you pull it all off after the hotel's flooding?"

"We have an amazing fiancée who doesn't back down in the face of trouble," Sean answers, grinning.

"She has lots of practice as she is usually the one *causing* the trouble," Maximus grins as we all laugh together.

"Well, however she managed it, she has done a wonderful job."

I'm about to agree when movement in my peripheral vision catches my attention. Layton walks into the tent, giving us all a wink before sitting beside a speaker and giving Lucinda a thumbs up. My heart leaps into my throat because if he's here, then so is Jasmine.

"Looks like we are ready," Lucinda says, smiling and looking from me to the brothers. "Are you all ready?" The four of us share a look, all looking a little more nervous than we did a moment ago. Taking a deep breath, my brothers follow suit and smile at each other.

"More than ready," I smile as she lifts up a thumb.

Layton grins and mouths, "Good luck", before fiddling with his phone.

"I Get to Love You" by Ruelle starts to play, making my heart swell and making me feel myself shake. Jason places his hand on my shoulder, but I can't bring myself to look at him, terrified I will miss her.

Little Luna comes into view first, beaming with a little basket. She's skipping and spinning as she throws flower petals around her. I hear her father's giggle as I grin. She is so precious, and I can't help but wonder if our daughter will one day be just like her.

As Luna reaches the front and stands beside Calvin on the other side of the aisle, she waves and smiles at the four of us, and I know we all smile back.

Looking back to the entrance, Abbi comes into view, looking beautiful in a long, light pink dress with a small bouquet in her hand. Shortly after, Danielle follows behind. The girls have handkerchiefs in their hands, and I can see they have been crying but are smiling at us like they are barely holding it together.

"If Danielle King is crying, I don't stand a chance," I hear Maximus whisper from behind.

"That's why we made sure to have extra hankies in your pocket," Jason answers. I can't help but chuckle in agreement because I feel like I'm barely holding it together as it is.

Verity comes into view as Danielle reaches halfway down the aisle. Her dress is a few shades darker than the others, but the same style. She looks beautiful, and one look at her fellas tells me I'm not the only one who thinks it. Verity grins at them before looking at us. The second our eyes meet, I realise how close to tears she is.

Suddenly, movement behind Verity draws my attention, and I hold my breath as I watch Jasmine appear on Terry's arm.

I forget how to breathe as I stare at my beautiful bride. Her hair is hanging down in loose curls, half gathered up, with a tiara holding it out of the way.

"Where did she get that dress?" Jason gasps behind me, but I can't answer because I'm speechless.

I can hear my brothers whispering behind me about how beautiful she is, but I can't tear my eyes from hers. The only other thing I see is the way Terry has his hand on hers as he walks her proudly down the aisle towards us. It feels like it takes forever to get her to us, and I don't think I take a breath. My face aches from smiling, but I can't move a single muscle.

"Breathe, Christian," I hear Jason whisper behind me,

and I manage to force air into my lungs as the others chuckle.

For a brief second, I remember the way the nightmare felt and half expect to see Connor Grant standing in front of me, but I manage to push it down as Jasmine finally reaches me. Terry turns to place a kiss on her cheek and whispers something in her ear. Jasmine drags her eyes from mine and looks at him with a smile.

"Thank you," she whispers to him. He turns to me, and I shake his hand.

"Look after her," he warns, giving me a firm look before turning his attention to my brothers. "All of you."

"Like you need to ask," I smile. Terry nods and places Jasmine's hand in mine with a nod. He shakes each of the others' hands before stepping back to sit beside Mrs Brown, who is a bubbling wreck.

I look deep into Jasmine's eyes as mine burn.

"You look … there isn't a word to describe how breath-taking you are, Sweetheart." Lifting her hand, I kiss her knuckles as her breath catches.

"You aren't looking too bad yourself," she teases before looking behind me. "All of you," she winks as we grin further.

"Shall we begin?" Lucinda asks, reminding me of her presence. I force myself to look away from Jasmine, and we both look to the front as I keep her hand in mine.

Chapter Fifty-Five

JASON

Standing beside Christian as the two of them exchange vows has me feeling all kinds of emotions, except the jealousy I was expecting. I thought I would stand here and watch the two of them become man and wife and be envious that our marriage isn't legal, but I don't. Even though this part of the ceremony is only for the two of them, Jasmine has also been stealing glances at the three of us. Showing how she really doesn't have favourites.

I look to Maximus and Sean, who have both been trying to hide the tears that fill their eyes every time they look at our girl, who is absolutely breathtaking. When she started walking towards us, I thought my chest would explode. I couldn't breathe, and one look at my brothers showed I wasn't the only one.

"This is the point I would ask you to exchange rings; however, I know you want to save that part for when it's the five of you in front of me."

Wait, that wasn't agreed with us. I frown at Jasmine and Christian as they nod and turn to us, smiling.

"It wouldn't be the same if it were only the two of us," Jasmine explains.

"Well, in that case, all that's left for me to do is announce you as husband and wife. You may finally k-" She doesn't get to finish as Christian grabs Jasmine, tips her back and kisses her so dramatically that everyone starts laughing and clapping.

Maximus whistles behind me as Sean cheers, both as happy for the two people in front of us as I am.

Glancing around at our friends, most of whom are like family to us, I see nothing but happiness and love on their faces. Christian finally lets Jasmine up for air as he stands her back up straight. The photographer we hired at the last minute rushes around, snapping pictures of them as they stare into each other's eyes lovingly.

Christian is the first to break eye contact as he turns to Lucinda and nods.

"Okay, before Jasmine and Christian sign the register, they would like for the other three grooms to step forward.

We move into position, Christian taking a step to the side as he makes room for Maximus to stand where he had just been. The two of them are now standing on one side of Jasmine, and Sean and I stand on the other. The twins are on either side of her and hold her hands, both placing kisses on her cheek.

"You are too beautiful for words, Shorty."

"A real princess," Sean adds as I lean in and kiss her lips.

"I'm loving the veil," I say, winking as Jasmine giggles.

"So this part is something I haven't done before." Lucinda smiles at us and then the small crowd. "So Jasmine, Christian and I sat together and devised a plan. Each of the

O'Reillys will say a little something, and yes, that includes you, Jasmine."

The bridesmaids start cheering loudly, and the rest quickly join in as the five of us laugh.

"God, I love this wedding," Lucinda laughs. "Anyway ..." she says a little louder, and everyone settles back down. "As I was saying, each of you will say a little something, and then you can exchange rings. Afterwards, I will end the ceremony, leaving you all to carry on the celebrations." She looks around at the five of us smiling, and I suddenly feel more nervous than I have all day.

"Shall we start at one end and go from there?" she asks, and all heads turn to me. "I think that's a yes," she laughs as Sean steps back, letting me get to Jasmine.

Stepping forward, I take a deep breath and look at my beautiful girl. My jaw clenches as I take in her radiant smile, realising how close I am to losing it. Taking both of her hands in mine, I take another deep breath before beginning.

"Jazzy, I have sat down every day for six months and tried to work out what I wanted to say, but nothing ever seemed enough, but then nothing in relation to you is. Because I will never get enough of your smile, your laughter, and how your eyes sparkle when you feel mischievous, I will never get enough of how you feel when you are curled up in my arms or how you always make me believe I can take on the world. But most of all, I will never have enough time to tell you how special you are to me.

"You have the biggest heart and have grown so much in our time together." Lifting her hand, I press a kiss on her knuckles. "You told me once I saved you, but Angel, you saved me too. I was lost before you walked into my life and gave me a purpose. You gave me a future I never thought I would have, so today, in front of everyone, I promise you that I will always love and protect you. I will save you every time you need me to. But most of all, I promise to be more than enough because there is nothing you could ever ask for which I would deny you." As I look deep into her eyes, I see her lip tremble a little.

"Daddy, you really did save me that night you followed me. You knew that if you demanded I leave the pub and go with you, I would fight and refuse all help. So, instead, you sat there, watching over me and letting me do what I needed to knock down the barriers and admit I needed help. You saved me in more ways than one, and you did it by being patient, loving, and comforting. When I cried, you held me and offered words of reassurance. You showed me that I wasn't a failure for asking for help. It was what I needed to hear. Every day since, you have showered me in support and told me time and time again that you will always guide me, and you have.

"You have always been more than enough, Daddy, and I know we will spend the rest of our lives saving each other because that's what we do. We are a team, and nothing or no one will ever come between us. That's a promise I want to make to you today in front of everyone who matters to us." A single tear escapes her beautiful bright eyes, so I reach up and wipe it away slowly whilst cupping her cheek.

"I love you, Jazzy," I whisper, leaning forward and kissing her lips.

"I love you too, Daddy," she replies just as quietly as my heart swells, and I fall even more in love with my girl.

Sean

Watching Jason and Jasmine, I realise I'm unsure if I can do this without crying. This amazing woman is here declaring herself as ours, and I don't deserve it, but I can't lose her, not now, not ever.

"Sean, would you like to go next?" Lucinda asks as Jason steps back, giving me room to get to Jasmine. My hands shake as I take hers. She smiles while giving my hands a reassuring squeeze, giving me the encouragement I need like she always does.

"Princess, I've had my promise written for weeks, but now I'm standing in front of you, like Jason; it doesn't feel like it's enough.

"From the first time I laid eyes on you, I knew you were the one for me. I stood in that hotel lobby and decided there was nothing I wasn't willing to do to make you mine. Within a few days of spending time with you, I had our whole future planned out. But when we discovered that all four of us had fallen for you, I never once thought you would choose them over me. Because I knew you had the other part of my soul. Everything with you is easy. Whether it's talking about absolutely anything until the early hours of the morning or watching you as you interact with my brothers, I never feel like I have to be anything I'm not.

"You told me I taught you to fight, but you taught me there was something worth fighting for. I have always done my own thing and held myself back as I compared myself to others. But you have shown me what I can achieve by fighting for what I believe in and want. Without your encouragement, I would have never had the courage to branch out and start managing fighters. Every time I hit a snag and feel like throwing in the towel, I wonder, what would Jaz do?

"You really are the brains of this family, and I, for one, couldn't be prouder of how you fight for us and yourself. You are a force to be reckoned with, and I can't wait to be by your side as you take on every challenge that comes your way, cheering you on and encouraging you to fight for what you want.

"Princess, you are my soul mate, my biggest supporter, my rock, my Princess, and now my wife, and I couldn't be happier and more excited to start this next part of our journey." Lifting her hands, I kiss her knuckles as she sniffles and takes a hankie that Verity offers her. She dabs under her eyes as everyone giggles around us.

"I'd been doing so well," she laughs between tears. Taking a deep breath, she slowly lets it out as she retakes my hands and looks deep into my eyes.

"Daddy, you have shown me what it's like to love wholeheartedly, accept what I can't change, and fight for what I can. You have made me a fighter, whether it's to protect myself and those I love or if it's just fighting to be seen and heard. I love you so much and hope you realise how proud I am of you and all you have achieved in your new role.

"I will always be your biggest supporter because I know there isn't a challenge you could face and not conquer. I have every faith in you and know you can achieve great things. I will always be by your side, pushing you when you need me to, but most importantly, I will be rooting for you." Leaning forward, I kiss her like I've wanted to since she walked into the tent.

"I love you, Princess," I whisper against her lips as we both attempt to blink back the tears.

"I love you too, Daddy."

Maximus

As Sean steps back and nods, signalling for me to step forward, I do what I've been longing to do since my girl walked down, looking like the Goddess she is.

Reaching for Jasmine's hand as Sean releases them, I spin her around to face me and kiss her whilst lifting her into my arms. Everyone around us bursts out laughing, including Jasmine, as I lower her to her feet.

"I couldn't wait any longer, and I'm not sorry," I smirk as Jasmine laughs, leaning into me, and I'm more than happy to hold her close.

"When have we ever done things the normal way?" she grins, looking even more radiant.

"Never," I answer, taking a strand of her hair in my finger and playing with it. "It's one of the reasons I didn't want to be the one to marry you legally," I admit as she frowns. Looking deep into her blue eyes, I let the hair slide from my fingers. "I don't think it is possible to call you anything but Shorty." Jasmine bursts out laughing as I wink. "That first day we met, I gave you a one-arm hug and immediately noticed how perfectly you fit against my side. Nothing has ever felt as perfect as you did that day and every day since. Even as you grew a few more inches, you still moulded perfectly to me, and I knew I had found the piece of me that had been missing for so long. You always have and always will be my Shorty." Lifting my hand, I run my knuckles down her cheek, unable to look away from her eyes and how they sparkle just for me in this moment.

"I thought I was your brat?" she teases as I burst out laughing.

"You are most definitely my brat, and I love you for it." Taking a deep breath, giving myself time to blink back the tears, I take her hand, which is resting on my chest and hold it to me.

"You told me I gave you the strength to finally stand up for yourself and be the real version of you, and I couldn't be prouder. But you need to know the truth, and I couldn't have done that without you showing me what it was like to care for someone. Before you, there were just my brothers and me. No one else mattered; all my strength came from the need to impress them. But then you danced your way into my life, and I no longer cared what they thought of me; the only person whose opinion I truly cared about was yours. There is nothing I'm not willing to do to protect you and show you how loved you are.

"I love you, Shorty. Even when you are not in my arms, you are the first thing I think about when I wake up and the last thing before I fall asleep and dream about. I love that I never know what you're going to do next or how you will make me laugh. You make me curse, but most importantly, you make me feel alive; you make me want to be more than the idiot who gets knocked around in the ring, and I want to promise you that I will always be more for you. I will be more than a husband; I will be your best friend, your biggest fan and, one day, the best father I can be to our kids. I may be far from perfect, but I will always do my best for you."

Jasmine reaches up and cups my cheek, wiping away a single tear that's slipped down my cheek.

"You are perfect, Daddy. There is not one part of us I would change. I know that no matter what is going on in our lives, you are the one who will help me laugh, with that mouth which has no filter," she teases as others laugh around us. "Even when all I want to do is cry. When I've had a bad day, and I want to escape reality for a while, I find you because, with us, there's no need to pretend; you accept me, whether it's the quiet version or the one who throws water over you because I feel like it." Throwing my head back, a laugh bursts from me, remembering that evening, which feels like a lifetime ago and yesterday, all at the same time. "I never worry that I will make you mad because you understand that side of me and have helped me accept that it's okay to be that version of myself. You've given me the strength to accept all parts of me, and for that, I love you beyond words. No matter how much of a brat I am for you, I know your love isn't something I have to earn. Your love for me is unconditional, no matter what. I love being your Shorty and will always be in your corner when you need me."

"Bloody brat," I mumble as I reach into my pocket and pull out a hankie to wipe my eyes and give myself a second to compose myself as Jasmine giggles in my arms.

Shoving the material back in my pocket and unable to hold back any further, I kiss my wife as I hold her body tightly against mine. Keeping her as close as possible without fucking her right here in front of everyone.

Christian

"Is there anything you would like to add, Christian?" Lucinda asks as everyone turns to me. Jasmine smiles as she turns in Maximus's arms and looks at me.

"I would like to say something first," Jasmine declares, smiling.

"Oh, of course," Lucinda grins.

Jasmine leans back in Maximus's arms as she reaches for my hand.

"If I don't say this now, there is a real chance I'll be too emotional to say it at all."

Reaching up, I wipe a tear from her cheek.

"I am so proud of you," she starts, taking me by surprise. "You take on so much and have let others drag you down to protect those you love, and I'm honoured to be one of those who holds your heart. There is nothing you wouldn't do for your brothers and me, and I can honestly say there is nothing we wouldn't do for you.

"You have taught me so much by your rules and guidance. Do you remember the bath we had that afternoon after the five of us made love for the first time?" I nod as Lucinda starts coughing beside us. But Jasmine just winks with that mischievous grin she gets before continuing. "You scolded me for not using my words, and I asked you to be patient with me, as I had spent nearly fifteen years being told to sit down and shut up. I could see how much that admission angered you. I saw it wasn't what you wanted for me, and it made me want to change for you.

"You might all joke that I'm a brat and talk too much and say the wrong thing, but before that afternoon, Daddy, I didn't use my voice, not in the way you have taught me to. You have shown me it's okay to say what's on my mind. To use my words and speak out. Because those words can make such a difference to not only my life but all of ours; by making me use those words, you have helped me to understand all the feelings I have pushed down all my life, and you have shown me that it's okay to have these emotions, even when they mean becoming a little childish; because my feelings matter too. Because of you, I will ensure I never lose my voice again and that our children are never silenced like I was. But most importantly, I have found my voice and will use it every day for the rest of our lives to tell you how much you are loved and appreciated for everything you do for us. But most importantly, I will be your voice when you lose yours."

"I am so proud of you," I whisper, squeezing her hands. Looking into her eyes, I know I have to say what I planned before I break down.

"Standing by and watching my brothers declare their love for you, I can't help but think back to that day when we all realised how special you were to us. There were so many ways things could have gone wrong from that evening, but they didn't." Stepping closer to her, Maximus releases her so she can lean into me as I hold her close and look at my brothers.

"You three have always been everything to me. All I cared about was looking out for you and fulfilling the promise I made our mum the night she died. I promised her I would protect you, and although I have failed in many ways, I have always done my best. But there was one thing I wasn't willing to do, and that was walk away from Jasmine without knowing if she returned my feelings or not." Kissing the top of her head, I tighten my hold on her.

"Deciding to share her wasn't an easy decision, but it always felt right. It could have made things so much harder, but we fell into our new dynamic quickly and without too many incidents." I look at Maximus and smile as he shrugs while trying to hide his grin. "This amazing woman has made us even stronger than we were before, and I know that whatever the future brings, the five of us will face it together. Because as I've always said, 'You hurt one O'Reilly, you hurt us all,' and now that includes someone who has not only become the brains of the family but, most importantly, the heart." My brothers nod in agreement as we all turn our attention to Jasmine.

"I love you, Sweetheart. We all do, and I think it's safe to say we all promise to ensure you have the best life, filled with fun and laughter, but most importantly, love. Because you have held all our hearts from the day we met you and deserve to be shown how loved you are every day."

"I love you all too," she whispers, turning to the others. "You are my family, and I promise to always have each of your backs. No matter what's happening, I will be in your corner, cheering you on and being there when you need to breathe. There is nothing that could ever come between us."

We all turn to Lucinda, who is wiping her eyes with a tissue.

"Here, they made sure I had extras," Maximus winks, holding a hankie for her as everyone laughs.

"Thank you," she smiles, dabbing under her eyes. "I think it's time for the rings." Jasmine steps out of my arms and meets the girls as they step forward, each with a ring box in their hand.

"I've got Uncle Jason's!" Luna calls out, smiling proudly, holding out the box.

"Thank you, Luna. You did such a good job looking after it for me," Jasmine grins, taking the box from her.

Jasmine opens each box one by one and slides the ring onto the relevant hand as the bridesmaids cry silently, watching their friend. Sean's is the last of the rings, and I place Jasmine's ring in his hand for him to present to her. The three of us take a place behind our beautiful bride as Sean holds her left hand.

"Princess, Jazzy, Shorty and Baby girl," he smirks as we

all laugh. "You have made all of us the happiest men in the world, and we can't wait to spend the rest of our lives showing you how much we love and appreciate you." He slides the ring onto her finger before pulling her into his arms and kissing her.

Everyone is on their feet as Lucinda shouts over the noise that the ceremony is over, and she presents Mrs O'Reilly and her four husbands.

We each get a few seconds with our girl before the bridesmaids pull her away, and people come over to shake our hands. For a few minutes, there was absolute chaos, and I couldn't be happier. Everyone is so happy for us, and there have been many tears shed, but the most important factor remains: Jasmine Rose O'Reilly is our wife, and there is nothing we wouldn't do for her.

"So, that's it," Jason smiles, stepping beside me. "We did it."

"We did," I nod, watching Maximus pick Jasmine up and spin her around as she tries to hold on to her veil. "I want out."

Jason's head snaps towards me as I continue to watch our family and friends.

"Define *out*."

"Out of the illegal shit. Out of the dark side of our lives. I want our wife and children to be free. No more constant bodyguards, no more lockdowns in our own home. I want to give that woman there the best life she could even dream of and to do that, I will get us out of the shit Tommy dragged us into."

"Is it possible?" Jason asks. I nod, finally looking away from our bride.

"It won't be easy, but I'm done, Jason. I'm tired of it all, and I just want to breathe again and live the life we deserve."

Jason nods as he places a hand on my shoulder.

"Then we do it. We return from the honeymoon and do what needs to be done to give our wife the best life."

Turning around, I pull my brother towards me and hug him. He has had my back all these years, and one word, and he has it again. Stepping back, I place a hand on the back of his head. And lean my forehead against his.

"Let's get our lives back."

Chapter Fifty-Six

ABBI

"Abbi, where are you going?" Danielle tugs at my hand, and I nearly lose my balance for a second.

"I need a drink!" I laugh, stumbling away from her and the others who are on the light-up dance floor the guys organised for the reception after the wedding. I thought it was terrific when I first saw it. However, I've changed my mind. Now I've had several very large drinks, and the lights are a little too bright and seem to be moving faster.

Sitting in my chair, I look at the table to find a drink, but they are all empty. The bar is only on the other side of the tent, but I have a funny feeling if I walk over there right now, a certain arsehole may see how drunk I am and start butting his nose in where it's not wanted; again.

Pulling my phone out of my bag, I search the screen, hoping for a message from Eddie, but there is still nothing. I haven't heard from him in four days, and I'm starting to think he's ghosted me. Things were going so well; I thought he cared. He even told me he loved me when we went to the bar the other night. How can he go from telling me he loves me to cutting all contact?

Opening the messages, I type out a new one.

Abbi: It's me again. Are you mad because I couldn't tell you where I was? I can now and will explain everything if you will let me. Please get in touch and let me know what I can do to make it up to you. I miss you.

My finger hovers over the send button, but I can't decide if it sounds too needy. I don't want to sound desperate, but looking around at everyone now, I can't help feeling lonely, so I send it.

All my friends are so happy, and I hate how jealous I am. Jasmine has four husbands, and Verity has her three fiancés. Danielle may be single, but she loves it, as apparently, the last person she dated turned out to be a cheating bastard; even Chelsea, Dad's old PA, has her three men surrounding her, placing hands on her growing stomach and making a fuss of her daughter; and then there's me. Desperate for someone to actually give a shit for once. However, that doesn't include the person whose eyes I can feel watching me from across the tent. There again, it's not like he actually cares; he just likes trying to control me.

Ever since Dad was killed, I've felt so lonely. He was my best friend. I spoke to him all the time, and he was there whenever I needed him, but he's gone and is never coming back. I miss him so much. My eyes start to burn as my heart pounds in my chest. Fuck, I need a drink.

Standing from my chair, I make my way over to the bar, thinking about each step and trying to hide how drunk I am already so no one will have another go at me. I almost manage it, but when I reach the bar, I find Christian leaning against it and watching me. He's lost his jacket and is now just in his shirt and waistcoat; his sleeves are rolled up to his elbow as he holds a whiskey glass in one hand and leans against the pop-up bar they booked in the other, talking to one of Chelsea's men.

"You okay, Abbi?" he asks, frowning.

"Absolutely," I smile, forcing myself to stand as tall as possible. "I'm having the best time," I add, quickly placing a hand on the bar to steady myself.

"I'm glad to hear it. It means a lot to Jasmine that you could be here today with her. She thinks very highly of you and has been worried," Christian points out. I know she's been worried; she tells me all the time it's getting tiring.

"She has nothing to worry about; I'm absolutely fine." I can feel how fake the smile I flash him is, and I know he can tell, too.

"What can I get you?" the bartender asks as he stands behind the bar.

"Vodka and cranberry juice, please. Make it a double."

"She will have a bottle of water, nothing else."

Every muscle in my body tightens. The bartender looks to the arsehole behind me, then to Christian.

"Water," he agrees, nodding to the prick behind me and turning his attention back to Chelsea's guy.

"I don't want water; I want a vodka," I order through gritted teeth.

"You're being cut off. It's soft drinks or nothing." *His* voice comes from behind me again, causing me to clench my teeth.

"If I want to drink, I will have a drink." I turn to give him hell, but my heel snags on my dress, and I nearly topple over; his arm around my waist is the only thing stopping me from landing on my arse.

"You have obviously had more than enough, Abigail. You can have water or head home; the decision is yours."

Stepping to the side and putting some much-needed space between us, I turn and glare at him.

"Stop telling me what to do; you are not my father," I snap.

"No, I'm not. He would have dragged you out long before you started making a show of yourself." His voice is quiet but deep as he chastises me.

"Don't you dare try to tell me what my father would be doing right now. He's dead because of you." A few heads turn in our direction, and I know I'm making a scene, but I don't care.

Alasdair McIntire stares at me, his eyes wide, and I know I'm meant to be scared of him, but I'm not. How everyone, the O'Reillys included, feels the need to suck up to him, I will never know. He's not the big, scary man everyone makes him out to be.

"Christian, Abigail is going home. Please pass on our congratulations again to the lovely Mrs O'Reilly. Abigail will be in touch soon."

His eyes don't leave mine as he takes hold of my arm and pulls me away from the bar.

"I'm not leaving," I hiss through my teeth, stamping my feet.

"I think it might be for the best, Abbi. Jasmine will call you tomorrow," I hear Christian say. When I look in his direction, he gives me a sad smile and nods before turning his attention back to the guy beside him. McIntire forcibly guides me towards the entrance to the tent, and I know there's no point fighting it. I don't want to cause a scene, not where Jasmine and the others might see at least.

"Aren't you even going to let me get my things?" I snap, trying to pull my arm from him, but his grip tightens further.

"So you can make an even bigger show of yourself? No. Roman has already gone to collect them." Roman, his security guard, is just as stuck up as the prick manhandling me. "Now, stop fighting me and get in the car, Abigail. The last thing you want is to cause Jasmine any more worry on her special day. You have done enough of that already."

"What the hell have I done?" I snap as I stop fighting and let him lead me away from the party. The second we are away from where people can see us, I pull my arm from his grip and storm away towards where I can see his car.

"Miss Young," his driver smiles as I approach and opens the door.

"Samuel." Climbing into the back seat, I cross my arms over my chest and look out the window, paying no attention to Alasdair, who sits beside me.

"Here are your things."

I take my shawl and purse, purposely not making eye contact. The car pulls away from the party, and I watch the house disappear from view. As the vehicle speeds up, I have to place my hand on my stomach as it starts to roll. The last thing I need is to throw up in front of him.

"Here, it will help." He holds out a bottle of water, but I ignore it. I don't want anything from him.

"Do you have pen and paper, please, Roman?"

I watch as he opens the glove compartment and hands me a notepad and pen. Thanking him, I write an address and rip it from the pad.

"Can you take me to this address, please?" I reach out to

hand the piece of paper to Roman to relay the address to Samuel, but it's snatched from my hand before he can take it.

"That's not for you," I snap, reaching for it, but Alasdair has already read it. I'm furious when he screws it up and places it in his pocket.

"There is no need for you to go there," he says matter-of-factly. I glare at him and his audacity to tell me what I can do.

"I don't remember needing your permission to go anywhere. If I want to see my boyfriend, I will."

"He's not your boyfriend, and you will not be seeing him again." I know I should be terrified by how he looks at me, but I refuse to bow to this man.

"Fuck you, arsehole," I snap, turning in my seat to look at him properly.

"Language, Abigail!" He gets a warning in his voice when I am pushing my luck, and right now, I don't give a shit.

"Stop treating me like a child. I am twenty-three years old, not three."

"Then start acting like it!" Alasdair roars, startling me. "If you don't want me to tell you what to do, then stop fucking things up and act your goddamn age! Because there is only so much I will be willing to do to protect you and clean up your messes."

"What's that meant to mean? What exactly are you trying to protect me from?"

"Yourself, Abigail, I have spent the last 2 days cleaning up yet another of your messes, and you don't even realise it." He leans forward, closing the gap between us. "Things need to change because you cannot carry on ruining not only your life but other people's."

"Whose lives am I supposed to have ruined now?" I yell, throwing my hands up in the air.

"How about young Jasmine? You know, the one who has called you daily, supported you, no matter what she was doing or going through."

"I would never hurt, Jaz."

"You ruined her wedding!" he snaps in my face.

"How?" Who the fuck does he think he is? There is no way I have ruined anything for her. I would never do anything that would cause her any type of pain or heartache.

"Who do you think was to blame for the flowers, the dresses, and the hotel? Your *boyfriend* and his sister were."

"You're lying, he would never-"

"Never what? Lie to you? Take you for a fool? Because he did, Abigail. He was only with you because he knew he could get information out of you when you've had a few drinks."

"You're lying."

"I can assure you I'm not because I tracked him down, and he confessed everything. Your drinking made everything so much easier for him. Apparently, you only need a few drinks inside you, and you become an open book. You told him everything he needed to know to help his sister to destroy your best friend's wedding."

He continues to stare at me, but I can't look at him without feeling sick. I want to believe he's lying to me, but I know deep in my heart that he is telling the truth. He has no need to lie to me, not about this.

Turning my attention back to the window, I think of all the times Eddie and I met up or when he called me. It doesn't take much persuading for me to drink these days. It's the only thing that helps with the pain.

"Where is he now?" I ask, already guessing the answer.

"Where he belongs, that's all you need to know." His voice is stern and to the point. My jaw clenches as I try to blink back the tears, but they escape anyway.

"Does Jasmine know?"

"She knows who was to blame for the damages, but I believe Christian was holding back on telling her any more than that." In other words, she probably doesn't know he's dead. Does she know I was the one giving him the information? I open my mouth to ask but close it quickly as I feel the urge to throw up. I will never be able to face her again.

"Abigail, I want to help-"

"Don't." I shake my head, unable to look at him. "Don't say another word to me."

The rest of the journey is silent. For the first time since I met him, he does as I say and doesn't try to talk to me again, giving me time to think.

But thinking doesn't help. It makes everything a million times worse. It gives me time to realise I am the worst friend in the world.

Since the day of Dad's murder, Jasmine has been by my side. She has held me as I cried, raged and screamed. She has called me at least once a day and messaged me constantly. Every time things became too much, she was the one to make me talk and help me through it, and this is how I repay her: by destroying her wedding day.

The car pulls up outside of my home, and I can't get out quickly enough. The second I'm on my feet, I lean over and throw up. The vomit keeps coming as I sob through the pain. Jasmine was hurt because of me. It was all my fault.

A hand touches my shoulders, and I instantly step away from him, stumbling slightly, thanks to the alcohol.

"Don't touch me," I snap, standing back up. When I

finally look at him, the hatred I feel towards him intensifies. "I fucking hate you," I snarl before storming towards the front door.

"I know, and I can live with that, Abigail. However, can you live with the hate you feel towards yourself?"

The door opens as I approach, and my mum stands before me.

"Abigail?" I can see from her face that she wants an explanation, but I'm not giving her one, not tonight.

"I'm going to bed." I snap at her, and I know I shouldn't, but I can't help myself. Storming through the entrance hall, I rush up the stairs and hide out of view as I try to catch my breath.

"I'm sorry Molly, she wouldn't slow down, and I had to intervene."

"I understand. Thank you for bringing her home, Alasdair," Mum sighs, and I know she will be close to tears; she always is these days. "Maybe this will be the one time she realises her actions have consequences and stops drinking so much."

"I'm afraid it will take more than this," he replies. "If there is anything I can do to help, you know I will."

"Thank you. You've been such a big help already."

What help has that bastard been? If he had been helpful, we wouldn't be in so much pain, and my dad would be alive.

Pushing myself away from the wall I'm leaning against, I head to my room, not wanting to be around the bastard for another moment. As soon as I'm in my room, I head to my wardrobe, where I have a bottle hidden. Pouring myself a strong drink I down it in one go before pouring another.

"If there is anything I can do to help, you know I will."

Why would we want his help? I want him gone. Even if

the others haven't clicked on to what an evil bastard he is, I have, and I'm going to make sure he stays as far away from my family as he can. Because I'm not going to stop until I've made sure he knows what pain feels like and is dragged from that throne he thinks he sits on.

Alisdair McIntire needs to be brought to his knees, and I will be the one to do it.

Chapter Fifty-Seven

VERITY

I haven't stopped laughing and crying happy tears all day. Everything has been perfect, just as my friend deserved. The O'Reillys have pulled out all the stops since we left yesterday morning. This evening was supposed to be a small gathering around a little speaker and bottles of wine and other drinks to help yourself to. But the O'Reillys found a DJ, a pop-up bar with a bartender and a light-up dance floor. To say it's been perfect is an understatement. They even managed to find a photographer who had been snapping our pictures all day, and I can't wait to see the photos from this morning and the wedding. However, I have a feeling the ones from this evening may be a little messier.

"I need to sit," Jasmine laughs, taking my hand and dragging me towards the area where everyone has pushed some tables together so they can all sit in one group.

Jasmine doesn't let go of my hand until she falls onto Sean's lap.

"There's my beautiful wife," he smiles, kissing her.

"Hello, my gorgeous husband," she grins back, wrapping her arms around his neck and kissing him back.

Rolling my eyes, I sit on Ethan's lap as he wraps his arms around me.

"Your feet hurting yet?" he asks, kissing my cheek.

"If I say yes, will you carry me to bed later?" I tease.

"Already planned on it, Baby girl," he winks, causing an inferno to start building between my legs.

"Where's Abbi?" Jasmine asks, looking around and pulling my attention back to the table.

"McIntire escorted her home about twenty minutes ago," Sean explains. Jasmine sighs as she leans into him.

"She is worrying me; she's not stopped drinking for the last week," she sighs. I know Abbi has been through a tough time, but it's getting out of hand.

"Hey," Christian says, placing a finger under Jasmine's chin and forcing her to look at him. "Don't worry about her. This is your day, and I don't want anything upsetting you. McIntire will ensure she gets home safely and get her help." His eyes soften a little as Jasmine nods her head in agreement. As he leans in to kiss her, I turn my attention to the rest of the table and nearly laugh out loud when I see a Luna curled up on Jason's lap.

"Someone has Uncle Jason wrapped around her little finger."

Jason smiles as he looks down at the little girl, who I realise has fallen asleep.

"She has a firm grip on his bank account, too," Drew laughs.

"It was a gift for being such a big help today," Jason argues.

"Jason, the necklace and earrings Jasmine got her were a gift. The thousand-pound doll house you have just ordered for her is far too much," Chelsea sighs, rubbing her belly as she looks at Jasmine. "I hope you realise your future children will be spoilt."

"Chels, he can't go more than a few days without spending money on Jaz; there's no way he will be able to hold back when they have kids," Calvin laughs.

"Yeah, well, we don't need to worry about that just yet." Jasmine grins at Christian, who hums under his breath. "No pressure, you promised," she adds.

"I also pointed out that your three other husbands have not made the same promise." He's trying to keep a straight face, but I can tell he's grinning on the inside.

"Well, I can't get pregnant until this one gets married," she states, pointing to me. "There is no way I'm being a pregnant maid of honour."

"You can't be maid of honour," Danielle announces from across the table.

"Why not?" Jaz and I ask in unison.

"Because you are married, so no longer a maid," she answers. "Which means I will have to take on the role," she adds with a big grin on her face.

"Yeah, because it's going to be the definition of traditional weddings," Layton laughs beside her.

"She's actually not wrong, though," Travis points out. "Jaz couldn't be named *maid* of honour; she would be *matron* of honour."

"As long as I'm by her side, I don't care what you call me," Jaz grins.

"Do you have any idea when you will get married?" Chelsea asks. Luckily, I had already told her everything I had discovered before Henry went 'missing', so everyone here knows the truth.

"As soon as she lets us marry her." Ryan smiles next to Ethan and me.

"He wants to tie her to him before she can take her millions and run." Maximus laughs before groaning when Ryan punches his arm.

"Arsehole," Ryan warns him playfully.

"Hey! Don't call my husband an arsehole!" Jasmine protests.

"Yeah, be nice, or I'll sic my wife on you, and trust me, you don't want to be on her bad side." Maximus winks at Jasmine as others laugh around us.

"I say we start planning as soon as I return from my honeymoon! How big are we going with it?" Jasmine asks.

"I don't want a big wedding, and I would like to wait a little while," I answer, picking up my glass of wine and taking a sip.

"How long?" Jasmine asks, frowning. I look at Travis, who smiles reassuringly.

"I want to track down my mum's guys, and find out which one is my father first." It's the first time I have mentioned finding them to anyone other than my men, and I hold my breath to see what everyone says.

"Thank god. I thought she was going to say nine months as she's pregnant!" Danielle exhales drastically.

"God, no, not yet! I'm all for waiting for that one!" I laugh as Travis and Christian share a look, and both laugh. I have no doubt they have had that discussion between them.

"Well, if there is anything I can do to help, just ask. Whether it's finding out who it is or the wedding. I'm always here," Jasmine smiles beside me. I don't know what I would do without this woman sometimes.

"I know," I smile, taking her hand. "Bratties before Daddies," I remind her, giving her hand a slight squeeze.

"Bratties before Daddies," she smiles, returning the squeeze.

As everyone around us starts talking among themselves and people start heading home, I sit back and enjoy seeing everyone happy and relaxed after a stressful week. My best friend has had the most wonderful wedding, which is what she deserves. There is nothing she wouldn't do for those she loves, and I'm lucky to be included in that list.

"So, has today made you think about what kind of wedding you would like?" Ryan asks as we head to the security hub, where we will stay again tonight.

"A little," I admit, as he places an arm around my shoulders. "I know I don't want a big one. Maybe something like this. Small and intermate.

"You can have anything you want, Sweetheart," Travis smiles. "All you have to do is say you are ready, and we can start planning."

"I would like to find my real dad first."

"Then that's what we will do, Kitten. You know we'll help you every step of the way," Ryan says into my hair.

"I know you will," I sigh, leaning into him while smiling at the others. They have been so amazing since everything has come to light, and I know there is nothing they wouldn't do to help me find peace. But to do that, I need to drag up the past, and I could never do that without them. There are so many unanswered questions, and I plan to get answers to them all. I owe it not only to myself but to my mum, too.

Also by D.E. Bartley

vinci-books.com/ladlingwithluke

Love wasn't on my holiday menu—until him.

Spending Christmas fake-dating my rival on his Alabama ranch? Not exactly what I had in mind. But between shared traditions, stolen glances, and one cozy bed, I might just find more than I bargained for.

Turn the page for a free preview…

Ladling With Luke: Chapter One

ELLI

"Hey girl, how did it go?"

I look away from my computer to see Grace standing behind me.

"I'm feeling positive. Hazel seemed pleased with my ideas and Anthony didn't doze off, which is always a good sign. I need to keep my fingers and toes crossed that I win this campaign and promotion" I reply, spinning around in my office chair to face her, holding up my crossed, manicured fingers.

"Girl, with those legs on show and your British accent, it's no wonder Anthony was paying attention." Grace smirks.

I smile as I look down at my grey pencil skirt suit and high heels. That's not why I wore this today, but I'm not going to tell her that.

"Looks like Luke's just come out from doing his pitch. He's looking very smug," Grace says as she looks across to the conference room, her smile quickly disappearing. "Fuck, he's coming over here," she mutters as I moan.

"Howdy, legs!" I hear his solid Southern accent come from behind me. I turn my chair and face Luke with a raised brow.

"I'm sure that's classed as sexual harassment in the workplace, cowboy," I reply, smiling. "Haven't you got anything better to do than spend your day looking at what you'll never get?"

Luke leans on my cubicle wall and looks at me with his sexy, playful grin. It'd be much easier to dislike him if he weren't so damn gorgeous, with his jet-black hair and blue eyes. Don't even get me started on his body.

"I've told you legs," Luke replies with a cheeky wink, "one day you won't be able to fight these desires anymore, and I'm going to show you just how much fun we can have with those long pins wrapped around me." I place my elbows on my desk before leaning my chin on my fists, smiling.

"The only part of you my legs will ever be wrapped around is your neck as I crush your windpipe," I reply. Luke runs his fingers through his hair as he flashes me a mischievous grin.

"I'm telling ya legs, you will succumb to me one day."

"That day will come when you stop being a royal pain in my ass. In other words, never!" I lean back into my chair and cross my arms over my chest.

"Ahh legs, you almost look like you mean it," Luke sighs as he places a hand over his heart and pouts. "Almost!" he adds with a wink before reaching over, picking up my coffee mug, which is half full and strutting off towards his desk on the other side of the floor. "Thanks for the coffee, legs!" he shouts as I flip him off.

"Bloody wanker!" I call after him, trying not to smile.

"I don't know why you don't report him for how he

speaks to you?" Grace says behind me. I turn to face her again as I laugh.

"Nah, he's harmless. He just needs somebody to keep him from getting too big-headed. It's all just friendly banter. Plus, it's fun when I win ad campaigns over him. He sulks for weeks and I get to gloat," I reply with a gleeful grin. "I've got this latest one in the bag; I can feel it."

Grace laughs as she picks up her bag from the floor. "Come on, it's the end of the day and I fancy a few glasses of champagne before we finish tomorrow for Christmas."

"Sounds great; let me grab my stuff, finish this email, and I'll meet you at the entrance," I reply as I turn back to my computer. After all the late nights working on the campaign, I could do with unwinding with a drink or ten.

Luke

"All hail Luke Johnson, the king of advertising. Long may he reign over us lesser peasants, especially those with long legs and British accents." Oliver calls out as he holds up his beer bottle, the other guys from the office all cheer as I shake my head.

"Hey! Only I get to talk about her legs! With me, she knows it's friendly banter; with you it's just perverted."

"Protective of her much, Luke?" Oliver teases, grinning.

"Someone has to watch out for her; she's only been in the States for six months, and that British accent is going to get her into trouble," I argue as I take a sip of my beer.

I'm surprisingly protective of Elli Clarkson. It's not just because she's gorgeous; with her long amber hair, hazel eyes, and curves that make me feel things I haven't felt in years. It's also because she's very quickly become a great friend. With us both having moved to Chicago within the last year, we're still finding our places in work and elsewhere. Plus, the banter is just plain fun.

I feel my phone vibrate in my pocket and quickly pull it out.

Anthony: A fantastic presentation today, Johnson. Be in my office at 9 A.M sharp to discuss how it can be improved so you can move forward with it.

I turn and show the message to Oliver, whose face lights up as he starts cheering.

"I fucking knew you would get it! I never had a single doubt! Time to celebrate, my brother; let's get on the shots!"

Ladling With Luke: Chapter One

ELLI

I look down at my phone and re-read the message from my boss Anthony for the hundredth time since receiving it last night. My heart's racing with excitement and nerves as I head up in the elevator to the fifteenth floor of the building, where the advertising agency I work for is based. I've worn my favourite trouser suit and my hair down - so it falls in long loose waves down my back - hoping to look as professional as possible.

I quickly head to my desk and dump my bag underneath it before pulling my portfolio from the drawer I locked it in last night. I look down at it and smile, my heart racing. This campaign will be the start of something big for me, I can feel it. It could be the one to push me closer to the life I've been dreaming about since I moved here from the UK six months ago.

It had been one of the scariest moves of my life; I left everything I knew and started afresh. The "starting anew" part wasn't the worst bit, I've done that my whole life. The scariest part of moving across the Atlantic Ocean was that this time I'd invested my life savings in my last ditch attempt to find a place I could finally call home.

I hear my phone vibrate across the desk. I pick it up and look at the screen.

Grace: Go get 'em, girl! Push for that pay rise so we can party in style!

I chuckle as I check the time. Anthony asked me to be at his office at nine, and it's five to now.

I place my phone in the bottom drawer of my desk with my bag and lock it before picking up my folder. I take a deep breath and head toward Anthony's office.

As soon as I get to his door, I knock. I hear him call for me to enter.

I take one last deep breath, open the door, and walk in.

"Sorry, I think I'm a little early," I say as I look at my boss sitting behind his huge mahogany desk with a smile.

"Take a seat, Elli, I'll just finish this call," Anthony replies as he holds his hand out to the two chairs in front of his desk. I take a seat and wait, trying not to listen to the conversation. A few minutes later, Anthony puts down his phone and looks up at me with a smile.

"I'm glad you're a few minutes early as I want to discuss something with you before…" he doesn't get any further as a knock at the door interrupts him. "Ah, I see I won't get to pre-warn you," he chuckles before calling for whoever's knocking to come in.

"Sorry. Am I early?"

I turn to see Luke standing in the doorway; he looks from Anthony to me and frowns.

"No, not at all Luke, please come in and take a seat so we can get started," Anthony says as I watch Luke walk cautiously into the room. I turn around and see our boss looking at us both, smiling.

"I can see you are both a little confused, so let me explain why I've called you both here together," he says as he leans forward in his chair and places his hands together on the desk in front of him.

"I'm going to be frank, as much as we loved both of your presentations yesterday, something was missing from them. I'm not saying they weren't good, but we want to try something new and get you both to work together on this campaign and see if you can come up with something bigger and better," Anthony explains as he looks between us. Luke and I glance at each other.

"You want us to work together?" Luke asks for confirmation. Anthony nods and looks at the two of us individually.

"The chemistry between the two of you has long been a subject of discussions on this floor, and I know you can't deny the fact that when you are competing against each other, you produce your best work. I want to see what will happen when you put that energy into something together," Anthony explains further, before staring at us both as if waiting for us to comment.

I know that Anthony's right; we probably would work superbly together, but a part of me wants to burst into tears. I need this campaign, plus the promotion and pay rise I would get from it. My funds are starting to run low, and living in the States is expensive.

"What about the promotion and bonus? Would it be offered to both of us? Would the money be shared 50/50?" Luke asks next to me. I watch as Anthony nods and slowly smiles, and my heart sinks.

"Yes, but we've asked the company for twice the amount

as they will have two of our best people working for them. They have agreed, so you wouldn't lose out on anything. As for the promotion, it will be offered to both of you," he explains as I let out a breath I didn't realise I was holding.

"What do you both think?" Anthony asks as he looks between us again. I hear Luke sigh next to me, but I still can't bring myself to look at him.

"I'm fine with it if Elli is," I hear him say. I turn to him and see him giving me a soft, reassuring smile. "Do you think you can handle working with me? Or would you end up pushing me out the window like you keep threatening to?" he asks with that lop-sided smile that puts me at ease. I nod before turning back to Anthony, hoping I can hide how fast my heart is racing.

"Okay," I answer as I force my shoulders to relax. "How long do we have to get this together?"

About the Author

D.E. Bartley lives in Wales, UK, with her husband, three feral boys, four cats, and a budgie.

To say her home is a madhouse would be an understatement, but she wouldn't have it any other way.

When she isn't running around after her tribe or driving her husband up the wall, she can be found reading and hoarding books like a dragon.

Nothing is as important to her as time with her family, and she loves her trips home to Cornwall with them more than anything in the world. What could possibly compare to sitting on a Cornish beach, with a glass of Cornish gin in one hand and an authentic Cornish pasty in the other, while the monsters, I mean children, play and bodyboard in the sea?

Absolutely nothing.

Acknowledgments

I don't even know where to begin. So much has occurred since I started writing this book, and honestly, I was beginning to think it would never happen.

When I started planning this story, I thought it would be a short and sweet novella based on the lead-up to the wedding and the day itself. Oh, how wrong I was! Never in my wildest dreams did I think so much could happen to five people. When I say I have no control over the O'Reillys, I mean it. They keep me on my toes, and Jasmine is just as hard to keep control of as the guys make out. But we got there in the end, and I can't wait for you all to read this book.

Now for the acknowledgements. Of course, the biggest thanks, as always, go to my husband and kids. They are always so supportive and help out in any way they can when I am writing. I know I could never do what I'm doing without their constant support. I love you to the moon and back and everywhere in between.

I would also like to thank my friend and biggest supporter outside my family, Karen. You know who you are and how much I appreciate everything you do to help me. One day, we will meet in person, and I will give you the biggest hug. Nothing I have achieved would have been possible without you.

To my amazingly talented bestie, Rochelle, who designed all the original covers for the O'Reilly series, you are an absolute legend and never let anyone tell you otherwise. The O'Reilly series wouldn't be as big as it is without you picking out the best models and graphics. The covers you created may not be the ones we are using now, but they will always be loved by those who have them. You have made me laugh when I wanted to cry and cry with laughter, you have had my back in so many ways, and we haven't even met face to face. It's true what they say, sometimes you can find the best of friends online and never get to meet them in the flesh, and that's what I have found with you. Thank you for everything, and know I always have your back.

To Sarwah, the O'Reillys wouldn't exist without you. You encouraged me to step out of my comfort zone and try something new, and it worked out better than I could have ever imagined. To this day, I don't know how that one story, which was split into two, has gone as wild as it has, but here we are. Without the original collaboration "Loved By Four," this series wouldn't have made it past my notebooks, so thank you. Thank you for the guidance and support when I needed it the most.

Most importantly, I want to thank each and every one of my readers. You have turned this exhausted healthcare worker into an author. Because of you, I was able to step away from healthcare and do what I love full-time. Without any of you, the O'Reillys would have never gotten their girl, and Jaz would still be stuck in the abusive loop. You have all made so much happen for not only me but my whole family, and I know I speak for not only myself but my husband and kids as well when I say thank you, and I love each and every one of you from the bottom of my heart.

www.ingramcontent.com/pod-product-compliance
Lightning Source LLC
Chambersburg PA
CBHW011741010726
47498CB00012B/2887

* 9 7 8 1 0 3 6 7 0 9 6 9 3 *